SIGNET ECLIPSE

W9-BRH-762

ISBN: 978-0-451-22936-6

9 780451 229366

50799

S ⟩ EAN

continued . . .

"Sassy, fun, and magical, *Wild & Hexy* is pure delight from the first page.... This novel is one you'll want to read in one sitting, and then you'll want to read it again."
—Romance Reviews Today

"A fun book to read from start to finish."
—Once Upon a Romance Reviews

Over Hexed

"A snappy, funny, romantic novel."
—*New York Times* bestselling author Carly Phillips

"Filled with laughs, this is a charmer of a book."
—The Eternal Night

"The same trademark blend of comedy and heart that won Thompson's Nerd series a loyal following."
—*Publishers Weekly*

"Thompson mixes magic, small-town quirkiness, and passionate sex for a winsome effect." —*Booklist*

"A warm and funny novel, you find yourself cheering. I would definitely recommend it." —The Road to Romance

"This novel was brilliant. I laughed until I cried and it was a very fast read for me. This genre is the beginning of a new series for Thompson, and if this novel is any indication of the following books, then Thompson has hit the jackpot."
—Romance Reader at Heart

"Vicki Lewis Thompson has a true flair for humor. Pick up *Over Hexed* and be prepared to be amused, delighted, and satisfied as Vicki Lewis Thompson takes you on an unforgettable ride." —Single Titles

"Vicki Lewis Thompson sure delivers with *Over Hexed* ... a lighthearted tale that won't soon be forgotten."
—Fallen Angel Reviews

Chick with a Charm

A Babes on Brooms Novel

Vicki Lewis Thompson

A SIGNET ECLIPSE BOOK

SIGNET ECLIPSE
Published by New American Library, a division of
Penguin Group (USA) Inc., 375 Hudson Street,
New York, New York 10014, USA
Penguin Group (Canada), 90 Eglinton Avenue East, Suite 700, Toronto,
Ontario M4P 2Y3, Canada (a division of Pearson Penguin Canada Inc.)
Penguin Books Ltd., 80 Strand, London WC2R 0RL, England
Penguin Ireland, 25 St. Stephen's Green, Dublin 2,
Ireland (a division of Penguin Books Ltd.)
Penguin Group (Australia), 250 Camberwell Road, Camberwell, Victoria 3124,
Australia (a division of Pearson Australia Group Pty. Ltd.)
Penguin Books India Pvt. Ltd., 11 Community Centre, Panchsheel Park,
New Delhi - 110 017, India
Penguin Group (NZ), 67 Apollo Drive, Rosedale, North Shore 0632,
New Zealand (a division of Pearson New Zealand Ltd.)
Penguin Books (South Africa) (Pty.) Ltd., 24 Sturdee Avenue,
Rosebank, Johannesburg 2196, South Africa

Penguin Books Ltd., Registered Offices:
80 Strand, London WC2R 0RL, England

First published by Signet Eclipse, an imprint of New American Library,
a division of Penguin Group (USA) Inc.

First Printing, March 2010
10 9 8 7 6 5 4 3 2 1

For Serra, who celebrates each visit to my house, tolerates pestering from my cat Eve, guards my door as if it were her own, and faithfully demonstrates the joy of living in the moment.

Acknowledgments

Special thanks to the amazing art department at Penguin. I've loved all my covers, but the last two really make me smile! As always, I'm extremely grateful for the support from my editor, Claire Zion, my agent, Robert Gottlieb, and my assistant, Audrey Sharpe. I'm lucky to be surrounded with such talented and savvy people.

Chapter 1

In all her twenty-six years, despite being somewhat of a rebel, Lily Revere had never cast a spell on anyone. But dire circumstances called for drastic measures. She'd had a crush on Griffin Taylor for three months now, and she was tired of waiting for him to make a move. She needed his devoted attention beginning tonight.

That required creating an elixir this afternoon before heading off to work, but her apartment manager would stroke out if she built a fire under a cauldron in the middle of her living room. Technically she could manage the fire without burning down the building, but she might set off the smoke alarm, which would alert the manager for sure. She was fond of this apartment, located a short bus ride from downtown Chicago.

To avoid possible eviction, she'd abandoned the cauldron and settled for a fondue pot on the floor as she brewed her adoration elixir. She didn't need much of it, anyway. A couple of drops slipped into Griffin's drink during happy hour tonight should start the process.

Her job as bartender would make that easy, and three hours after sipping his drink, Mr. Handsome would be fixated on her. If they had sex within twelve hours, the spell would strengthen, growing more powerful with each sexual encounter. Yummy prospect.

Lily wouldn't have to worry about being too tired

to have sex with Griffin after work tonight. Performing magic jacked her up more than chugging down three triple espressos in a row. It was a side effect not experienced by many witches, but she'd inherited the tendency from a great-aunt and she'd learned to live with it.

While Daisy, her golden retriever, watched expectantly, Lily opened the magic circle that contained the steaming fondue pot and a small basket of herbs.

"Come, Daisy." Lily beckoned the dog into the circle and guided her to sit on one side of the fondue pot. Daisy was critical to the project. She doted on Lily, and that was the quality Lily intended to transfer to the elixir.

It seemed like the only way to get Griffin off the dime. He'd been a happy hour regular for weeks, and only a stupid woman would miss the heat in his hazel eyes when he looked at her.

When he'd failed to go beyond those burning glances, she'd asked around, thinking he was engaged or married. Nope. Finally she'd taken the initiative and suggested meeting for coffee. He'd politely—and with obvious regret—turned her down.

Lily wasn't much given to analyzing a guy's motives, but Griffin flipped all her switches, so she'd made an exception in his case. She'd concluded that his lawyerly self had decided they weren't a good match based on her nontraditional job and cheeky personality. Lily thought that was plain dumb, especially considering the chemistry between them.

Lily hadn't been this interested in a guy in ages. On top of that, her older sister Anica's budding romance with Jasper Danes had become annoying. If conservative, predictable Anica could end up with a hot guy like Jasper, then Lily should be able to snag someone of similar sex appeal.

Griffin Taylor, for example. His close-cropped brown hair and square jaw made him look like a jock, an impression intensified by the way his suit jacket hugged his broad shoulders. Lily knew from barroom conversation that Griffin worked out and would probably look great naked, but he was also smart, and Lily really liked smart men.

Anica and Jasper's engagement party loomed on the horizon, and Lily wanted to go on Griffin's arm. The elixir should guarantee it.

Closing the magic circle, she sat on the opposite side of the fondue pot and gazed at her dog. She'd always wanted a dog and Anica had convinced her to adopt Daisy, probably hoping that would take Lily's mind off her obsession with Griffin.

Daisy was great—Lily couldn't ask for a better companion, especially because the dog had turned out to possess more than a touch of magic herself. She seemed to understand every word Lily said and apparently could read a bit, too. If Lily asked Daisy to bring her *Vogue* from the magazine rack in the living room, the dog sorted through the rack and brought back *Vogue*.

No doubt about it, Daisy was special and Lily was grateful to have found her. But when all was said and done Lily still wanted what Anica had: a guy who adored her.

"Okay, Daisy, this is it. You must stay very still." Taking a deep breath, Lily picked up a handful of herbs from the basket, sprinkled them in the steaming water and began to chant.

"Pure devotion fills me up. I have found it with this pup."

Daisy regarded her with that wise, brown-eyed stare that was her trademark. Because Daisy was seven years old, she might not appreciate the *pup* reference, but Lily had discovered that very few good words rhymed with *dog*.

She continued with the chant she'd created specifically for this spell. *"Pure devotion, strong and true, makes a lover stick like glue. From the dog into the brew!"*

The mist that had hovered over the fondue pot gradually rose and swirled around Daisy's head.

Lily hadn't tried this particular spell before, so she was pleased that at least something was happening. Daisy snorted, as if the moisture had gone up her nose, but she didn't move from her assigned spot.

Both Lily and Anica, a powerful witch in her own right, had evaluated Daisy after retrieving her from the animal shelter, and they'd concluded Daisy was an unusually sensitive dog in addition to being very smart. Apparently she was used to creating spells, because she'd taken Lily's magical activities in stride.

After the mist had swirled around Daisy's head a while longer, it changed direction and dove into the fondue pot exactly the way a genie would disappear into a magic lamp. Lily was gratified with the results. Anyone watching would have to conclude that something from Daisy had been transferred into the liquid in the fondue pot.

Lily hoped it was the devotion she'd talked about in the chant, and not some other doggie trait like ear scratching or tail wagging. By tonight she would know.

As Griffin walked into the Bubbling Cauldron on Rush Street with his friends from work, he wondered for the hundredth time why he tortured himself. The brown-eyed, dark-haired beauty who tended bar wasn't for him. He was looking for steady and serene, and Lily Revere was neither.

After witnessing the destruction of his parents' marriage when he was eleven, he'd concluded two things: A guy should pay lots of attention to a woman's personality before he walked down the aisle with her, and everyone in a divorce could end up the victim of an unscrupulous lawyer.

Griffin had gone to law school to become a better divorce lawyer than those who had handled his parents' split. In his practice he'd come to realize that many couples with totally opposite goals had been lured by something, usually good sex, into a marriage that never should have happened.

If he were a different kind of man he might have had an affair with Lily. But he didn't believe in purely recreational sex. When he went to bed with a woman, he wanted a connection that went beyond lust.

He couldn't see making that sort of connection with Lily. From everything he could tell, she was more interested in having a good time than planning a future. Griffin didn't want a party girl, even if the blood sang in his veins every time he looked at her.

He'd made love to her many times in his fantasies, though. Knowing that he would never act on those fantasies, he should steer his law-firm buddies to a different bar for happy hour and quit putting himself in temptation's way. So far, for some reason he didn't care to examine, he hadn't been able to do that.

Usually Lily stayed behind the bar and mixed drinks while the waitstaff served them. But she'd fallen into the habit of coming over to take orders personally from Griffin's table of lawyers—Kevin, Miles and Debbie.

Debbie was a recent addition to the group. When she'd invited herself along a couple of weeks ago, Griffin had thought Miles was the draw. But Miles was sure Griffin was her target.

If so Griffin should be happy to fall in with that plan. The tall blonde was focused and smart. He'd love to be interested in her, but when Lily was around he couldn't seem to think about any other woman. He really should suggest a different happy hour spot.

But not tonight. Lily, dressed in a tight black top, skinny jeans and boots, was already on her way to their table with smiles for everyone and an extra wink for Griffin. One wink and his cock grew stiff as a swizzle stick.

After depositing a bowl of mixed nuts in the center of the table, Lily positioned herself next to Griffin's chair, which meant that her spicy perfume quickly transformed him into a man with no brain. She took everyone else's order before turning to him.

"Griffin, the usual?"

This close, he could feel the warmth of her body, and it was all he could do not to respond with a suggestion that would have shocked everyone at the table. Her full lips were slightly parted as she gazed down at him.

Tonight she wore glossy red lipstick. He wondered if it would smear if he kissed her, or if she'd invested in the long-lasting kind. He'd bet that lipstick would carry her through a make-out session with no worries. She was the sort of woman who would know all about cosmetics and how to use them to full advantage.

"Griffin?" she prompted. "The usual?"

Wonderful. She'd caught him staring brainlessly at her, probably with undisguised lust in his eyes. "Thanks." His voice sounded rusty. "That would be great." He always ordered a vodka tonic with a twist.

"Or maybe you'd like to shake things up a little? I make a great Harvey Wallbanger."

He shouldn't have looked into those brown eyes when she said that. Once he did, all he could think of was wall-banging sex, which probably had been her intention. She was wicked that way, and he shouldn't like it.

She'd also cornered him. If he stuck with his tried-and-true drink, he'd look stodgy. His ego couldn't stand to take the hit.

He smiled at her. "Sure, why not? I haven't had a Wallbanger in years."

She laughed. "That's a shame." Then she whisked off toward the bar.

Kevin, short and on the stocky side, shook his head as he glanced across the table at Griffin. "You're an idiot, Taylor."

"No kidding." Miles, who looked like a surfer, thanks to sessions in a tanning booth, grabbed a handful of the mixed nuts. "Only a moron would pass up that kind of opportunity."

"Thanks, guys," Griffin said. "I think you're both swell, too."

On Griffin's right, Debbie sighed. "Did it ever occur to you bozos that Griffin prefers a more subtle approach?"

"Exactly." Griffin glanced at Debbie and wished like hell he could feel the same groin-tightening excitement for her that he felt every time he looked at Lily.

Debbie met his gaze. "We should have dinner sometime."

So there it was. Miles was right and she was after him. Maybe he should explore that option. "That's a good idea," he said. If he put some effort into getting to know her better, he might find excitement lurking under the surface. Still waters and all that. "Saturday?"

"Sounds good."

"Don't mind us." Miles grabbed another handful of nuts. "Conduct your personal business right under our noses. We don't care, right, Kevin?"

"Right. We can conduct personal business, too. Hey, Miles, want to catch the Cubs game Saturday night?"

Miles nodded. "You bet. I'll see if I can score some tickets."

Griffin knew he was in trouble when he suddenly wished he could go to the game with the guys instead of spending the evening with Debbie. He turned to her. "You like baseball?"

"Not especially." She must have seen something in his expression, because she hurried into a disclaimer. "I mean, I don't know a lot about the game, but if you want to go, maybe you could coach me on the finer points. I'd be okay with a Cubs game."

Now Griffin felt like a total louse. Debbie sounded

way too eager to please, which meant she was into him much more than he'd suspected. He didn't want a woman who was willing to immediately alter her behavior to make him happy. He shouldn't have agreed to dinner.

Peripherally he noticed that Kevin and Miles were watching with poorly disguised interest to see how he got himself out of this little jam. Saturday was still four days away. He'd figure this out. "We'll do dinner," he said. Better that than watching her pretend to enjoy a baseball game for his sake.

He caught Lily's scent as she approached, but he didn't look up. He didn't have to. The mental picture of her balancing a tray one-handed, which further stretched the material of her blouse over her breasts, was a vision he'd committed to memory weeks ago.

"One Wallbanger for Mr. Taylor." She placed a cocktail napkin in front of him and set the tall glass of orange liquid squarely on the napkin.

Was it his imagination or did she sound winded? She hefted trays all the time, so he knew the exercise hadn't taken her breath away. Was she breathing hard because she was close to him? That was an arousing thought, as if he needed another one.

After delivering the other three drinks, she returned to stand beside his chair. "Anything else I can get for you folks? Appetizers? A sandwich?"

No, it wasn't his imagination. She *was* breathing faster, as if she was excited about something. Or someone. Jesus. Now he was imagining how she'd breathe if she got really excited, like during sex.

"Onion rings would be good," Miles said. "How about an order of onion rings for the table?"

"Coming right up." She left again.

Good thing, because Griffin didn't need to hear her breathing fast and saying things like *coming right up.* She looked so hot she seemed to be giving off sparks. Kevin and Miles stared after her, obviously fascinated.

Lily in normal mode was sexy enough. Lily charged up about something was damned near irresistible.

But he would resist, because he'd been observing her behavior for weeks. He'd listened carefully to her casual comments. Lily might be the sexiest woman he'd met in years, but she was also impulsive and unfocused. Hooking up with her would be asking for a repeat of his parents' messy history.

His mom had told him that she'd been blinded by his dad's charisma and enchanted with his spontaneity. She'd never stopped to think what it would be like to live with someone who never planned beyond the present moment. Griffin intended to stop and think about all those things.

That was one reason he was careful how many drinks he had at the Bubbling Cauldron. He always took public transportation back to his apartment, so driving wasn't an issue, but losing concentration definitely was. Too much alcohol and he might forget why hooking up with Lily was a bad idea.

"Gonna drink your Wallbanger or just look at it?" Miles asked. "Because if you really don't want it, pass it over."

Griffin picked up the chilled glass. "Sorry. If you want a Wallbanger, you'll have to get your own." He took a hefty swallow.

Wow, that was amazingly good.

"I thought you were gonna let it go to waste," Miles said. "You were doing that staring-into-space routine again."

"Just thinking about a case." Griffin took another drink of his Wallbanger and practically smacked his lips. He couldn't remember when he'd enjoyed a cocktail so much.

"I guess you like it," Kevin said. "I haven't seen you looking that happy since the Carletons decided to settle out of court."

"Yeah, that was a damned good day." Griffin had managed to keep the Carletons from wasting money in a nasty court battle. He wasn't sure the senior partners appreciated his efforts to save his clients money, but fortunately he brought in enough business that they didn't bitch.

"And this is a damned good drink," he added as he savored the combination of orange juice and Galliano. "I might have to switch my regular order from now on." He loosened his tie and unfastened the button at the collar of his dress shirt.

"Now I'm curious about your fabulous drink." Debbie leaned toward him. "Let me have a sip to see what it tastes like." She reached for his glass.

"Onion rings!" Lily moved between Griffin and Debbie, knocking the other woman's hand away from the Wallbanger as she plunked the basket down on the table.

If Griffin hadn't known better, he would have sworn Lily was deliberately trying to keep Debbie away from his drink. He appreciated the interruption. Sharing a drink with Debbie was the sort of intimacy that would only encourage her. Damn, he wished he hadn't agreed to dinner. It had been an impulse, and he knew that following impulses only led to trouble.

Lily glanced at Debbie. "I'll be happy to mix you a Wallbanger, too."

"Yeah," Griffin said. "Let me buy you one, Debbie. You don't want to drink from my glass. My throat's kind of sore. I might be getting a cold."

Debbie looked alarmed. "I sure hope not. I'd hate for us to miss dinner on Saturday night." She gazed up at Lily, and there was unmistakable triumph in her eyes. "Griffin and I have dinner plans for Saturday."

Lily's expression tightened. "How nice. Can I get you that Wallbanger, then?"

"No, I don't think so. Not tonight." Debbie basked openly in her status as Griffin's future date. "Maybe I'll have one Saturday night with Griffin, since he seems to like them so much."

Griffin pretended not to hear the muffled snicker from Miles, who seemed to be enjoying the byplay immensely. He'd known Miles and Kevin since law school, and both guys could read him like a book. The *I'm coming down with a cold* routine was something they'd all used in the past to get out of a sticky situation with a woman.

"I'm glad you like the drink, Griffin," Lily said. "I put special effort into that one. And the orange juice should be good for your cold."

"I'm sure it'll help." Griffin took another drink.

"Want another?"

"No, I think one will do it."

Lily smiled at him. "Yes, it probably will. They tend to be fairly potent, at least the way I make them." Then she went back to her bartending duties.

There had been something secretive about that smile of hers, and Griffin wouldn't put it past her to have doubled up on the vodka. He was feeling extremely mellow. Now would be a good time to leave before he said or did something stupid, like proposition Lily.

Finishing the drink, he pulled out his wallet. "That's it for me. I'm heading out."

Kevin blinked. "Hey, don't you want some onion rings? You love onion rings!"

"It's been a long day." Griffin put money on the table. "I'll see you all at the office in the morning."

Debbie didn't look happy about his sudden departure. She caught his arm. "About Saturday night: You'd better make reservations soon. It's tough to get into the good restaurants, especially now that the weather's nicer."

Griffin nodded with as much enthusiasm as he could muster. "I'll do that." He wanted to jerk his arm away, but he eased out of her grip so as not to seem rude. Somehow between now and Saturday, he'd find the courage to tell

Debbie they wouldn't be going to dinner. Dating her when he felt no attraction and she had an obvious crush wasn't fair to either of them. He'd tell her privately, though, so he wouldn't embarrass her in front of Kevin and Miles.

Then he'd fix this nagging problem of his inappropriate craving for Lily.

The solution was blindingly obvious. He would never set foot in the Bubbling Cauldron again. Yes, that was the answer. Great Wallbangers or not, he vowed to keep away from the place. Yep. A new happy hour spot was in order.

Chapter 2

Lily watched Griffin leave the bar without looking back. He had all the signs of a man on the run. Was he really so afraid of his attraction to her? Apparently so.

If the elixir worked the way it was supposed to, she'd have the chance to find out why. Her heart was still racing from the usual high she experienced after doing magic, plus the excitement of taking this bold step with Griffin. She'd worked many spells in her life, but she'd never purposely tried to alter someone's behavior.

There was a reason for that. The magical world frowned on spells that messed with the concept of free will. But if she left Griffin to his own devices, he'd be going to dinner with that Debbie person on Saturday night.

He didn't want Debbie. Any fool could see that. He wanted Lily, but for some unexplainable reason he wouldn't allow himself to have her. In a sense, her spell would simply remove his self-imposed blocks and allow him to be true to his own nature. It was a noble act on her part.

Well, maybe not so much. She intended to benefit a lot from that spell, and noble acts were supposed to be about self-sacrifice. Lily had never been into self-sacrifice.

She wasn't good at waiting, either, especially when jacked up on magic, but somehow she'd have to get through the next three hours to find out whether her spell had taken hold or not. It could work in less than three hours, of course, which meant that Griffin could show up at any time, ready to rumble. That thought was enough to send shivers through her already revved-up system.

"Hey, Lily, you up to making a few drinks, or are you on permanent break?"

Lily looked down the length of the bar at Sherman, a waiter with long hair and a smart mouth. "Cool your jets, Sherman. What do you need?"

"An appletini, a Black Russian, and two Wallbangers, if it wouldn't disturb your moment of Zen."

She ignored the crack. "Who ordered the Wall-bangers?"

"The lawyer dudes."

"I'll get right on it." Lily smiled. Little did Miles and Kevin know that their Wallbangers wouldn't taste nearly as great as Griffin's. The elixir was designed to enhance the flavor of any drink to increase the chances it would be drained to the last drop.

But Lily decided to add a little extra vodka to the drinks for the boys, which would be some consolation. She worked with practiced efficiency, sailing each drink down the bar toward Sherman as it was finished. She'd filled the last order when her sister, Anica, burst through the door and hurried over.

She wore her favorite blue sweat suit because the spring nights were still on the chilly side. Her wind-blown blond hair looked as if she'd run all the way from the bus stop, and her blue eyes were filled with anxiety as she spoke to Lily in a low, urgent tone. "Tell me you haven't done it yet."

"Done what?" Although Lily pretended not to understand, she had a good idea Anica was talking about the elixir. Anica must have found out about Lily's plans through some sort of magic of her own.

"Made an elixir for Griffin."

Yup, that was it. "What makes you think I would?" Lily could guess what had happened. Anica, a hovering big sister worried about Lily and her crush on Griffin, had taken magical action.

"All right. I admit I asked Dorcas and Ambrose to—" Anica's confession screeched to a halt as Sherman appeared by her elbow. "Hi, Sherman."

"Hey, there, Anica. Lily, can I get a Singapore Sling and a cosmo?"

"I'm on it." Lily flicked a glance at her sister, who had the good grace to blush. Yep, Dorcas and Ambrose Lowell, a matchmaking witch and wizard who lived in Big Knob, Indiana, had been peeking into Lily's life, courtesy of Anica's meddling. Lily had a right to be upset about the invasion of privacy, but she knew Anica was acting out of concern. Lily couldn't find it in her heart to be angry, especially because Anica was too late to stop her.

Sherman leaned against the bar and looked over at Anica. "So, where's Jasper?"

"The place we picked for the engagement party, Donatello's, had a last-minute conflict, so he's gone there to talk about alternatives and pick up a refund if they really can't work it out."

"That sucks," Lily said. "How are you supposed to book another place in four days?"

"You should have it here," Sherman said. "I wondered why you didn't do that in the first place."

"Well, I could tell Lily wasn't too crazy about that idea."

And that was why Lily couldn't be angry with her sister about the scrying session. Anica did try to do the right thing. "It's true that I wasn't crazy about having it here," Lily said.

"I don't see the problem." Sherman grabbed a bar rag and wiped up a wet spot on the bar. "It's not like Lily would have to work. Chad's the bartender on Sunday nights."

"But we're talking about this Sunday," Lily said. "Devon wouldn't rent out the place on such short notice."

"Sure he would." Sherman waved aside that protest. "Sunday night's dead, anyway. And Chad will be overjoyed to get the extra money for a party like that."

"But if Chad ran into any problems, he'd want me to help." And if Lily's plans worked out, she'd be in a killer dress, escorted by a very attentive Griffin. She didn't want to end up behind the bar, mixing drinks.

"Hey, I could fill in if it came to that. I know enough, and I think it would be a cool venue for the party." Sherman was obviously warming to the idea. "I could haul out the mirrored ball from the back room."

Lily chortled. "Anica, you should see the look on your face. She doesn't want a revolving mirrored ball, Sherman. It wouldn't go with her ... uh, style." She'd been about to say *in-laws*. Jasper's parents were on the stodgy side and would be horrified if they ever discovered that their future daughter-in-law was a witch. But Lily wouldn't criticize them in front of Sherman.

"Okay, forget the ball, although it would look amazing. Considering the family connection, Devon would probably give Anica and Jasper a good rate."

"Probably." Lily finished filling the drink order. Devon was a wizard, and he'd love the prestige of having his bar used for a party that would include Dorcas and Ambrose, both members of the Wizard Council.

"Maybe Donatello's will work out," Anica said. "But if we consider coming here, Lily has to be okay with it."

"I get that." Sherman picked up the drinks Lily scooted over toward him. "If you do decide, then request me, okay? I really could be backup behind the bar. It'd be fun."

Anica smiled. "I promise to request you, Sherman." Her smile faded as she turned back to her sister.

"I'm sorry about the snag with the party." Lily had been to the Italian restaurant, and it was perfect for Anica and Jasper's event—snowy tablecloths and lots of potted trees decorated with white lights. The Bubbling Cauldron had rough-hewn wooden tables, neon beer signs, and wall sconces that gave the room a reddish glow. "If you have to have it here, then—"

"Never mind that. Listen, the reason I hired Dorcas and Ambrose is that—"

"You care about me. I know." Lily started washing glasses. "It's okay."

"Anyway, Dorcas called to tell me you were planning a spell that would transmit Daisy's qualities into an elixir for Griffin. I came right over, hoping you haven't made it yet."

Lily looked her sister in the eye. "I have."

"Oh, Lily. I should have known by that slightly manic look in your eyes, the one you always get when you do magic."

"I like to think of it as a glow instead of a manic look."

"Whatever. You haven't given it to him, have you? Surely you wouldn't actually . . ." Anica searched her sister's expression. "Dear goddess, you gave it to him."

"Uh-huh. About a half hour ago."

"Oh, no! Didn't you learn anything from my horrible experience with Jasper?"

Lily's hackles rose. After all, she'd helped bail Anica out of that situation. Not long after Anica had started dating Jasper, she'd had a fight with him and become so angry at his arrogant attitude that she'd transformed him into a cat. At first it hadn't seemed reversible, but it had all turned out okay in the end, partly because of Lily.

"What's to learn?" Lily said. "You're getting married, aren't you?" She heard the envy in her voice and winced.

Anica must have heard it, too, because she softened her tone. "Jasper and I went through hell to get to this point," Anica said quietly.

"Yeah, I know. But it's not like I'm changing Griffin into a cat." Lily felt justified in bringing that up now that Anica was acting all righteous.

"Maybe it's not quite as bad as what I did," Anica said. "But you're still messing with his free will. You know that violates the magical realm's guidelines."

"He already likes me. He just won't let himself act on it. The elixir will give him a nudge in the right direction."

"A nudge, huh?" Anica gazed at her. "If I understand the adoration elixir, it's more along the lines of pushing him off a cliff."

"I didn't give him much. Besides, those perfume ads promise the same thing."

"I need a mudslide, two Bud lights, and a chocolate 'tini," Sherman said as he came up behind them.

Anica sighed and plopped down on a bar stool. "A chocolate 'tini sounds like a good idea about now."

Sherman grinned at her. "Don't tell me the bride's getting the jitters?"

"No, I— Whoops, there's my phone." She pulled it out of her purse and twisted the stool around, leaning over and covering her other ear with her hand.

Lily took advantage of Anica's phone call to make her a chocolate 'tini with some high-end vodka, which might mellow her out. Anica wasn't happy with her, but after the stunt her sister had pulled on Jasper, she wasn't in a position to lecture Lily about proper witch behavior.

If Lily had more time, she might not have slipped a potion into Griffin's drink. But she had less than four days before Anica and Jasper's engagement party, and tonight Griffin had asked Debbie out. That called for immediate action, and Lily was glad she'd brewed the elixir and had been prepared to use it. Dawdling around could have meant losing him completely.

Besides, another deadline loomed. Lily and Anica's parents were arriving back in town on Thursday, and Lily wanted a boyfriend in place before that. Her parents would prefer a wizard to a nonmagical person, but Lily wasn't worried. Anica had already blasted through that barrier by choosing Jasper. Lily would be happy to ride on her big sister's coattails in that department.

Anica closed her phone and swiveled back to face Lily. "Donatello's is out."

"This should help." Lily set the chocolate 'tini in front of her sister.

"Thanks." Anica took a sip. "Mm. That's great."

"So, did Jasper get his money back?"

Anica nodded. "At least there's that. We're short on options, though, so if you're okay with it, maybe I should talk to Devon."

"I'm okay with it. I was just worried that this place isn't quite what you had in mind."

Anica glanced around at the noisy bar. "Not exactly, but we can make it work."

"With a little magic?" Lily relished the idea.

"Some, although we have to be careful. This will be a mixed crowd, some magical, some not. I don't want to tip my hand to the in-laws."

"We can do a lot without magic. We can round up some tablecloths, and I have a few strands of white lights in my box of Christmas decorations."

"You know what?" Anica tapped the side of her glass with her finger. "I don't think we should try to transform this place into a mediocre version of Donatello's. We should play up what it is—a rowdy bar. The mirrored ball might not be such a bad idea. I'm thinking balloons and streamers, and maybe a few tiny illusions."

"Ready to shake up those in-laws, after all?"

Anica shared a conspiratorial smile with Lily. "Yeah, I am. They'll never guess what's going on, anyway."

"Nonmagical people never do." Lily savored the moment of witchy bonding, but it soon passed and Lily could see the wheels turning as her big sister circled back to the subject that had brought her over here in the first place.

Anica took another swallow of her 'tini. "Dorcas told me that if you fail to consummate the union within twelve hours, the spell simply wears off."

"*Consummate the union?* Ugh. It sounds like something you'd need rubber gloves for."

"You can joke about it if you want, but the bottom line is that you can't have sex with him."

Lily blew out a breath. "And waste all that work I put into the elixir? Aren't you curious about whether it works or not?"

"Sure I am, but not at the risk of—"

"Here's an idea. I'll just keep him for the weekend. Then I'll let the spell wear off. How's that?"

"No good. He's a cutie-pie, and I'm guessing once you shag him you'll want to keep it up. That will make the spell grow even stronger, so it'll take a long time for it to wear off. It's much better if you don't get started down that path in the first place."

Lily went back to washing glasses. She had to concentrate, because when she was high on magic she tended to break them. "Easy for you to say."

"Hey, there'll be a bunch of single guys at the engagement party. You could meet someone."

"I've already met someone. I think Griffin and I could turn out great together."

"All the more reason to let the spell wear off!" Anica reached across the bar and clutched Lily's arm. "Seriously, Lil. What if he's your one and only? If you start out this way, you'll always wonder if it's the spell or if it's real."

Lily dropped a glass in the sink and it broke.

Anica released her arm immediately. "Hades, did I make you do that?"

"Sort of. Not really. It's what happens when I'm a little jiggy because of the magic and I don't concentrate. And what you said . . ." She sighed. "I suppose you have a point."

"I do. Watch yourself with that broken glass."

"Right." Lily carefully fished out the broken pieces and threw them in the trash.

"I just don't want you making a huge magical mistake like your big sister. Learn from my error and let the spell wear off. I know Griffin turned you down for the coffee date, but some time's gone by. Try again. Invite him to the engagement party."

Lily wiped her hands on a towel. "Maybe I will."

"Without benefit of the spell."

Lily was torn. To take Anica's advice or not? That was the question.

Within an hour, Griffin's mellow sense of well-being had disappeared. He paced his apartment, unable to settle down to anything. He nuked a frozen pizza and tried to watch TV while he ate it. The remote got a workout, but in the end he turned off the TV.

He wanted . . . something. After searching the refrigerator he decided it wasn't food he craved. A survey of his liquor cabinet told him it wasn't booze, either. None of the books on his shelves sounded interesting.

As the minutes ticked by his restlessness grew. He hadn't been to the zoo in years, but he remembered going as a kid and watching a male lion pace endlessly in his enclosure. Griffin felt like that lion.

There was no reason he should, though. The lion had been trapped behind bars, but Griffin was free to go wherever he wanted. He could go to the gym, for example, but that didn't appeal to him, either. A run, though—that sounded better. He changed into sweats and a T-shirt and left the building.

He was cold at first, but in about three blocks he was feeling just fine. Moving was the answer to whatever ailed him tonight. Feeling the blood pump through his veins felt good. Heading toward Lake Michigan, he ran in place whenever he had to stop at a traffic light.

He wondered if Lily liked to run. She had the legs for it, long and supple. He pictured her in black Lycra. Maybe her running gear would have a purple stripe down the side that would undulate as she ran.

In his fantasy her hair was loose, streaming behind her like a banner. Her long strides caused her breasts to jiggle enticingly under her sports bra, and made her breath come hard and fast, the way it would when she was nearing a climax.

Arousal came upon him slowly, subtly, and he fought it off by running faster. Now was not the time to indulge in fantasies about Lily. He'd vowed to eliminate her from his life, and that meant clamping down on the fantasies, too.

But this one was more persistent than most. In it they were running along the edge of the surf until they were both exhausted. Climbing to higher ground, they threw themselves down on a soft beach towel, where he peeled away the Lycra inch by inch, revealing her flushed and responsive body.

He was desperate for her in the fantasy, and that desperation began to carry over into the here and now. Without realizing it, he'd changed course and was now moving in the direction of the Bubbling Cauldron. The need to be with her grew stronger the closer he came to the place where she worked.

But he wouldn't let this need ruin everything. He was more disciplined than that. A strategy began forming, one that seemed to make perfect sense. He was giving her up, no question about that. But that was tomorrow. Tonight he could go to her and explain that all he wanted was one night.

Surely the two of them could handle one night together, knowing they'd never see each other again. One night wouldn't change the whole course of his life or hers, but it would ease this tremendous ache. After that he would be strong. He would abandon thoughts of Lily and look for someone who didn't make him think about sex all the time. He didn't want to fall into the same trap as his parents had and base a relationship on lust alone.

Lily had talked to him and his friends enough for him to know that this bartending job was the latest in a series of jobs for her, none of which had much of a future. Griffin had been goal-oriented all his life. He and Lily were on very different paths.

Turning the corner, he spotted the sign—a cauldron outlined in red with golden bubbles rising from it. He stopped to rest his hands on his knees and catch his breath. Once he stopped running lust nearly swamped him. She was in there and her heat called to him. He wasn't sure how he'd manage to seduce Lily tonight, but he had no doubt that he would succeed.

Chapter 3

Although Lily hadn't known what to expect from this elixir experience, Griffin standing in the doorway, wearing gray workout pants and a sweat-dampened T-shirt didn't fit any of her preconceived scenarios. She'd hoped he'd show up, but she'd halfway expected him to appear bearing flowers and candy. She'd thought he'd be freshly shaved and that he'd look eager. Instead he looked manic.

Sherman had just placed the last orders of the night when Griffin walked over to the bar, his gaze intent on Lily. Sherman lifted his hand to signal a high five. "Way to time it, buddy! You snuck in under the wire."

Griffin ignored him and focused on Lily. "How soon can you leave?"

She was taken aback by his abrupt question. "Why?"

"I need you ..." Griffin paused, as if struggling to sound reasonable. "I need you to help me with something. Please."

Alarm raced through her. She'd hoped that he'd be excited, but instead he seemed desperate. "Are you feeling okay?"

His hazel eyes burned with lust. "I'm ..." He cleared his throat. "I'm fine. I—" He glanced over at Sherman, who regarded him with obvious curiosity. "We need a moment."

"Hey, sure, sure." Sherman raised both hands and backed away. "I can take a hint."

Lily's hands were shaking, so she grabbed a bar rag and started wiping down the surfaces to hide her nervousness. Griffin's intensity was a wee bit overwhelming.

Griffin placed his forearms on the bar and leaned toward her.

She couldn't help noticing how muscled his arms were, which made her think of how delicious the rest of him would feel pressed against her body.

"I can't explain what's happening," he said, "but I have an overpowering urge to be with you. You asked me out once, so I know you're not indifferent to me."

Lily breathed in a combination of sweat and faint traces of aftershave and soap. Underneath that, like the low note in a glass of fine Bordeaux, was the unmistakable scent of aroused male.

Her mind was still sorting through the ramifications of this spell, but her body, still high on magic, had zoomed past all the intellectual junk and was happily responding to the idea of Griffin as a potential bed partner. "No, I'm not indifferent." Now, there was an understatement.

"This will probably come out wrong, but I think the attraction is mostly sexual."

It certainly is now. She couldn't deny the flash fire being generated between them. "Maybe," she said.

"I'm not looking for anything long-term."

How very doglike of him, to want to live for the moment. She kept her voice low. "What are you suggesting?" As if she didn't know.

"No strings, no promises. Just come home with me tonight."

Poor man, he thought they could have a one-night stand and he'd get her out of his system. But instead, once they had sex he'd become even more enmeshed than he was now. She felt the first twinge of guilt.

Sherman edged closer. "I don't want to interrupt

whatever you two have going, but I need those drinks, Lily. The customers are getting restless."

"Right away, Sherman." Lily glanced at Griffin. "I need to mix some drinks. Would you like one?"

He dragged a hand over his face. "Yeah, sure. But not a Wallbanger, just a beer. That Wallbanger had aftereffects. I couldn't concentrate on anything."

But he's concentrating now, she thought as she quickly drew him a draft and set it on a napkin in front of him. He was concentrating on getting her into bed. And wasn't that exactly what she'd wanted?

As she worked quickly to fill the order Sherman was waiting for, she could feel Griffin's gaze on her. She was no stranger to having men look at her with obvious sexual interest, but this was different.

Griffin's laserlike focus touched off little bonfires all over her body until she was so hot she wanted to rip off her clothes and fling herself into his arms. His response would be a guaranteed conflagration. Goddess, but it was tempting to consider what he'd proposed.

She reminded herself that he was only acting that way because she'd given him the elixir. Well, not entirely because of the elixir. The chemistry between them had always been there, simmering beneath the surface. The elixir had heated it to the boiling point in Griffin, and the lust was quickly spreading to her.

Good thing she could mix drinks in her sleep, because she was paying no attention to what she was doing as she completed the order and slid the drinks down to Sherman. For the first time she wondered what Griffin would do if she rejected him. How determined was he?

She had to admit the thought of being relentlessly pursued pumped up her heart rate. And it was already faster than normal because she'd done magic today.

As she finished mixing the last drink, her cell phone, which she always kept stashed in her backpack under the counter, played "Witchy Woman." Anica was calling her, and she knew why, too.

She could ignore the call, but Anica had her own brand of persistence. If Lily didn't answer, Anica would find some way to communicate. Ignoring a witch wasn't a wise move, even when you were a witch yourself.

Lily plucked the phone from inside her backpack and flipped it open. Then she turned away from Griffin's seductive stare. "Hi, Anica."

"What's happened?"

"He's here."

"And?"

Lily decided not to mention that Griffin had run all the way to the bar from his apartment and that he was wearing very few clothes. "He invited me to come home with him."

"For goddesss's sake, don't do it!"

Lily felt as if she'd been paraded in front of a display of chocolate truffles and then told she couldn't have any. It wasn't fair to have a man like Griffin panting for her and have to turn him down. But Anica had made some potent arguments.

Lily didn't want to be a pariah in the wizard world because of this. Griffin's response to the elixir was exciting but might be difficult to control if she let things go any further.

The thought of not having sex with him tonight was killing her. But she had to remember that doing magic always clouded her better judgment. Anica was watching out for her. Anica probably knew what was best.

"Okay," Lily said. "I'll shut him down."

"And you're not just saying that because you're high on magic, right? You know how you tend to be more agreeable when you have a magic buzz going."

"I mean it, Anica."

"Just remember that in another nine hours, he'll be

back to normal. Then you can ask him to the engagement party and find out if there's any real connection
between the two of you."

Lily had the most horrible feeling that Griffin
wouldn't accept an invitation to Anica and Jasper's engagement party once the spell wore off. If she let him go
now, that would be the end of her chances with him.

"Lily? You're with me on this plan, right?"

"Sure." Lily glanced back at Griffin and her heart
thumped in triple time. It would be so sweet if only—
but no, she wouldn't go through with it. "You bet."

"Good," Anica said. "And remember, he'll try to talk
you into going to bed with him, and you have that tendency to be agreeable when you're like this, so watch
out."

"Okay."

"I just wish I knew whether you'll agree with me now
and turn around and agree with him later." Anica sighed.
"Anyway, I'll talk to you tomorrow. If we're going to
have the engagement party at the Bubbling Cauldron,
we have plans to make."

"Absolutely."

"Be strong, Lil."

"I will. Talk to you tomorrow." Lily closed the phone
and tucked it into her backpack.

"Your sister?"

Lily turned, enchanted by the sexy resonance in his
voice. She would love listening to him murmur sweet
words in her ear while they were making . . . no, she
wasn't going to do that tonight. "Yes, that was Anica."

"I met her and her fiancé here."

"That's right." She could ask him to the engagement
party now and he'd say yes. He'd say anything to gain his
objective of luring her into his bed. The invitation to the
party was on the tip of her tongue, but she couldn't ask
him to the party and then refuse his advances tonight.
That would seem weird.

Sherman came over with money and credit cards to settle the last of the bar bills.

"Let me pay for my beer now, too." Griffin pulled some bills out of a hidden pocket in his sweats.

Lily waved away the money. "It's on the house." Paying for his beer was the least she could do considering that she planned to deny him satisfaction when she'd created the craving in the first place.

"Thanks." Griffin put the money away.

Sherman glanced at Griffin, then back at Lily. "If you two have plans, I'll close up tonight. All I need you to do is take care of the register."

Lily sighed with regret. "That's okay, Sherman. I can do it."

Griffin lifted his eyebrows in a silent question.

"Suit yourself," Sherman said. "I'll start stacking chairs. Let me know if you change your mind."

After Sherman walked away, Lily gazed at the man she had lusted after for weeks and said what needed to be said. "Griffin, I can't go home with you." How she hated saying that!

"Sure you can." He leaned toward her and his hazel eyes coaxed her to agree. "You know we'd have a great time."

"I'm sure we would, but I have ... responsibilities." For one thing, she had responsibilities to the wizard community, which wouldn't appreciate the spell she'd cast on him, but she couldn't tell him that.

"Such as?"

She resisted the temptation of his heated gaze as she moved to the cash register to close it out for the night. "My dog. I can't go off and leave Daisy. She has to be walked and then fed in the morning."

"No problem. I'll go home with you and help with the dog. We could stay at your place if you'd rather."

"That's not a good idea." It sounded like a wonderful idea, but she dared not tell him so. Picking up his glass, she washed it, being very, very careful. Now was not the time to break another glass.

"Why isn't it a good idea?"

"Daisy isn't used to strangers." It could be true. Lily hadn't had her long, and no strangers had visited the apartment since Daisy had arrived.

"That's okay. I'm good with dogs. I had a golden retriever when I was a kid."

"Daisy's a golden." Lily said it before she'd stopped to think that the information would only encourage Griffin. "But she's really not very sociable."

"That's hard to believe. golden retrievers usually love people."

Belatedly she remembered what he did for a living. A lawyer would be very good at arguing his case. She was matching words with someone who was far more skilled at wordplay than she was. "Sorry. I can't take the chance. She might bite you." More likely Lily would be the one biting him during a passionate, very naked moment. Love bites could be a lot of fun.

"Then I'll wait outside your apartment for you until you've taken care of your dog."

"No, I can't have you doing that." Lily took a deep breath and faced him. Anica would be so proud of her right now. "I'm not spending the night with you, Griffin."

He took the ultimatum without blinking. "All right. Then we'll just have coffee."

She was totally confused. "But . . . but I thought you wanted to . . ."

"I did. I do. But if that won't work for you, then we'll walk your dog and then we'll go get coffee and talk."

Lily could see advantages in that. She'd finally have a chance to get to know Griffin, and as long as they didn't have sex, the relationship might build naturally, carrying over after the spell had disappeared. Anica had made

Lily promise not to have sex with Griffin, but she hadn't made her promise not to have coffee with him.

"I guess that would be okay," she said. "Let me go tell Sherman." Lifting the hinged part of the bar top, she walked over to where Sherman was stacking chairs on top of tables. "If you wouldn't mind closing up, then—"

"Be happy to." Sherman grinned at her. "I noticed a long time ago that you'd taken a shine to that guy. I think it's cool that he finally grabbed a clue."

"We're just going for coffee."

Sherman's grin widened. "Yeah, that's what they all say."

"No, really. Just coffee."

"You trying to convince me or yourself?"

"I'm not trying to convince anyone. I just—"

"All I'm saying is that you're sounding a little out of breath, which usually means there's more at stake than coffee."

Lily deliberately slowed her breathing as she met Sherman's gaze. "Nope. Just coffee. Thanks for locking up." With a wave, she walked back to the bar and retrieved her purse.

Griffin slid off his bar stool. "All set?"

"Yep." She tried to sound nonchalant. "By the way, I usually take the bus home. The bus stop's only about half a block from here."

"We can take a cab this time."

"That's not necessary." Plus a cab ride had more potential for hanky-panky. How ironic that she was in the crazy position of holding him at bay.

"A cab will actually be easier for me. I don't have any tokens and the bus won't take cash at this hour."

She used a bus pass, so she didn't have tokens to give him, either. Apparently they had no choice but to ride together in the back of a cozy, intimate cab. At least they couldn't have sex there. Well, technically they probably could, but Lily wasn't a fan of backseat sex. She couldn't imagine Griffin would like it, either.

"Okay, we'll take a cab," she said.

His hand closed over her arm in a warm, possessive grip. "Then let's go."

His heat penetrated her sleeve and made a quick journey through the rest of her body, finally settling smack-dab between her thighs. Well, so what? She was a twenty-six-year-old woman who didn't have to act on every arousing thought that passed through her mind. She could handle this. She hoped.

As they stepped out of the bar, a chilly wind whipped down the deserted street.

Griffin yelped. "Jesus, it's cold out here!"

"Then let's go back inside and call a cab from there."

"Nah." He grabbed her hand. "We'll run down to the corner where there's more traffic."

"I'm not exactly dressed for a run." She lifted one foot to display her high-heeled boot.

His gaze traveled slowly from her boot up the length of her tight black pants. He seemed to have forgotten all about the cold breeze, the cab, even their surroundings. His grip on her fingers tightened. "I see what you mean."

Whew. That was some elixir she'd brewed. The look in his eyes was hot enough to scorch the material right off her body. "We could jog up to the corner," she said.

He cleared his throat. "Not now."

That's when she noticed the sizable bulge easily detected under the soft fleece of his sweats. She quickly looked away, but it was too late. She was already turned on.

"Let's walk." His voice was low and rough.

"Can you?"

"Barely. But if we don't move out, I'm liable to shove you and your do-me boots up against the nearest wall."

Chapter 4

The cab ride was torture as Griffin fought the urge to take Lily right there on the worn upholstery. The exotic spice of her perfume drove him crazy in the close confines of the cab's backseat. He hugged the side door, afraid that if he touched her at all he'd soon be ripping at her clothes. At his current level of desire, the presence of the cabdriver made no difference to him.

In fact, all social restraints were falling away, while his senses had sharpened considerably. Underlying the tang of her perfume, he breathed in the unmistakable scent of her arousal. He wanted his nose right there, right between her thighs. He wanted his tongue there, too. Moisture pooled in his mouth at the thought.

He recorded the pace of her breathing, which he guessed she was unsuccessfully trying to control. He was in the same boat. If not for the thin veneer of civilization, he'd be panting like a damned dog.

He wanted her with a ferocity that alarmed him. His lust was an immediate thing, a craving that he needed to satisfy tonight. He couldn't plan beyond that, because taking her to bed didn't fit in with any of his long-range goals.

Worse yet, he didn't believe in one-night stands. Yet that's exactly what he had in mind. She'd balked at the idea and he could hardly blame her. He wasn't wild about the concept, either.

But for some reason his libido had taken charge tonight, and he *had to have her.* He wasn't proud of his single-minded pursuit of one night in her bed. He'd never thought of himself as a selfish bastard, but he was acting like one now.

He'd coaxed her into taking him home with her by promising a coffee date. The truth was he had no intention of leaving her tonight without having sex. He would be willing to have it right now in the back of this cab, but he had no condoms and a small part of his brain was still operational, thank God. He was counting on her to have condoms in her apartment.

From inside her trendy backpack lying on the floor of the cab, Lily's cell phone played the opening bars of "Witchy Woman." She leaned down to pull out the phone, which made her scent swirl in the backseat.

Griffin clenched his teeth as a surge of desire made him long to grab her. It was amazing to him that he'd never kissed those full lips.

She flipped open the phone. "Hi, Anica."

He had to look away, because the sight of her mouth moving as she talked to her sister made him long to grab the phone away and thrust his tongue in deep. And that would only be the beginning. He had plans for that mouth she loved to decorate in lipstick the color of ripe cherries. Before the night was through, he wanted cherry-red lipstick marks all over himself.

"Yes, everything's cool," Lily said. "I'm on my way home."

Nothing on Griffin was cool. He'd waged a constant and often unsuccessful battle during the cab ride to keep his penis calm.

"Never mind," Lily said. "It's all under control."

Griffin had the oddest feeling they were talking about him, but that made no sense. How would Lily's sister know about this sudden fixation of his?

"Yeah, I promise I won't do anything you wouldn't

do. Talk to you tomorrow. Bye." She closed the phone and reached over to tuck it into her backpack.

Then she glanced over at Griffin. "Anica worries about me. She knows I'm ... uh ... interested in you."

"It sounded as if she might be warning you away from me."

"She just doesn't want me to do anything I'd regret. She's my big sister, after all. But I can't see how she'd object to us going out for coffee."

"Then why didn't you tell her we were doing that?"

Lily looked away. "Let's just say I have a history of flying in the face of good sense. It's better that she doesn't know we're together. She wouldn't believe I could keep it to a coffee date." She faced him again, her expression resolute. "But that's what we're going to do."

Like hell. He waited for his conscience to kick in, but nothing happened. It seemed that he was determined to seduce this woman whether she wanted him to or not. Funny thing, his instincts told him she did want him to, no matter what she said to the contrary.

After what seemed like the longest cab ride in history but had taken less than ten minutes, they pulled up in front of a four-story brick apartment building that resembled many others that were sprinkled throughout the city.

Griffin dug in the inside pocket of his sweats and came up with the fare. If they actually went for coffee, which he doubted, he could cover that, too. He followed Lily out of the cab and up the cement steps to the front door.

His heart was going crazy with anticipation, but he'd have to keep his cool until the issue of the dog had been settled. They couldn't get naked until the dog—was her name Daisy?—had been allowed out to do her business. Griffin liked dogs a lot and he didn't want to put this one through misery.

Lily paused in the small hallway where the mailboxes

took up one wall. "I'm on the third floor, and there's no elevator. You can wait down here if you want, while I go get Daisy."

"That's okay. I'll go up with you." But as he followed her up the stairs, he regretted the decision. He'd wanted to see her apartment, sort of get the lay of the land where this seduction would take place later on, but doing so meant having the chance to ogle her shapely rear all the way.

It meant following the trail of her scent, both her spicy perfume and her pheromone-laden woman's aroma. The exertion of climbing made him breathe all the more deeply, until his impulse control began to dwindle. Much more of this, and he might—

"You don't have to go all the way up." She paused on the second landing and glanced back at him.

He was partway up, in more ways than one. "I'm fine."

"Seriously, you can wait here. I'm used to this climb."

"I'm okay, really."

"No, you're not. You're panting worse than Daisy does."

Terrific. He could tell her the truth, that he was panting out of sexual frustration, or he could end up looking like a wimp incapable of handling two flights of stairs. Or he could lie.

"I'm training for a marathon," he said. "Mounting . . . I mean *climbing* the stairs is good for me." Damn, even his vocabulary was skewed toward sex.

She shrugged. "If you say so." She started up again, her heels tapping seductively on the wooden staircase.

Watching her fanny sway from side to side as she climbed was heaven. Dealing with the painful condition of his cock was hell. He shouldn't look at her. He should simply put his head down and make the trek up the stairs like a blind man.

Of course he could no more look away than fly to the

moon. Instead he created scenarios in which he caught up with her and they had doggie-style sex on the stairs. Or he joined her on the next landing, backed her up against the wall and took her standing up.

Apparently weeks of denying the attraction he felt for her had built up a hunger of monumental proportions. He couldn't remember ever being this focused on sex with a woman, not even as a teenager. Besides that, his obsession was specific to Lily. He didn't just need to have sex with someone ASAP, he needed to have it with her, and only her.

"Almost there," she called over her shoulder.

Because he was worried about the telltale bulge under his fleece sweats, he forced himself to look at the stair treads instead of her backside for the last few steps.

"This is it." She put her key in the lock of apartment 333. "I can hear Daisy whining."

Too bad it was socially unacceptable for him to whine or he'd be doing it. God, how he wanted her. But the dog had to go out first. He got that.

As he stood hesitantly at the door to the apartment, mindful that the dog might not take to him right away, he wondered if she had a fireplace. There was a smoky scent in the air. Then, across a room that was filled with eye-popping primary colors, he spied the incense burner on the coffee table. That must be what had generated the smell.

Daisy was obviously ecstatic to see Lily. Lily dropped to her knees and wrapped her arms around the wiggling, whining dog. "I missed you, too, sweetheart," she murmured. "Now, I'd like you to meet my friend Griffin."

He hadn't been sure what to expect, given Lily's warning about Daisy not being used to strangers. He'd thought maybe she'd look wary or back away, or maybe even growl a little.

Instead she lifted her head and looked him straight in the eye. It was eerie the instant connection he felt with her, as if they had some prior history. "Nice to meet you, Daisy," he said.

She gave a short bark, as if in acknowledgment. Then she walked over to him with that same knowing gaze in her brown eyes. Her tail wagged slowly, and Griffin could swear she was smiling.

Crouching down, he held out his hand for her to sniff. She did, quite thoroughly; and then she gave his hand a lick.

"I guess it's okay if I pet her," he said.

"Apparently so." Lily seemed slightly bemused herself. "She seems quite taken with you. I'll get her leash."

"Okay." Griffin sank his fingers into Daisy's soft golden fur and scratched behind her ears as she continued to stare at him. He was probably projecting thoughts on her that she wasn't having, but she looked for all the world as if she'd seen him somewhere before and was trying to place him.

He had a similar feeling, as if he knew this dog. But that couldn't be. "Where did you get her?" he called out to Lily.

"From the animal shelter. Why?"

"She acts as if she knows me, and she seems familiar to me, too. But none of my friends have—or had—a golden." He stood as Lily arrived with Daisy's leash and a black nylon jacket she held out to him.

"This is big on me," she said. "If we're going for coffee, you should have something."

"Thanks." He had planned to have coffee at her place because he didn't have a jacket, but Lily had neatly solved that problem. "What about Daisy? Is she going for coffee, too?"

"There's a café about a block away. They have outdoor seating and heaters. Daisy will be fine there. I wish we could go to Anica's shop, Wicked Brew, but it's not all that close and she isn't open at night, anyway. She caters to the office crowd. So this is my second favorite spot."

Apparently he'd have to drink some coffee tonight, after all. It didn't really matter. The evening would still end the same, with both of them naked and enjoying a simultaneous orgasm. But that would take a little longer to accomplish than he'd figured.

They retraced their path down the stairs, this time with Daisy in the lead, Lily coming next and Griffin bringing up the rear. The jacket smelled like Lily, which wasn't helping keep his mind off sex.

The dog was a distraction, though. Griffin decided to concentrate on Daisy in order to get through this coffee-date foreplay. "Was Daisy a stray?" he asked.

Lily took the steps quickly to keep up with Daisy, who seemed eager to get outside. "No, a family left her at the shelter. According to her record, they moved to England and decided not to try and take her."

"Hard to imagine anyone leaving a beautiful dog like this."

"Their loss is my gain. They didn't appreciate her the way I do, or they never would have left her."

"So your apartment allows pets?"

"Luckily they do. I didn't think of that when I moved in, but now I'm really glad."

"It's funny; I made sure my apartment complex allows pets because I wanted to get a golden after I got settled in there. But then I . . . just never did." He wondered now how he'd let that plan slip away.

Sure, he worked long hours, but he had the money to afford a pet sitter who could let the dog out once during the day. If he skipped the happy hour habit, he'd have plenty of time to get in a run with a dog each evening. But if he'd skipped happy hour, he never would have met Lily, and he sure as hell didn't regret that.

"Maybe you just needed someone to nudge you." Lily opened the front door and followed Daisy down the concrete steps. "My sister's the one who convinced me to adopt a dog. I didn't think I had time, but you make time."

"Exactly." Griffin decided then and there to get a dog, a golden like Daisy. By some twisted logic, he might have been waiting until he met the right woman so they could pick out a dog together, but that was nuts. The right woman would like the dog he chose, or she wouldn't be the right woman, would she?

They paused so Daisy could pee in a little patch of gravel about halfway down the block.

"My only worry is that she doesn't get enough aerobic exercise," Lily said as she waited for Daisy to do her thing. "I'm not into running."

"I'm surprised." Griffin remembered his fantasy—tight black Lycra covering her long legs and a black sports bra. "You seem so—"

"Fit? Well, there are the stairs."

"Unless you go up and down them twenty times a day, that's not enough to keep you . . ." How could he describe the perfection of her body? ". . . looking that good." Lame, totally lame. She looked more than good. She looked like a centerfold, someone he wanted to lick all over.

She laughed. "Then I guess it's magic."

He had no problem believing that. Some people were born with the kind of metabolism that kept them in wonderful shape. Lily's kids could very well inherit that metabolism, which would be a bonus for them. And whoever had the privilege of creating those children with Lily would be one lucky bastard sharing her bed every night.

Griffin blinked. Where had all of that come from? His plan was for one hot night with Lily. Nothing in the plan included thoughts about sharing a bed long-term and making babies. In fact, he needed to be absolutely certain she had condoms so there wouldn't be any chance of babies. He needed to get back on track.

The neighborhood coffee shop with the outdoor tables and heaters beckoned from the corner. A yellow neon sign told him it was called Harvey's Hangout. With barrels of red geraniums defining the space and red umbrellas anchoring each wrought-iron table, the place was appealing, although Griffin was more interested in privacy than appeal. This spot offered no privacy whatsoever.

Two of the four sidewalk tables were occupied by couples. Romantic couples, at that, despite the lack of privacy. One pair was simply holding hands across the table while they talked, but the other couple had scooted their chairs close together and looked as if they might kiss at any moment.

Griffin thought that might be a good thing. Watching other people kiss could flip some switches for Lily, and he wanted that. Coffee, with its jack-you-up qualities, wasn't going to help much. Wine would have been better, but a quick check of the chalkboard menu told him he didn't have that option here.

"If you'll grab a table, I'll get our order," he said. "Do you want anything besides coffee?"

"No, thanks. But a tall mocha cappuccino would be great."

He tried not to put any significance on the fact that he always ordered the same thing. "Whipped cream?"

"A little."

There it was, a grown-up version of the hot cocoa he used to love as a kid. It was what he always ordered when he had coffee in the evening. So Lily liked the same kind of coffee drink and the same kind of dog. So what? That didn't mean they were compatible, that they had similar goals in life.

Lots of people probably liked mocha cappuccinos and golden retrievers. And had great bodies with a killer metabolism. It was natural that he wanted to undress her and have sex with her all night, but the relationship didn't have to mean more than that.

He didn't want to make it into more than it was. That had been his parents' mistake, and he didn't plan for history to repeat itself. He just needed to scratch this one, persistent sexual itch, and he'd be good to go.

The coffee shop smelled terrific. He'd been in dozens of coffee shops, and he couldn't remember ever being surrounded by so many heartwarming scents. Coffee, chocolate, steamed milk, cinnamon, hazelnut, and vanilla all combined to give him a sense of rightness and well-being.

He gave his order to the nerdy guy behind the counter whose name tag identified him as Thomas.

"You must be here with Lily," Thomas said.

"Yeah." Griffin discovered a certain pride in admitting that. She might not be right for him long-term, but she was the kind of date a man could feel good about because she was . . . okay, he'd just admit it to himself and try not to feel like a shallow bastard: She was extremely hot. When men looked at Lily, they thought of tangled sheets and slick, naked skin.

As did Griffin, but the more he considered the nerdy guy imagining Lily like that, the less he liked it. All things considered, Griffin had no right to be possessive about Lily. He was in for the short haul.

That meant not caring who else was interested in the lovely Ms. Revere. Thomas wouldn't stand a chance, anyway. He was too young, and not at all Lily's type.

"She always orders this," Thomas said. "I almost started making it when I saw her out there, but since she's here with someone else, I thought she might change her mind."

"Guess not." Griffin recognized the adoration in Thomas's eyes. Poor lovesick kid. Griffin tried not to feel smug. But any smugness vanished when another guy came out from the back, someone who was probably the owner.

He was casually dressed without being sloppy. Jeans

and a white shirt, loafers, good haircut, midthirties. He could easily be Lily's type. He breezed past Griffin, went out the front door and straight over to Lily.

She glanced up and smiled. The interloper, which was how Griffin thought of him, crouched down to pet Daisy, who thumped her tail on the sidewalk. The nerve of the guy, talking to Lily and petting her dog when she was out on a coffee date with someone else.

Griffin's jaw tightened and his fist clenched. And that was ridiculous, because he had zero claim to Lily. Yet he continued to observe the interaction and continued to hate every second of it. He could hardly wait for his order to be ready so he could go out and break up that cozy little chat.

The mocha cappuccinos with a small amount of whipped cream appeared on the counter set into a cardboard tray. Griffin picked it up and made for the door. He couldn't justify his behavior, but he planned to let the guy know right here and now that he was no longer welcome to hang around Lily. Not tonight, anyway.

Chapter 5

Lily had known Brad Harvey for a couple of years. Three months ago they'd gone out on a date, which had convinced Lily of what she'd suspected before—she had no chemistry with Brad. He'd tried to change her mind, but in the end he'd had to settle for being friends.

She was afraid he still carried a torch. Staying away from his shop seemed silly when he could use the business and his was the only decent late-night café within walking distance of her apartment. She'd never brought a date here, though, thinking that would be mean. Maybe not. Maybe it was a good idea for Brad to realize she was interested in someone else.

Brad's smile never wavered when she told him she'd come here with Griffin, but his gaze sharpened. "So he's a customer at the Bubbling Cauldron?"

"Initially. He's more than that now, of course." Or she hoped he would be. From the corner of her eye she saw the café door open and Griffin emerge with their coffee drinks. "Here he comes. Let me introduce you."

"Absolutely. Consider me the big brother you never had, the one who gives your dates the third degree."

"Good luck with that. He's a lawyer." She turned as Griffin approached. "Griffin Taylor, I'd like you to meet Brad Harvey. Brad owns the café."

Balancing the tray with his left hand, Griffin shook hands with his right. "Nice place."

Lily couldn't fault Griffin for the comment, which was perfectly polite, but she was amazed at the curt way it was delivered, without even the hint of a smile. Despite the brief handshake, Griffin wasn't being the least bit friendly.

"Thanks." Brad stuck his hands in his pockets and rocked back on his heels. "It works for me. I'm a night owl like Lil. We've spent many a wee hour together talking and drinking coffee."

Lily almost choked. Between his saying her nickname, something he seldom used, and his implication they were really close friends, he was trying to one-up Griffin. She hadn't seen that coming. But she hadn't expected Griffin to be borderline rude, either.

"I'm something of a night owl, myself." Griffin set the cardboard tray on the table and pulled out the chair nearest Lily. "Great to meet you, Brent," he said with a total lack of enthusiasm.

"It's Brad." Brad made no move to leave. "Lily says you're a lawyer."

"That's right." Griffin didn't look up as he took the drinks out of the segmented tray and placed one in front of Lily.

"Can't be much of a night owl when you have to be in court bright and early."

Griffin looked up at Brad. His gaze was direct. "I recover fast."

Openmouthed, Lily stared at the two men. She'd never seen either of them act this way. They were both normally easygoing and affable. But tonight they were behaving like ... She realized what they were behaving like and had to press her lips together to keep from laughing. They were behaving like two rutting elks vying for a female.

She had no intention of sitting here while the two of them pawed the sidewalk and locked antlers. Pushing back her chair, she untied Daisy's leash from the table leg, stood and picked up her coffee. "Daisy's had almost no exercise today," she said. "If you don't mind, Griffin, I think she needs a longer walk."

"Great idea." Griffin came out of his chair so fast he almost knocked over his coffee. "Let's go."

"See you tomorrow night, Lil," Brad said.

"I may not make it tomorrow night," she said. "My life seems to be on fast-forward these days. Take care, Brad." She turned Daisy toward home because she didn't want to continue down the street and have to pass Harvey's on the way home.

"Right!" Brad called after her. "The engagement party! Can I pick you up?"

"Uh, thanks for the offer, but I'll . . . I'll probably have to go early." Lily squeezed her eyes shut. She'd forgotten that Anica had invited Brad, but only as a friend, someone who knew Lily and was in the same coffee shop business as Anica. Lily had been fine with it until now.

"You come here every night?" Griffin fell into step beside her as they started back toward her apartment.

"No. I don't know why he implied that I do."

"Don't you?" He took her hand and laced his fingers through hers.

Lily sighed. "Yes, I know why he implied that. We went on one date. One. It didn't work out."

"But he wants a second chance."

"Yeah." Now would be the time to ask Griffin to be her date for the engagement party, but she was still afraid he'd reject the idea. They hadn't spent enough quality time together.

She'd envisioned lingering over coffee and discovering all sorts of interesting things about each other. Well, they could do that while they walked.

"If you don't mind, let's go down to the dog park," she said. "Daisy really could use the exercise."

"All right." He didn't sound overjoyed by the prospect.

"You can head home, if you want. I brought my cell, so I could call a taxi."

His grip on her fingers tightened. "I'll stay."

Guilt swept over her again. He was probably sticking around because he hoped that eventually he'd be able to get her into bed. She had the opposite goal. She wanted them to become friends tonight, not lovers.

She took a fortifying drink of her coffee. "I'm going to be straight with you, Griffin. You can hang around until dawn if you want, but I'm not going to bed with you. If that's all you want from me, then maybe you should take a cab home."

"I won't pretend I don't want to have sex with you."

"Thanks for being honest."

"But I've never forced a woman in my life. I'm not about to start now."

She glanced over at him. "You think you'll wear me down, don't you?"

The corners of his mouth twitched, as if he might be trying to control a smile. "That's a very unromantic way of putting it."

"You think you can seduce me, then."

The smile broke through, a confident grin of male pride. "It could happen."

If only he knew how easily. Just talking about having sex with him had dampened her panties. But she understood the consequences and she would be strong. He had no idea that he was dealing with a magic spell that could turn him into her love slave. If he knew, he'd be running in the opposite direction instead of walking along with her, hand in hand, casually and somewhat arrogantly talking about luring her into bed.

They reached the dog park, a grassy area dotted with young trees and enclosed by a chain-link fence. Releasing her hand, Griffin tossed his empty coffee cup in a nearby trash can, opened the metal gate, and motioned them through ahead of him.

"Thank you." Lily waited for him to shut the gate before unhooking Daisy's leash. Daisy had never shown the slightest indication that she'd run away, but Lily wasn't taking any chances. "There you go, Daisy. Knock yourself out."

Daisy circled around in front of them and stood gazing up at them, her tail wagging.

"Go on," Lily said. "Run around. Stretch your legs."

"There aren't any other dogs. She needs someone to play with."

"That's where you're wrong. I've brought her here when there are gobs of dogs, and she acts as if they're beneath her. Sometimes she'll take off running, but it's usually her idea and not because she's chasing or being chased."

Griffin searched the ground at his feet. "Maybe this will work." He picked up a short stick. "Fetch, Daisy!" He tossed the stick several yards away.

Daisy followed the direction of the stick with her gaze but she didn't chase it. Instead she looked expectantly at Griffin, tail wagging.

"What do you want?" he asked. "A tennis ball? I don't have one."

"She wouldn't do any better with a tennis ball. I've tried sticks, chew toys, tennis balls. She has no interest in playing fetch. It's almost as if she's too smart to do that kind of repetitive game."

"Then maybe she'd like to run with me." Griffin took off the jacket Lily had loaned him and handed it to her. "Let's see what happens if I invite her for a run. Daisy, would you like to jog around the park with me?"

Daisy gave a short bark.

"I feel as if I'm in the middle of *Lassie Come Home*," Griffin muttered. "Okay, come on, Daisy! Let's run!" He took off and Daisy bounded beside him, mouth open, tongue flapping.

Lily had never seen her dog so happy. If a running partner was what Daisy needed, then Lily would have to become that running partner no matter how much she loathed the activity. On the positive side, she'd have to go shopping for running gear. Any activity that required shopping wasn't all bad.

Meanwhile, Daisy and Griffin looked like a clip from a dog food commercial. The security lights surrounding the dog park illuminated their joyful romp around the perimeter. Griffin zigzagged as he ran, challenging Daisy to figure out which way he'd go next. At one point he spun in a circle and charged back the other way. Daisy turned like a professional sheepdog and was instantly back at Griffin's side.

His laughter carried across the distance between them, and Lily was reminded how much she loved his laugh. It was the first thing that had drawn her to him. She'd heard that laugh in the din of the Bubbling Cauldron and wanted to know the man it belonged to.

When she'd spotted Griffin, she'd been struck by how well he matched his laugh. She would have pictured a man like him—solid of build, the kind of cropped hair favored by athletes and a good-humored twinkle in his hazel eyes. That good humor had gone missing when Griffin had encountered Brad, though.

She had to assume the elixir had made him uncharacteristically territorial. As she thought back over the meeting, she decided Griffin had opened the hostilities by being less than gracious during the introduction. Brad had escalated the unacknowledged battle, and then both of them had completely lost their charm.

Griffin's charm was back in spades at the moment as he cavorted with Daisy. Lily wished she could have a video of this. Maybe if things worked out between them, she could bring a camera to the park some Saturday morning and get footage of Griffin playing with Daisy. They did seem to get along exceptionally well.

Well, duh, they should. Griffin was currently operating under a spell that included a massive dose of Daisy's essence. No wonder he felt such a kinship with the dog, and she with him. Maybe once the spell wore off, they wouldn't delight in each other so much. That was a depressing thought.

Griffin spread his arms and started zooming around like a stunt plane, complete with sound effects. Daisy loved it. When Griffin crouched down as if going into a dive, Daisy gathered herself and leaped over him. He tried it again, and she repeated the trick.

"Did you see that?" Griffin called out to Lily.

"I did!"

"This dog could be in a show!" Griffin made a large half circle using both arms, and sure enough Daisy leaped neatly through it. Griffin let out a whoop and dropped to his knees to ruffle her fur and scratch behind her ears.

Lily snorted softly to herself. All she had to do was learn to jump through hoops like Daisy, and Griffin would be enthralled. Just like a man.

Griffin and Daisy trotted up, both of them panting.

"How about that?" Griffin beamed at her. "Did you know she could do those tricks?"

"Can't say that I did."

He stroked the dog's head. "Makes me wonder what else she knows."

You would be amazed. But Lily thought it was a little early in the relationship to reveal her witch status and what she'd learned of Daisy's magical tendencies. Lily had a theory about the leaping tricks. Daisy was bored with the usual doggie games like fetch, but once a human started playing with her, she became inspired to show off.

Not being the athletic type, Lily hadn't brought out that side of Daisy. "Thanks for giving her such a great workout."

"It was fun." Griffin continued to fondle Daisy's ears, but his caress slowed the longer he gazed at Lily. "I thought maybe if I wore myself out I wouldn't want you so desperately."

She didn't have to ask how that was working out. His hazel eyes had once again begun to glow with lust. And his obvious emotional heat stirred an answering response in her. She swallowed. "We should walk to the corner and hail you a cab."

"Please don't." He moved toward her. "At least not until I've kissed you. We can't end this night without at least one kiss."

"I think kissing would be a really bad idea." Even so, she stood right there and let him pull her into his arms.

"I think it would be a really good idea." His head lowered.

Behind him, Daisy whined.

"Daisy thinks so, too," he said.

No doubt Daisy did think so. Lily wondered if by using Daisy's essence for the spell, she'd unwittingly made Daisy a coconspirator in this match-up.

Then Griffin's mouth touched hers, and every coherent thought melted. All her concerns, all her reservations, were swept away in a river of sensation. Needs that she'd been desperately trying to control flooded through her at an alarming rate.

She'd been kissed before, kissed a lot, in fact. Nothing had prepared her for Griffin's all-out assault. From the moment his lips touched hers, she had no doubt of his ultimate objective. The urgency of the kiss delivered by any other man would have turned her off.

But Griffin knew what he was about. The skill with which he kissed her telegraphed the skill he would exhibit in the bedroom. What a dizzying prospect. She would be able to abandon herself to the experience because she had found a man who knew what he was doing.

Was it the spell that allowed him to know exactly how she needed to be kissed? Would it also guide him as to exactly how she needed to be loved?

As pleasure swirled through her, as she fought to keep her sanity, one question kept bubbling to the surface of her fevered brain. If she denied him on this fateful night, if she sent him away and allowed the spell to wear off, they might both miss the best sex of their lives.

Surely, given that circumstance, she would be forgiven for surrendering. Every woman, and especially every magical woman, deserved one perfect night.

Griffin lifted his mouth a fraction away from hers. His breath was warm and scented with chocolate-flavored coffee. "We need to go home."

In some ways it was an odd thing to say. It was her home, not his, and certainly not theirs. But at the moment *home* meant being alone with him in a place where they could explore, taste, enjoy. She couldn't refuse him.

"Yes, it's time. Let's go."

Chapter 6

This time Griffin barely noticed the climb to the third floor. He was running on pure adrenaline and in sight of his goal. Once they were inside Lily's apartment, he made sure the door was locked while she dragged Daisy's bed out into the living room.

"Stay," she said to the dog.

Then she caught Griffin's hand, pulled him into her bedroom, and shut the door.

He took a quick inventory of his surroundings, noting the black enameled headboard and dresser, mood lighting that cast a fiery glow, red linens and a purple blanket. If Lily made love the way she decorated, he was in for one hell of a ride.

She might very well be that dramatic. He'd ditched the jacket in the living room, and she was already sliding her soft hands under his T-shirt. That gentle caress had incredible consequences. His cock instantly jerked to rigid, quivering attention.

It demanded to be served, but before his control disappeared entirely, he had to take care of business. Cupping her face in both hands, he leaned down to nibble her lower lip. "Condoms," he murmured.

She tickled her fingers through his chest hair and brushed them over his nipples. "Left-hand bedside table drawer."

He groaned at the sensation of her hands on him. "That's all I needed to know." From that point on he was a man on a mission. His single-mindedness soon had her stretched on the red coverlet, wearing nothing but the silver hoops in her earlobes.

He'd kept her far too busy to undress him, so he nudged off his shoes, pulled off his T-shirt, and climbed into bed with her. The rest of his clothes would disappear in due time, but for now, he wanted to feast on the banquet that was Lily.

She was a study in contrasts—alabaster skin tinged with the rosy glow of arousal, accented by the midnight-black triangle concealing his ultimate destination.

His hungry gaze swept over her, lingering on the tempting pout of her nipples and the sweet indentation of her navel. His gaze dropped lower to a flash of dew-dropped pink amid the black curls. His pulse rate sky-rocketed. Yes, there.

Her voice was low and sultry. "Let me see you, Griffin."

"I'm not nearly as exciting to look at as you are."

She smiled. "That depends on your perspective. Take it off, Griffin. Take it all off."

He did, and was gratified by the blatant eagerness in her expression.

"Now let me touch," she said.

As if he would object. Stretching out on the bed next to her, his cock pointing at the ceiling, he invited her to explore. He'd never been with a woman who enjoyed the process this much. By the time she'd stroked, nibbled and licked her way over his hot skin, he was ready to explode.

At the very moment he decided to make her stop so he could salvage some staying power, she seemed to sense that he'd reached the end of his sexual rope. That kind of awareness in a woman was hard to find. He knew. He'd looked.

She slid up next to him, her body like velvet, her warmth issuing a siren's call. "If I thought you could take it, I'd suck on your dick."

He rolled to face her. "If I thought I could take it, I'd let you. But I have a better idea."

"Ideas are good."

"This one's outstanding." Easing her to her back, he began kissing his way down the length of her body.

Her breathing quickened the closer he drew to her flash point. "I think I know where this is going," she said.

"Or coming." He reached the object of his quest, a spot fragrant with pheromones. Gently he probed with his tongue, and she arched upward with a sharp gasp. This wouldn't take very long.

He wanted—*needed*—to give her an orgasm before he lost himself completely in her heat. Once that happened, he couldn't guarantee what he'd do. Knowing the urges driving him to bury his cock in her, he could become completely oblivious to her pleasure. He hoped not and that wasn't like him, but with this woman, this level of lust, he couldn't be sure.

And so he opened his mouth over her moist sweetness and used his tongue to send her into a frenzy. He loved the way she moaned, deep in her throat, as if his caress touched off a primitive reaction she couldn't control. He didn't want her to control it.

From the first moment he'd glimpsed her in the bar, he'd sensed something wild in her. That very wildness had made him back off and decide she wasn't the one for him. Apparently he wasn't that strong, because tonight he'd been blindsided by the compulsion to have her.

If this was to be his only night with Lily, he was going for broke. He was determined to arouse her wild side and discover what sort of woman she would become when the veneer of civilization had slipped away.

Making her climax was no challenge. But he wanted more than a mere orgasm. He wanted to turn her inside out and shatter her world, because he sensed that she was about to shatter his.

The ache in his loins was more powerful than anything he'd ever experienced. In order for her to be ready for that kind of intensity, in order for her to accept the vigor of his first thrust, she had to be wide open, her womb already pulsing in welcome.

And she would be. He felt the surge of orgasmic power building within her. She began to pant and utter breathless, pleading cries, as if she couldn't get there fast enough. Sliding both hands under her hips, he lifted her up, which gave him even better access.

Her fingers dug into his scalp as she urged him on. He gloried in the force of her wanting as he plundered her riches, sucking her in, stroking her relentlessly with the flat of his tongue. She trembled, drew in a sharp breath, quivered again. He pressed down hard with his tongue and she came noisily, in a juicy, wonderful rush that filled him with even greater lust.

Another time he would kiss and lick and soothe her trembling vagina, but not now. Now marked that moment of desperation when he would die if he didn't plunge into her. Leaving her moaning and undulating in the aftershock of her orgasm, he located the condoms in record time and put one on faster than he ever had in his life.

Quickly he moved between her quivering thighs, found that hot, wet center that he'd so recently abandoned and drove home. He barely recognized the bellow of triumph coming from him. The next few minutes were a blur of sensation as he began to thrust with increasing speed.

He was vaguely aware that she was tightening around him with every stroke, but he'd lost the ability to gauge whether she was ready to come or not. He no longer cared. His world centered on the pistonlike motion that carried him closer and closer to his personal nirvana.

Almost there. He pumped faster, breathing hard. Now. Yes. *Now!* He hurled himself into her, his body racked with tremors that left him gasping for air.

She cried out and lifted her hips. The constrictions of her climax stimulated his cock even more, increasing the pleasure until it bordered on pain. He groaned and sought to push even deeper into her rippling chamber. He couldn't get enough of her. He'd never be able to get enough. Never.

Lily drifted in and out of sleep, but something wasn't right. A heavy weight pressed her down and breathing normally was a struggle. Not only that, a warm breeze was coming from somewhere and it tickled her ear.

Eventually she roused herself enough to realize the weight was Griffin and he was out like a light. His head lay tucked against her shoulder, and that's why a breeze tickled her ear.

She wasn't surprised that he was asleep. That had been some session, and if he weren't sprawled on top of her like a stone, she'd be asleep, too. Great sex could have that kind of effect on a person.

But this had been more than great sex. This had been life-altering sex, and it was all her fault. She waited for guilt to extinguish her post-great-sex glow, but for some reason, that didn't happen.

Maybe she hadn't done something so terrible, after all. She and Griffin liked the same coffee drink. They liked the same kind of dog. Sexually they were a terrific match. Relationships had been built on less than that.

Then again, she might not be thinking straight because she couldn't get enough oxygen to her brain. Somehow she had to move Griffin before he crushed her. She'd like to move him without waking him, though.

All her rationalizations aside, she was slightly nervous about what life would be like for each of them now. With Griffin still asleep, she could paint a rosy picture of two compatible people enjoying each other's company. She could forget about Anica's dire warnings.

But she also had to breathe. She began by giving his shoulder a nudge. It was like trying to move a statue in Grant Park.

She might have to wake him up a little bit, just enough to get him to shift over on his own. If she shook him . . . She tried her best to accomplish a decent shake, but nothing happened. He wasn't moving. She'd always liked the fact that he looked so solid, but now that he was both solid and unconscious, she faced a problem.

Wiggling out from under him didn't work, either. She was pinned to the bed and her chest hurt. She called his name, but he didn't respond. She called louder. Still no movement from Griffin.

If the sleep clinic at the University of Chicago needed a poster boy, Griffin would be their guy. She'd known good sleepers in her life but he was a world champion. Of course, this particular deep sleep might have more than a little magic going for it. After all, he'd just had the most significant sexual experience of his life. That sort of thing probably induced all sorts of heavy-duty sleep needs.

Unfortunately, she'd have to wake him up. Somehow. Reaching up, she took hold of his ear. "Griffin, wake up." She pinched his ear gently.

He moaned softly but didn't move even a centimeter.

"Griffin, sweetie, you have to move." She threw the *sweetie* in there because she was about to inflict more pain. She pinched his ear really hard.

"Ow!" Scrambling up, he stared down at her in shock, his hazel eyes filled with accusation. "You pinched my ear!"

"Only because I couldn't get you to move any other way. I'm sorry. I was suffocating with you lying on top of me."

As he gazed down at her, all the irritation faded from his expression. "You're so beautiful."

She smiled. "Maybe sometimes, but not at the moment. At the moment I'm sure my makeup's smeared and my hair's a wreck. That's nice of you to say, though."

"I'm not saying it to be nice. You're gorgeous. I could eat you up. But I need to grab a shower. Then I'll follow up on that thought."

Before she could open her mouth, he'd left the bed and disappeared into her bathroom. She turned her head and checked the bedside clock. Two fifteen in the morning, and Griffin sounded as if he was ready to go another round. Whew. Well, she could probably manage that, especially if she showered herself.

While she could sleep in, however, she'd be surprised if he could. She wasn't a lawyer, but she'd watched TV shows about lawyers, and the job seemed to include a lot more pressure than her bartending duties. She didn't think Griffin could afford to show up exhausted.

If the spell had worked, and by his reaction she had a feeling it had, then they'd have many more nights like this. They didn't have to experience everything immediately, and they'd both probably enjoy themselves more if they got some rest.

The shower was already running by the time she worked up the energy to climb out of bed. In theory, making love all night sounded great. In practice, for a couple of working folks, it could cause problems.

She walked into the steamy bathroom, but even with the mirror fogged, she could see that her hair was sticking out in all directions. Not what she'd call gorgeous. But his comment had been good for her ego.

From inside the shower came the sound of a washcloth

slapping against damp skin. Her libido perked up, but she told it to calm down. She and Griffin needed several hours of sleep more than they needed to dance another horizontal mambo.

"Griffin?"

"I'm almost done."

"Listen, I'm flattered that you want to pick up where we left off, but you have to get up early for work. What if we make a plan for tomorrow night after I'm finished at the Bubbling Cauldron?"

He turned off the shower and slid back the curtain decorated with red and black swirls.

She gulped. There was nothing quite like a fine specimen of manhood standing in a girl's shower to ruin all her noble intentions. His muscled body glistened in the overhead light. Droplets of water clung to his chest hair and the dark curls surrounding his penis.

As her gaze wandered in that direction, his balls tightened and his penis swelled. He had quite a package there, and she was mesmerized by the rapid inflation going on.

"I can't wait until tomorrow night," he said quietly.

Her brain stalled. She'd been trying to make a point, but damned if she could remember what it was.

"Stay right there." He stepped out of the tub and left the bathroom. "I'll put something on."

"Don't do that on my account." She couldn't have moved if she'd wanted to. The sight of his tight ass when he'd walked away had rooted her to the spot. No doubt she'd had her hands on that very fine part of his anatomy earlier tonight, but she must not have been paying proper attention. That was the kind of feature a girl needed to worship with both sight and touch.

When he returned, she realized what he'd meant by *putting something on.* He was nicely dressed in another condom. His eyes were hot as they roamed over her.

Suddenly sleep was the farthest thing from her mind.

Her nerve endings began to hum and her vagina grew slick with anticipation. "I take it you have a plan?"

"Uh-huh." Circling her waist with his big hands, he lifted her to the bathroom counter. "Lean back on your hands and spread your legs for me."

She did as he asked, feeling wanton and daring as she gave him a full, well-lit view.

"Nice." He ran his knuckles gently over her moist folds.

She closed her eyes as his lazy touch carried her closer to an orgasm than she cared to admit. She'd never been this responsive with any man, and she shocked herself a little.

"I think you like that," he murmured.

"Mm." She fought to steady her breathing, but it was no use. The more he casually brushed her with his knuckles, the more her control slipped.

"I think you might like this, too." Using one hand to steady her on the counter, he began to caress her more deliberately. Parting her, he slid two fingers in partway as his thumb settled with devastating accuracy over her clit. "Look at me."

Opening her eyes, she discovered his were heavy lidded with passion.

"I want us to be looking at each other when I make you come." He circled her clit with his thumb as he curved his fingers and stroked her G-spot.

"That's a bad idea." She groaned as her climax bore down on her at breakneck speed. "Nobody . . . oh, that's good . . . nobody looks good when they're coming."

"You will."

"No. Let's both . . . close our eyes." She squeezed hers shut as she felt the wave about to crash over her.

"Lily, look at me."

She could hardly refuse him when he was doing such a lovely thing for her. She opened her eyes right before the first contraction. She opened her mouth, too, so that she could give vent to the pleasure. Her cries echoed in the small bathroom.

His face was a fierce mask of triumph; and then his image blurred as her orgasm rolled through her and rolled through her again. But as he'd demanded, she kept her eyes open. It was the least she could do.

As he had the last time, he entered her while the walls of her vagina were still flexing with her climax. The exquisite timing of his penetration meant that with each stroke, he took her surely and confidently back up the mountain she'd so recently hurtled down.

Instinctively she wrapped her legs around his waist, increasing the friction.

"Yeah, like that. Good." He pumped faster, his big hands clutching her tight so the force of his thrusts wouldn't send her sliding right across the counter into the large wall mirror behind her.

She gasped, ready to fly apart once again. "Griffin, I'm—"

"Me, too, babe." He increased the pace a fraction more. "Ah yes."

"I'm coming!"

With a shout, Griffin pushed deep one last time and held her tight as his large body quaked and his chest heaved. Through it all he held her gaze, as if keeping that connection was even more important than keeping the tight connection between their bodies.

When they'd both caught their breath, he withdrew and disposed of the condom. Then he picked her up and carried her to bed.

Her back to him, she snuggled against him, spoon fashion. "Now we'll sleep." Her eyes drifted closed.

"Maybe." He tucked her in close and cupped her breast. "No guarantees. I seem to be obsessed with you."

Her eyes snapped open and she stared into the darkness. Then she told herself to relax. The novelty would wear off and then he'd be more like a regular boyfriend, one who liked sex but could do without it sometimes so that each of them could get on with their normal routine. At least she hoped it would work out that way.

Chapter 7

After years of needing to be at the office before nine, Griffin had trained himself to wake up at seven, which he did, right on schedule. Waking up naked wasn't unusual—he wasn't a pajama kind of guy—but waking up with a naked woman on a weekday wasn't his usual pattern.

After the first jolt of surprise he felt a sense of rightness, as if he was supposed to be here with Lily this morning. He might just call in sick to the office. Sure, he had the Altman hearing this morning, but he could ask Kevin to handle that for him. Estelle Altman should be fine with that.

Propping himself up on one elbow, he gazed at Lily, who was still fast asleep. If he remembered correctly, her shift at the Bubbling Cauldron didn't begin until four in the afternoon. She was probably used to staying up late and sleeping in. He didn't want to disturb that routine.

Naturally, though, as he watched her sleep he got a hard-on. He briefly considered waking her up so they could have sex again, but that seemed like a damned selfish thing to do, no matter how much he wanted to. Besides, if he played his cards right, he might be able to spend most of the day in bed with her.

He'd sacrifice short-term for long-term gain. She would probably sleep for at least another couple of hours. That left him plenty of time to prepare for a day of hanging out with Lily.

Something niggled at him, a thought having to do with his original plan regarding Lily. Had he figured on one night with her to get her out of his system? If so, he'd seriously miscalculated. He had no intention of ending this relationship after one night.

In fact, he had no intention of ending this relationship anytime soon. That was weird, because Lily was no more right for him today than she'd been yesterday, and yet he couldn't imagine giving her up. Eventually he would have to, but not in the near future.

That being the case, he needed to take a cab home, grab a change of clothes and come right back. He'd borrow her key. Maybe he should have an extra one made while he was at it. That would simplify things, because he expected to spend quite a bit of time in her apartment.

Moving carefully so as not to disturb her, he climbed out of bed and gathered his clothes and shoes. Then he crept, naked, into the living room and was greeted enthusiastically by Daisy. Oh yeah. He'd nearly forgotten about the dog.

She danced in front of him, obviously wanting to go out. Logically, she shouldn't be desperate if she lived on Lily's schedule. The dog would be fine until he came back with fresh clothes, maybe even croissants. He'd check to make sure Lily had a coffeepot and coffee before he left.

But as he pulled on his clothes, including the jacket Lily had loaned him, Daisy pranced around him, tongue out, as if she just knew they were going to play some more in the park. In the end, he couldn't leave without her.

Scribbling a note on a pad saying he'd taken Daisy for a walk, he left the note on the table in front of the sofa. He'd checked the kitchen and found a coffeemaker, a grinder and a jar of fresh beans that smelled exactly like the ones he had at home.

Daisy's leash and Lily's keys were on a small table next to the front door. Griffin snapped Daisy's leash on her collar, pocketed Lily's keys and headed out the front door, locking it behind him.

On the street, people were heading off to work. Horns blared and people in business clothes whistled for cabs. Griffin felt very strange being out here in his sweats, walking a dog on a Wednesday morning. Maybe he should let Daisy do her business, take her back to Lily, and return to his apartment.

He still had time to change and make it to work on time. The Altman hearing was important, and Kevin hadn't been briefed on it. Griffin needed to be there to make sure the agreement they'd hammered out didn't get mucked up somehow.

But Daisy didn't seem interested in doing her business. She pulled on the leash, urging him in the direction of the dog park. Oh, what the hell. Estelle Altman would be fine. He'd ironed out all the issues, and a robot could handle the hearing. Kevin wouldn't mind helping out.

Once Griffin had made up his mind, he approached the dog park with relish. He'd had a great time with Daisy the night before, and he looked forward to testing out her abilities even more.

The place wasn't deserted this morning. A guy in jeans and a sweatshirt had brought a standard poodle to run, and a matronly woman was trying to get her cocker spaniel to play with the poodle. Neither dog seemed interested in the other.

Considering the time of day, Griffin didn't expect either the guy or the woman to recognize Daisy. Daisy was probably lucky if she got to the dog park by noon, so he wouldn't have to explain why he was here instead of Lily. Not that he minded advertising his relationship with Lily, but he wasn't quite sure what the nature of it was yet.

He wanted to be with her. That much he knew for

sure. But if someone had asked him to explain why that was, after he'd specifically decided against going out with her, he wouldn't have been able to offer an explanation. A logical guy like Griffin found that perplexing. For the first time in recent memory, he didn't understand his own actions.

The connection with Daisy was far easier to understand. He'd always loved goldens, and Daisy was an exceptional example of the breed. After he opened the gate, she walked into the dog park as if she owned the place.

Griffin unsnapped her leash, curious as to what she'd do regarding the other two dogs. Lily had said Daisy hadn't seemed interested in playing with other dogs, so now he had a chance to witness that for himself.

First Daisy took care of her necessary business in a small gravel area near the trash cans and the convenient dispenser of disposable bags. Griffin handled his part of the chore as Daisy pranced over toward the standard poodle.

So much for Lily's claim, Griffin thought as Daisy and the poodle greeted each other in the familiar head-to-tail routine.

"Pretty dog," said the guy in jeans.

"Thanks." Honesty prompted Griffin to explain. "She's a friend's dog."

"I wondered. I haven't seen a golden around this time of day."

"I'm sure Lily brings her later." Griffin discovered he was happy about that. The guy in jeans might appeal to Lily, and Griffin didn't want them bonding over their dogs.

He didn't want Lily bonding with anyone, come to think of it, other than him. He wasn't sure what he and Lily were to each other, but when he thought of another man showing interest, he felt like growling. Funny; he wasn't ordinarily the jealous type.

"I hope she takes to Max," the guy said. "The cocker spaniel doesn't want to play, and Max loves to run."

"So does Daisy." He remembered the thrill of chasing around the park with her last night. She'd seemed to read his mind, which was crazy, but he hadn't been able to shake the idea, especially after he'd executed his airplane maneuver with the thought that if she leaped over him it would be very cool. Then she'd leaped.

"Will you look at that?" The guy stood, hands thrust in his jeans pockets, as Daisy led Max over to the cocker spaniel. "It's almost as if she's introducing them."

"It is. But I'm sure we're assigning motives that aren't there." In his line of work, he saw that all the time. It was one of the principle reasons for divorce.

"Could be. So, are you self-employed?"

Griffin glanced at him. "Why do you say that?"

"You have the look of a professional, but you're here on a weekday morning. I peg you as a consultant."

"Actually, I'm a lawyer who decided to take the day off."

The guy laughed. "So you could walk your girlfriend's dog?"

"Something like that." Examined in the cold light of logic, his behavior made no sense. The dog didn't need to be walked right now, and he didn't have to spend the day with Lily. Or did he? His urge to do that was one of the strangest ones he'd had in ages.

"All I can say is, your girlfriend has a very unusual dog. Somehow she's coaxed Max to play with the cocker while she stands on the sidelines."

"As if she's admiring her handiwork," Griffin said.

"I was thinking the same thing. But like you said, we're probably assigning motives that don't exist. She's only a dog."

"That's true, but I'd love to know her background. Lily adopted her from an animal shelter, and I have the feeling this dog was trained in ways that most aren't."

"Maybe so." The guy turned and stuck out his hand. "Mitch Adams. Semisuccessful novelist."

Griffin shook his hand. "Griffin Taylor. Divorce lawyer." Now he was doubly glad Lily slept late. A novelist would pique her curiosity for sure.

"I probably should have met you a year ago when I was going through my divorce. In any case, thanks for bringing Daisy this morning. She's an excellent matchmaker."

Griffin laughed. "No problem." Daisy had trotted over to him as if she was ready to leave. "Guess we're outta here."

"Maybe I'll see you again," Mitch said.

"Probably not during the week. Most of the time I really do have to work."

"I'm here every day," Mitch said.

"All righty, then. I'll probably be around this weekend." As he snapped Daisy's leash onto her collar, he wondered how he could be so sure that he'd be at the dog park this weekend. Yet he knew he probably would.

He was at a loss to explain it, but somehow, some way, he'd become hooked up with Lily Revere. That reminded him that he needed to break that date with Debbie. He definitely wouldn't be going out with her on Saturday. He was involved with Lily, now.

Lily woke and stretched, feeling the unfamiliar twinges that accompanied a night of good sex. The who and the why didn't come to her right away. Then she remembered. Griffin. Griffin!

She sat up and looked at the bedside clock. After ten already. Griffin must have decided to leave without waking her. That was considerate of him, but she wondered where they stood. Was he coming back? Had the spell worked the way it was supposed to?

Then the aroma of coffee drifted through the bedroom door, which was now open. She listened more closely and heard the rustling of paper. Surely Griffin wasn't still here? He had a job, obligations. He couldn't hang around her apartment.

Slipping out of bed, she took a red silk robe from the back of her bedroom door and put it on. They'd been very intimate during the night, but waltzing out in her birthday suit wasn't her style. She didn't know what sort of discussion they would have this morning, either, and the robe gave her a measure of psychic protection. She'd inherited it from her great-aunt Violet, the powerful witch and spell maker from whom she'd inherited the tendency to get jacked up whenever she did magic.

Still, she winced at the picture she probably made. She hadn't taken off her makeup last night, and her hair was probably in even worse shape than when she'd glimpsed it in the bathroom mirror hours ago. She could use a magic spell to repair the damage, but that would require her wand, which was somewhere in the living room.

Dear goddess, she hoped she hadn't left her wand lying about. The last thing she wanted was for Griffin to discover she was a witch. She had a few books in the bookcase, but those could be the result of idle curiosity. Her crystal ball could be dismissed as a trinket.

She might even be able to explain the wand, but the more things in plain view, the more questions he might ask. She'd rather avoid all that, at least for the time being. In her experience, men didn't like thinking they'd been hoodwinked, and in a manner of speaking, that's what she'd done to Griffin.

The fact that he was still here meant the spell had worked better than she'd even imagined. She'd have to make sure he returned to work, though, because an unemployed boyfriend wasn't her idea of a good situation. It wouldn't impress her parents, either, who were arriving tomorrow.

The coffee smelled delicious, though. She wasn't used to waking up to the smell of coffee in her apartment.

If she wanted coffee in the morning, she had to make it herself or take the bus over to Anica's shop, Wicked Brew.

Anica. She would have a royal fit at this turn of events. Lily had to pray that she hadn't called this morning, and that if she had, Griffin had let it ring. Surely he wouldn't answer her phone. Surely not.

She walked into the living room to find him in jeans and a chambray shirt, lounging on her sofa, reading the *Tribune.* A cup of coffee sat on the lamp table beside him. Daisy lay at his feet looking quite pleased with herself.

He glanced up from the paper. "Your sister called."

"And you let the machine get it, right?"

"No, I didn't. I was afraid the phone would wake you, so I answered."

She closed her eyes. "Zeus's balls."

"What?"

"Never mind." Opening her eyes, she took a deep breath. "What did Anica say?"

"She was surprised to hear me answer."

"I can only imagine how surprised she was."

"She said the two of you had planned to get together to discuss the plans for moving her engagement party to the Bubbling Cauldron. She asked if you'd call her when you got up."

Now, there was a call Lily didn't want to return. "I'll do that in a little while. But first, not to be rude or anything, but don't you have to be at the office?"

"I told them I was taking the day off."

"Really." She appreciated the impulse, sort of, but she had things to do today. For example, she needed to talk to her sister about the engagement party. That conversation would now be made much more difficult because Anica would want to know what the hell Griffin had been doing answering her phone first thing in the morning.

"I thought we could hang out here for a while, ease into the day. Daisy's been walked, the coffee's made, and I have fresh croissants in the kitchen."

All this was a little metrosexual for her, but she hated to seem unappreciative. "Thank you. That's great."

His gaze swept over her. "Nice robe."

"It's a hand-me-down."

"I doubt the previous owner filled it out like that."

"Thanks." Her traitorous body reacted to his heated look, but she didn't have time for hanky-panky. If she didn't call Anica soon, her sister was liable to show up here. Lily tightened the sash on her robe. "I need to shower and get dressed."

"Go ahead and shower. Want me to bring you some coffee?"

From the way he was looking at her, she could guess that bringing her coffee would result in shower sex. After all, he knew where the condoms were. She couldn't deny the jolt of excitement at the thought of Griffin using the hand-held shower head on her willing body, but she couldn't indulge either of them right now. As it was, she'd have to do some fast talking to convince Anica everything was fine.

And it was fine. Griffin might be going slightly off the deep end, but she'd correct his course. Once she got him back into his normal nine-to-five routine, all would be well.

In the meantime she had a few fires to put out. She could do that more efficiently once she was showered and dressed.

"That's okay," she said. "I'll grab some coffee and a croissant on the way out."

"You're leaving?" He looked stunned. "I thought the two of us could—"

"Nice idea, but it won't work today. I need to meet Anica at the Bubbling Cauldron. We have to make plans for her party, and we can't do it while the place is open for business. That would be awkward."

"I see."

"Taking the day off is a nice gesture, Griffin, but it's sort of impractical right now. This is a busy time." And it would get much busier once Anica started chewing her ass for letting Griffin spend the night.

Griffin folded the paper, set it on the sofa, and stood. "Then maybe I should head on over to the office."

"I think that's a wonderful idea."

He crossed the room and took her by the shoulders. "Tonight, then."

"Tonight?" She was confused. She didn't remember making a date with him, and besides, she had to work.

"I'll come by the Bubbling Cauldron near closing. I'll take you home." He looked into her eyes as he gently kneaded her shoulders. "And then I'll take you to bed."

Heaven help her, but she wasn't going to refuse that offer.

Chapter 8

"You spent the night *where*?" Kevin sat with Griffin at their favorite hot dog joint half a block from the office.

"I guess I just snapped." Griffin scrubbed a hand over his face. Lack of sleep was catching up with him. He'd ordered black coffee to go with his kraut dog. "All of a sudden I couldn't stay away from her another minute."

Kevin nodded. "She's hot, I'll grant you that. She must be *really* hot for you to call in sick."

"Yeah, well, that was pretty dumb." Griffin still felt sheepish about assuming he and Lily would spend the day together. Of course she had plans. And he had an important court hearing he'd almost missed.

"I've never been so glad to see anybody as when you walked into the hearing this morning. Estelle Altman almost peed her pants when she found out I'd be taking your place."

Griffin glanced across the table and grinned. "Maybe she was just excited to be working with you."

"'Fraid not, buddy boy. You're the one she wants as her lawyer, and I think she'd take you in every other way, too, if you were open to that. If you wanted a hot cougar, she'd be there for you. Mark my words."

"I have enough troubles with Lily."

"Listen, anytime you have too many women hanging

all over you, let me know. I may be short, but I have a helluva package." He waggled his eyebrows.

Griffin laughed. Kevin's overabundance in that department had been a running joke all through college. "You do all right for yourself. You don't need me to pimp for you."

"I have reasonable success, but I've never run into the woman who could inspire me to call in sick when I had major things going on at the office. So how did that all shake out? Obviously you went back to the bar later on."

Griffin described his restlessness, the need to run, and then the overwhelming urge to see Lily.

Kevin's eyes widened. "That doesn't sound normal, man. I mean, it wasn't like you had a relationship going on."

"Only in my head. And I kept telling myself she was the wrong woman for me, so I stayed away."

"Note to self: Denying a strong sexual attraction can make normal guys act in irrational ways. You *ran* from your apartment to the bar?"

"Yeah, but—"

"That's got to be a good five miles, maybe closer to seven."

"I suppose." Griffin hadn't taken the time to figure out the mileage. "It didn't feel that far."

"No, because your gonads were providing rocket power. I have to hand it to you, Griff. You worked a full day, made that run and then played mattress bingo the rest of the night. Keep up that shit and you'll be a legend in your own time."

"I'm a little bushed, to be honest."

"Glad to hear it; otherwise I'd be totally intimidated. So I guess you've changed your mind about Lily, huh?"

Griffin blinked. "What do you mean?"

"I know your MO, buddy. You don't have sex with a woman unless she's a possibility for that walk down the aisle."

Griffin choked on his coffee and then had to spend time mopping up the mess.

Kevin's gaze was filled with speculation. "Judging from your reaction, you haven't given a whole lot of thought to matrimony during this gig."

"No." Griffin cleared his throat. "No, I haven't, and you're right, that's not like me. I don't let myself get carried away by the sex. Or I haven't, until . . ."

"Now," Kevin finished for him.

"Right." He mopped up the last of the spewed coffee. "I need to take a look at that."

"If you're open to a little advice . . ."

Griffin glanced up. He'd been friends with Kevin for more than ten years. They'd seen each other through drunken frat parties, brutal final exams, pressure-filled job interviews, and the tricky world of office politics. Miles was a good buddy, but Kevin was the one Griffin would seek out in a crisis.

That's why they were sitting here having lunch. Griffin had needed a reality check, and Kevin was offering him one. "Yeah," he said. "Shoot."

"Cut yourself some slack. You're allowed to have a relationship that's based on sex. People do it all the time. Hell, I do it all the time. Just because you have a little fun doesn't mean you're going to make the same mistake your folks did."

"How do you know I won't?"

"Because Miles and I won't let you."

As Lily got off the bus and rounded the corner, she spied Anica pacing back and forth in front of the Bubbling Cauldron. Her flowered dress looked happy and springlike, but Anica's rapid pacing indicated the exact opposite of happiness. And it was all Lily's fault.

To make matters worse, the original plan of meeting at the bar before it opened had been scrapped because Lily had overslept and then she'd had to deal with Griffin. She'd managed to get him out of her apartment without having sex again, but it had been a challenge. She'd been so tempted, but she knew they'd end up spending the whole day in bed if they started it there.

Finally she'd returned Anica's call. Her big sister had been upset by the turn of events but hadn't wanted to talk about it on the phone. Anica had already contacted Devon, the magical owner of the Bubbling Cauldron, and, as Lily had predicted, he was thrilled to host her engagement party.

Lily had been relieved that at least that much was working out well. Considering how late it was already, she'd suggested meeting Anica there for lunch. She'd told Anica to go on in and order if she got there first.

Anica always beat Lily whenever they met anywhere, and she'd done it again. But she hadn't gone inside. Obviously she wanted a chance to chew Lily's ass in private before they walked into the bar.

To fortify herself for this encounter, Lily had worn a short denim skirt, thigh-high boots, and a short-sleeved red sweater. A snug red sweater. Anica would never wear something so sexy in public, and Lily felt like proclaiming her individuality.

She had more than a chip on her shoulder. She walked up to Anica with a railroad tie balanced there.

Anica ruined the whole rebellion shtick by taking one look at her and grinning. "Hey, it's your funeral. If you want to screw up your life beyond belief, that's up to you."

Lily stared at her sister. "Who are you, and what have you done with Anica?"

"Okay, I was upset at first, but I got over it."

"What are you talking about? You were upset two minutes ago! I saw the way you were pacing. Pacing is never a good sign."

Anica held up the cell phone in her hand. "I was talking to Jasper, and I needed to be outside so I could hear him.

He's getting more uptight by the minute, which is making me uptight, too. He's convinced that because we're holding the party at the Bubbling Cauldron, his parents are going to realize that I'm a witch and all Hades will break loose."

Lily felt the railroad tie of belligerence slip from her shoulder. "I'm sorry, An. Do you want to tone down our plans? Eliminate the magic elements?"

Anica widened her eyes in disbelief. "Uh, *no*. The more Jasper frets, the more I want to do a couple of outrageous things. Like you said, nonmagical people won't notice anything except cool special effects."

"I must be rubbing off on you."

"Too bad I'm not rubbing off on you."

"See, see? You are upset with me."

Anica sighed. "How can I be? I've seen the way you look at Griffin. I gave it my best shot last night but I had a feeling you'd cave. After you do magic, you'll agree with whoever's talked to you last, and that wasn't me."

Lily decided not to mention that talking hadn't been the main mode of coercion. "It might work out okay."

"It might. But if it doesn't, I hate to watch you go through the same kind of agony I did with Jasper. Eventually Griffin will find out about the spell, you know."

"Maybe not. Maybe I could put a moratorium on us having sex until the spell gradually wears off. In the meantime, we could do fun things together. We could bond the way couples do during that montage in the middle of a movie, where there's no dialogue or anything, just romantic music."

"Lily, you're demented. You and I both know you're not going to stop having sex with him."

Lily thought about the way Griffin looked naked. "Yeah, probably not."

"So he'll get more and more attached to you, and then your conscience will bother you so much you'll confess about the spell. He won't be happy. I can vouch for that. Jasper was furious with me."

"Because you turned him into a *cat*. Hel-*lo*. Griffin's still very much a man." And how. "So what does he have to complain about? I put a spell on him so now all he wants to do is have lots of sex with me. I'm good at sex. What guy would complain about an arrangement like that?"

"The guy who likes to believe he's in control of his own destiny. And that's all of them, by the way."

Lily wished her sister didn't sound so wise, so blasted *right*. Then there was the other teensy problem, the one Anica didn't know about yet. Griffin showed signs of invading Lily's time and space. She hadn't figured on that.

She should have. Daisy would be with her night and day if Lily allowed it. But Daisy was a dog, so Lily could make her stay at the apartment while she went to work. Daisy didn't have the freedom to show up whenever. Griffin did.

"I guess I'll take it one day at a time," Lily said.

"You could always try reversing the spell."

"Are you crazy? I'm not going to try a spell reversal on Griffin right before Mom and Dad arrive. Just my luck I'd screw it up and they'd be here to witness the whole thing. You're lucky they were out of the country when you had your little episode with Jasper."

"I was definitely lucky." Anica gazed at her. "Are you still coming with me to the airport in the morning to pick them up?"

"You bet. Did you get a rental car?" Neither of them owned a car, both because of the expense and the trouble with parking. They made do with public transportation except for unusual situations, like picking up their globe-trotting parents from O'Hare.

"I did. Jasper offered to let me use his car and loan it to them for the weekend, but . . ."

Lily laughed. "I know. Dad's driving. Wizards don't make the best drivers in the world. You got insurance, right?"

"All they offered." Anica fidgeted with her cell phone, flipping the cover open and shut. "Speaking of Jasper, um . . . you won't tell on me, will you?"

"I won't tell on you if you won't tell on me."

"I promise not to tell Mom and Dad, but I have to warn you that Dorcas and Ambrose know."

"Anica! What'd you do, call them up right after you found out Griffin had spent the night?"

"*No.*" Anica looked insulted. "Dorcas called me. She knew you were thinking about it and she wanted an update. I'm not going to lie to a member of the Wizard Council, Lily."

"I wish they didn't know. They're coming to the party, which means they'll be talking to Mom and Dad."

"They won't tell Mom and Dad."

"How can you be so sure?" Lily tried not to panic, but she *really* didn't want her parents to know what she'd done.

"First of all, Dorcas and Ambrose aren't the kind of people who go around spilling other people's secrets, which is good for me because they know about me turning Jasper into a cat."

"True." Lily hadn't thought about the fact that the Lowells were keeping secrets for both sisters.

"And second of all, they're not allowed to interfere unless somebody asks them to, like I did when we couldn't figure out how to turn Jasper back into a guy."

"And you didn't ask them to do anything regarding me and Griffin, right?"

Anica gazed at her. "No, because this is your deal."

"Thanks, An. Thanks for letting me handle it."

"I couldn't have asked them, anyway. It would have to be either you or Griffin who asks."

"Oh." Lily laughed. "I see. You're being noble by default."

"No, I really wouldn't have asked, even if I could!"

"Right."

"Anyway, your secret's safe with them. They won't tell, and I won't tell as long as you'll keep my secret."

Lily smiled at her. "Blackmail is a glorious thing, isn't it?"

"Uh-huh. Now let's eat. I can't plan a magical party on an empty stomach."

Griffin had found a private moment at the office to tell Debbie he wouldn't be going out with her on Saturday night. He'd explained that there was someone else. From the way she'd rolled her eyes, he thought he probably knew who that was.

She'd made a snide remark about men who preferred blatant sexuality to women with a more refined appeal, and he'd said nothing. Intellectually he preferred subtle to blatant himself. But his mind wasn't running the show these days.

Debbie didn't join the group when Kevin, Miles and Griffin headed over to the Bubbling Cauldron for their normal happy hour. Griffin had given Kevin permission to bring Miles up to speed on the situation, so both friends were eager to see how the new status would affect their routine.

"You're welcome to take her into the storeroom for a quickie," he said, "as long as I get my drink first."

Griffin knew that sparring with Miles would only make him ramp up the teasing. "I'll see if she'll go for that," he said as they walked in the door. "I've never had storeroom sex."

"Oh, I have," Miles said, looking worldly.

"Here?" Griffin was trying to picture that happening without him or Kevin knowing.

"Not here. At that bar we used to go to back in college."

Kevin didn't look convinced. "Yeah, right."

"I have! I have great memories of storeroom sex. The smell of cardboard boxes can still get me hot. And it would work great in this setup, too. I've noticed that the storeroom isn't off the kitchen, like in some places. It opens off the same hall as the bathrooms."

As they sat at their usual table, Kevin shook his head in obvious disbelief. "If you've made it with a chick in a storeroom, then I'm Clarence Darrow."

Miles stuck out his hand. "Nice to meet you, Clarence."

Their banter made little impression on Griffin. All his attention was focused on Lily. She stood behind the bar and leaned casually against the polished surface while she talked with the long-haired waiter. What was his name again? Sherman. Yeah, that was it.

Lily had glanced over at him when he'd first come in and given him a brief but dazzling smile. That smile coupled with the low-cut black tops she favored when she was tending bar had him salivating. He'd needed every last ounce of his self-control to keep from marching over to the bar, cupping his hand behind her head and French-kissing her blind. But this was her work environment and he wouldn't compromise that.

Sherman was entirely too friendly for Griffin's taste, though, and Lily seemed perfectly happy in Sherman's company. The guy was a little young for Lily, but some women liked younger guys. Maybe he should wander over to the bar and give her their order.

"Earth to Griffin. Come in, Griffin." Miles waved a hand in front of his face.

He turned to Miles. "What?"

"I asked you twice if you wanted to order a sandwich. There's not a huge selection, but it's better than my alternative, which is to go home and nuke a frozen pizza. We figured you'd go for that plan. Am I right?"

"Sure. Let's do that." Griffin swiveled back to continue watching Lily, who was busy mixing drinks. Sherman had left and was now on the far side of the room, taking orders. Griffin didn't expect Sherman to take theirs, however.

Any minute now Lily would come over and take their order, the way she always did. Pretty soon he should figure out how he wanted the evening to go. He hadn't thought about spending the whole night at the bar, but on the other hand, he didn't want to go home until Lily was ready to leave.

He also had to decide what to do if he spent the night at her place again. Waking up with no change of clothes, no razor and no toothbrush wasn't his idea of suave. Maybe he and Lily should go home, pick up Daisy and anything Lily would need, and then go to his place. If he was going to work the next day that would make it easier.

"You know, it's like sitting here with a robot, a robot who looks like Griffin Taylor," Miles remarked.

At the sound of his name, Griffin turned his attention back to his friends. "Excuse me?"

"Kevin and I were wondering if you were going to partake in any jovial guy talk tonight, or if we could expect you to spend the entire happy hour staring at Lily."

Griffin didn't like appearing to be a lovesick fool in front of his friends, so he leaned back in his chair and loosened his tie. "What sort of jovial guy talk did you have in mind?"

"Oh, the usual. Whether the Cubs are likely to move up in the standings this weekend. Whether Britney Spears is hotter than Jennifer Lopez. Whether you're aware that your fly's down."

Instantly Griffin checked, and just as instantly knew he'd been had. "Funny. You guys are a real riot."

"So are you," Miles said. "Kev warned me about the state of your brain, or what's left of it, and I thought he was exaggerating."

"As you can see, I wasn't," Kevin said.

"Nope." Miles folded his arms. "But I predict we'll see the old Griff in another week or so. He's been depriving himself, so this reaction is natural. Pretty soon sex won't be this shiny new toy, and then we'll have our buddy back."

Griffin took comfort in Miles's matter-of-fact evaluation. He was feeling a little out of control, but Miles was probably right. He hadn't been indulging in sex recently, and then he'd repressed his attraction to Lily. Now that he'd turned those urges loose, he was feeling consumed by them.

But it wouldn't last. Nothing this exciting ever lasted. That was the whole point. You didn't build a life on the basis of a momentary infatuation. His buddies would keep him grounded so he wouldn't do that.

Even so, when he caught Lily's scent and knew she was on her way over to the table, his pulse leaped and his groin stirred. He thought about Miles's joke about storeroom sex, and it wasn't such a joke anymore. Griffin wondered if he could tempt her to go back there.

He hadn't brought condoms, but every bar worth its salt and lime had a condom dispenser in the men's bathroom. It was a thought. Not a particularly noble thought, considering that he'd recently vowed not to bother her on the job. But a thought nevertheless.

"So, gentlemen, what will it be tonight?"

Griffin looked up and his face was level with her cleavage. If he grabbed her around the waist he could bury his face there. He wouldn't do that, of course. But the storeroom was looking like a better option every minute.

Chapter 9

Lily was good at her job, which allowed her to do it while only part of her brain was focused on tending bar. The other part was absorbed with watching Griffin. She could tell from the way his friends teased him that they knew about her. That was an encouraging development. If Griffin had told his friends, then he wasn't ashamed of the connection.

Tonight she'd ask him to Anica and Jasper's engagement party on Sunday. If nothing else, she'd have a cool date for that party, and she'd been worried about that ever since the plans were made. She should be past the point of competing with Anica, but when she was completely honest with herself, she admitted she wasn't past it.

When her parents came, Anica would be introducing them to her fiancé, a really great guy even if he wasn't magical. At the very least, Lily wanted to show up with a really great boyfriend. Her parents had always predicted she'd end up with a bad-boy type, and she would be delighted to present Griffin, who was everything her mom and dad could want for their daughter.

Well, except for the fact that Griffin wasn't a wizard. But mixed marriages were becoming increasingly common in the magical world, and her parents would just have to get in step with the new millennium. Whoops. Had she just let herself think about the M word?

That was making quite a leap. She might have bound Griffin to her sexually, but marriage was a huge step beyond that. She must be influenced by Anica's upcoming wedding.

Still, as she served hot pastrami sandwiches and beer to Griffin and his friends, she pictured Kevin and Miles as groomsmen. Kevin might be Griffin's best man, because he seemed a little closer to him than Miles. But both of them would definitely be in the wedding.

She'd have Anica as her matron of honor, and Jasper might be a groomsman. That meant coming up with a couple more women, but Lily would have no trouble with that. She had two girlfriends from high school that had moved out of the Chicago area, but Lily still kept in touch with them. They'd expect to be in her wedding. Oh yeah, they'd be excited for her.

"Lily?" Sherman reached across the bar and touched her shoulder. "Are you about finished with those margs?"

Lily jerked out of her wedding daze and looked at the two margarita glasses in her hand. They had salt on the rims, and that was about the extent of her preparation on those two drinks. "Coming right up," she said brightly, as if she hadn't been standing there daydreaming about a wedding that might never take place.

When Lily was a little girl, she'd loved pretending to be a bride. Then puberty had hit with a vengeance, and she'd differentiated herself from her sane, responsible sister by being a wild child. She hadn't stopped to figure out that men don't usually propose to the wild child.

After Kevin, Miles and Griffin finished their food, Lily expected them all to leave as they usually did. Kevin and Miles did leave, giving her a wave as they went out the door into the spring night. Griffin, however, moved his base of operations over to the bar and perched on a stool.

Lily glanced at her watch. She had another four hours before she could go home. Surely Griffin wasn't planning to sit at the bar for four hours?

But she was the consummate bartender, so after he sat down, she placed a napkin in front of him. "What can I get for you, stranger?"

He gave her a heart-melting smile. "I don't really need another drink, but I guess if I'm going to sit here I need to order something."

"The management likes that, yeah."

"Then get me another beer. I'll nurse it."

She kept her voice low. "Griffin, aren't you going home?"

"I thought I'd stick around until you got off work."

"But that's four hours away." She considered this scenario stretching on, night after night. "Your liver can't take it."

"I realize it's not the brightest plan in the universe, but I . . ." He reached out and traced a finger along her arm. "I can't seem to leave."

She knew why, too. She'd given him an adoration elixir, and he wasn't happy unless he was breathing the same air she was. That made her think of Daisy, and how much Griffin had loved taking her out.

She had an idea, one that might benefit them all. "You know, whenever I'm here at the bar, I worry about Daisy and wonder if she needs to go out."

"She's probably fine. I'm sure you took her out before you left for work."

"I did, but it was quick, and then I fed her. You know how that can jump-start things." She reached under the counter and unzipped her backpack. "Take my key. You can let her out, go down to the dog park and then wait for me at the apartment."

"I was thinking maybe we'd pick up Daisy and take her to my place."

Lily thought about her commitment to ride to O'Hare with Anica first thing in the morning. "That won't work. I'm doing an airport run with Anica in the morning, and I need to be at home so I can get ready for that." She paused, wondering how much to say. "My parents have been on a yearlong research trip to Peru, and they're making a special trip home for the engagement party and wedding. Anica and I need to be on time."

He looked worried. "When your parents arrive, will that mean we can't spend as much time together?"

"Unfortunately, that's likely. Of course, I'd love for you to go to the engagement party with me on Sunday."

"I'll be happy to go wherever you go."

She gulped. That sounded good on the surface, but it might not work so well in practice. "Actually, I'll be down here most of the day, decorating with Anica, so if you could hang out with Daisy part of Sunday, I'd really appreciate it."

He didn't seem overjoyed to be substituting Daisy for her, but he nodded. "I can do that."

"And if you take care of Daisy for me tonight, then you and I will have more time to . . ." Instead of spelling it out, she gave him a heated look and let him fill in the blanks.

He sucked in a breath. "Got it. Tell you what. I'll head to my place, pick up a few things, go to your apartment and take care of Daisy, and have the bed warm by the time you get there."

That scenario wasn't half bad. If only he weren't being driven by the spell she'd cast, she could look forward to having a man waiting in her bed for her when she got home. Zeus's balls, she could still look forward to it. She'd created this situation, and she might as well enjoy herself.

* * *

Griffin took time to change into jeans and a sweatshirt. Then he picked up clean clothes, his toiletry kit and the condoms he preferred before leaving his apartment. As he stood in the living room with a garment bag over his shoulder and a small duffel in one hand, he wondered what Lily would think of the place. He hadn't so much decorated as he had simply moved in and bought some necessary furniture.

Unlike Lily's apartment, which glowed with color, Griffin's apartment was filled with shades of beige. He'd never felt comfortable with the whole decorating concept, so he'd stuck with neutrals because they were safe.

His whole damned life had been safe, now that he thought about it. He'd been so desperate to avoid the chaos of his parents' impulsive choices that he'd avoided taking any personal risks at all. Until Lily.

The more he thought about it, the more pleased he was that he'd taken that risk, followed that impulse that had made him run all the way to the Bubbling Cauldron last night. His life had been colorless until then, but he'd taken steps to pump the color back in.

He didn't kid himself that he and Lily had a future. They were still very different people, set on very different paths. But for some crazy reason she wanted him. And for obvious reasons, he needed her. He'd walked the straight and narrow for too long.

Thinking about what they'd share later tonight, he set down his garment bag and duffel so he could rummage through a kitchen cupboard. Ah, there they were. A former girlfriend, one who hadn't inspired him half as much as Lily had already, had given him a box full of various sizes of candles.

The relationship had ended before he'd used any of the candles. He tucked the box into his duffel, along with a book of matches. He'd never been much of a romantic, but Lily was the kind of woman who seemed to invite the romantic approach.

He was almost out the door when he remembered the bottle of red wine he'd bought months ago and tucked in a cupboard, thinking he needed to have some on hand. Because he'd been so damned picky about his dates, he'd never brought anyone home to sample that wine.

Lily would appreciate it. And he knew instinctively that she'd have wineglasses and an opener. Lily knew how to enjoy herself, and it was high time he learned how to do that, too.

Fortified with his supplies, he caught a cab over to her apartment. The place was already starting to feel familiar, and Daisy greeted him, wiggling and panting with joy. Maybe she really did need to go out.

Setting down his duffel and garment bag, he located the leash and clipped it on. Once he was out the door, he discovered that he looked forward to romping with Daisy. He truly needed to get a dog.

Out on the sidewalk, Daisy found a patch of gravel and took a quick pee. Then Griffin pointed her toward the dog park, but Daisy tugged him in the opposite direction.

"Daisy, it's this way." He pulled on her collar, but she wouldn't budge, and she was stronger than he'd realized. Short of carrying her to the dog park, which seemed idiotic, he would have to go along with her new plan.

God, this was getting more like a Lassie episode every time he interacted with this dog. She definitely had a mind of her own. "Look, I don't want to go see your friend at the coffee shop, okay? He's way too interested in Lily."

Daisy whined and gazed down the street.

"Oh, what the hell. I suppose it doesn't matter. I have

the inside track. I can take this opportunity to inform what's-his-name that he can look elsewhere. Let's go."

The retriever's tail lifted like a banner as she trotted down the sidewalk. Once again, she seemed to be smiling.

"You are some kind of dog, Daisy. I doubt there's another golden at the animal shelter quite like you, but one of these days I'll have to go down and take a look."

Daisy gave a short yip, as if she approved of that plan.

Warning himself not to turn her normal doggie responses into more than they actually were, he continued to talk to her. "Just think, if I hadn't gone home with Lily last night, I never would have met you. There were plenty of obvious benefits to going home with Lily, but I hadn't thought I'd find a new friend in the process."

Daisy whined and wagged her tail.

"Same here, Daisy. Same here."

The neon sign for Harvey's Hangout glowed at the end of the block. Griffin wondered if he should buy a cup of coffee. Probably. It would be rude to bring Daisy for a visit and not buy any coffee.

As they approached, he noticed that tonight's crowd was different, mostly teenagers hanging out. Then again, he was here a couple of hours earlier, so maybe that made sense. He paused, thinking he'd tie Daisy to the leg of one of the wrought-iron chairs.

Daisy didn't pause. She kept right on walking.

"Well, I'll be damned." Puzzled, Griffin followed her to the corner. When he stopped to wait for the light to change, she sat down beside him.

He glanced across the street toward a neighborhood grocery store that was still open. He wouldn't have noticed it the night before because they'd been here much later. Maybe Daisy had a friend over there, too. He'd have to ask Lily about Daisy's habits so he'd be forewarned about the places she liked to go and the people she liked to see.

The light changed, and Daisy pranced across the street, towing Griffin. Her tail waved in delight the closer they came to the corner store. On this spring night the double doors stood open and the owner had displayed colorful fruit and vegetables in tiered bins.

The array almost made Griffin wish he could cook. Besides the produce, the display included one section of bouquets in a riot of color. Griffin considered the flowers and decided that would be a nice addition to the candles and wine.

"Thanks, Daisy. This was a great idea." As he stood by the door, wondering whether to tie Daisy to a nearby bike rack, the owner came out wearing a green bib apron.

The small Asian man of indeterminate age was grinning so widely that the rest of his face almost disappeared. "Daisy!" He stooped down and scratched the dog behind both ears. "So good to see you, honored friend."

Daisy whined in delight and gave his face a lick.

"She must make friends fast," Griffin said. "Lily hasn't had her long."

"Oh yes, she makes friends very fast." The small man gave Daisy one last pat before standing. "She's a great dog."

"Smart, too. She was determined to come down here and say hello."

"Of course." The man reached down to stroke Daisy's soft fur. Then he winked at Griffin. "I give her soup bones."

"I see. So she has ulterior motives."

The little man gazed at him. "Don't we all?"

Griffin had to smile at that. "I suppose. I thought I'd get Lily some flowers, and my ulterior motive is to impress her with my thoughtfulness." He had a sudden inspiration. "Maybe I should buy her lilies."

"No, not lilies. Buy her these daisies." The owner plucked a bouquet of red gerberas from the display.

Griffin congratulated himself on knowing they were gerberas. He'd always liked that flower, too, and a few weeks ago he'd finally taken the time to look it up. "Maybe I should buy lilies *and* daisies."

"No, go with these. She goes nuts over these, and I just got a fresh batch today. She always liked them before, but when her new dog turned out to be named Daisy, she decided this was the flower for her."

"Sold." Griffin reached in his hip pocket for his wallet. "I wasn't sure where to tie Daisy so I could come in the store."

"Tie her?" The man blew out a breath. "She can come with you. Daisy never bothers anything in my store. She's a good dog." He turned and started back inside. "I'll get her soup bone."

"Okay." Griffin had never taken a dog in a grocery store, but Daisy seemed to be the exception to most dog rules he'd ever known about. Nevertheless, he tightened his grip on her leash. "Behave," he said.

Daisy snorted as if he'd just insulted her. Maybe he had, because she walked carefully through the store without bumping a single display or sweeping anything off a shelf with her tail. Even when the owner handed Griffin the soup bone in a paper bag, Daisy kept her tail wagging to a minimum. But she was smiling to beat the band.

"Thanks so much," Griffin said as he pocketed his change and picked up the flowers and the bag containing the bone.

"Now both your girls will be happy."

"Uh, right." Griffin was taken aback by the assumption that Daisy and Lily were *his girls*. That implied a deeper connection than he was comfortable with. But, after all, he was walking Lily's dog and buying Lily flowers. The guy had a right to make assumptions.

"See you around," the store owner said. "My name's Bruce."

"Nice to meet you, Bruce. I'm Griffin."

Bruce nodded. "It's a good name. Lily and Griffin. Sounds good together."

Griffin had no idea what to say to that, so he simply nodded. For a man who was just in this for the sex, he sure was getting chummy with the neighbors.

Chapter 10

All the way home on the bus Lily thought about Griffin in her apartment, waiting for her. She'd never encouraged a man to hang out in her space, but the idea of coming home to a warm bed and a hot man was appealing. Anica had been pretty negative about this spell, but Lily thought it had a positive side. Griffin was a little overeager, but she was managing that so far.

She had no key, so she had to buzz the intercom when she reached the front door.

His voice drifted through the speaker, soft and intimate. "Hi."

She went up in flames. "Hi, yourself. Think you could let me in?"

The lock buzzed and she walked into the foyer. Without her keys she couldn't check the mail, but she was more interested in the male upstairs. Of course, he could be propped in front of her TV with a beer, watching whatever sports were on at this hour. He might already have strewn some of his belongings around, the way men tend to do.

She didn't know Griffin well enough to be familiar with his habits, and he'd had a couple of hours to settle in, make himself at home. She was curious as to what that would look like. That was another perk of this spell. She could find out whether Griffin was easy to be around or a royal pain in the ass.

Carrying her backpack by the shoulder strap, she tested the apartment door and discovered he'd unlocked that for her, too. Daisy was there to greet her, as always, but the dog seemed calmer than usual. That made sense if Griffin had taken her to the dog park. Besides, Daisy was a social dog. She'd probably enjoyed having Griffin around for a few hours.

Griffin wasn't in the living room. One of her lamps was turned on low, but the TV was off. Points to him for not being sprawled in front of it. Most guys would have been.

She saw a note on the coffee table and picked it up. *Lock up and come to bed. I'm waiting. Griff.*

Short and sweet. To the point. Lust swirled through her as she let her backpack slide to the floor. The bedroom door was closed. Daisy's water dish was filled.

Lily secured the front door and switched off the lamp he'd left burning for her. She could get used to this. What was Anica so worried about? Maybe she was jealous, especially now that she had Jasper agonizing over how his parents were going to react to the engagement party. Anica might want to slip him a little something. Life with a man under the influence of an adoration elixir could be wonderful.

Lily started to open the bedroom door and paused. She could imagine the scene that awaited her, and she might want to step into it without being encumbered by her boots. Unzipping them, she slipped them off and left them in the hall.

Then she wondered why she should leave on her slacks and her top. She wasn't quite ready to walk in there naked, but her underwear was black and sexy. She could make an entrance in that.

Piling her clothes next to her boots, she slipped off her watch and her bracelet, setting them on top of the pile. She was left with her lace underwire and a pair of black lace bikini briefs. She opened the bedroom door.

Griffin was propped up on her bed reading, but he'd only taken off his shoes and socks. At first she felt foolish standing there in her underwear, but as his gaze swept over her and his chest heaved in anticipation, she felt less foolish.

The bedroom looked fabulous. He'd set candles on every available surface, and he'd bought her favorite flowers and found a vase in her cupboard. Between the flowers on one of her bedside tables and an open bottle of wine on the other, she felt a romantic interlude coming on.

She wondered what he'd found to read. She had a brief glimpse of the title before he laid the book on the floor beside the bed. *Modern Magic.* Dear goddess, was he suspicious?

"I see you've discovered my hobby." She hated lying to him, but he wasn't ready for the truth. He might never be. "I'm an amateur magician."

"Do you perform at parties and stuff like that?" He swung his jeans-clad legs to the floor.

"Not usually. But I might do a couple of tricks for the engagement party on Sunday."

He grinned. "Are you gonna show me how it's done?"

She decided to deflect the conversation by giving him a suggestive smile. "Are we talking about magic or ... something else?"

His gaze smoldered. "I'd love to talk about something else. I *really* like your outfit."

So he wasn't terribly curious about her interest in magic. That was fine with her. Trying to field questions from a practicing attorney who had probably studied debate in college would only get her in trouble.

She glanced at his jeans and sweatshirt. "I, uh, thought you might be wearing a similar outfit."

His smile was endearingly modest. "Maybe I don't have your confidence."

The picture of him standing in her shower was permanently burned into her brain. "You should."

"Thank you."

"I love the candles, the wine and the flowers. The only touch needed to complete this bedroom scene is a naked Griffin Taylor as the centerpiece."

"You know, I never did have an eye for decorating." He reached behind his back and pulled his sweatshirt over his head, tossing it on the floor. "I can tell from the way you've done the apartment that you have a gift for it. Any tips?"

"Well, you need a major accent, something that gives the whole thing oomph." She eyed his jeans. "Taking those off would be a good start in that direction."

"If you say so." He unfastened the metal button at his waistband and slowly unzipped his jeans.

It was a wonder the zipper hadn't stuck, considering the sizable bulge Griffin had to work around before he could ease the zipper all the way down.

Lily's chest tightened in anticipation as her gaze locked on that bulge. "That's what I'm talkin' about."

"Waiting for you has been a special kind of torture."

"I can tell." She glanced into his eyes, a devilish urge prodding her to tease him. "I'm surprised you didn't resort to . . . alternative methods of satisfaction while you waited for me to get home."

"I thought about it, but I realized it was pointless."

"Really? Why?"

"I can't imagine being satisfied by sexual pleasure without you."

She gulped. That was the effect of the elixir binding him to her. "Does that seem . . . strange to you?"

"Yes, but everything about this compulsion seems strange. I guess I waited too long to give in to the attraction. Now I'm dealing with a fixation. It's not your fault, so don't worry about it. I'll figure it out."

"I'm sure you will." Yes, it was completely her fault. The elixir had made him dependent on her for sexual gratification, and she'd known that would happen.

But now that it had, she didn't feel comfortable with that kind of responsibility. She couldn't guarantee she'd be available, for one thing. She didn't like to think of him in a constant state of arousal because she wasn't around to take care of that for him.

He shucked his jeans. "For tonight it's not a problem. You're here."

She was so there, taking in the sight of him clad only in his briefs. Maybe she'd worry about the issue of her responsibility later.

He hooked his thumbs in the elastic waistband in preparation for taking them off.

"Wait." She stepped forward. "Allow me."

He paused and let his hands fall to his sides. "I'm all yours."

And that's what she'd dreamed of when she'd created the elixir. She couldn't change things immediately, so she might as well savor the experience and not let it be ruined by guilt. Sliding her fingers under the elastic, she lowered herself slowly to her knees.

His sharp intake of breath told her he understood her intent. She'd been thinking about this ever since she'd seen him fresh from the shower, his pride and glory nestled in a wreath of dark, moisture-tipped curls. Now she would have him exactly where she wanted him.

She pulled the briefs down with slow deliberation, easing them past his very erect, very solid, very tempting penis. She planned to give in to temptation.

Once the briefs reached his knees, she leaned forward and placed a kiss on the tip of that jutting statement of desire.

He groaned. "If you do this, I'm not sure I'll be able to control—"

"Sure you will." She licked the ridged underside, running her tongue along the vein that pulsed there.

He sucked in another breath. "That ... may not be possible."

"It will if you concentrate." She shoved his briefs to the floor. "We'll have a little contest. I'll try to make you come, and you'll try not to. It'll be fun."

"God, Lily, I—"

"There are no losers in this contest." Curling her fingers around his cock, she cupped his balls in her other hand. Yes, this was how she wanted Griffin Taylor, right in her grasp. And in her mouth.

He tasted like desire, and the more she licked and sucked, the more she wanted him. While she used her tongue and lips on his cock, she gently massaged his balls, and she was gratified to feel them tighten. She wouldn't mind making him come. Knowing the power of his lust, he'd recover soon and give her everything she needed.

She challenged him, though, and he fought valiantly for control. His breathing grew labored and his thighs quivered. From the corner of her eye she could see that he'd clenched his hands into fists.

The contest wasn't all one-sided. The longer she ministered to him, the greater desire teased her with the possibilities he offered. She was drenched with wanting him, aching to feel him pounding into her.

If she made him come, she'd have to wait for that sweet penetration. If she stopped now, she could have what she wanted within the short time it would take him to pull on a condom. Ah, but she'd lose the triumphant moment when he lost control. She wanted to enjoy that, wanted—

"No!" With a roar he lifted her up off her knees and

pushed her unceremoniously toward the bed. It was pure caveman, and she loved it.

She fell back on the mattress, her legs dangling to the floor. She cried out for him, not caring whether she had him in her mouth or in her vagina, just knowing she needed him back, needed ... and then he was standing over her, rolling on a condom, ripping away the panties she'd never taken off, lifting her up, up, until only her arms and shoulders rested on the bed. She wrapped her ankles around his neck and he drove into her.

They joined together in the kind of wild abandon she'd only dreamed of, their cries and groans echoing off the walls, her bed creaking with every thrust. His face was a mask of total concentration, the cords in his neck standing out, his jaw clenched. She focused with equal intensity, glorying in the powerful friction as he stroked relentlessly.

His big hands held her hips off the bed, his fingers pressing into her thighs. His voice was a hoarse croak. "Come for me!"

"I will," she promised, her body already trembling, her breathing a series of quick gasps.

"Yes, you will." Panting, he adjusted his grip just enough that his thumb reached her clit. He pushed down hard.

The spasms hit with unbelievable force as he kept pushing down and thrusting, thrusting, thrusting once more. Her cries became sobs of pleasure. Nothing had ever felt that amazing.

And then he climaxed, great shudders racking his body as he groaned and cried out her name. Dazed as she was by the tumult surging through her, she heard that precious sound, the sound of her name on his lips. Emotion spilled like warm honey, flooding through her.

And then she knew the depth of her problem. She wanted him to want her. Oh yes, definitely that. But more than merely wanting, she wanted him to love her. But because of the elixir, she would never know for sure if he did.

Griffin no longer had to worry whether he was taking enough risks in his personal life. Spending time with Lily was like being on a thrill ride. His adrenaline level spiked on a regular basis, and he felt more alive than he had in years.

Once they'd taken the edge off their lust, they'd sampled the wine he'd brought. Griffin had never sipped on wine naked or in bed, for that matter. He realized that the women he'd dated had been too conservative to think of it.

"Great wine. Thanks for bringing it." She set her empty goblet on the bedside table and turned her head on the pillow she'd propped lengthwise against the headboard so she could sit up. "And the flowers are my favorite kind. How did you know?"

"Daisy told me."

"I can almost believe that."

"It's almost true." The vase of flowers sat on the bedside table next to him. He reached out and plucked one up, letting the water from the stem drip back on the remaining flowers. "When I took Daisy out for a walk, she led me to the corner grocery to see her friend Bruce."

"Let me guess. He gave her a soup bone."

"Yep. The remains are somewhere in the kitchen." He twirled the daisy between his thumb and forefinger. "Bruce told me you like these."

"I do. They're so cheerful and full of life. Like my dog, actually."

"And like you."

She smiled at him. "That's a nice thing to say. Especially considering you must be exhausted. It's nearly two in the morning. Want to get some sleep?"

Griffin's gaze swept over her, from her tousled hair to

her bright red toenails. "I can't say I feel sleepy." Neither did his dick.

She laughed. "We could put out all the candles so we can't see each other. That might help."

"I doubt it. I'd just use my imagination." His imagination had been getting a workout in the past twenty-four hours, and he was grateful for every sexual idea that had come to him. "Do you want to go to sleep?"

Her dark eyes glowed with a secret fire. "Maybe not, but I'm used to this schedule. You're not."

As if he could resist that sparkle in her eyes. He turned so that he could trail the flower over her breasts. "Then I need to get in shape for it."

"That tickles."

"Are you ticklish?" He suddenly wanted to know every little detail of her ticklish places.

"Certain places."

Sitting upright, he moved so that he could brush the flower over the soles of her feet. "Here?"

"No."

Circling her ankle with his fingers, he lifted her leg so he could get at the back of her knee. "Here?"

She giggled and twisted until she was flat on the bed as she tried to get away from him. "Yes."

"Score one for me." Moving quickly, he straddled her thighs and twirled the daisy over her navel. "Here?"

"Nope."

"Here?" He ran the flower up and down her side, and she erupted with laughter as she tried to move him off her.

"Ah, I have you in my power." He tickled her other side.

Tears of laughter streamed down her cheeks. "Stop it! No fair! I— Oh, what have we here?" She took a firm hold on his penis, which had reacted predictably to her wiggling around between his knees. "You'd better stop tickling me, or I'll . . ."

"You'll what?" He grinned. "Damaging that particular piece of equipment wouldn't be in your best interests."

She moved her hand up and down in a steady rhythm. "Who said anything about damaging you?"

"I get your point." He'd completely lost interest in tickling her. But when he came again, he didn't want it to be like this. The decorating discussion had suggested a visual that he craved to make happen.

Laying the flower beside him, he grabbed her wrist and pried her fingers from his dick. Then he captured her other wrist. Bracing her hands on either side of her head, he leaned down and captured her mouth.

She tasted of wine and sex, and he could have gone on kissing her for a long time, but he had other activities on his agenda. He lifted his mouth a fraction away from hers. "I want to try something with that daisy. I can't guarantee what shape it'll be in afterward, though."

Her breath was warm on his lips as she answered him. "Go for it, big guy."

He took another condom from the stash on the bedside table and rolled it on. Then he picked up the daisy and broke off most, but not all, of the stem. Settling the corona of red petals on her dark triangle of curls, he tucked the remainder of the stem into her cleft. It rested gently against her clit but wasn't long enough to reach her vagina.

"That feels . . . interesting," she murmured.

It was a mental picture he would never forget, Lily decorated with a red gerbera daisy. Holding the daisy gently in place by pressing his forefinger against her clit, he propped himself above her with his other arm, giving thanks for all those workout sessions and one-armed push-ups. He entered her slowly, and the daisy quivered.

Her voice was breathy. "Are you having fun?"

"Uh-huh." He began to stroke and watched the daisy

petals dance in time with his movements. At times the stem would come in contact with his dick, like a light scratch of a fingernail. He used his finger to move the stem around a little, which brought whimpers of delight from Lily.

"I don't know what you're doing down there, but it feels wonderful."

"I'm playing." Had he ever played at sex before? Probably not. He was playing now, and that flower was really beginning to dance. He'd never look at gerbera daisies the same way again.

As he quickened the pace, he felt her tighten around him. Good thing, because he wasn't going to last much longer. Poised above her, able to watch that red daisy vibrate, had him right on the edge of his climax.

He held on until she arched her back and cried out. As her climax rolled over his aching penis, he came in a rush, surging forward and crushing the flower in his frenzy to be deep inside her. To think he'd tried to avoid getting involved with Lily. What an idiot he'd been.

Chapter 11

The night had been perfect. The morning . . . not so much. Lily wasn't used to getting up early, which to her meant eight o'clock. She'd set her alarm so that she'd have no trouble meeting Anica at the coffee shop at nine thirty for the airport run.

Griffin was awake and whistling in the shower by seven fifteen. It wasn't a recognizable tune, either—more of an aimless, wandering kind of whistle. Lily wondered how he'd enjoy having a gerbera daisy shoved in his pursed lips. The shower was one thing. Tunelessly whistling was a whole other thing, a noisy thing that she could do without.

Pulling a pillow over her head, she tried to drown out the sound. When she'd envisioned Griffin under her spell, she hadn't projected exactly how that would work out. The sex was a given, but staying all night and jumping in the shower and *whistling* at seven fifteen . . . she hadn't figured on that at all.

She tried to soothe herself by imagining how great he looked in that shower, how the water would stream off his pecs, cascade down his washboard abs, and sluice down his sizable penis. It was a good image, but it didn't go with the tuneless whistling. Tuneless whistling made him seem less than sexy, even less than bright.

Oh, she knew he was very smart or he wouldn't be

pulling down big bucks as a lawyer. But his clients who paid him all that money wouldn't be impressed if they could hear him in the shower this morning. She could storm in there and ask him for the love of all that was holy to please stop, but that would be like kicking a puppy. He wouldn't understand what he'd done wrong.

Finally she gave up, left the bed and took her black robe out of the closet. She could make coffee, which would go a long way toward rescuing this morning. When she emerged from the bedroom, there was Daisy, overjoyed to see her.

Lily rubbed the top of Daisy's head. "One thing about you. You don't whistle."

Daisy shoved her wet nose against Lily's hand and gave a little moan of ecstasy that she could be with her human again.

"Yeah, I'm crazy about you, too." And she was crazy about Griffin. Everybody had irritating little habits. Lily acknowledged that she might have a few. So maybe whistling in the shower wasn't the worst thing in the world. Opening the blinds, she discovered a sunny spring morning. The blue sky paired with her memory of an outstanding night made her inclined to forgive Griffin for whistling.

She fed Daisy and gave her fresh water. As the coffee hissed and dripped into the pot, she drank a glass of orange juice and wondered whether she should throw on some sweats and take Daisy out now or wait until after her shower.

About that time, Griffin walked into the kitchen, smelling like heaven. He looked pretty damned good, too, freshly shaved and wearing a crisp white shirt and slacks. She preferred the buns-hugging jeans he'd worn the night before, but he couldn't very well wear jeans to work.

Daisy leaped up from where she'd been lying near the breakfast nook table and bounded over to Griffin as if she hadn't seen him in months. Griffin crouched down to give her a good head rub, and the picture of dog and man brought a smile to Lily's face. Then she noticed how Griffin's position stretched his slacks nicely over his sculpted ass, and that picture brought a smile to a part of her lower down. She decided he could whistle in the shower any damned time he wanted to.

If only they had time for her to coax him out of those slacks and change his mind about going in to the office. That was the exact opposite of what she'd wanted the day before, and it was still an unworkable plan. So she waited for him to finish loving Daisy. When he stood, she smiled at him. "Good morning."

"Good morning to you, too." His gaze swept over her, his expression telegraphing plainly that he wanted to know if she was wearing anything under her bathrobe.

"Want some juice?"

"Is that a trick question?"

She was so tempted to unfasten the sash and answer him that way, but then she glanced at the kitchen clock hanging on the wall behind him. "No, it's a real question."

"Damn. I was hoping it was code for—"

"I know. But we can't." She gestured toward him. "For one thing, you're all spic-and-span."

He took a step closer. "Don't let that stop you."

"For another thing, neither of us can be late, especially me. Coffee will be ready any minute." Draining her orange juice glass, she set it in the sink. "And I need to take Daisy out."

He closed the short distance between them. "I'll take her. But first I need a kiss."

As he pulled her into his arms, she had a feeling they shouldn't risk getting this chummy. Sure enough, while his lips were busy plundering hers, his hand was busy untying her sash. She made a halfhearted attempt to stop him, but when he kissed her like that, her brain turned to mush and her body instinctively wanted to be naked.

And, oh, how her body wanted his big hand on her breast, then wanted it roving lower until his fingers tunneled through her curls and discovered what kind of power his kiss had over her. If her cell phone sitting on the kitchen counter hadn't started playing Anica's tune, "Witchy Woman," no telling what would have happened next. Correction: Lily knew exactly what would have happened next.

But instead of having sex on the kitchen table with Griffin, Lily wiggled out of his arms and answered the phone.

"I just wanted to make sure you were up," Anica said. "I checked the flight and it's on time."

"I'm up." She looked over at Griffin.

Me, too, he mouthed.

Lily pressed her lips together to keep from laughing.

"I'm warning you." Anica was in full big-sister mode. "If you're not here by nine thirty, I'm leaving without you. Use magic to get cleaned up if you have to. Just make sure Griffin's out of there beforehand."

"Don't worry. I won't do anything stupid, and I'll be on time." Lily rolled her eyes. "You always get like this when the 'rents come home."

"Get how?"

"Frantic, bossy, anal . . . oh, wait, I forgot. You're anal all the time."

"I am not. So how is Griffin, anyway?"

Lily recognized that as a retaliatory dig. Anica was reminding her about the spell. "He's good." Lily was happy to have Anica take that as a double entendre. Griffin was *very* good in one particular way. "So how's Jasper? Still the same cool cat?"

"You know he's fine. He's permanently changed back, and unless you, Dorcas or Ambrose spill the beans, Mom and Dad never have to be the wiser."

"Like you said, big sis, blackmail's a—" She suddenly remembered that Griffin was standing right there listening to every word. "A nasty business. Well, gotta go. Wouldn't want to be late." She flipped the phone closed. "I need to get going."

"I could tell, although I'm curious about that blackmail comment."

"Just an inside joke."

"Okay. You go get ready, and I'll take Daisy out."

"Thanks, Griffin." She wondered if he'd be this considerate if she hadn't put a spell on him. She'd like to think so. "While you're out, you're welcome to make a copy of my key. That way you don't always have to be borrowing mine."

He looked pleased about that. "Okay."

She headed toward the bedroom as he went into the living room to get Daisy's leash. Daisy followed right at his heels, as if she understood that Griffin would be the one taking her out this morning. Lily wasn't so sure she hadn't understood. Many times she reacted as if she fully comprehended human speech.

Griffin paused by the front door to clip on Daisy's leash. "What do your parents do, anyway? I should probably know something about them before Sunday."

"They're researching ancient herbal remedies in Peru." Lily didn't mention that they were on a sabbatical from teaching at the International Academy of Magic.

"They're scientists, then."

"Yes."

"They sound like interesting people."

"They are." A little intimidating because they were so accomplished, but definitely not boring. Lily wondered if the day would ever come when she'd tell Griffin about their special powers . . . and hers.

Try as she might, she couldn't imagine a good reaction to that news, so chances were she wouldn't tell him. If she never told him, then he would never know one of the most important things about her. That didn't make for a very complete relationship. As usual, Anica was right. Lily hadn't thought this through very well.

About two hundred and fifty miles south, in the small town of Big Knob, Indiana, Dorcas Lowell stood in the kitchen of her quaint Victorian, attempting to fry eggs the regular way, without magic. Her black cat, Sabrina, sat on the windowsill, tail twitching, as she studied Deep Lake, hoping for a sight of her beloved friend Dee-Dee, the lake monster who lived there.

"I don't think she'll be out today, Sabrina," Dorcas said. "Her baby twins weren't feeling well yesterday. Her partner, Norton, might show up later, but I think Dee-Dee's staying with the kids this morning."

Sabrina meowed forlornly. Since Dorcas and her husband, Ambrose, had transported a male lake monster to Deep Lake, Dee-Dee hadn't had as much time for her friend Sabrina. In the old days Dee-Dee used to let Sabrina ride on her head as they sped around the lake on misty mornings when no human locals from Big Knob were around. Nobody in Big Knob suspected there was even one giant creature in the lake, let alone a family. Dorcas planned to keep it that way.

The residents of Big Knob thought they lived in a conservative, if somewhat quirky, town. They didn't question why the streets were laid out in the shape of a pentagram, or what caused the strange noises in the Whispering Forest. Dorcas and Ambrose had been assigned to manage the dragon who lived there. Thanks to them, George had given up most of his high jinks and had earned his golden scales so that he was a True Guardian of the Forest.

Life in Big Knob was more peaceful these days than it had been when Dorcas and Ambrose had first arrived and the dragon George was out of control, playing poker with the raccoons and causing mischief. Dorcas would go so far as to say it had become boring. She needed something to challenge her.

Ambrose strolled into the kitchen. "I smell eggs. Yum."

"Don't get your hopes up. I'm determined to make them without magic."

Ambrose sighed. "Why put yourself through it?"

"Because I watch nonmagical women cook without magic, and that makes me feel like I'm cheating." She nudged the frying eggs with a spatula. Sure enough, they were sticking. "Ambrose, what are we going to do about Lily and Griffin?"

"I don't recall being asked to do anything."

And that was driving Dorcas crazy. When she'd checked with Anica and discovered Lily had, in fact, administered the elixir, she'd wanted to jump right in. "Lily needs our help," she said, working to slide the spatula under one of the eggs. She liked them sunny-side up, but Ambrose insisted on over easy. That was the tricky part.

"I think Griffin's the one who needs the help," Ambrose said. "But that's out of our jurisdiction up there. We can't help if no one asks us to."

"Maybe someone will ask us during the engagement party on Sunday." Dorcas gave up on being tentative with the eggs. She shoved the spatula forcefully under the sticking egg, and yoke oozed out from the bottom and spread over the rest of the pan. "Hera's hickeys! Why is this so hard?"

"Because you're not using magic." Ambrose walked over to the stove, mumbled a Latin phrase and four perfect eggs appeared in the pan, two sunny-side up and two over easy.

"I didn't want to use magic!"

Ambrose wrapped both arms around her waist and leaned down to place a kiss on her neck. "And I'd like to eat my breakfast. I need to get down to Click-or-Treat, update my MySpace page and see what's happening on eBay with my scooter."

Dorcas leaned against him with a sigh of defeat. "Okay. But I hope you know that nobody's going to pay the ridiculous price you're asking for that scooter." And how she wished they would. She hated that dorky red thing. A Harley would be cool. A red scooter just looked lame.

"You never know." He gave her a squeeze and released her. "Maybe I'll talk it up at the engagement party. Somebody there might want it."

"Don't you dare." She dished up the eggs and set the plates on the kitchen table while Ambrose buttered the toast. "That party's designed to celebrate Anica and Jasper, and for their parents to meet each other, and . . . for us to get a look at Griffin Taylor."

"You need to forget about Griffin Taylor."

"But—"

"I'll make you a deal." Ambrose poured them each a mug of coffee from the pot on the counter. "I promise not to talk about selling my scooter if you promise not to find a way to offer unsolicited advice to either Lily or Griffin."

"All right." Dorcas got out napkins and utensils. "But if someone asks, then it's our magical duty to help."

Ambrose gave her a warning look. "They have to ask without prompting, Dorcas."

"I know." But she was very adept at steering conversations. She intended to steer a few on Sunday.

Lily and Anica stood at the end of the concourse, watching the stream of passengers for the familiar sight of their parents. They wouldn't be hard to spot. Both were tall and slim, and they favored exotic, colorful outfits, often purchased in the country where they'd been working.

"I'm glad you're getting married." Lily meant it, even if she was a little jealous. "For many reasons, of course, but also because it means Mom and Dad are coming home for a few weeks. I've missed them."

"Me, too, but they love what they're doing, and they can't research ancient tribal remedies parked in their condo. I'd rather have them out there living an exciting life than see them hunkered down at home being couch potatoes."

"True. Oh, there they are!"

"Are they ever," Anica said. "Mom's wearing a hat like a flying saucer, and Dad's wearing a feathered headdress."

Lily took in the arresting headgear, made even more dramatic because her parents were five-nine and six-two, respectively. Lionel Revere wore a blousy turquoise shirt, loose pants, and sandals, along with a bronze pendant around his neck. Simone Revere was in a peasant blouse decorated with a red ribbon, plus a full skirt in bright blue with a band of elaborate embroidery around the hem. "I guess it's good that Jasper didn't come along."

"Yeah. Maybe we can tone them down before they meet him."

"Good luck with that." Lily admired their style. Not everyone's parents came off a plane sporting saucer headgear and feathered headbands.

She and Anica hurried forward and were soon enveloped in laughter and welcoming hugs. Then they all headed for baggage claim.

While they stood a little apart from the crowd waiting for the luggage, Simone stood back and beamed at her daughters. "You girls look fabulous. I know Anica's in love, which explains that glow, but Lily, you're sparkling, too. What's up?"

Leave it to her mother to zero in on a change in her. "Well, there is a guy. You'll meet him on Sunday."

"Is he a wizard?" Lionel sounded hopeful.

"No, Dad, sorry. He's a lawyer."

Simone glanced from Anica to Lily. "Neither of you ever wanted to marry a wizard, did you?"

Anica gazed at her sister. "I can't speak for Lily, but I've always admired nonmagical men. No offense to you, Dad, but I'm impressed with what a nonmagical man can accomplish with sheer grit and force of will. Jasper can't wave a magic wand and make things happen, and so when he does something for me, it's special."

Simone gazed at Anica. "Yes, but . . . does he truly accept that you are magical? That *we* are magical?"

"He does." Anica hesitated. "But I'm not sure if his parents would, so I'd rather they didn't know."

Lionel sighed. "I was afraid of that. So no levitating the wineglasses, I suppose."

"Probably not." Anica smiled. "But Lily and I have a few little tricks planned for the party, things that will look like movie special effects but are really magic at work."

"They'll be very cool," Lily added.

Simone nodded. "Excellent. So, Lily, does your lawyer . . . what's his name?"

"Griffin Taylor."

"Griffin. I like that name. Does he know you're a witch?"

"Not exactly."

"Which means he doesn't." Simone eyed her younger daughter. "Are you serious about him?"

Lily wasn't sure how to answer that. "I guess."

"That doesn't sound very committed." Simone waved a hand. "If he's a passing fancy, then no need to tell him, I suppose. But if it's anyone you think will be a long-term relationship, then you know where the magical world stands on that."

Lily felt like a five-year-old caught stealing cookies. "Full disclosure."

"It's the reasonable thing." Lionel draped an arm around Lily's shoulders. "I'm sure it's not an easy conversation to have, but those who date nonmagical people need to remember that it can be a shock, so the sooner the nonmagical person is informed, the better."

Lily had trouble accepting this sage advice from a man wearing three feathers attached to his forehead with what looked like a macramé headband. But she nodded, anyway. "You're right, Dad."

"I'm sure Lily will do the right thing," her mother said.

That made Lily feel even more guilty. She could feel Anica's eyes on her, but they had a pact. Neither would tell on the other. It was a workable method of mutual coercion.

"My goodness, I almost forgot." Simone rifled through the colorful carrying bag on her arm. "I'm giving this to Anica and Jasper as an engagement party gift. I'll wrap it up, of course, and make a proper presentation, but I had to show it to both of you first. You'll love it."

Lily was prepared for something bizarre. Her parents never gave ordinary gifts. But she wasn't quite ready for the eight-inch carved onyx figure with the abnormally huge penis.

Anica seemed equally dumbfounded as she stared at the generously endowed statue. His dick was bigger than his leg.

"It's an Incan fertility symbol!" Their mother seemed so proud of her gift that Lily couldn't help but respond. "It's magnificent, Mom."

"Yes." Anica sounded slightly faint. "Truly magnificent."

Lily almost felt sorry for her sister, who would have to witness this gift being opened in front of her future in-laws. But at least Anica had taken care of business and told Jasper that she was a witch. Lily was running on borrowed time, and she knew it.

Chapter 12

When Griffin walked into the Bubbling Cauldron that night with Kevin and Miles, he paused just inside the doorway. "You guys go on over to our table. I need to talk to Lily."

"Do whatever you have to do," Kevin said. "We know you're obsessed with that woman, right, Miles?"

"*Obsessed* is the right word." Miles shook his head as he gazed at Griffin. "Biddle was remarking on how distracted you seemed today."

Griffin knew he should be worried about that. Nobody liked negative attention from a senior partner. But he was more concerned about how Lily's day with her parents had turned out. "I'll talk to Biddle tomorrow," he said. "Everybody has days when they're a little off, even Biddle. See you guys at the table in a few minutes."

"Right." Kevin gave him a searching look. "See you in a few."

Griffin knew that look. Kevin was worried about his involvement with Lily. And maybe it was somewhat on the obsessive side. He had to admit that he'd found concentrating difficult today. He'd wanted to call Lily on her cell, but he didn't want to do that while she was interacting with her parents.

Having them arrive so soon after he'd hooked up with her put a whole new spin on the situation. He didn't

feel ready to meet her parents, but he couldn't avoid it
with the engagement party coming up on Sunday. For all
he knew, they'd stop by the bar tonight, especially if they
wanted to get a look at their daughter's new boyfriend.

Griffin was sure they were perfectly nice people. But
parents tended to pick up on things, like whether a guy
was sleeping with their daughter. Once they figured that
out, they'd want to know his intentions. He had no intentions, no long-range plans.

He just wanted to be with Lily . . . a lot. Her parents
might think he only wanted to use her for sex, and that
wasn't true. Or was it? Why else was he hoping for all
the sex he could get without any plan for the future? A
not-so-noble part of him was hoping her folks had been
delayed . . . indefinitely.

Lily was dressed in her usual bartending outfit, tight
black blouse and snug black pants. Her hair was piled on
top of her head, and a strand that had come loose curled
at the nape of her neck. He found that incredibly sexy.
In fact, he was having storeroom fantasies again.

"Hi, Griffin." She smiled at him, but her brown gaze
looked a little harried. "I'll be over at your table right
after I finish making these two daiquiris."

"I'm not here to bug you. I wanted to ask how it
went—picking up your folks and everything."

"Okay."

"Good." So they'd made it to Chicago. There went
one of his cherished hopes.

"'Scuse me a sec." She flipped on the blender.

Griffin waited until the whirring stopped and she
poured the drinks into glasses. "So, uh, are they coming
by the bar tonight?"

"No." Lily garnished the drinks with a cherry. "They
went out to dinner with Anica and Jasper so they could
get to know their prospective son-in-law. Then I'm sure
they'll go straight to bed. They've had a long day. Here
you go, Sherman." She slid the glasses down the bar to

the waiter, who had walked over from the far side of the room.

"Thanks." Sherman loaded the drinks on a tray. "Hi, Griffin. How's it going?"

"Great." He could say that now that he knew Lily's parents wouldn't be showing up tonight.

Lily wiped the bar. "Griffin, as long as you're here, can I ask you something?"

"Sure."

She glanced up at him. "Do you read your horoscope?"

"No, why?" Maybe she'd read it and thought the prediction was significant. But that couldn't be right. He hadn't told her his birthday. He didn't know hers, either. That was something he should find out. Women expected a guy to pay attention to that kind of stuff.

Or rather, they did if the relationship was serious, which brought him back to his original dilemma—the nature of this thing he had going with Lily.

"A Miller draft and a gin fizz," Sherman called from the end of the bar.

"Coming up!" Lily put down her bar rag and picked up a beer glass from the rack under the counter. "I just wondered what you think of that kind of thing," she said.

"You mean astrology?" She'd told him she was an amateur magician, which was more of a party trick than a philosophy, but still, he decided to tread lightly. "I don't know a lot about it. Do you?"

She drew the beer and started making the gin fizz. "Some. I guess I'm wondering how you feel about . . . you know, stuff you can't rationally explain but that happens, anyway."

"Like aliens?" He couldn't figure out what she was trying to say. "Area 51 and all that?"

"Well, no." She finished up the gin fizz. "Never mind. It's not important."

He had a feeling it was important, but she wasn't making the conversation easy to follow. "Well, I should probably get back over to the table so we can figure out our order. Want me to come back here and give it to you?"

Her eyes sparkled. "Just how do you mean that?"

Instantly he was aroused. "How would you like me to mean it?"

She met his gaze and she flushed. Then she lowered her voice and leaned closer. "You can probably guess, but we're in the middle of a crowded bar, so it'll have to wait. I'll come over and take the order, the way I always do."

He reached over and rubbed his thumb against her full lower lip. "Later, then."

Her voice was husky. "Yeah, later."

Knowing that she wanted him, too, fueled his store-room fantasies even more. But he forced himself to think about something neutral so he could walk back to the table without embarrassing himself. He settled on baseball stats as the safest way to go.

He mentally reviewed the ERA stats for all the starting pitchers in the Cubs lineup as he approached Kevin and Miles. "Her folks made it to town okay," he said.

Miles looked sympathetic. "Too bad for you. I've always thought dating orphans was the way to go."

"Speak for yourself, loser." Kevin leaned back in his chair. "Parents always like me a lot."

"Sometimes better than the girl likes you," Miles said.

"That only happened once, and it was because they had their heart set on a lawyer for a son-in-law, and she had her heart set on a punk rocker. They still send me a bottle of Scotch every Christmas."

Griffin sat down with a sigh. "I'm not ready for this."

"No man is ready for this," Miles said. "You're sleeping with their daughter, so naturally they'll expect you to be looking at rings. It's the way it is."

"Maybe they don't have to know I'm sleeping with their daughter."

Kevin shook his head. "Don't kid yourself. They'll know. Parents have radar for such things."

"You're right." Griffin glanced at his friends. "I'm not planning to marry their daughter, so what do I say to them?"

Miles loosened his tie and unfastened the top button of his dress shirt. "Say what you usually say in this situation."

"The thing is, our buddy Griffin hasn't been in this situation," Kevin said. "He's only slept with potential wives."

Miles stared at Griffin. "Is that true? I didn't know that."

"It's true," Griffin said. "This is the first time I've slept with someone just for the hell of it, because I wanted to."

Miles blew out a breath. "I'm still back on the *sleeping with potential wives* part of this conversation. You were considering marrying Sharon?"

"Sort of. For a while."

"Jesus, man, I had no clue or I would have stepped in. Sharon was pretty and all, but she would have been a disaster. Neurotic as hell."

"Yeah, well." Griffin shrugged. "She had career goals. She knew what she wanted out of life. Whereas Lily—"

"Did someone call my name?" Lily appeared at his elbow. He hoped to hell she hadn't heard any of that discussion, but as he glanced up, her expression was open and friendly, so she probably hadn't.

After she left with their order, Kevin leaned toward him. "Okay, here's what you say to her parents: You and Lily are just getting to know each other, and you think she's fantastic, but you don't want to rush into anything and neither does she."

"Sounds good," Miles said. "And another tip. Don't flaunt your sexual relationship in front of them. Keep your hands pretty much to yourself, and definitely no lip-locks in their presence."

"I think that's why I'm so nervous about meeting her parents. I've never dated anyone who turned me on this much. I'm afraid I'll forget and grab her right in front of them."

"You won't," Kevin said. "You're a lawyer, for God's sake. You know how to put on an act when you have to. We all do."

"I suppose." Griffin glanced over at the bar where Lily was mixing their drinks. "At least I don't have to worry about it yet."

Lily watched as Kevin and Miles left for the evening. Griffin stayed at the table, but she expected him to wander over to the bar soon. She'd debated suggesting that he go back to her apartment again tonight and take Daisy out, but now that her parents were in town, she felt like making the most of whatever time she had with Griffin when her folks weren't around, even if it was at work.

Business at the bar had slowed, as it usually did once happy hour was over. Maybe she'd buy Griffin a drink and he could sit at the bar and talk to her for a while. She liked talking to Griffin, liked hearing his voice. She wouldn't bring up anything paranormal this time, though.

Her horoscope question had gone nowhere, and she shouldn't have been surprised. Griffin had never struck her as the kind of guy who would head for the tarot booth at a county fair. But after her dad's comments, she'd decided to find out if Griffin at least had an open mind about events outside his own experience.

She'd have to come at it from a different direction next time, though, because astrology didn't click with him and they'd totally derailed when Griffin thought she might be talking about aliens. Maybe she could mention a couple of movies as a lead-in to the subject.

But not tonight. Tonight she wanted to flirt and have a good time. She wanted to enjoy the good parts of this spell and stop worrying about the potentially bad parts. She wanted to enjoy the experience of being into someone who was also into her.

"You're smiling."

She glanced over and was surprised to see that Griffin had come to the bar and slid onto a stool without her noticing. She turned toward him and discovered the only other customer who had been sitting at the bar had paid up and left. "I was thinking about you," she said honestly.

"And smiling." He seemed happy about that. "I'll take that as a good sign."

"It is." She met his gaze and allowed herself to bask in that admiring glow for a few seconds. Heat spiraled through her and settled in a predictable spot. Too bad they weren't alone. "A very good sign."

"Did you want me to go take care of Daisy?"

"She'll be okay for a little while longer. I could buy you a drink, if you'd like to stay and talk to me until my break."

"You have a break coming up?" He looked interested in that.

"In about twenty minutes. Sherman handles the bar for me so I can get off my feet for a little while."

"And how long is that?"

"Oh, about fifteen minutes. But I can't really leave, if that's what you're asking."

He shook his head. "Just wondering how long I could have you to myself."

The intimate way he said it, along with his steady

gaze, sent more heat flooding through her. "You'd better stop looking at me like that, or we're liable to cause a scene."

"Sounds like fun."

She laughed. "Oh, it would be, until I got fired. So, what would you like?"

He just smiled.

Wow, the man packed a punch. "Besides that."

"I guess I'll make do with a bottle of Heineken, then. And I don't need a glass." He pushed money across the bar.

"Seriously, this one's on me."

He pulled the money back. "Thanks. Remind me to do something nice for you soon."

"I will." She winked at him as she opened the bottle and handed it to him. About that time Sherman arrived with a couple of orders, and she busied herself filling them while Sherman went to check on another table.

"If there's anything special you want to watch on TV, Griffin, say the word and I'll change to that channel. You're the only one sitting here so you might as well please yourself."

"There's nothing on TV that beats watching you move around doing your job."

She flushed with pleasure. "That has to be boring. All I'm doing is mixing drinks."

"With great efficiency." He leaned closer. "But also when you work fast, your breasts shift just enough to make the view really interesting."

She smiled but kept her eyes on her work so she didn't mess up the order. "So you're ogling."

"Yes, ma'am, I sure am. Does that bother you?"

"Uh-huh." She didn't dare look at him or she'd never get this order filled. "I'm not only bothered, I'm hot and bothered."

"Too bad we can't do something about that."

She finished the drinks and set them on the bar for Sherman. "It is a shame."

"Not many private spots in a place like this. I don't suppose there's a storeroom or anything."

She laughed. "Griffin Taylor, you know there's a storeroom. You have to pass it to get to the bathrooms. You've been plotting this all along, haven't you?"

"Maybe. Any chance my devious plan would work?"

She shouldn't think about the possibility, but now she couldn't help it. If they were quiet and nobody needed anything out of the storeroom, it could work. The guys in the kitchen had often complained that there was no door from the kitchen to the storeroom, so they had to go out in the hall and through another door to get anything. Funky old buildings like this one sometimes had odd layouts.

"You're crazy." But she hadn't said she wouldn't do it. In fact, her body was telling her to go for it. "You'd have to go into the men's room and get a—"

"I know." Griffin looked at his watch. "By my calculations, I should do that pretty soon, if we're going to take advantage of your break."

She was already planning how they could do it. The thrill of the forbidden had always appealed to her, and doing something wild like this with Griffin was icing on the cake. "Go make your purchase," she said. "I'll call Sherman over and tell him I need him to cover for me while I take inventory of the liquor supply, so I'll know what we need to order from the distributor."

"Will he buy that?"

"He should. I've done it plenty of times. I like my job and I like it to run smoothly. I'll admit planning ahead normally isn't my strong suit, but when not doing that will affect how the bar operates, then I jump in there. Devon's not big on keeping track of supplies, so Syd makes sure we have everything we need for the kitchen and I take care of ordering the booze."

"Which is a lucky thing right now."

She trailed a finger down the side of his face. "Very lucky."

"Lily, you are the hottest, most amazing—"

"Hey, Lil." Sherman came toward them. "Things have slowed down, so I was thinking of taking a break."

Lily gave Griffin a secret smile. "If you can wait a little longer, I need to take inventory in the storeroom. Griffin's offered to help." She reached in her backpack and pulled out her set of keys.

Sherman looked from Lily to Griffin. "Oh." He opened his mouth as if to say something else, but apparently changed his mind. "Okay. Take off, then. I'll hold down the fort."

What a rush, Lily thought as she lifted the hinged part of the bar and walked out into the main serving area. She was meeting her dream guy in the storeroom for sex. No matter what else happened because of the adoration elixir, she'd always remember this unbelievably wild stunt. If she was this turned on by the idea of taking a chance, she wondered how Griffin was able to walk.

He might have been having some issues, because he wasted no time disappearing down the hall toward the men's room.

Lily unlocked the storeroom and reached inside to turn on the light. In the glare of the overhead bulb, she took stock of the situation. Shelves full of cardboard containers lined the walls of the narrow room. The empty space in the center was about seven feet across. The place smelled musty, which made it all the more exciting.

She envisioned how this would work, and the only way would be with one of them braced up against a row of boxes. There would be no lying down in this place. They'd have to do it upright. Cool.

"Sorry I took so long. The machine was acting up."

She turned to find Griffin standing there in his suit. "But you were successful?"

"There was never any doubt."

She gestured around the storeroom. "You could get a little dusty with this plan."

He stepped toward her. "I hope to hell I do."

"Then I guess we'd better lock the door."

Chapter 13

Griffin hadn't ever done anything remotely like this, and it felt damned good to be acting on a wild impulse. Lily closed and locked the door, which muted the rock music coming from the bar but didn't eliminate it. The music would help cover the sound of their activities.

And he was more than ready for those activities. Pulling her into his arms, he satisfied his immediate need to kiss her. Kissing only threw gasoline on a fire that was already out of control.

He lifted his head and glanced around at the starkly lit interior of the storeroom, searching for the best place.

"We don't have much time." She reached down and unbuckled his belt.

"Let's go over there. Up against that stack of boxes."

She was breathing quickly. "Fine." She unfastened his slacks and started to pull down the zipper as he backed her toward the boxes. "Where's the con—"

He grabbed her hands as she fumbled with the zipper. "I'll do that. You take off your pants." He sounded more like a drill sergeant than a lover, but they had so little time and he was desperate to be inside her. All he could hear from the muffled bar music was a steady drumbeat that would be perfect accompaniment.

"Right." She stepped away from him long enough to

unzip her tight black pants. "Oh, Hades, the boots. I have to take off the boots if I'm going to—"

"Just take off one." He fought the red haze of lust that made his fingers tremble as he ripped open the condom packet. All the while he prayed that they'd have enough time to finish this. It had become the single most important thing in his life, to bury his cock in her hot, slick vagina.

And he knew it would be hot and slick. The sweet aroma of aroused woman floated up as she tossed her boot aside and pulled one leg free of her pants and panties. He had the condom on by the time she accomplished that.

He'd love to be able to feel her breasts against him, but they didn't have time for taking off anything else. He'd never had sex with his suit jacket on, either, but this was a night for firsts. With his pants down around his ankles on a dusty floor, he reached for her.

She put both hands on his shoulders and looked into his eyes. "Can you hold me up?"

"I could hold up Wrigley Stadium if it meant I could be inside you."

Her laugh was breathy. "Adrenaline is amazing, isn't it?"

"Yeah, it most certainly is."

She moistened her lips.

He picked her up, and she demonstrated the agility of a gymnast, tucking her legs around him as she clutched his shoulders. His penis reacted like a Scud missile, homing in on her moist heat, finding the target and sliding in as if they'd practiced this for hours.

"Mm." She closed her eyes. "That's very good."

"Outstanding." He felt so strong he imagined he could hold her like this forever.

She leaned back on the boxes, and he liked that she was urging him on, but he sure as hell didn't need any urging. Something about the harsh overhead light made this all the more illicit, all the more erotic. He was turned on as he'd never been turned on before.

The rhythm he initiated followed the pounding beat of the music seeping through the walls. He gave it to her fast and he gave it to her hard. Vaguely he wondered if the steady thumping against the boxes could be heard outside the storeroom, even with the rock music playing, but he was so lost in the experience that he didn't much care.

"Oh, Griffin . . ." She moaned and clutched his shoulders. "Griffin . . . I'm . . . yes, like that. Like *that.*" She arched her back. "Mustn't yell, mustn't yell."

"Then . . . talk to me." He pounded into her. "Tell me how it feels."

"Like . . . like fireworks . . . like a whirlpool . . . like . . . *there, Griffin. Right . . .*" She closed her mouth against the cries that threatened to give them away.

When her climax undulated over his aching cock, he let go. He couldn't yell, either, so he shuddered and swore softly and eloquently. The sensation of coming in this urgent way was incredibly exciting. He knew he'd never forget it, which meant he'd probably never forget Lily, either.

As that thought drifted through his passion-soaked brain, a repetitive noise interrupted his postcoital glow. At first he thought it was the music, but it didn't have a musical beat.

Who was messing with this most excellent moment? It wasn't Lily, who had sagged back against the boxes, eyes closed, while her legs were still wrapped firmly around his waist. It wasn't him, because once his orgasm took over, he'd stopped moving, except for the occasional quiver of aftershock.

Lily's eyes slowly opened. Her words came out in a hoarse whisper. "Someone's knocking at the door."

"That's—" Griffin cleared his throat and tried again. "That's not good."

"No. No, it's not."

"Lily!" Sherman's voice penetrated through the locked door.

She took a deep breath. "What is it?"

Griffin was impressed at how calm and rational she sounded, as if she'd indeed been in here taking inventory of the booze supply instead of boinking him senseless.

"Someone's out here to see you," Sherman said.

"Who?"

"Your parents."

Griffin had never much believed in reincarnation, but he wondered if there wasn't something to it, after all. It would explain why this was happening. He must have done something very bad in another life.

Miles had given him some excellent advice—not to flaunt his sexual relationship with Lily in front of her folks. Apparently he was now being punished for his past-life transgressions, because here he was, with his cock still buried in Lily's warm vagina, and her parents standing somewhere beyond that door.

He could only hope they were in the bar having a drink and not in the hallway waiting to come into the storeroom to see their beloved daughter. But if he were truly being punished, they'd be right there with Sherman, waiting for Lily to come out of the locked storeroom with her new boyfriend Griffin, who was willing to risk getting her fired because he had to have sex with her during her break at work.

To her credit, Lily didn't immediately pull away from him and scramble into her clothes. He appreciated that. In her shoes, or in her boots, or in this case, one boot, he wouldn't have been so cool and collected.

"Tell them to order anything they want on the house," she called out to Sherman. "I'll be out in a few minutes, when I've finished up the work."

"We'll see you soon, then, Lily," said an unfamiliar male voice.

Griffin looked at Lily.

My father, she mouthed.

So it was official, Griffin decided. Reincarnation was a fact, and in some previous life he'd been a really, really bad boy. "This is somewhat awkward."

"It's not a problem." Holding on to his shoulders, Lily eased herself free and lowered her feet to the floor. "I have it covered."

"How? Sherman knows we were both in here, and when we come out all rumpled with dust on our clothes, and the inventory not done, he'll know." Griffin tucked the used condom in his handkerchief. What he'd do with the handkerchief he had no idea. Then he saw a trash can and tossed it in there. "And your folks will know, too. Parents have a sixth sense for when their daughter is having sex."

"Calm down." Lily stepped into her pants and pulled them up. "It'll be okay."

"I was hoping we could gloss over the fact that we're sexually involved." Griffin pulled up his pants. "I think that train just left."

"Not necessarily. Let me look at you." Lily surveyed him and smiled. "You look like you've been having sex in a storeroom."

He groaned. "Exactly. And so do you. You have dust all over that black outfit, and your hair's coming down in the back."

"Let's take care of you, first." Lily circled him, brushing at his clothes and muttering something.

"What are you saying?"

"It's a little poem my mother used to recite when she helped me get ready for parties when I was little. When I was nervous it helped me calm down. I think we both need that now. *Clothes so wrinkled, clothes so messy, magic sprinkled, now you're dressy.*"

"Cute, but I think I need a dry cleaning service."

"Actually, you look very good."

He glanced down at his slacks. To his surprise, they did look good. "Huh. I'll have to buy another suit like this. I had no idea it could shed dirt and wrinkles that fast." He smoothed a hand down his shirt, which felt as if it had been freshly pressed. "Huh," he said again. "I'll need to pick up a few more of these shirts, too."

She arched her eyebrows. "Because you plan to have lots more storeroom sex?"

"I wouldn't mind." He gazed at her and decided any embarrassment involving her parents was worth it. "Thank you for one of the best times of my life."

Her smile warmed him. "Same here."

"Listen, you still look pretty much like you've been . . . doing what we've been doing."

"I won't after I have a few minutes in the ladies' room. We probably shouldn't come out together, so you can wait here for about five minutes, which will give me time to go meet them."

Griffin didn't like the image of him cowering in the storeroom while Lily faced the music. "I'm good to go. I'll go first."

"But you've never met them."

"I can handle it." Griffin decided it was time to man up. "Tell me their names and what they look like."

She gave him a look of gratitude. "Their names are Lionel and Simone Revere. They're both tall. My dad has dark hair like me, with a little gray in it, sort of salt-and-pepper. My mom's still a blonde, with a little help, of course. I take after my dad in looks, but I'm more like my mom in personality. Anica's got my dad's conservative streak but my mom's blond coloring."

Griffin nodded. "I shouldn't have any trouble spotting them."

"I guarantee you won't. My dad's taken off his Peruvian feather headdress, or he had last I saw him, but I'll bet he's still wearing the peasant pants, shirt and sandals he got down there. Oh, and he'll have a huge Incan medallion around his neck. You could give somebody a concussion with that thing."

"Let's hope he doesn't use it on me."

She laughed. "Sorry. I didn't mean it like that. My dad isn't ordinarily a violent man."

"Finding your daughter in a locked storeroom, having sex with a guy you don't know isn't all that ordinary."

"Don't worry. They'll both be cool." She frowned. "Although I hope my mom's ditched the red Peruvian flying-saucer hat, but last time I saw her she was wearing it. She said if she took it off, she'd have hat hair."

Despite the nobility of his gesture, Griffin felt a headache coming on. Out of all the parents in the world, he had to make an impression on a couple of certified flakes who wore Incan medallions and weird Peruvian hats. Logically, he shouldn't care what they thought of him. Jasper was the one who had to get on their good side, not Griffin. It wasn't as if they were his future in-laws. That was Jasper's territory.

Then again, if Lily's parents didn't like him, then Lily might be influenced to kick him to the curb. That was totally unacceptable. He needed to be with Lily in the same way he needed to breathe. He wasn't sure how long that condition would last, but for now, Lily was essential to his well-being. He didn't want to muck that up by getting crossways with her folks.

"Griffin, you look as if you're about to step in front of a firing squad. If you'd rather not do this, then—"

"No, I'm going." He took a deep breath. "But first I'll help you brush off some of that dust. There's a lot of it, and your hair—"

"I can handle all that." She walked over and unlocked the door. "Trust me, when I come out of this storeroom, no one will suspect a thing."

He doubted that. "See you out there, then." Squaring his shoulders, he walked into the hall, which was deserted, thank God.

He decided to duck into the men's bathroom and double-check that his fly wasn't open or he didn't have lipstick smeared somewhere. Lily might have missed something that would be really embarrassing. To his surprise, he looked almost as fresh as when he'd arrived at work this morning. Yep, he was definitely buying another suit of this brand and some more dress shirts. They could take anything.

Fortified with the knowledge that he was presentable, he walked into the main area of the bar. He tried for an air of cool confidence, but not so confident that he seemed arrogant. Somewhere along the way it occurred to him that he'd indeed had storeroom sex, and not every guy could say that.

He wouldn't be saying it, either. Miles could talk about his sexual experiences if he wanted to, but Griffin wouldn't. What he and Lily had shared was private, their own business and nobody else's.

Sherman came toward him carrying a tray of drinks. As he went by, he said something out of the corner of his mouth. It sounded a lot like "Way to score in the storeroom, dude." But Griffin could have misheard him.

A quick scan of the room sent him to a corner table where a middle-aged man wearing a large medallion sat with a blond woman whose red hat did look a lot like a flying saucer. Unless Griffin was mistaken, they were both drinking his favorite, vodka and tonic with a twist. He'd take that as a good sign.

Lionel Revere stood as Griffin approached. Either Lily had described him to her folks or Lionel was acting on what were probably well-honed instincts. Lily's father held out his hand. "You must be Griffin."

"I am." Griffin looked into the man's dark eyes as he accepted his firm handshake.

"This is my wife, Simone."

"Pleased to meet you, Griffin." Simone didn't get up, but she held out her hand. Her grip was as firm as her husband's, her blue gaze equally direct. "I have the feeling we interrupted something in the storeroom."

Griffin's face grew hot. So much for cool and confident. "Um, well, that is, Lily and I—"

"Sit down, sit down." Simone waved Griffin to a chair. "You and Lily are young and vital. If you weren't enjoying a little hanky-panky, I'd wonder what was wrong with you."

Lionel resumed his seat. "But since you are, it's our parental duty to give you the third degree. Lily says you're a lawyer, so I figure you can take it. What are you drinking?"

As much as I can gulp down in a short time. "Vodka and tonic with a twist."

Lionel glanced at him with approval. "Good answer. Ah, there's Lily on her way over here. We can just give her your order."

Griffin turned in his chair. If he'd been a cartoon character, his eyes would have bounced out of his head on springs. Lily didn't look even slightly rumpled. Her hair was neatly done up and her black outfit unwrinkled and free of dust. Even her makeup was perfect.

Simone got out of her chair to hug her daughter. "Surprise!"

"You surprised me, all right," Lily said. "I'm surprised you two are still awake."

"We're tough old birds." Her father came around the table to hug her after Simone was finished. "And now that we've stumbled on the nitty-gritty of your relationship with Griffin here, we feel free to interrogate him."

Lily's eyes widened. "What nitty-gritty? Griffin was helping me take inventory."

Simone winked. "I'm sure he was, dear."

"No, really." Lily waved a sheaf of papers. "Here it is, all catalogued."

Griffin's jaw dropped. "When did you do that?" When Lionel started laughing, he realized he'd just screwed up.

"I mean, yeah, that's what we were working on. That's the list, all right."

By now Simone was laughing, too, which made her saucer hat bob uncontrollably. "Lily always was the best cover-up artist I've ever known. Didn't matter what she got herself into, she'd make you believe she was completely innocent."

"*Mom!* That's a huge exaggeration. I—"

"Don't get all huffy, sweetheart," her father said. "You're creative and we love you for it. Now if you'll bring Griffin a vodka and tonic with a twist, the three of us will get down to business."

Lily looked uneasy. "Haven't you two ever heard of jet lag? You should be completely whipped."

"Ah, but we're not," her father said. "After all, we've been studying ancient herbal remedies, including ways to boost energy."

"Besides," her mother said. "You didn't think we'd go to bed without meeting Griffin, did you? I could tell by the way you talked about him that he's special."

Griffin couldn't quite get his head around all of it. Lily had come out of the storeroom, looking perfect and with an inventory list in her hand. Her parents didn't believe that she'd actually been in there doing the inventory, but nevertheless she'd produced an official sheaf of papers. How had she done that?

Lily turned to him. "They might not be tired, but I'll bet you are. You don't have to sit here and be grilled unless you—"

"I'll stay." Griffin sensed things going on under the surface with both her parents and with her, things he didn't understand. He'd been sexually fascinated by Lily from the beginning. But he was intrigued by more than that now. "I'd like to get to know your folks."

She continued to look wary. "Just don't believe everything they tell you."

Chapter 14

Lily watched her mom and dad laughing and talking with Griffin and hoped they wouldn't tell him too much. Now she wished she hadn't used magic to make both her and Griffin presentable after their interlude in the storeroom. She hadn't fooled her parents, and Sherman seemed to know exactly what had been going on in there.

That meant she'd taken a risk for no good reason. She'd have to figure out how to explain the completed inventory to Griffin, and she was reasonably sure he'd ask her later on tonight, when they were alone.

Her mom and dad stayed until close to closing time, and she couldn't get over how animated they were. Obviously they'd found some interesting herbs in Peru in addition to unusual outfits and an engagement party gift that was sure to cause a comment. She wondered how Anica planned to spin that.

As if she'd conjured up her sister, her cell phone in her backpack played "Witchy Woman." Lily grabbed it and held it between her shoulder and her ear while she made a mai tai and a Singapore Sling. "Hey, big sis."

"Are they there?"

"Yes, and I think they discovered the secret to eternal life down in Peru, because after all those hours on the plane, they're still upright and making intelligent conversation. At least I assume they are. They're having drinks with Griffin." She considered telling Anica about the storeroom incident and decided against it. Every sexual encounter strengthened the spell, so Anica would no doubt worry about the state of Griffin's involvement.

"Jasper's watching a TiVo of the Cubs game, so I sneaked into the bedroom to call you."

"I still can't get used to you living where there's cable and everything." Lily knew Anica had made a compromise about TV when she and Jasper had picked out their new place. Lily didn't mind having one, but Anica had lived without a television for years, preferring to use her leisure time to work on her magic.

"I'm gradually transforming this condo so it feels more like home. Listen, I called because I need some advice about that fertility symbol the folks plan to give us at the party. I haven't told Jasper about it because he's already imagining total chaos when his extremely traditional parents meet our extremely untraditional ones. Now that he's spent time with Mom and Dad he's even more nervous. The statue will be the crowning blow."

Lily garnished the drinks and set them on the bar. "Mom was very excited about that statue. I'll bet she met the artist and paid a small fortune for it. If you don't accept it with profuse gratitude, she'll be crushed."

"Thanks for telling me something I didn't already know. If Jasper's parents weren't going to be there, I'd just roll with it. It's not something I'd put on the coffee table in the living room, but as a bedroom accent, it could be . . . stimulating."

"No kidding. I actually like the silly thing. It's funky. All it really means is that Mom and Dad are hoping you'll come up with some grandchildren."

"I know, and that's sweet. In their usual twisted way, they're saying they love me and want me to have babies."

"That's exactly right," Lily said. "So here's my advice.

On Sunday, we'll get the bartender, Chad, to double up shots on Jasper's mom and dad."

Anica gasped. "Your plan is to get Jasper's parents drunk?"

"You got something better?"

"No."

"Until you come up with something better, I say we'll go with Chad doubling the shots."

"I'll keep thinking," Anica said. "So are the folks interrogating Griffin?"

"Apparently they came specifically for that purpose." Lily smiled at Sherman as he came by with an order written on a slip of paper. Whenever he noticed that she was on the phone, he did that, which was nice of him. She was also convinced he knew about the storeroom sex but she trusted him not to say anything to Devon, the owner.

"And?" Anica prompted.

"The three of them are having a confab at a corner table and seem to be getting along great. I only hope they aren't letting those vodka and tonics loosen their tongues to the point they let something slip about the magic."

"They do know you haven't told him anything, right?"

"I tried to make that clear today. But you know Dad. He's always on that Full Disclosure kick."

"Well, you could tell him while he's still under the influence of the adoration elixir," Anica said. "You'd have a captive audience, so to speak."

Lily filled a glass with beer and poured red wine into a goblet. "Yes, but if I tell him, he might begin to wonder if I've cast a spell on him. I'd rather keep the status quo for now, at least until after the party. Actually, until after the wedding would be terrific. I could deal with it after that."

"The wedding's not for three weeks. Can you keep a lid on things that long?"

Lily glanced over to the table where her mom and dad were sharing a laugh with Griffin. She'd always dreamed of this—the man she'd chosen enjoying time with her parents. Now it was happening, and within a month her folks would go back to Peru. Then she could figure out this thing with Griffin.

"Yes," she said. "I can keep a lid on it that long. You bet."

Griffin's time with Lily's parents flew by. After being worried that he wouldn't get along with them, he discovered they were fascinating to be with. They'd quizzed him a little about his background, but apparently after deciding that he had no huge skeletons in the closet, they'd dropped their line of questioning and gone on to relate their experiences in Peru.

Somehow they'd moved from that subject to Lily, and they'd entertained Griffin with stories about what she'd been like as a little kid. He listened to the stories with a touch of envy.

Lily had been outrageous from an early age, but around ten, close to the age when he'd turned into a cautious kid because of his parents' divorce, Lily had become the prankster of the neighborhood. Anica had been their steady, obedient daughter, while Lily had loved to douse people with water balloons and prank call strangers.

Griffin realized he could credit this wild streak for the fun they'd recently had in the storeroom, and the sense of adventure she'd shown in the bedroom, too.

After telling the story of how Lily had smuggled whoopee cushions into a school board meeting and placed one on every school board member's chair, Lionel wiped tears of laughter from his eyes. "She was a handful, all right."

She still is. And Griffin loved that energy now that he'd surrendered to it. A thought came to him, a blindingly obvious conclusion. She was forbidden fruit, the kind of woman he'd told himself to avoid. That's why she drew him like a magnet.

He'd have to be careful, but he had a safety net. Kevin had promised to make sure he didn't do anything stupid, so he'd felt free to pursue his interest in Lily, the most daring woman he'd ever dated. Kevin wouldn't let him crash and burn.

Toward closing time, when it became obvious Lionel and Simone would soon head home, Griffin decided to ask a few questions of his own. The more he knew about this fascinating woman he was involved with, the better prepared he'd be to deal with her. "Has Lily ever had a dream, something she wanted to pursue?"

Simone leaned her chin on her fist and gazed at him. "Not really. She's all about having fun, but I've always wished she had more direction. Obviously you have direction, considering that you made it through law school and are now working in your chosen field."

"I was lucky to find out early what I wanted to do." Now, there was a concept. He'd always considered his background a negative, and yet it had prodded him into a career, one he liked.

"I don't think Lily knows yet what she wants to be when she grows up," Lionel said. "Although I have to say she's excellent at this bartending job. I've been watching her, and she's in her element back there, mixing and measuring and creating concoctions."

"So she could be a chemist," Griffin said. "If she went back to school, of course. Or maybe a pharmacist."

Lionel shook his head. "I think she's too free-spirited to be in either of those professions. She's not crazy about being a student, either."

"What about her magic?" Griffin asked.

Lionel and Simone put down their drinks and stared at him as if he'd just suggested they all get naked and make a quick circuit of the room.

"You do know she's an amateur magician, right?" From their reaction, he wondered if maybe he wasn't supposed to reveal that. Her parents might not approve, although with their open-minded attitude toward life, he found that hard to believe. His question had startled them, though. He could tell that much.

Lionel coughed. "I suppose we knew a little something about that."

Griffin warmed to his idea. "I can see her perfecting her act through parties, maybe even gigs at malls, and then taking it on the road. She's gorgeous, so I doubt she'd have trouble getting bookings."

"It's something to think about." Simone finished her drink. "Magic is tricky, though. Earning a living with it isn't always possible."

Griffin wasn't sure why they were acting so weird about this. "I haven't seen her perform," he admitted. "Are you trying to tell me she's not very good at it?"

Lionel chuckled. "Oh, she's very good at it. You should get her to show you what she can do."

"I absolutely will." Lily's parents might not be excited about a potential performing career for their daughter, but Griffin thought it was a great idea. She might be a good bartender, but he thought she had way too much potential to do that for the rest of her life.

By the time Lily's parents stood to leave, they were treating Griffin like an old friend.

Simone even gave him a hug. "Be sure to let us know how it goes if you talk Lily into doing some magic for you."

"Is she shy about it?" Griffin still couldn't get a handle on this situation. He couldn't imagine why a person would train themselves to be a magician if they never intended to perform for anyone.

"Am I shy about what?" Lily had come out from behind the bar to tell her parents good-bye.

"Your magic," her mother said.

The expression of outright fear in Lily's eyes took Griffin aback. Did she really have stage fright?

She swallowed. "What have you been telling him?"

"That it's tough to make a living as a magician," her mother said. "Griffin thinks you should take your amateur magician act on the road."

"But . . ." She seemed to be casting around for something to say. "But he's never seen me do magic."

Her father nodded. "That's what he said. Maybe it's time you showed him a little of it."

Lily glared at her father. "I'm not ready to do that, Dad."

He seemed unperturbed by her anger. "Oh, I think you are."

"You don't understand. It's not the way you think."

Simone moved closer to Lily and wrapped an arm around her daughter. "Your dad has a point, but we won't push it, will we, dear?" She gave her husband a quelling glance.

"Not tonight," Lionel said. "But Lily knows how I feel about this. And the guidelines are quite clear on the subject."

Griffin was completely at sea, and really sorry he'd brought up the magic thing in front of Lily's parents. For some reason it was a touchy subject for all of them, and damned if he knew why. The comment about guidelines made no sense at all. Their daughter was teaching herself magic tricks. No big deal.

Or it shouldn't have been, but there was still some tension evident as Simone and Lionel said their goodbyes and left the bar.

Griffin turned to Lily. "That was my fault. I'm the one who mentioned your being an amateur magician."

Her smile was strained. "It's not your fault. This is between me and my folks."

"Do they have something against you performing in public?"

She shook her head. "It's not that. Listen, let me close out the register and then . . ." Her voice trailed off, as if she couldn't decide what would come next.

"Then we can go back to your place." He sure hoped this little tiff with her folks hadn't screwed that up.

"That might not be such a good idea."

Hell and damnation! If only he hadn't opened his big mouth. "I don't know exactly what's going on here, but I'll bet I could find a way to make you forget all about it."

"You probably could, but I . . . I need to be alone tonight."

He hadn't realized how much he'd counted on going home with her until she took away that option. "Lily, don't do this. Hey, if you don't want to have sex, that's okay. I just want to be with you."

"It's better if we have some time apart."

"No, it's not!" He felt an unfamiliar panic gripping his chest. He needed to go home with her. He *needed* to.

"Griffin." She laid a hand on his arm and her gaze was pleading. "We've moved pretty fast. Don't you think it's time to take a break, give ourselves a chance to catch our breath?"

Inside he was screaming *No* and *Hell, no*, but he struggled to sound reasonable, civilized and rational when he was none of these things. "As I said, we don't have to have sex. I can give you a foot rub. I'll bet after all the hours on your feet you could use one."

She gazed at him for what seemed like forever while he went slowly nuts wondering what her decision would be. He was on the verge of begging, and only a deep sense of pride that had been ingrained at an early age prevented him from doing exactly that.

"Please go back to your place tonight, Griffin. We each need some time alone."

"I don't." He was ashamed at how needy he sounded, but he couldn't seem to help himself.

"You may not think so now, but you do. We both do. I'll see you tomorrow night." She turned away and walked back to the bar.

He was so upset he thought he might puke. Somehow he got control of himself. As he walked out of the Bubbling Cauldron, he wondered how he was going to survive until tomorrow night. He would be counting the minutes. Hell, he'd be counting the seconds until he could be with her again.

Lily had a very bad night. Worse yet, she figured Griffin was having a really bad night, too. And that was all her doing. Once again, she was the black sheep of the family.

She'd thought having her parents catch her having sex with Griffin wouldn't matter too much. And it wouldn't, if she would agree to tell him she was a witch. They'd accepted Anica and Jasper's relationship because Jasper knew everything there was to know about his future wife. Anica wasn't trying to pretend to be somebody she wasn't.

Lily, however, had used magic on Griffin without telling him anything. He thought the attraction between them was simple lust. Her parents thought that, too, which was why they couldn't understand Lily's reluctance to fill him in on her magical abilities.

They'd spent the evening with Griffin and liked him. That made them even more determined that Lily should come clean, because they didn't like seeing someone they respected being duped. Unfortunately, they had no concept of how thoroughly Griffin had been duped.

As Lily tossed and turned in her bed, Daisy padded over and laid her head on the mattress, as if wanting to give Lily comfort.

"Thanks, but I don't even deserve a good dog like you," Lily said.

Daisy whined and wagged her tail.

"Seriously, I don't." She stroked the dog's silky head. "This is way worse than what Anica did, because when she turned Jasper into a cat, she did it impulsively, without thinking. I *planned* this, Daisy. I had plenty of time to reconsider, but I charged ahead, the way I tend to do."

Daisy licked her hand.

"I should reverse this spell. That's really what I should do. But you know what? I don't have the guts. If I reverse it, Griffin will take off, and I don't want him to do that."

Daisy put both paws on the bed so she could lean over and lick Lily's face.

Lily buried her face in the dog's ruff. "Oh, Daisy, I don't know what to do. If you truly are a magic dog, I could use some help."

Chapter 15

Griffin didn't sleep much, and when he did, he dreamed constantly of Lily. He woke up with an erection, of course. After a cold shower he thought about calling her, but he knew she wouldn't be awake yet. Thinking of her in bed made him want to go over there. He had a key, so he could let himself in and ... no. She'd made it plain she didn't want him there right now.

He wondered if Daisy would get her morning romp in the dog park. When she'd gone home without Griffin the night before, had she taken Daisy down to Harvey's Hangout? The thought of her talking to Brad Harvey made his blood boil, so he decided to stop thinking about it.

Dragging himself to the office, he debated his next step, and decided to send her flowers. He'd just placed an order for three dozen red roses when Kevin walked in carrying two mugs of coffee.

He set one in front of Griffin. "It's hot and it's strong. I didn't dilute it with any cream, even though you like it that way. From the way you looked in the elevator, I decided you needed straight caffeine, so drink up."

"You were in the elevator with me?"

"Yeah, along with about four other people from the office. You didn't say anything to any of us."

"Sorry. I didn't sleep well."

Kevin took one of the two chairs positioned in front of Griffin's desk. "That's obvious from the red eyes and dark circles. Did you spend the whole night going at it with Lily? If so, I hope you had fun, because I doubt you'll have much fun here today."

Griffin picked up his coffee and tried to act nonchalant. "What's up?"

"When I was getting your coffee in the break room, I ran into Biddle. He's on the warpath, so I wanted to warn you before he calls you in. And he will."

"About what?" Griffin was trying to focus on what Kevin was saying, but mostly he wondered if the florist would get the order right and if the roses would be partly opened buds, as he'd requested.

"Apparently one of your clients, Jack Schooner, called him this morning to complain that you missed an appointment yesterday. Schooner's the one—"

"Yeah, I know. The one Biddle turned over to me as a special favor." Griffin winced. "I'd agreed to meet him at the end of the day."

"You didn't say anything about that when we left for the Bubbling Cauldron."

"That's because I forgot about it." Griffin looked down at his desk, and there, tucked in his blotter, was a note written by his secretary, Marcie, before she'd left at five. *Jack Schooner, 5:30.* She'd done her job. He hadn't done his.

Worse yet, he didn't much care about Jack Schooner. He was more worried about Lily's state of mind today, and if the flowers would help, and whether she would let him stay over tonight.

"No, you didn't forget," Kevin said. "What happened was, I got this shooting pain in my left arm, and there's a history of heart problems in my family, so you, Miles and I took off for the ER. We were there most of the night. Fortunately it was a false alarm."

Griffin stared at him. "*Do* you have a history of heart problems in your family?"

"No, you moron. That was the best I could come up with on short notice. I wanted to make sure you knew what I'd told him. And if I were you, I'd call Jack Schooner and kiss ass."

"I'll call him."

"Griff, you're going off the deep end." Kevin said it gently, but he wasn't smiling.

Griffin gazed at him, unable to argue that point. "Lily wanted some time apart last night. We weren't together."

"And you look like this? What'd you do, stay up all night pining for her like a loser?"

"Something like that."

Kevin groaned. "I thought you could have a little fun for a change, date somebody who is certifiably hot, but this is not good. You've been involved with her for three days! Nobody gets that hooked on a person in three days. It's like she's cast a spell over you, man."

Griffin almost laughed at that. "Well, she is an amateur magician."

"Hey, maybe she hypnotized you! Think back. Was there ever a moment when that could have happened?"

"No."

"I once dated a stripper who could twirl tassels with her tits. I damn near got hypnotized watching those tassels go round and round. Are you *sure* something like that wasn't part of your bedtime routine with her?"

"No twirling tassels, Kev."

"Even so, that magician angle could be the clue to what's going on. They're trained in the fine art of misdirection. I'm going with my hypnosis theory, and maybe she's so good that she can hypnotize you without any pendulum swinging."

"I hope to hell I would have noticed if she'd hypnotized me."

Kevin sat forward in his chair. "Seriously, what's in

her apartment relating to this magician thing? Is there a ticking clock? She could have used that."

"I don't remember a ticking clock."

"Aha!" Kevin pointed a finger at him. "It was probably there and you were so involved with her you didn't notice that thing going like a metronome, putting you under her spell. Now she's got you in her clutches. She could probably make you cluck like a chicken."

Griffin put down his coffee and scrubbed both hands over his face. His chin hurt where he'd nicked himself shaving. His head ached from all the thinking about Lily. He was a disaster.

"That's just it," he said. "I want to be in her clutches, but instead she rejected me last night."

"That could be a tactic. You know, to see whether or not the hypnosis worked. I'd love to get a look at her apartment, check out the scene of the crime, so to speak."

"Kevin, for the last time, she didn't do anything like that."

"I'll be damned if I have a better explanation. You're not yourself at all. And Miles agrees with me. If you don't snap out of it soon, you're gonna jeopardize your job."

Griffin noted that he wasn't nearly as worried about that as he should be. "You're being overly dramatic."

"You're being overly complacent. Do you have a key to her place?"

Griffin hesitated. "Why?"

"Because something's going on, and you're too lovesick to figure it out. Do you have a key or not?"

"Maybe."

"So you do have one. That's a break. We need to go over there this afternoon while she's at work and check for a ticking clock, and look around for . . ."

"For what?" Griffin didn't like this idea at all. "Magic

potions? Voodoo dolls? I knew you shouldn't have gone to New Orleans for Mardi Gras. You're too impressionable about stuff like that."

"Look, make fun of my suspicions if you want to, but I promised you I'd keep you from making a huge mistake. I take that promise seriously, and I now see you in the process of making one. We need to investigate her apartment. Miles should come, too. He's stealthy."

"We're not doing it. I can't violate Lily's trust like that."

Kevin pointed at him again. "Think about this, buddy boy. Has she been completely straight with you? Do you feel as if you know everything there is to know about this woman?"

Griffin remembered the whole weirdness with her parents last night, which, come to think about it, had centered on a discussion of magic. But magic was just a parlor trick. Wasn't it? Anyway, Lily hadn't wanted to explain that discussion to him, so she wasn't being totally open.

"Griff, if you were drowning in a deep lake, I would jump in and try to save you."

"I know that, and I appreciate that you're thinking about my welfare, but going into Lily's apartment when she's not there to snoop through her stuff feels very wrong."

"We're not going to ransack the place. You'll be right there. You can direct the action."

"I don't like it."

Kevin wore his hard-ass lawyer expression. "What about this compulsion you have to be with her all the time? Does that feel normal?"

Griffin had to admit it didn't. He'd never been so tied to a woman, never forgotten his responsibilities because he was so absorbed in the relationship. Yet he couldn't imagine how Lily had done anything to him that would explain his behavior.

"Think of it as easing my mind," Kevin said. "I'm worried about you, and if I get a chance to look around Lily's apartment and don't find anything unusual, then I can conclude that she's got you by the balls because she's the sexiest woman on the planet. I just want to make sure we're dealing with normal lust and not something more exotic."

Griffin knew Kevin was only trying to watch out for him. The guy had already told a whopper this morning to protect him from Biddle. Griffin knew Kevin, and now that he had this hypnotism theory he wouldn't let it go until he could be proved wrong. "So if we spend ten minutes there, you'll get off my case?"

"I'd rather have twenty."

"Ten."

"Fifteen."

Griffin sighed. "Okay, fifteen minutes, and you don't touch anything without asking me first."

Kevin held up both hands in surrender. "I will be the soul of discretion." Picking up his coffee, he stood. "Call Jack Schooner."

"I will. And thanks for watching my back."

"Always. It's what friends do."

The roses had shown up at eleven, breaking into a morning that had turned into a frenzied attempt on Lily's part to forget about Griffin. She didn't even have her folks to distract her today. Jasper's parents were arriving this morning, and Anica had planned some touristy things for the afternoon and evening so the two sets of in-laws could get to know each other.

Therefore Lily had filled her hours with a long session in the dog park, exercising Daisy, and way more cleaning than she usually bothered with. She could have cleaned her entire apartment with magic, of course, but usually that wasn't worth the extra adrenaline that doing a cleaning spell pumped into her system. Besides, magic wouldn't have taken any time, and she needed to take up time.

She'd been washing windows when the florist truck pulled up outside. With a sense of inevitability, she watched the driver haul an enormous bouquet of red rosebuds out of the back of his van and walk toward her apartment building's front door.

If she'd hoped that a few hours away from her would dial back the power of the spell on Griffin to a more reasonable level, she was now disabused of that notion. She was afraid she'd put Griffin—and herself, truth be told—through a night of misery for nothing. The store-room sex probably had contained a double dose of binding ability because it was so illicit.

She went downstairs to get the flowers, not wanting to put a harried delivery guy through the process of carrying them up three flights. But as she climbed the stairs, cradling the mammoth vase and surrounded by the heavenly scent of roses, she realized she'd have to call Griffin. More than that, she should ask him to lunch.

Of course, lunch would be the perfect venue to tell him that she was a witch. But she couldn't do it yet. After this weekend, after the engagement party was over, then she would figure out a way to tell him.

She'd be doing Anica a favor by holding off, she told herself. It wasn't really rationalizing, because if she told Griffin now, he might go a little crazy. She didn't dare try to break the spell prior to the weekend, in case she goofed it up.

So telling him would do nothing except placate her father, who had no clue about the elixir. Griffin would still be bound to her by the adoration elixir, but he wouldn't be happy about it. He might cause a scene at the party, which could ruin what was supposed to be a wonderful celebration.

Convinced that she had to let this weekend play out as if she and Griffin were a normal adoring couple, she set the roses in the middle of her coffee table. She decided to read the card before calling him, but the roses couldn't be from anyone else. She pulled the small envelope from its plastic holder and opened it.

Please don't shut me out of your life. I need you. Griffin

The words made her heart ache. The poor guy was pitiful, and all because of her. She'd thought this kind of adoration would make her feel good, but instead it made her feel like a manipulative bitch, and that rhymed with *witch*, and that stood for *trouble*.

With a sigh she went in search of her phone, which she'd left somewhere in the kitchen. Then she realized that she had no phone number for him—not for his cell or his work. She hadn't needed to contact him, because ever since he'd taken the elixir he'd been the pursuer.

She could call information if she knew the name of his law firm, but she'd never taken note of that, either. Unless she wanted to forget her plan of calling him and inviting him to lunch, she'd have to use magic to get his number at work. Well, why not?

She knew why not. Doing magic, even a light information-gathering kind, caused her to get a little high. She wasn't always totally rational after a magic session, and she tended to be way too agreeable and to forget things.

But then she looked at that gigantic vase of flowers and knew that the man who sent those was desperate to hear from her. He probably didn't realize that she'd never paid attention to where he worked and had never asked for his number. She pictured him waiting to hear whether the flowers had arrived and getting only silence.

After all he'd suffered already, and knowing that nothing would happen this weekend to change that, she couldn't let him agonize over the flowers. She'd use her crystal ball to find out where he worked.

Her crystal ball needed cleansing, though, and she didn't have time to let it sit in salt water or put it out in the sun for a while. She'd use a smudge stick. Rummaging around in a cupboard where she kept all her magic supplies, she found the smudge stick and lit it with her small butane torch.

She'd always wondered if the makers of those little torches had been magical folks, because the lighters were so much handier than matches. She'd have to ask her dad, because he'd written a paper about the contributions magical people had made to society. He'd told her that wheeled suitcases had been invented by a wizard, and microwave popcorn had been dreamed up by a witch.

Waving her smudge stick over her crystal ball, she mentally divested it of any negative energy it might have picked up in the past couple of months since she'd used it. Once she was satisfied the ball was clear, she moved her furniture to the perimeter of the room and set the ball in the middle of her living room floor. Then she placed candles in a four-foot circle around it.

Daisy watched from the corner, where she lay with her head on her paws. She seemed curious but not particularly surprised.

Lily glanced over at the dog. "I haven't worked with my crystal ball since you arrived."

Daisy thumped her tail on the floor.

"I know this seems like a lot of trouble for one silly phone number, but I honestly don't know how else to get it. I can hardly go through all the law firms in Chicago asking if Griffin Taylor works there."

Daisy lifted her head and whined.

It was the strangest thing—at moments like this Lily could swear she could understand what the dog was trying to tell her. Lily tended to respond to those intuitive thoughts. "I don't dare go over to Anica's and use her computer to look him up, either. I don't know her schedule for sure, and it would be just my luck I'd get there at the same time as her in-laws, which means it would take forever to get what I need and leave."

Daisy sighed and settled back down.

"Trust me, this will be faster." Lily walked around the circle, lighting the candles. Then she mentally closed the circle and faced the crystal ball. "Smoky orb, where secrets lurk, show me Griffin's place of work."

Crouching down, she stared into the depths of the crystal ball and finally made out a brass plate, one of several on the elevator wall of a large office building. "Biddle, Ryerson and Thatcher. Thanks, Crys." She patted the ball. "You're a pal." She put out each candle with a snuffer, opened the circle and went to get her cell off the kitchen counter.

Within a few minutes she'd obtained the number, reached Griffin's secretary and was now waiting, her fingers drumming on the kitchen counter, for him to pick up. As usual, working the spell had put her on edge. Patience was never one of her strong suits, and after performing magic, she was absolutely no good at waiting for anything.

"Lily?" He sounded eager, way too eager. "Did you get the flowers?"

"Yes, and they're—"

"The buds were supposed to be just opening. Is that how they look?"

"They're perfect, Griffin. It's the most beautiful bouquet of roses I've ever been given in my life. You didn't have to do that."

"I wanted to."

"Well, thank you. Listen, I—"

"Meet me for lunch."

The low urgency in his voice sent shivers of desire up her spine. She'd missed him more than she cared to

admit. And he'd asked her to do something. She liked
agreeing to do things. "Where should I meet you?"

"There's a nice little restaurant in the Hilton, and
that's close to my office. I'll meet you in the lobby at
noon, if that's okay."

"I should be able to make it there by noon. But go
ahead in and get us a table."

"I'll do that," he said, "but I'll still meet you in the
lobby."

There was no point in staying on the phone, arguing
with him, and in her frame of mind she didn't want to
argue, anyway. She would have trouble getting ready
and down to the Hilton on time as it was. "I'll be there
as soon as I can. Bye."

Racing back through her living room, she realized
that the candles and crystal ball were still in the middle of the room. Oh, well. She'd clean that up when she
came back to get ready for work.

Chapter 16

Griffin gave himself permission to be devious. Critical times called for critical measures. When Lily walked into the hotel lobby, he knew any man in America would forgive him.

Her hair was down around her shoulders, and she wore a short red dress and red sandals with at least a three-inch heel. A delicate silver anklet of moons and stars circled one slim ankle, a tiny detail that excited him almost as much as her low-cut neckline.

Judging from the fit of the dress, he'd be willing to bet she wasn't wearing a bra. His nerves sizzled. He supposed she didn't own any frumpy outfits, but she couldn't walk around looking like that when he was feeling like *this* and not expect something to happen. Something would.

He walked over to meet her. "Hi."

Her smile was as warm as ever. Whatever had made her decide they should stay apart the night before seemed to have melted away. Her brown eyes sparkled as she gave him the once-over. "Hi, yourself. That navy suit looks good on you."

"I like that dress on you." And he'd like it even better when it was off her. He cupped her elbows and pulled her in for a kiss that wouldn't get them thrown out of the lobby but would let her know he'd been thinking of her . . . a lot.

She kissed him back with enough enthusiasm that he decided he'd be wise to end this activity before she shorted out every brain circuit he possessed. He eased back and gazed at her, drinking in the sight of her flushed cheeks and full lips. "It seems like forever."

"I've missed you, too." Her glance roamed over his face. "I suppose we'd better go in and order our lunch. You probably have a tight schedule."

"I do, so I thought I'd save time and order for us."

"Good idea." She started toward the restaurant.

He caught her arm. "This way." He turned her in the opposite direction.

"Griffin, I don't mean to be difficult, but the sign says the restaurant is—"

He guided her toward the bank of elevators. "I ordered room service." If he hadn't been holding her arm he might have missed the slight quiver that went through her. But he didn't miss it, and it made him smile.

Her reply was deceptively casual, though. "You did, huh?"

"Yeah." He turned to look at her. "We have an hour."

"Mm." She nodded calmly as if they were discussing the length of a business meeting, but her breathing was a little faster than normal. "Do you think that's long enough?"

"I hope so. I have an appointment at one fifteen."

"So, what . . . ah . . . what did you order for us to eat?"

"Mostly finger food. Things that taste okay even if they're cold or room temperature. Things that you don't have to fool with, unless you want to fool with them."

He let that suggestive thought dangle as the elevator opened and he guided her inside. He would have loved this to be a private elevator ride so they could continue the discussion of food. He hadn't told her about the strawberry shortcake with whipped cream.

But a middle-aged couple, hotel guests who had been

out shopping, judging from the bags they carried, joined them.

"So, where are you folks from?" the man asked.

Griffin's brain stalled. He shouldn't care what the people on the elevator thought, but he'd been a straight arrow for too long. He didn't want to tell them he was from Chicago, which might lead to conclusions that would be completely accurate, such as he was checking into the hotel for a nooner with this gorgeous, sexy woman.

"Actually, we're from Peru," Lily said. "Just got back from studying native herbal remedies down there."

"Really?" The woman gazed at Lily in obvious disbelief. "Were you tramping through the jungle, then?"

Griffin decided to jump in and help. "I did most of the tramping. Lily stayed in camp and . . . and . . ."

"Sorted through the data," Lily said. "I'm a top-notch data sorter."

"She sure is." Griffin nodded. "I was lucky to have her on the dig—uh, I mean, in the field, or rather, not in the field but in the camp, where she sorted data. Lots of data to sort on one of these trips." Sheesh. He should have kept his mouth shut. He was terrible at lying.

"Well, that's interesting," the man said. "I've never been to Peru. What's the climate like?"

At the same time Griffin said *hot* Lily said *cold*. She widened her eyes at him before turning to the man. "It depends on the time of year, of course. Like here, it's hot in the summer and cold in the winter."

The woman was gazing at them with barely disguised suspicion. "Except aren't their seasons the opposite of ours?"

"Technically, that's true," Griffin said. "So what Lily meant was, during our winter, it's their summer, so now that it's almost summer here, it's—"

Mercifully, the elevator jerked to a stop and the doors opened before he could dig a deeper hole for himself.

"That's our floor!" The man ushered his wife out and gave them a wave. "Nice talking to you."

The doors stayed open for a few seconds, which allowed Griffin to hear the woman's voice as it floated down the hall.

"Jerry, those two are no more from Peru than my cat Fluffy."

"Gabby, shh! They might hear you."

"I don't care. I'll bet they're . . ." The elevator doors slid closed, blocking out the last of her comment.

Lily grinned at him. "Here's a tip. If anyone asks you to take a job with the Secret Service, just say no. You suck at espionage."

"You, on the other hand, could get a job as a spy with no problem." Although he was teasing her, he was also thinking about Kevin's suspicions. How much of herself was she hiding from him?

He could ask, of course. But the elevator had just stopped at their floor, and asking her to explain herself wasn't going to help his cause any. He hadn't been able to keep his mouth shut before, but he sure as hell better do it now if he wanted the next hour to go well.

"This is it." He slid his hand beneath her silky hair, cupping the back of her neck as he guided her out of the elevator and toward the room number he'd been given. Touching the bare skin of her nape made his pulse jump with excitement.

Their footsteps whispered on the thick carpeting of the hallway. Griffin wondered if he'd make it to the room or whether he'd have to throw her down right here. He was just that desperate.

"This feels decadent," Lily said.

"It's supposed to be." Amazingly, his voice sounded normal and civilized, while inside he was battling his inner caveman. Primitive urges made him think of taking her by the hair and dragging her into the room so he could have his way with her.

"When did you set it up?"

"Right after I talked to you." He couldn't dial that phone fast enough. He'd considered reserving the penthouse, but decided that should be saved for a day when they had more time.

"And what did you say?"

"That I needed a reservation, that I'd be there a little before noon, and I wanted them to have food waiting in the room when I got there."

"Wow." She glanced at him as he paused in front of the door to their room. "You sound quite experienced at this kind of thing."

"I've never done this before in my life."

"Then I'm honored."

"You inspire me." He pulled the key card out of his pocket and noticed that his hands were trembling as he inserted the key in the lock. Finally he would get to hold her again, and it couldn't be soon enough.

He opened the door and gestured for her to go in ahead of him. "Are you hungry?"

"Starving."

"Then maybe we should have some of that food to start with." He closed the door, flipped on the privacy lock, and turned back to her. "I—" Whatever he'd been about to say vanished from his mind without a trace.

In the time it had taken him to lock the door, she'd slipped out of her dress, and she stood there in her high-heeled sandals and red thong. As he'd suspected, she'd worn no bra.

But she'd chosen to put on that slender ankle bracelet. Some people called it a slave bracelet, but if either of them was a slave, it was him, not her.

She walked toward him, her gaze fixed on his. He tried manfully to keep his eyes on her face, but he'd never watched the movement of her bare breasts as she walked. She had firm, high breasts, and the gentle sway was subtle, which made it all the more riveting.

Did she hypnotize you? Kevin's question popped into his head, and he hated that. He wasn't hypnotized by her almost naked body, but he sure as hell was fascinated and aroused by it.

"You said we only had an hour," she murmured. "So I decided to get this party started."

She seemed to be lit from within. Her fiery energy called to him, and he wanted her with such intensity that he was nearly speechless. But not completely speechless. "I love you," he said.

He hadn't expected to say that, but once the words were out of his mouth, he knew they were absolutely true. He loved her. That would explain everything.

She stopped and stared at him. Then, to his dismay, her dark eyes filled with tears. "You do?"

"Yes." He stepped forward and cupped her face in both hands. "I don't know why it's taken me so long to realize it."

Her voice was choked with tears. "Griffin, it hasn't been very long, not . . . not really." Tears dribbled down her cheeks.

"Don't cry." He brushed her tears away with his thumbs. "Loving someone is a good thing."

"I know!" Her reply came out as a wail. "Oh, Griffin."

"You don't know if you love me back, do you?" He kissed her damp eyes, her damp cheeks, her trembling mouth, but softly, not urgently. For now, the urgency had been replaced with the tender knowledge that he loved her. "Don't worry if you don't love me yet. I can wait for that to happen. It will happen."

She gazed up at him with brimming eyes. "You're a good person, Griffin Taylor, and I don't deserve you."

"That's ridiculous." He captured her mouth with his, this time with more insistence. If she was having a crisis of confidence, he would have to show her how much he worshipped her, and maybe that would take the tears away.

She might be crying, but she still wanted him. He could tell by the way she unknotted his tie and tugged it free. Her hands were everywhere and he loved it. Her eagerness to undress him bolstered his hope that some-day soon she'd admit to loving him, too.

He shrugged out of his clothes as she got them loose. They were so frantic to get naked and into the bed that it became funny. She laughed as he fumbled with his shoes, and he laughed with her. God, this was so great, to be here with her, each of them eager for what was about to happen.

In a frenzy they made their way to the big bed with its mound of pillows and rose-colored comforter. By that time he was down to his briefs and his socks. Her thong panties had been tossed to the far side of the room.

Gasping, she pulled her mouth away from his. "You take off your socks and I'll take off my shoes."

"Leave the shoes."

Her eyebrows arched and she laughed again, breath-lessly this time. "All righty, then." She flung herself back-ward onto the rose-colored comforter.

The picture she made lying there, gazing up at him in welcome, would be burned into his memory forever. He decided that she loved him, whether she knew it or not.

She giggled again when he hopped on one foot so he could get rid of the blasted socks. She was so full of life. How could he not love her?

Shucking his briefs, he grabbed his slacks and fished in the pocket for the condom he'd put there earlier. He tore open the wrapper and started to roll on the condom.

"Wait."

He glanced up to find her gazing at him with the kind of admiration that did wonders for his ego.

"We've never done this in the middle of the day," she said. "I want to take just a moment to look at you. You're . . . magnificent."

He could live with that. In fact, few things in his life stacked up to having Lily Revere say that his package was magnificent.

Her smile trembled on her full mouth. "Thank you. I needed that. Now, if you have that little raincoat handy, we're burning daylight."

He was just burning, period. Climbing onto the bed, he slid his arms under her knees. Those do-me shoes of hers flashed red in his peripheral vision as he cupped her bottom and angled in for that first glorious thrust. He took it slow, enjoying the way her pupils dilated and her cheeks flushed as he eased into her.

Then he was locked in tight, and her sigh of pleasure made her nipples quiver. He liked this position, where he could watch her as he stroked lazily back and forth, but he also craved more body contact. Shifting while staying deep within her, he propped his forearms on either side of her shoulders.

There. Now he could lean down and nibble on her mouth, which he did, relishing the velvet feel of her lips and the tiny puffs of warm air as her climax drew near and she began to pant. He could lower himself just enough that his chest brushed her puckered nipples with every thrust. She wrapped her legs around his waist, and those crazy shoes rubbed against his butt as he moved within her.

There was nowhere else on earth he'd rather be than right here, making love to Lily. He kissed her again as the mounting tension urged him to go faster.

Then he lifted his mouth to gaze down at her. "I love you."

She moaned and closed her eyes. "Don't say that."

"Then I'll say this." He pumped faster. "I love being naked with you. I love pushing deep inside you and making you come. I love the sounds you make and the way you clench around my cock when you're ready to . . . like that . . . just like . . . *that*." He came in a rush at the same moment that she cried out and arched upward, pulling him deeper, letting him feel the steady pulse of her climax.

He covered her body with his, wanting to absorb her tremors, wanting her to feel his. And while he tried to keep some of his weight on his arms as he braced them on either side of her, she wouldn't let him. She hugged him to her, as if desperate for the contact, as if even one milliliter of space between them was unacceptable.

She might not want to talk about love, but her body was expressing every emotion she didn't want to admit. He didn't know what demons she was fighting that kept her from acknowledging her feelings toward him, but eventually he'd find out. Until then he'd just keep on loving her.

Chapter 17

Lily knew that when the man of your dreams says he loves you, it should be cause for celebration. It should be, unless you've given that man a potion that has altered his perceptions and so his feelings for you aren't real. Then it is cause for misery.

As miserable as she felt, she shouldn't be able to enjoy sex this much, but she blamed the magic buzz she still had going on. Sex was a great pastime when you were feeling both high and agreeable. Besides, she hated for the finger food to go to waste.

Now that their immediate lust had been satisfied, they took the remaining time to play with what Griffin had ordered. He smeared cream cheese on her nipples and licked it off, which she found quite stimulating, so much so that she agreed to have him try the cream cheese lower down.

After she recovered from that successful experiment, she commandeered the whipped cream. "I'll make this quick," she said. "You have a meeting."

He groaned as she smeared whipped cream on his firm penis. "Forget the damned meeting."

"No." She began to lick away the whipped cream. "You'll make your meeting."

"As if I care. Ah, Lily . . ."

She reapplied more whipped cream to the very tip.

Then she closed her mouth over that treat and sucked in deep. He gasped and clutched the sheets in his fists.

She released him for a second. "Now, concentrate, Griffin. We're going to take it on home."

"I don't care if I'm late. I don't . . . oh, dear God . . . that's incredible. Sweet lord, but you know how to . . . ah . . . *ah*!" With a groan of surrender he came.

She loved knowing she'd given him pleasure. It was the least she could do under the circumstances. She coddled him a little as he came back to earth, and then she nudged him until he gave up and went in to take a quick shower.

She didn't join him there. On top of her other sins, she wasn't about to add career sabotage. Instead she stretched out on the bed and pulled the covers up to her chin. She hadn't slept much the night before, and all this great sex had relaxed her.

Sure, she still felt guilty as Hades, but she had no immediate solution for her problem, and the sheets were soft and Griffin was whistling in the shower. For some reason it didn't bother her so much this time.

He came out of the bathroom and dressed quickly. Then he crossed to the bed and leaned down to kiss her. "You make me very happy."

"Thanks. Same here." She wondered if making a man happy was such a crime. He hadn't seemed particularly happy before she'd given him the elixir. Now he was enjoying great sex and thinking he was in love. Was that so bad?

With a sigh of regret he moved away from the bed. "Gotta go. But relax here for as long as you want." He shrugged into his suit coat. "The room's reserved for the rest of the night." He paused. "Too bad you have to work, or we could hang out here."

"Except I do have to work, and there's the matter of Daisy."

"Right. Didn't mean to forget her. So I'll see you at

the Bubbling Cauldron, then." He looked adorably uncertain. "And later? Is it okay if we—"

"Yes. That being-apart thing didn't work out very well."

"It sucked." His smile was brilliant with joy. "Okay, then." He touched two fingers to his forehead in a mini salute. "See you tonight."

As he left, she thought the phrase *a spring in his step* described Griffin's exit. And she had put that spring in his step. Sure, eventually she'd have to straighten this whole thing out and get right with Griffin. It wasn't as if they could live their whole lives with a huge secret between them.

But for now, with the engagement party coming up and her parents in town, maybe a small deception could be forgiven. Maybe, even though he'd been given the elixir, he loved her a little bit on his own. It could happen.

With that thought cheering her, she snuggled under the covers and dozed, telling herself she wouldn't take more than an hour's nap. She had to go home, take care of Daisy, and change for work. But she had time ...

Two hours later, she had almost no time. She'd slipped into a deep sleep and only a knock on the door, which turned out to be someone with the wrong room number, saved her from an even worse disaster. Ignoring the expense, she took a cab back to her apartment.

In record time she showered, changed, took Daisy for a quick trip outside and then fed her. She glanced at the crystal ball and candles in the middle of the living room floor as she ran out the door. Griffin might think it was a little strange, but she'd make something up. She'd tell him she was practicing a routine for Anica's party on Sunday night.

She wouldn't use her precious crystal ball at the party, though. Just her luck it would get broken. Instead she planned to do a couple of tricks with her wand. It would be real magic, which the magical people in attendance would know, but the nonmagical folks would assume she was very good at sleight of hand and let it go at that.

Griffin arrived back at the office, determined to talk Kevin out of his idea of investigating Lily's apartment. But he was in meetings until nearly four, when they'd agreed to go over to Lily's.

Kevin breezed into Griffin's office with Miles right behind him. "Ready to go?"

"No. It's a bad idea. We can't do this."

Kevin turned to Miles. "Told you he'd try to back out."

Miles stepped forward. "We gotta go over there, Griff. I was talking to Biddle today. He wants to know what's up with you. You were the golden boy until this week, but now . . . he asked if you had some psychiatric problem he should know about."

"Jesus." Griffin shook his head. "So I missed an appointment. One lousy appointment and he's convinced I'm a nutcase. If he's that touchy maybe I should just quit."

Kevin and Miles exchanged a glance.

"You missed more than the appointment, buddy," Kevin said. "You were supposed to have lunch with Biddle at his club today. He was looking all over the office for you, but you were AWOL. I don't have to think very hard to imagine where you were or what you were doing."

"That lunch was today?" Griffin looked at the calendar on his desk and groaned. "I completely spaced on that. Man, I need to apologize. Is he still here?"

"Nope," Miles said. "He's gone home for the weekend. Said he's taking his yacht out on the lake tomorrow for the first time, and you know what a big deal that is."

"Yeah, I do," Griffin said. "He loves that boat."

"Yeah, well, apparently he was going to ask you to

join him," Miles continued, "but when you didn't show up for lunch, he bagged that plan. He asked me to go, but I get seasick."

"He didn't ask me," Kevin grumbled. "But then the short guy always gets passed over for you tall sonsabitches."

"The point is," Miles said, "you aren't your normal self, Griff. A week ago you would never have forgotten that lunch date. Biddle's treated you like a long-lost son, but that isn't going to last if you keep up this bullshit."

"Look, it's my fault, okay? Lily didn't hypnotize me or anything. I'm in love with her. Simple as that."

Miles and Kevin stared at him, their mouths open.

"Don't look at me like that. Lily's a wonderful woman. Why wouldn't I be in love with her? I know this is a little sudden, but sometimes love is like that. It strikes when you least expect it to."

Kevin continued to stare at him as if he'd grown horns. "You love her."

Griffin smiled, thinking of Lily snuggled into the king-sized bed at the Hilton. "Yeah, I do."

"You've been dating her for three days, and now you love her? You're thinking with your pecker, man. This isn't love. This is exactly what I promised to save you from—letting sex screw up your life like it did to your parents."

That jangled a warning bell in Griffin's brain, but he ignored it. "This is different."

"It is different," Miles said. "This fixation seems like it's more than just sex. Kev told me about his hypnotizing theory, and I'm all over that. If she's studied how to do magic tricks, guaranteed she's fooled around with hypnosis. Have you asked her about this whole magic shtick?"

"She . . . um . . . didn't want to talk about it." Griffin realized how damning that sounded.

"No duh," Miles said. "I'm sure not, since she used

her tricks to rope a lawyer who makes four times what she makes at the bar."

"It isn't like that!" Griffin wasn't about to stand there and let his friends sully the reputation of the woman he loved.

"If it's not like that," Kevin said, "then we'll find no evidence of her manipulating the situation if we pay a quick visit to her apartment. If we go there and find nothing, then Miles and I will do our best to keep you from shit-canning your career while you work through whatever is eating your brain."

Griffin gazed at his calendar, with the Biddle lunch written in red, and had to concede that he wasn't functioning optimally these days. In that case, he'd need his friends to keep him from making huge mistakes, and they wouldn't agree to do that unless he allowed them to explore their pet theory. Once they discovered that was a dead end, they'd settle in to protect him from himself.

"All right," he said. "We'll go over there for fifteen minutes. If she ever finds out, I'll say that I was worried about Daisy, and you two offered to go along while I let her out."

Kevin frowned. "Who's Daisy?"

"Lily's golden retriever. She's a great dog."

Miles looked worried. "Does she bite?"

Griffin saw his opportunity. If he portrayed Daisy as unpredictable, Miles might reconsider the plan, and Kevin might not go if Miles backed out. But then they'd both still think that Lily had somehow used magic to make him want her, and that was ridiculous. He'd enjoy proving them wrong.

An hour later as they took a cab back to the bar, he still couldn't believe that they'd walked in to find a crystal ball in the middle of the floor and at least twenty candles in a circle around it. Worse yet, a closer inspection of the magic books showed that they focused on more than just parlor tricks. There were incantations, spells, potions.

Miles had found an underlined section in a book on potions, and that underlining had been the nail in the coffin. It was called an adoration elixir, and it could be added to any normal beverage. He'd also found a potential remedy for the spell that involved sprinkling salt around the bed.

"But I don't believe in this stuff," Griffin kept insisting as they took a cab back to the Bubbling Cauldron. "Witches don't exist. Magic spells aren't real."

Miles waved a hand at the sign over the door of the bar. "Do you think she works here by accident? I don't think so. It probably fits in with her skills, mixing drinks for people."

"For all we know, she puts stuff in everybody's drinks so they'll tip more," Kevin said.

"Okay, that's enough. Lily is not the sort of person to use whatever special talent she has to wring money out of people." That much Griffin knew for sure. Everything else was up for grabs. "Anyway, I'm going to ask her about the magic. I'm going to ask her straight out."

"That's the worst idea you've had recently," Kevin said. "And you've had some doozies. You can't just ask her. If she knows you're on to her, she's liable to work some other spell on you."

"Look, she cares about me. I know she does. She wouldn't want to hurt me or anything."

"Oh, I think she cares about you." Kevin paid for the cab while Miles and Griffin climbed out.

"I don't know," Miles said as they stood outside the bar. "If she cares about him, why would she slip something into his drink?"

"Because he wasn't paying attention to her, and she was crushing on him."

Griffin wished his friends didn't make such logical sense. He wished he hadn't let them into Lily's apartment so they could find the crystal ball, the candles, and the books. They might have snooped around some more, but he'd made them leave.

Daisy hadn't liked them being there. Griffin had noticed her confusion, because she was happy to see him but suspicious of his friends. Obviously she hadn't known quite how to act, whether she should be guarding the house or welcoming the new guests. Mostly she'd paced.

It had been a nasty business, this spying on Lily. Griffin didn't want to know what he knew. He didn't want to think that Lily, the woman he'd felt such a connection with, the woman he'd declared his love for, had engineered the whole thing by doping his drink. That went against everything he believed was possible.

And yet . . . he couldn't deny the effect she'd had on him recently. There was something fishy about the whole thing, now that he looked at it more carefully.

Kevin lingered on the sidewalk outside the bar, as if reluctant to go in until they had a plan. "I think the potion was in the Wallbanger," he said. "Remember Tuesday night you were going to order your usual vodka and tonic with a twist, and she suggested the Wallbanger."

"I absolutely remember that." Miles pointed a finger at Kevin. "That was the night Debbie was there and Griff asked her out. Lily wouldn't have liked that, no sir. She fixed it so Griff wouldn't go out with Debbie."

"You're making her out to be some sort of relationship Nazi," Griffin said. "She's not. She may be outrageous sometimes, but she's also very sweet, and she loves her folks and her sister, Anica. They—"

"Wait a minute," Kevin said. "Wait. A. Minute. Spells and incantations. What if she's a full-fledged, bona fide witch?"

"I'm not ready to pin that label on her," Griffin said.

"Okay, you don't count." Miles waved him away. "You've had amazing sex with her, so you want to believe she's exactly as advertised. It's up to Kev and me to ferret out the truth."

"As I was saying," Kevin continued, "if the spells and magic turn out to mean she's a witch, then her sister is a witch, her mother's a witch, and her father's a wizard."

Griffin's head hurt. "I wish to God you hadn't gone to Mardi Gras."

"You're going to be glad I did, buddy boy. Because my knowledge of witches and wizards is going to save your ass."

"What if I don't want to be saved?" Griffin was feeling irritable, to say the least. "What if I like the way my life is right now, with lots of great sex with an amazing woman?"

Kevin had the bulldog expression that he got sometimes when he wasn't about to let go of an idea. Juries hated to see that expression. So did Griffin.

"I promised to keep you from making a mess of your life with the wrong woman," Kevin said. "I didn't expect to have to deal with a witch who had given you a love potion, but that's life. You are not going to fall prey to her scheme."

"And that goes double for me," Miles said. "We're going to be your watchdogs, keep track of you, be your monitoring system. Oh, except for tomorrow night, of course. We'll be at the Cubs game tomorrow night, so you're on your own then."

Kevin glared at Miles. "We will leave the Cubs game if we deem it necessary."

"What?" Miles looked outraged. "I got primo tickets from StubHub! It's gonna be an awesome game!"

Kevin regarded him with disdain. "This is more important than a Cubs game."

"But they're leading the division!"

"Miles, we have a friend who has found himself smack-dab in a real-life version of *The Witches of Eastwick*. Are you going to abandon him at a time like that?"

Miles seemed chastened. "Guess not." He glanced at Kevin. "So what's the plan?"

"You make this sound like some kind of battle," Griffin said.

Kevin nodded. "It is."

"Bullshit. We don't need a battle plan. You're talking about the woman I love."

"No," Miles said. "She's the woman you *think* you love because she gave you a magic potion. There's a huge difference."

"What if I really love her? What if I've overpowered the potion she gave me, and now what I feel for her is actual love?" Griffin wanted to believe that scenario. It was far better than thinking he was some puppet on a string.

"If that's true, then you'll be willing to try the antidote I found. If you still feel like you love her after you try that, then maybe we'll start to believe you." Kevin pulled a piece of paper out of his pocket. "I would have liked to have more time, but you rushed us out of there."

"You know I hated the snooping idea from the beginning."

"That's because you're under a spell and don't know what's good for you," Miles pointed out.

"Right." Kevin consulted the notes he'd made. "Maybe we can research this online. Anyway, as I told you back in the apartment, the first thing you have to do is sprinkle salt around the bed and see if that makes you less attracted to her."

Griffin blew out a breath. "That should be subtle. She's ready to do the deed, and I'm busy with the carton of Morton Salt. Do you think she'll get suspicious?"

"You get in there and sprinkle the salt when she's not looking, moron." Kevin shook his head. "I should go over there and do it tonight while you're still with her at the bar. You could give me your key."

"No, absolutely not." Griffin cringed at the idea of his

friends invading Lily's apartment when he wasn't even there.

"Yeah, that's a bad idea," Miles said. "The dog would eat you."

"Then you have to do it." Kevin gazed at his notes. "It says sea salt. Tell you what. Miles and I will bring that to you at the bar later tonight."

Griffin rolled his eyes. "Also a subtle move. You and Miles show up with a container of salt. How are you going to explain that?"

"We'll figure out a different delivery system," Kevin said. "We'll get it to you in a package you can conceal until you're ready to sprinkle it around the bed. Surely you can take ten seconds to accomplish that."

"It's dicey," Miles said. "She is one hot tamale. Once she gets naked, Griff might not have ten seconds to spare."

"Will you two knock it off?" Griffin had taken about all he could. "I swear to you Lily is not out to get me. There's an explanation for all this that will demonstrate she's a decent person."

Kevin sighed. "Buddy, your best hope is that she's a decent witch."

Chapter 18

Lily had mulled over Griffin's declaration of love ever since she'd arrived at work. She knew it could be bogus, a product of the elixir she'd given him, but she didn't want to believe that. She wanted to believe that the incredible times they'd shared in the past few days had created a loving bond that had nothing to do with the elixir.

That's what she wanted to believe, but she had no confidence that it was true. Spending time with Griffin tended to reinforce that belief, so she was eager for him to arrive at the Bubbling Cauldron. He and his buddies seemed later than usual, and she hoped everything was okay at the law offices of Biddle, Ryerson and Thatcher. Now that she knew the name of the firm, it seemed more real and she felt a more personal concern about Griffin's fate there.

At last Griffin walked in with his two buddies. Maybe she was being paranoid, but she could swear they looked at her more closely than they had in the past. She'd even say they scrutinized her.

So maybe Griffin had told them he was in love with her. That would make sense, if the three were as close as she thought. With a confession like that, Griffin had moved her from girlfriend to serious girlfriend. Men who admitted to being in love tended to propose.

Yikes. She hadn't exactly thought about that. Her father would give her no end of grief if she accepted a proposal from a man under an adoration spell. She wouldn't feel particularly comfy about it, either. Enjoying good sex was one thing, but making a lifetime commitment was something else.

Because happy hour had started about thirty minutes ago, the first rush had subsided, so she had time to go over to Griffin's table and take the order. She just wasn't sure she wanted to. Kevin and Miles weren't joking around the way they usually did when they first came in the bar. The whole table was way too serious.

But if she didn't go take the order that would seem strange, so she lifted the hinged section of bar and walked through it. All the way over to the table she could feel Kevin and Miles evaluating her as a potential wife for their friend. If they knew the truth about her . . . but she didn't intend for them to find out about her magic.

Griffin was a different story. If she ever hoped to take this relationship further, she had to tell Griffin. But she didn't want to tell him yet, so she hoped he wasn't working up to a proposal. That would change the timetable considerably.

"Hi, guys!" She gave them all a bright smile.

Kevin and Miles responded with what looked like really fake grins, as if they'd suddenly decided they needed to look cheerful. Griffin didn't even try to look cheerful. In fact, he looked depressed.

She wasn't about to address that. "What's everybody having?"

"A draft," Miles said.

Kevin nodded. "Make that two."

Griffin glanced up at her. "I'll take a draft, too."

His expressive hazel eyes gave her a jolt. Instead of being filled with love, they reflected pure misery. How had that happened? Earlier today he'd seemed so full of good cheer.

She could think of only one explanation—his friends didn't approve of her. They must have romped all over his declaration of love and maybe even tried to talk him out of sticking with the relationship. And that just made her mad. What right did they have to judge whether she'd make Griffin a good life partner?

"Anything to go with the beer?" She asked the question with as much energy as she could pump into it. She'd be the perfect bartender tonight, and if that wasn't good enough for them, that was their problem.

She had never been anything but nice to them. She'd served them with enthusiasm and made sure their orders came out fast and right. She'd even given Kevin and Miles an extra shot in their Harvey Wallbangers on Tuesday night.

"Nothing for me, thanks," Kevin said.

Miles and Griffin followed along, shaking their heads and mumbling that they weren't hungry.

Lily was working up to a real fit of anger when she realized it might not be about her at all. Something might have happened to one of them, or there might have been a tragedy at work. She was obviously on edge and had leaped to a conclusion that might be wrong.

"You guys seem a little down tonight," she said. "I hope everything's okay."

Griffin's head snapped up and both Kevin and Miles looked guilty.

"Everything's fine, just fine," Miles said. "It's been a long week, I guess."

Kevin jumped in. "Yeah, a really long week. You know what? Maybe we should have some onion rings. What do you say, Miles, Griff? Onion rings and maybe some pub fries?"

Miles nodded enthusiastically. "You bet. That goes great with beer." He clapped Griffin on the back. "Join us in some onion rings and pub fries, buddy. In fact, don't they have garlic fries on the menu?"

Lily was totally confused by the sudden attempt to be jovial. Whatever was going on with these three, they didn't want her to know what it was. That could mean she was the topic of conversation, or it could mean they had some other issue going on. She'd have to ask Griffin when he wasn't with them.

She got her chance an hour later. After Kevin and Miles left, Griffin made his way over to the bar and sat on a stool near where she was working.

She glanced up at him and smiled. "Hi there."

"Hi." His expression didn't seem so tortured now, but then he'd had a couple of beers.

She continued to mix drinks so she wouldn't get behind. "So what's your pleasure tonight? Want to go back to my place and hang with Daisy, or stick around here until closing?"

"I'll stick around."

"Good." She wanted to talk to him, anyway, and try to find out what was up with Kevin and Miles. Him, too, for that matter. "But I need to warn you that we can't try the storeroom trick tonight. Devon's here, and I'd rather not get fired."

"That's okay."

She glanced up and found him watching her with an unnerving intensity. "What?"

"Nothing."

"I don't buy it." She slid the drinks down the bar toward where Sherman was waiting for them. "Something is going on with you and your friends. There was a whole different mood at your table tonight." She wiped down the bar as she talked. "Can you tell me about it, or is it confidential lawyer stuff?"

"I can't really tell you."

She could accept that. After all, the three of them dealt with issues that shouldn't be the subject of barroom gossip. "But I'm not wrong, am I? You three are upset about something."

"No, you're not wrong."

"I'm feeling a little paranoid." She stopped wiping the bar, which she'd already polished until it shone. "At first I thought whatever had upset all of you had to do with me."

The silence that followed that remark turned her heart into a lead weight. "Oh, dear. I was right. They don't like me."

"No, they do like you!" He reached across the bar and covered her hand with his. "They just think we're moving too fast."

She gazed into his eyes. "You told them you were in love with me, didn't you?"

"Yeah, I did."

"So what is it you can't tell me? Your friends are upset because you say you're in love with a woman you've been seeing for three days. I'm not particularly flattered, but I guess I can understand that. What's the big secret?"

"Well, uh . . ."

She had another horrible thought. "Omigod." She wrenched her hand away from his. "I'll bet you're married and she's in the military or something like that. Or you're separated and not quite divorced yet. Is that what you don't want to tell me? You're legally bound to someone else?"

"No! What kind of a guy do you think I am?"

From the corner of her eye she saw her boss, Devon, coming toward the bar. She immediately started washing glasses. "We need to keep it down. Devon's on his way over, and he doesn't like us conducting personal business while we're working."

Griffin drew back. "You'd better fix me a drink, then."

"What do you want?"

"Another beer will be fine."

Lily finished washing the glass she'd been holding

and dried her hands so she could draw a beer for Griffin. Setting a cocktail napkin in front of him, she placed the beer glass squarely on it. "There you go, sir."

"Thanks."

"Hey, Lily." Devon leaned on the bar several feet down from where she was working. That meant she was supposed to walk down to meet him.

She clenched her jaw. When she'd first come to work here, Devon had made a pass and she'd deflected it. He was an okay-looking guy, but he spent a little too much time worrying about whether his dark hair was combed just so, and he had an air about him that reminded Lily of the old-time Chicago mobsters.

When she'd turned away from his attempted kiss, he hadn't fired her, which was a blessing because she liked the job. But now he tended to play power games with her. Calling out her name and expecting her to walk over to where he stood was one of them.

But she did it because he might have seen some of her interaction with Griffin, and that could be a firing offense. He'd especially hate it because Lily was interested in a nonmagical man, when a perfectly acceptable wizard—Devon himself—had tried to make it with her and had been refused.

Devon would have a royal fit if he ever found out about the storeroom incident. He'd tried to seduce her in the storeroom himself, so he'd be doubly furious that she'd taken personal pleasures during her work hours. She felt safe, though, because Sherman wouldn't tell on her, and she'd fixed everything back the way it had been with a little touch of magic.

"So you and your sister are going to throw a bash in here on Sunday." He was chewing gum. Devon always seemed to be chewing gum, and he liked to snap it, too.

Maybe that was why Lily thought of him as a gangster type. All he needed was a pinstriped suit and a tommy gun and he'd fit the profile. "That's right, we are," she said. "Anica really appreciates you taking on the challenge at the last minute."

"I had to shuffle a few things, but seeing as how it's your family, how could I not? I came to find out if there's anything special you'll need. Will you use the sound system we have or bring in a DJ? Personally, I recommend a DJ if you're going to have dancing."

"We will have dancing. There also will be a little entertainment, compliments of me."

"Oh yeah?" Devon snapped his gum and looked her up and down. "Like what?"

She could almost read his mind, and knew he was picturing her pole dancing. "A few magic tricks."

"Is that so? I thought this would be a mixed crowd."

"It will be." Lily lowered her voice. "But it's a magic act."

"Ahhh." Devon nodded. "A magic act." He leaned in close. "Only with real magic," he murmured.

"Right." Overwhelmed by the scent of his cinnamon gum, she backed away. "Listen, I'll check on the DJ idea."

"It so happens my brother-in-law is a DJ," Devon said. "I could probably get him on short notice."

Now she understood his eagerness for the DJ. His brother-in-law needed the work. But it wasn't a bad idea. Sherman had already suggested the revolving mirrored ball, and a DJ would make the party more festive. "Let me check with Anica and I'll get back to you."

He tapped her on the forearm, to show that he could get away with it. "You do that." Then he walked away.

She rubbed her forearm as if she could wipe away the unwanted touch. Suing him for harassment on the basis of a touch on her forearm would be a lot of trouble, and besides, she wanted to keep working here. So she let it go.

"I don't like that guy," Griffin said as she returned to finish washing the glasses. "He's inappropriate."

"Yes, he is." She smiled as she realized that a lawyer sat right across the counter from her. He'd probably take the harassment case in a heartbeat, even if that wasn't his specialty. "But I like tending bar here and it isn't worth getting into a legal battle over his behavior toward me."

"I wasn't thinking of taking him to court. I was thinking of going back to his office and telling him to leave you the hell alone."

"Well, thank you." Having a champion, even if he was under the influence of an elixir, felt nice. "But that would only draw his attention to our relationship, and he could get ugly about that. As I said, we have a policy about no fraternizing with the customers during business hours."

Griffin smiled for the first time since he'd walked in the door tonight. "If he only knew."

"Yeah." She smiled back at him and felt the tension between them ease. "You know, your friends are right about us taking this kind of fast. You may think you're in love with me, but we should probably give ourselves some time before making any promises."

Amazingly, he agreed with her. "Absolutely. Let's take some time. But can we still have sex?"

She laughed. "You bet."

Kevin showed up around ten, looking furtive. Griffin wished Miles had come, instead. Miles could pull off secretive stuff, but Kevin was too much like Griffin, meaning he was no good at lying.

Fortunately Lily was down at the far end of the bar, talking to Sherman, and didn't seem to notice Kevin. Griffin left his seat at the bar, where he'd been eating a pastrami sandwich, and walked over toward Kevin. "You look like a bad imitation of Maxwell Smart."

"I love you, too. I have the salt. It needed to be organic and coarsely ground, so that's what we got."

"Where's Miles?"

"He struck up a friendship with the girl at the organic foods store, and they went out for drinks. It'll probably be something awful like organic persimmon juice, but Miles doesn't care because she's built."

If Griffin hadn't been so keyed up about the whole salt concept, he might have laughed. "Where's the salt?"

"Like we talked about, I couldn't come in with the actual container, which is the size of a Polish sausage, so I put some in a plastic Ziploc bag for you." He pulled it out of his pocket.

"Good God, Kev. It looks like you're dealing crack." Griffin shoved it in his pocket, where the unfamiliar bulk reminded him of all he didn't want to know regarding Lily.

"You should probably chant something while you're sprinkling it around the bed."

"Like what?"

"You know. Like *Bubble, bubble, toil and trouble.*"

"That's Shakespeare, and I don't know how Shakespeare is going to help this situation. I'll be lucky if I get it sprinkled in the first place without Lily seeing me."

"You have to find a way. This is important." Kevin gazed at him. "How're you doing?"

"I still want her more than any woman I've ever known."

Kevin nodded. "That's how it's supposed to work."

"Oh, and her boss is an asshole who tries to intimidate her sexually. I have the urge to rip out his throat."

"I wouldn't do that if I were you, Griff. It's the elixir causing you to have those primitive emotions. Modern guys take assholes to court."

"You know what?" Griffin flexed his hands. "Being uncivilized is a lot more fun."

"Oh, boy." Kevin looked nervous. "Well. We'll do what we can. Sprinkle the salt around the bed. Then I'd advise you to sneak a peek at her magic books if you can this weekend and find out what else you can do. Barring that, go online. I intend to do the same. Then we'll compare notes."

"I've been thinking—is this really so bad? I have great sex with an amazing woman and I feel terrific, except that you and Miles keep telling me I have to get away from her because she's ruining my life."

"She could. You're not doing so great at work, remember?" Kevin took him by the shoulders and gave him one of his *I'm serious* looks. "This is a strong magic spell."

"Do you realize how ridiculous that sounds? I still wonder if it's you who's lost it here and not me."

"Sprinkle the salt. If it changes the way you feel about her, you'll know there's something going on."

"Since you went to so much time and trouble, I'll sprinkle the salt, although how I'll explain it if she catches me, I have no idea."

"Tell her it's room deodorizer."

"That's insulting, like I think her apartment smells bad."

"Okay, then tell her it's an aphrodisiac you found at the local sex shop. Make up whatever you need to, but sprinkle that damn salt!"

"Okay. Thanks, Kev."

"I have your best interests at heart."

"I know." But as Griffin watched him leave, he wondered if Kevin had ever had sex this good. Probably not. Maybe nobody in the whole world had sex this good.

Chapter 19

Once again Griffin treated them to a cab. Lily told herself not to get used to such luxuries because she didn't know where the relationship with Griffin was going, but for now the cab ride was nice. It got them home quicker.

As they walked into the apartment, the lamp in the living room that she left on a timer illuminated the scene, reminding her that she'd moved the furniture against the wall so she could set up her crystal ball with the candles around it.

Instinctively she walked over to her crystal ball and picked it up. That crystal ball meant the world to her, and now she regretted she'd left it in the middle of her living room.

"I know this looks strange." She cupped her beloved ball and the quartz warmed, reacting to her magic vibrations. "But I can explain it."

"I'll admit to being curious." Griffin tossed his suit coat over the arm of a chair. He'd removed his tie earlier in the evening and tucked it into his coat pocket, so he looked relaxed and endearingly at home in her apartment. "It looks sort of ritualistic."

"It's part of my magic act." Lily wasn't sure how convincing this sounded. "I think my act will be more effective if I have candles and a crystal ball involved, don't you?" She felt the warm crystal vibrate in her grip, and it seemed unfair to imply that such a powerful tool would be part of a mere act.

Daisy walked over and shoved her nose against Griffin's hand. He petted her, but his attention remained on Lily and there were questions in his hazel eyes. "I'm not much of an expert on magic acts. I guess candles and a crystal ball would be good."

"I'm hoping they will." Holding the crystal ball always centered her and brought her into balance. Being balanced meant divesting herself of all falsehoods.

She was involved in an enormous one tonight. The crystal grew warmer in her grip, and that warmth worked on her. She wanted to confess everything. She wanted to in the worst way.

But she knew once she did all Hades could break loose, and this was a critical weekend for her sister. But it wasn't all about Anica, and she admitted that to herself. She didn't want to lose Griffin. Not yet.

"Does that crystal ball have a laser embedded in it somewhere?" Griffin stepped closer.

"No, why?"

"It seems to be glowing."

"A trick of the light, I guess." Turning her back to him, she carried the crystal ball over to its metal stand on her bookcase. "I'll just put it back where it belongs."

"Lily . . ."

"Yes?" She placed the ball carefully in the stand.

"Nothing. We'd better take Daisy out."

"Good idea." She would love to walk Daisy with Griffin by her side, and she was relieved that he didn't ask any more questions about the crystal ball. If she hadn't fallen asleep in the hotel room this afternoon, she would have cleared everything away. Maybe he'd accept her lame excuses for now.

"In fact, I have a better idea," Griffin said. "You take Daisy out, and I'll move these candles into the bedroom. I have the urge for some candlelit sex tonight."

She couldn't very well tell him that those were special candles that she used exclusively for spell work. She wasn't sure what would happen if she and Griffin made love while those candles burned. If anything, it might heighten the effect of the elixir. No telling what that would mean. He might want to elope to Vegas.

But she couldn't think of any logical excuse to keep him from setting up his romantic bedroom scene using those candles. She'd have to go with it and see how it all turned out. One thing was for sure: The sex would be outstanding.

She picked up Daisy's leash from the hall table as he started collecting the candles. For some reason her mind flashed back to a scene in the bar, something she'd forgotten to ask him about. "By the way, what did Kevin want?"

Griffin glanced at her with a look that was definitely secretive.

She noted that with great interest. So she wasn't the only one hiding things.

"Kevin?" Griffin's attempt to appear nonchalant failed miserably.

"He came back around ten. I saw you talking to him. He never comes back in, so I was curious about why he did tonight."

"Oh." Griffin glanced away, another sure sign he was making it up as he went along. "He wanted to confirm that I wasn't going with him and Miles to the Cubs game tomorrow night. I told him you and I would probably plan something to do together."

You're lying. Her own recent attempts to hide the truth had probably made her more sensitive to Griffin when he tried to do the same thing. Besides, she'd already established that he was a terrible liar.

That meant that Kevin hadn't come back to question Griffin about the Cubs game. She'd bet money he'd come back with instructions about how to deal with Lily, how to put the brakes on the relationship. Yet here they were in her apartment, and Griffin wanted to have sex by candlelight.

That wasn't putting the brakes on. That was stepping on the gas. She decided to think about it while she took Daisy out.

"I won't be long." She opened the apartment door as Daisy danced around in excitement. "I won't go all the way to the dog park tonight, just down the block."

"To Harvey's Hangout?" Griffin's expression darkened.

"No, not that far, either." She could tell her friendship with Brad Harvey bothered him. She hadn't planned for possessiveness to be part of the spell, but it made sense. Dogs guarded the person they loved. Griffin wouldn't want anyone encroaching on his territory.

Her short walk with Daisy wasn't enough time to sort out all the reasons Griffin might have lied about why Kevin had shown up at the Bubbling Cauldron. She thought maybe Kevin was operating in the same capacity Anica had when Lily had first set her sights on Griffin. Anica had come into the bar to talk Lily out of having sex with him.

Maybe Kevin's objectives were the same, to convince Griffin that he should spend the night in his own bed instead of going home with Lily. If that had been Kevin's objective, he'd failed. But then, he didn't know what he was up against. The magic grew more powerful with every sexual encounter.

The thought was a little intimidating. If Griffin was this attached now, what would he be like after they had sex a few more times? Lily had never checked to see if the power of the elixir had any limits. That might have been a good idea before she'd administered it to an actual man.

Sad to say, checking out all the angles wasn't her strong suit. When she was feeling positive about herself, she said that's why her life was so exciting. When she was feeling more negative, she said that's why her life was a disaster in the making.

Tonight was a toss-up between the thrill ride aspect and the impending disaster aspect. But she wasn't about to throw Griffin out of her bed or out of her apartment, so she might as well enjoy what he had in mind.

She waited until Daisy took care of business, and then they started back toward the apartment building.

Griffin dropped the candles on the carpet and took the plastic bag of salt out of his pants pocket the minute Lily went out the door. Sprinkling salt around the bed seemed like a dopey thing to do, but Kevin had insisted and he meant to prove his friend wrong.

Having never done such a thing before, Griffin felt no level of competence. He dumped too much of the salt on one side of the bed and ran out before he got around to the other side. That also meant that on the one side, which happened to be the side where Lily slept when they were together, a person could easily see the salt on the carpet.

A person, namely Lily, would probably notice the salt if she happened to step on it, especially in her bare feet. Griffin went in search of a dustpan and whisk broom, which he found in the kitchen pantry. In the process he noticed the pantry was loaded with all sizes of glass jars with labels like MUGWORT, VERVAIN and MANDRAKE.

Maybe they were herbs for cooking. And maybe not. He was also positive that the glow he'd seen coming from the crystal ball had not been a trick of the light. The moment she'd picked up the ball it had started giving off funky flashes and twinkles.

He hated to admit it, but the evidence was mounting that Lily was a practicing witch. And she was practicing on him. Returning to the bedroom, he set about brushing some of the salt into the pan so he could sprinkle it more evenly.

As he worked he cursed softly under his breath. That probably wasn't the magical chant that Kevin had in mind, but it worked for him. Most guys ended up with normal women, and it seemed that he'd become entangled with a certified witch. What were the odds?

In some ways he couldn't complain. Lily was great to look at and great in bed. But if she'd taken away his right to choose, if she'd slipped him some kind of magic drug that made him want her no matter what, that wasn't good.

He swept faster and soon had a dustpan full of coarse salt. Moving his hand over the carpet, he decided that it wasn't quite as gritty and maybe she wouldn't notice. If she did notice, he had no idea what to tell her. None of Kevin's suggestions had sounded worth anything.

Besides, what sort of reaction could he expect from an actual witch? Would she take out her magic wand and turn him into a toad? All the stories from his childhood came rushing back. He should just leave, but he . . . couldn't. That was the most telling evidence of all.

About the time he'd emptied the dustpan along the other side of the bed, the key turned in the lock. He shoved the dustpan and the whisk broom under the bed and walked back into the living room, where the candles he'd dropped still lay on the floor.

She unhooked Daisy's leash and glanced at the candles. "Problems?"

"You know what? I love the effect of candles, but when you get right down to it, they're a fire hazard."

She lifted her eyebrows. "If you say so."

"Let's just forget the candles." Now that she was back, now that she was within range, an ache of extreme longing took over. She was steps away, this woman who could satisfy that ache. Was that so bad, to want someone this much and have the prospect of amazing sex close at hand?

Maybe he shouldn't have sprinkled the salt around the bed. This kind of sexual excitement had never happened to him before. Kevin couldn't possibly know how Griffin felt, so of course he wanted to interfere and remove the spell. He might even have acted out of jealousy, come to think of it.

When Griffin listened to Kevin, he agreed the spell had to go, but now, gazing at Lily, he was enjoying the hell out of being magically transformed. It was flattering that she'd chosen him, and he wished he hadn't sprinkled the salt around the bed.

But he couldn't very well take it back now. Lily might get suspicious if he had a sudden inclination to vacuum.

So they'd make love in that bed with the salt around it, and maybe he'd feel differently about the experience. And maybe he wouldn't, which might mean that Kevin and Miles were wrong. Lily might be an amateur magician and nothing more.

Yes, he was ignoring the strange items in the pantry and the glowing crystal ball. Big deal. Now seemed like a good time to forget about those things and concentrate on taking Lily to bed.

Lily put Daisy's leash on the small table by the door. "I picked up another soup bone for her yesterday and forgot to give it to her last night. Let me set her up with that. I'll be right back. Come on, Daisy. Soup bone time."

Daisy pranced happily after her into the kitchen.

Griffin looked down at the candles, which lay scattered, some on their sides, some even upside down. That wasn't very considerate of him, to leave them like that. Dropping to his knees, he began to gather them up.

Lily walked back into the room. "Here, let me help get those." She got down on her hands and knees next to him.

The moment she did he became intensely aware of her. Her scent drifted toward him, beckoning him to touch her. Sitting back on his heels, he reached over and cupped his hand over the back of her neck, massaging gently.

She glanced at him over her shoulder and smiled.

That smile tripped some sort of switch, and the urge to have her swamped every logical thought. With a low, primitive growl, he slid his hand down her spine and wrapped it around her waist.

"Griffin?" She looked back over her shoulder again.

"I want you." He tugged her back against his thighs, and the candles she'd been holding tumbled back onto the carpet as she braced her hands on the floor. He settled her against his erect penis.

"I can tell you want me." Her laughter was breathless. "Does that mean you're no longer on candle detail?"

"That's right." Leaning over, keeping her sweet backside in contact with his cock, he scraped his teeth against her neck. "I want you right here. Like this."

She shuddered. "That's a long way from candlelight."

"I don't need candlelight. I need you." Pulling her blouse from the waistband of her slacks, he reached under the stretchy material to release the front catch of her bra. Her breasts spilled into his hand, silky and full.

She moaned softly as he caressed her.

"I can't seem to get enough of you," he murmured against her neck. He loved touching her, stroking her nipples until they became tight with desire, but he had other needs that drove him to release his hold and unfasten her slacks.

Sliding his hand inside her panties, he discovered she was wet and ready. He stroked her, wringing a whimper from her as she arched against him. Heavy with need, he pushed back, wanting more, so much more.

He nipped the soft skin of her neck as he plunged his fingers in deeper. She moaned and pleaded for release. Something snapped within him. In an instant he'd wrenched down her slacks and panties, ripping the seams.

She gasped and looked over her shoulder. "What . . ." Her gaze took in his open fly. "Griffin, we can't—"

Oh yes, they could. Seizing her around the waist once more, he plunged deep, crying out at the intense pleasure of entering her without any barriers between his heat and hers.

"Griffin, no . . ." Her protest was weak, and even as she made it, she surrendered to the moment and lifted her hips to give him greater access. Then she was moving with him, meeting each thrust with a backward push that had them coming together with a force that sent his blood surging through his veins in triumph.

Glorious. She tightened around him as the pace quickened. Her soft cries kept time with the rhythm of his strokes. He drove deep and she seemed to flower, as if she was one of the budding roses he'd sent her that had been bathed in sunlight and opened its petals to the light.

This was what he'd craved every time he'd been with a woman, and this was what he'd been denied, this ultimate connection, this complete joining of two bodies and two souls. Her climax propelled him into his, and he poured himself into her with a shout of exultation.

He clung to her, panting and spent. Gradually he became aware of his surroundings, which had faded with the first blossoming of passion. Now the setting clicked into place. He'd never found himself in this position in the middle of a woman's living room. He'd never destroyed her outfit to get to her.

And he'd never, in the entire course of his sexual life, failed to use a condom. Yet he didn't regret anything. He should be filled with remorse, but he wasn't. She was his love, his mate, and this was the way it was supposed to be between them.

Holding her fast, he eased them both down to the
carpet and held her, spoon fashion. "I should apologize,"
he said. "But I can't make myself do that."

"Aren't you ..." She paused to catch her breath.
"Aren't you worried about ... getting me pregnant?"

"No." He nuzzled behind her ear. "I'd love to get you
pregnant."

She sighed. "No, you wouldn't. Right now it might
sound like a great idea, but eventually you'd come to
your senses."

"I feel as if I've come to my senses for the first time in
my life. Marry me, Lily. We could fly to Vegas tomorrow,
get married and fly home Sunday morning in plenty of
time for the engagement party."

"That's a tempting offer."

"Then let's do it." His heart raced as he anticipated
the thrill of eloping with her and coming back to Chicago on Sunday as a married couple, deed done.

"I can't."

He snuggled her closer. "As they say in the movies,
you might be carrying my child."

"No, I'm not."

He was devastated. He'd had no idea how much he'd
counted on that as a deal maker until she'd shot it down.
"You're taking birth control?"

"Um ... yes."

"Well, we could still fly to Vegas and get married. It
just wouldn't require a shotgun."

Her body quivered as she chuckled. "No, it would require a lobotomy."

"On who?"

"Me. I can't marry you, Griffin. I don't know you well
enough. And you sure don't know me well enough. But
thanks for the offer."

"The offer stands. Let me know if you change your
mind."

"I will. Now let's get off the living room floor and into

a real bed." She disentangled herself and sat up. "This has been fun, but an innerspring's a little cushier, don't you think?"

That's when he remembered the salt he'd scattered around her bed. He'd forgotten it when she crouched down next to him on the floor, which had led to the most excellent episode they'd just enjoyed, which had led to his proposal.

He wondered if having sex without a condom and suggesting an elopement to Vegas were more signs that she'd bewitched him. Probably. As mellow as he felt right now, he'd didn't give a damn if she was a witch or not.

But he was a little curious as to whether the salt would make any difference for the next round. As he stood and followed her into the bedroom, the only thing he knew for sure was that there would be a next round.

Chapter 20

Lily kept an antipregnancy potion in her medicine cabinet. The potion also protected against STDs, although she doubted Griffin had any issues in that department. Many witches kept the potion on hand. It made sense to do that, because it was the simple and easy solution should an unexpected event occur. As it had tonight.

She'd never had to take the potion because she'd always insisted that a man wear a condom. She could ingest the liquid at any time within twelve hours of having unprotected sex and there would be no baby. The potion was an insurance policy against unwanted pregnancies.

As she walked into the bedroom, her slacks and panties in tatters, she realized she could easily excuse herself and take the potion. Griffin had obviously assumed from her comment that she was taking some kind of traditional birth control pill, but a practicing witch never bothered with prescriptions. Because she wasn't ready to admit her magical status, she'd let him assume she was using something more conventional.

They'd entered dangerous emotional territory, and she knew it even if he was too besotted by the spell to understand the problems he faced. She could surely see how the elixir was having a more powerful effect with every sexual encounter. This afternoon's hotel experience had fostered this latest session on the floor of her apartment.

He'd abandoned the idea of condoms and even seemed to relish the idea that she could get pregnant. That moved them to another whole level of involvement. And now, after a session on the floor of her apartment with her unlit spell candles strewn around, he'd suggested eloping to Vegas.

If Lily were more of a scientist, she would be keeping notes as the elixir experiment unfolded. But she wasn't a scientist and she'd rather keep these developments to herself. At some point she might confide in Anica, but even that was risky.

She should, however, take the antipregnancy potion. And she would. But her comfy bed called to her, and Griffin was shucking his clothes in preparation for climbing under the covers. She wanted to cuddle with him, and once they were recovered, she wanted to make love some more.

Actually, it made sense to wait to take the potion. Having sex with Griffin without a condom ranked right up there in her list of peak experiences. She'd like to do it again, which meant she'd have to spend the morning making another batch of the potion. That was just inefficient.

Instead she took off her boots, which had remained on during the living room interlude, and started peeling off what was left of her panties and slacks.

"I shouldn't have wrecked your clothes," Griffin said as he climbed under the covers. "I know what. We could go shopping together tomorrow and I could buy you new clothes. And as long as we're out, we could look at rings." He propped himself on one arm and gazed at her adoringly.

Well, of course he looked at her adoringly. She'd given him an adoration elixir. That reminder depressed her so she decided not to think about it anymore. She

would also ignore his suggestion about buying a ring. No
matter how much part of her might want to, they were
so not doing that.

"Unfortunately I don't have the day free," she said,
"or I'd take you up on the clothes-shopping idea. I love
looking at clothes. But I'm supposed to spend some time
over at my folks' condo tomorrow. They've got it in their
heads that Anica and I should come over and help them
decide who inherits what. I think it's ridiculous when
they'll be around for a long, long time, but they're determined to do it."

"So I won't get to see you tomorrow?"

"You'll see me when you wake up in the morning,
and you're welcome to come by work tomorrow night."

He sighed. "I guess that'll be okay." He sounded extremely disappointed, as if she'd wrecked his whole day.

Much as she liked having his adoration, that kind of
neediness didn't work for her. "I'm sure you have things
you usually do on the weekend."

"Well, yeah, but that was before we got together."

And his neediness was all her fault, she reminded herself. No point in blaming him for something he couldn't
control.

Right before she climbed into bed, she noticed that
the carpet beside her bed felt gritty under her feet, as if
someone had been tracking in sand. "Griffin, have you
been down to the beach today?"

"No. Why would I go down to the beach on such a
cold day?"

"I don't know, but there's sand or something on the
rug." She crouched down and ran her fingers over the
carpet. "This isn't sand, it's . . ." Her hand stilled. *Salt.*

Her pulse beat erratically as her mind raced back
over the evening's events—his friends with their serious
expressions, Kevin coming back into the bar later on,
Griffin begging off from going on the walk so he could
light candles. But he hadn't lit any candles. Instead he

must have sprinkled salt, probably provided by Kevin, around the bed.

He knows about the spell and he was trying to break it.

"Lily?" Griffin propped himself up higher so he could see what she was doing. "Is anything wrong?"

She had to decide what to do, and decide quickly. Should she tell him that she knew what he was up to, or pretend ignorance? A little salt wouldn't break the spell. In fact, no amateur methods he might find in books or online would break it. He might dilute it, though.

Considering how powerful it had become already, that might be a good thing. She hadn't realized how wearing it could be to have a man so eager to please her and so desperate to be with her night and day. She wouldn't mind dialing that back some.

Keeping her discovery a secret would mean playing a game of cat and mouse, though, at least through this weekend. In the process, if she treated him well enough as the spell grew less powerful, he might start falling in love with her for real.

He lay on her red satin sheets, looking incredibly yummy and incredibly worried.

"I figured out what was on the floor," she said. "That's where I spilled some bath salts the other day. I forgot to clean it up."

His expression of extreme relief almost made her laugh. He climbed out of bed. "That can't feel very good under your feet. How about if I run the vacuum so you won't have to step on it in the morning?"

Aha. So he'd sprinkled the salt, but the power of the spell, especially after they'd had such unrestrained sex in the living room, made him regret that he'd done it. A picture of a naked Griffin vacuuming her bedroom carpet would make an awesome centerfold for a racy women's magazine. Who wouldn't want household help like that?

But she didn't want him to get rid of the salt. In fact, she was curious as to how it would affect them if they made love surrounded by it. "Never mind." She pulled back the sheets and slipped under them.

Then she patted the vacant spot next to her. "Come to bed with me. I have plans for you." She was gratified that her suggestion had an immediate effect on his penis, which began to swell.

Still, he looked uncertain, as if he really would like to break out the vacuum and get rid of the salt. He also looked as if he might be on the verge of a confession. "Lily, I—"

"I'm waiting." She threw back the sheet and slid her hand between her thighs. "Impatiently, I might add." She didn't want him to confess. That would only bring about a discussion she wasn't prepared to have. They were definitely in a don't-ask-don't-tell situation, at least through the weekend.

With a groan of surrender he came to her, as eager as he'd ever been to kiss her, touch her, arouse her to fiery heights. Apparently the salt had no immediate effect on the spell. But she wanted to take charge this time, and once she had him in her arms, she rolled him to his back. Not having to worry about a condom was a bonus she intended to exploit.

She began by sliding down his body and letting him feel the weight of her breasts throughout the journey to her destination. Once there, she settled between his thighs while she made love to his cock.

Judging from his moans and sharp inhalations, he was having an excellent time. She wanted him to have a good time, but not *too* good. She stopped just short of making him come, changed her position and straddled him.

Immediately he bracketed her hips and tried to guide her where he wanted her.

She resisted. "Wait," she murmured, bracing her arms

on either side of his shoulders and leaning down to brush her mouth over his. "Let me do it."

"I want—"

"I know what you want. And I'll give it to you ... eventually." She eased down on his rigid penis, but not very far.

"More."

"Not yet." She withdrew and repeated the motion.

"I'm dying."

"And what a way to go." She treated him to a few more teasing penetrations that only went so far. Then she returned to her first position nestled between his thighs and loved him with her mouth.

Whenever she thought he couldn't take any more, she circled the base of his penis with her fingers and squeezed until his trembling thighs relaxed. Then she began all over again.

She lost track of how many times she changed positions, but obviously the combination was driving him around the bend. His gasps and groans became more pronounced, and he began to thrash around on the bed.

Finally she straddled him for the last time and leaned down to nibble at his mouth as she slowly took the tip of his penis into her slick channel. "Now," she said.

He took her hips in a viselike grip and pulled her down with a low, guttural sound of satisfaction.

"Mm." She'd been submitting herself to the same sweet torture she'd portioned out to him, and now she was right where she wanted to be at last. She lifted her head so she could look into his eyes. "That's very good."

He gazed back with laserlike intensity, as if he wanted to discover all her secrets. "I love being inside you."

Inside my body or inside my mind? Or maybe she was reading too much into his searching gaze. "I love that, too. But I thought it would be fun to build up to it."

His laughter was hoarse. "Oh, it was." He continued to hold her captive with his eyes. "It is." He loosened his grip and smoothed his hands over her thighs, creating fire wherever he touched. "Ride me, Lily."

"That's what I had in mind." She needed no more urging as she began a steady rhythm. Arms braced, she allowed herself to delve into the depths of his eyes.

"I do love you," he said.

"I know." And for this moment, as she took them both toward a shattering climax, she allowed herself to believe it. If he didn't love her now, he would. She'd find a way to replace every bit of that fake love with the real thing.

The next morning, Griffin woke up wondering what the hell he'd been thinking, making love to Lily the night before without a condom. The salt must have worked at least a little bit, because he was feeling much saner today and much more worried about his out-of-control behavior.

He'd had unprotected sex with Lily before she'd told him she was on the pill. What an idiot. And he still wasn't sure if she'd been straight with him, because after they'd taken Daisy for a run, he'd opted for the first shower and had a chance to check the bathroom cabinets. He'd found a couple of bottles of liquid with strange-sounding labels that had been hand lettered, but no birth control pills. Of course, she could be using something else.

Later, over breakfast, he decided to bring up the subject. Surprise pregnancies weren't his idea of a good time. At least they weren't this morning. He vaguely remembered actually relishing the idea of making her pregnant last night, which was crazy. Once a woman was pregnant the options narrowed.

This whole witch thing had him worried, and although he still felt completely bonded with her, he didn't want to be rushed into anything. Sure, lots of couples decided against getting married right away when they discovered an unexpected pregnancy, but Griffin wasn't made that way. He would want to marry the mother of his child immediately. And then he'd be married to a witch, or at least that's what it looked like more and more.

As they munched on bagels slathered with chive cream cheese from the corner market and sipped fresh-brewed coffee from ground whole beans, Griffin wished he didn't have to bring up a touchy subject. The morning together had been great, congenial. He hadn't felt a desperate need to have sex with her, probably another sign the salt was working. As a consequence, they'd had several actual conversations.

The mood was mellow, with Daisy snoozing on a bed in the corner of the kitchen and soft music coming from a radio on the kitchen counter. Lily had dressed casually in cropped black sweatpants, running shoes and a lime green V-neck shirt. She'd pulled her hair back in a pony-tail and she wore very little makeup.

He liked this understated version of Lily almost as much as he liked the potent vixen who worked behind the bar at the Bubbling Cauldron. Today she seemed ready for a relaxed Saturday. Griffin could get used to beginning his weekends like this, but he didn't want to be forced into domesticity because he found himself accidentally the father of her child.

He took a drink of his coffee, set the mug on the table, started to say something and picked up the mug again. But after another slow sip, he couldn't put off his questions any longer. Soon she'd have to leave for her parents' condo.

"You . . . ah . . . said you were on the pill."

She glanced up, her dark eyes alert. "Last night, you didn't seem to care one way or the other."

He acknowledged that with a nod. "I got a little carried away."

"We both did." She drained her coffee mug. "But you

don't have to worry about a thing. There's no danger I'll end up pregnant."

He wanted to take her word for it. He really did. But he'd feel a lot better if he'd found a container with the pills in it. "Are you taking that daily kind or something else?"

"Something else."

"Oh." Now he was a little lost. He realized there were other options, but he wasn't completely up on what they were. "I guess there's a shot or something."

She laid a hand on his arm. "Griffin, it's okay. I promise you won't get a tearful phone call saying the test was positive."

"I just wondered what you were on, exactly. You know, whether it was safe for you. Some of this experimental stuff makes me nervous." She obviously was avoiding a discussion of her birth control method, and he couldn't figure out why. As part of the sexual partnership, he had a right to know, didn't he?

She gazed at him steadily for several seconds. "Wait here and I'll go get what I use so you can see it for yourself."

Okay, maybe she kept the pills in some special place where he wouldn't have thought to look. All he needed was to see a familiar package, a delivery system he'd recognize. Then he could forget about the issue of pregnancy.

She came back with one of the two bottles he'd seen in the mirrored medicine cabinet. She set it on the table. "I took a tablespoon this morning. It works like a charm."

A charm. She would have to use that wording. He picked up the bottle. "It looks homemade."

"That's because it is. I brew it up using a special blend of herbs."

I brew it up. He couldn't very well deny the truth now, could he? She was a witch who could make a love potion to bring him into her bed and an antipregnancy potion to prevent any unwanted consequences.

As he held the bottle in his hand, he remembered the thrill of having no-condom sex with her. As long as she took this potion, they could keep up that program. He should be worried about continuing a relationship with a certified witch, but damn, the sex was great.

"Trust me on this, Griffin. You're off the hook."

He chose to believe her, because the potion she'd used on him had certainly worked. The bottle was small, though, and what she'd taken this morning had left it only half full.

He held up the bottle. "So can you make more?"

She smiled. "Yes. I can make as much as you want."

"Then I recommend you make a bathtub full." He leaned over and gave her a kiss that would have led to more, except that she had to leave, and he had to report back to Kevin as promised. He planned to tell Kevin—nicely, of course—to take a flying leap. Sex with Lily was too good to give up, and if Kevin didn't understand that, too bad.

Chapter 21

Lily usually looked forward to spending time with her parents, but today was an exception. Guaranteed they'd be quizzing her about whether she'd leveled with Griffin yet. She could tell a half-truth and say that Griffin was now aware of her magical abilities. But they would have preferred that she tell him, which she hadn't.

Plus the whole exercise in choosing items to inherit freaked her out. Her folks could be a trial sometimes, but she didn't want to think about them not being around to give her a hard time.

Anica arrived before she did, of course. When her dad answered the door, she could hear Anica and her mom talking in the kitchen.

Her dad was dressed in another peasant shirt and loose-fitting pants, but he wasn't wearing a headdress today. Instead he had on his reading glasses and had stuck a pencil behind his ear. He held a clipboard in his hand. "Come on in."

"I guess you decided against the headdress for today."

"Yeah, it gets in the way when I'm working. Which reminds me, should I put you down for the headdress? Anica didn't sound excited about getting it. I'm taking inventory so we know what we're talking about."

Lily walked into the small entryway and turned to

him as he closed the door behind her. "Let's not talk about it at all, okay? You two will be around for a long, long time, and dividing up your stuff now feels creepy."

Her dad looked at her over the top of his glasses. "It's not creepy. It's practical. Your mother and I got to talking during our trip up here, and while we intend to stick around long enough to teach magic to our great-grandchildren, we do travel a lot on commercial airlines. Something could happen that we couldn't control."

"Oh, that's cheery." Lily took off her backpack and set it by the hall table. "Now I get to worry about you crashing on your way back to Peru." But mostly she was thinking about his reference to great-grandchildren.

She and Anica would have to be grandparents before that could happen. There was a concept. But at the rate Lily was screwing things up, her sister would be a grandmother long before Lily took her first walk down the aisle.

"You know me, Lil," her father said. "I like to anticipate problems and solve them before they come up. Your mother and I have had wills for some time, but we never got around to designating where the little stuff goes." He walked to a bookshelf crammed with knick-knacks from their travels and continued with his list.

"You have wills?"

"Yep. Anica has copies." He moved a wooden statue of a pig and peered at the carved monkey behind it. "Anyway, I'm sure she'd show them to you or even make you your own copy if you—"

"That's okay. Now that you mention it, she might have said something about having them. I'd rather not read through those, either, thank you very much."

Her father glanced at her. "It does you no good to stick your head in the sand. It's much better to figure these things out in advance, so that when you're faced with something like the death of a parent, you—"

"Not *listening*." She stuck her fingers in her ears and

began to sing. "La-la-la-la. Do-wa, diddy-diddy-dum-diddy-dum."

Her dad's dark eyes, so like hers, began to twinkle. "You look about five when you do that." He grinned and reached over to tug on her ponytail. "Have it your way, but that means Anica gets to be totally in charge."

"Oh." She hadn't thought about that. "I suppose she's like the executor or something, huh?"

"She is now, but I think we should talk about that. I'd like to modify the will while we're home and make you both coexecutors, if you're up to it. But if you want to plug your ears and pretend you're a little kid again, then I guess being a coexecutor isn't for you."

She had to admit the idea of being on equal footing with Anica for a change had a certain appeal. "Can I think about it and get back to you?"

"Sure. By the way, have you told Griffin about your magical abilities?"

She'd thought about her answer to that question all the way over on the bus. "You know, I was so worried about how he'd take the news, but he seems fine with it." She'd practiced that sentence several times, and she thought it sounded pretty convincing.

It wasn't exactly a lie. Even though Griffin had a good idea what was going on, he hadn't run away screaming. That translated to his being fine with her magic, didn't it?

"Just so you make sure he really *is* fine with it. Your mom and I like him a lot, Lil. I think you'd be good for each other."

That comment surprised her. "I can imagine how you think he'd be good for me, but how would I be good for him?"

"You'll keep him loose. He looks as if he'd have a tendency to be a little too conservative and driven, to the point where he forgets to have fun. I never have to worry about that with you, and that's a relief."

She stared at him, blown away by the unexpected compliment. "It is?"

"Sure. See, I have that anal tendency, too."

Gazing at the neatly lettered items on his notepad, she smiled. "Really?"

He smiled back. "As if you haven't noticed. But you've probably also noticed that your mom makes sure I don't turn it into a religion. She buys me things like headdresses and Incan ceremonial medallions so I don't take myself too seriously."

"So you think I should buy Griffin a headdress?"

He laughed. "Or the equivalent. And for balance, he'd be a steadying influence on you."

"Aha! You do think I'm too wild."

"I'm just saying it's a good combination. I hope it works out for you two."

That's when she knew why he'd suggested the coexecutor gig. She'd hooked up with a responsible guy, and her father had taken that as a sign that she was growing up. Hera's hemorrhoids. If he knew how she'd lassoed Griffin, he'd take back every compliment he'd just given her.

Her web of deception was threatening to strangle her. The urge to confess and break everything wide open was strong, but that would be selfish. Even negative attention was still attention, and Anica deserved center stage this weekend.

Lily decided that she and her dad needed a change of venue. "Let's go see what Anica and Mom are up to in the kitchen," she said.

"You go ahead. I want to finish cataloging everything on this bookshelf." He turned and picked up a particularly ugly carving of a llama.

"That one has Anica's name written all over it," Lily said.

"I think you're right," he said with complete seriousness. "I'll make a note."

A rush of tenderness for her goofy, anal father brought tears to Lily's eyes. She turned away so he wouldn't see. How could she tell him what she'd done? How could she ruin his newfound faith in her?

Now she wanted to hold on to Griffin for two reasons—because she was crazy about him, and because her father probably saw in him a vision of the son he'd never had. Yes, using that elixir had been underhanded, but if she hadn't done that, her father and Griffin would never have gotten to know each other. She had a feeling they could be great friends, and didn't that count for something?

Kevin had insisted on coming over to Griffin's apartment to strategize, and nothing Griffin could say made any difference. Miles would have been there, too, except that he'd hooked up with the clerk at the natural foods store and they were spending the day at her place.

"Typical," Kevin said over beer and burgers. "My friends are both getting laid while I, the one with the most outstanding package, sit home alone."

"At the moment you're sitting on my couch watching baseball with me," Griffin pointed out. "But if that's not exciting enough for you, I can find out if Lily knows any other witches."

"I almost wish you could, but I don't think you want to tip your hand and admit you know she's a witch."

"I think she knows I know, which makes for some interesting sex."

Kevin picked up his bottle of beer. "So you've said." He tipped the bottle in Griffin's direction. "You've also admitted to a serious lapse in judgment last night, and I blame that potion she gave you. You're in dangerous territory, buddy."

"Yeah, but I think the salt helped. Last night I didn't know it was a stupid thing to do. This morning I did."

Kevin swallowed a mouthful of beer and shook his

head. "It's still too close for comfort. I worry that you'll buy two tickets to Vegas and get married by Elvis."

Griffin choked on his bite of hamburger.

"You've already considered it, haven't you? Good God. We need something more powerful than a few handfuls of salt."

Griffin cleared his throat and took a swig of his beer. "Like what?"

"This is the point where you'll be happy to have a friend who graduated summa cum laude, because I've applied my considerable brain power to this problem, and I have some ideas."

"Do tell." Griffin took another bite of his burger.

"You could sound a little more grateful and eager about hearing them."

Griffin finished chewing and swallowed. "It's tough to get motivated when the sex is better than anything I've ever had."

"Yes, but don't forget that was your parents' downfall."

Griffin went completely still. "You're right. Jesus, you're absolutely right. Give me what you've got."

"Two things. The first is this." Kevin reached in his pocket and pulled out a polished black stone about the size of a silver dollar. "I got it at a New Age store."

"Yeah, and what do I do with that?"

"Put it in your pocket. It's called jet, and it protects you when your emotions are out of control. At least that's what the woman told me. Just my luck she was old enough to be my mother."

"What about when I don't have a pocket, if you get my meaning?"

Kevin rolled his eyes. "Rub it in. You're getting naked with a gorgeous woman and I'm not."

"I think you should see if Debbie's interested."

"Maybe I will. Anyway, when you don't have a pocket for this, I guess you could slip it into the pillowcase." He handed the stone to Griffin.

The stone fit neatly into his palm, and as his fingers closed over it, the stone grew warm. He wondered if something that small could handle a craving so big.

"I don't think the jet alone is enough to solve the problem, if that's what you're wondering," Kevin said.

"I was, yeah."

"I thought it would make a good stopgap measure. If you really want some help, you should go to Jasper Danes."

"Anica's fiancé?"

Kevin nodded. "I don't know if you remember, but Miles and I met him a few weeks ago. He came in the bar with Anica."

"Right!" Griffin had been having his usual happy hour with Miles and Kevin. Jasper had come over claiming to know him from the gym where Griffin used to go. Griffin didn't remember Jasper at all, but it didn't matter. They could have once belonged to the same gym.

"You'll see him Sunday, obviously."

"I think that's a given."

Kevin picked up the last of his hamburger. "He's about to marry Lily's sister. Chances are he knows Anica's a witch and probably has some pointers."

"I have to admit that's brilliant."

His mouth full, Kevin simply nodded his agreement.

Griffin smiled. No false modesty for his buddy Kev. "I think you're on to something," he said. "Those two sisters are close. I'll bet Anica knows about the potion. The night Lily gave it to me, Anica called her twice that I know of. I don't think she wanted Lily to have sex with me."

Kevin swallowed. "That's the rest of my theory. From what I read online when I was researching this stuff, I'll bet every time you have sex with Lily, the spell gets stronger."

Griffin thought back over the past few days. That theory made a lot of sense. "Are you saying that in order to break the spell, I need to stop having sex with her?" Even though Lily wasn't with him, his body cried out in protest.

"Even I wouldn't expect that kind of sacrifice," Kevin said. "After the fun you've had, you can't go cold turkey. But maybe the salt and the jet will help you taper off."

Griffin sighed and slipped the smooth piece of black stone in his pocket. "Do you think there are couples who have great sex *and* a dynamite relationship?"

"I'm sure there are," Kevin said. "But when you're under a magic spell, there's no way you can evaluate whether you have the good relationship to go along with the fantastic sex. You're not playing on a level field."

Griffin gave him a long look.

"I mean that in the most helpful way."

"Right."

"Seriously, Griff. If you ever want to find out whether you have something special with Lily, you have to break the spell."

"Yeah." Griffin blew out a breath. "And I may never forgive her for putting it on me in the first place."

Lily realized she'd never seen Griffin in the bar on a Saturday night, so she had no idea when to expect him. When he was coming from work, he and his buddies would arrive sometime between five and six. But he wasn't coming from work and she doubted he'd show up with his friends, either.

She tried not to watch the door, but that proved difficult. Every time it opened, she glanced over, hoping to see Griffin. She suspected he'd conferred with his buddies today and might have more plans for how to counteract the effects of the elixir.

Well, bring it on. For every measure he took to break the spell, she'd ramp up the sexual excitement. Her father had said they'd make a good combination. Her instincts had told her so from the beginning, but her dad was a smart man. If he thought she and Griffin fit together, she'd work all the harder to make it happen.

But first he had to show up. She couldn't believe he'd be able to affect the spell so strongly that he wouldn't feel the urge to be with her. Even without the spell, he had the promise of sex without condoms, which should be enough to bring him back to her tonight.

He was taking his own sweet time, though. Nine o'clock came and went with no Griffin. The bar was full of people, but not the one person she wanted to see. She was so distracted that she messed up an order, something she never did.

Sherman stopped back to get the revised tray of drinks. "You okay?"

"Sure. I just—"

"You wonder where Griffin is. I've seen you watching the door. Is he due at a certain time?"

She shook her head. "We didn't set a time. It's only that he's usually here by now."

"So call him on his cell. Tell him to get his butt down here."

"Yes, maybe I will." But she was embarrassed to admit to Sherman that she didn't have Griffin's cell number. She'd had to use her crystal ball to get his work number. Their relationship had moved so fast and he'd been so devoted, coming by the bar every night, that she hadn't thought to ask how to get in touch with him.

For that matter, he didn't have her cell phone number. She realized that if he simply failed to show up, she would have only one point of contact for him—his office—and that would do her no good on the weekend. She had no home address and no cell phone number. He was the most important man in her life right now, the most important man in her life ever, and she couldn't get in touch with him unless she did another spell with her crystal ball.

As she was in the midst of vowing to find out his cell

number the first chance she had, her own cell rang from the pocket of her backpack. It was the generic, unassigned ring, so she knew it wasn't anybody she usually talked to. She checked the number and didn't recognize it, so that might mean . . .

Her heart beat faster as she tucked the phone against her shoulder so she could continue making drinks while she talked. She'd have to keep a sharp eye out for Devon, who would fire her if he found her talking on her cell phone when she was supposed to be concentrating on her job.

She hardly ever did that, but if the voice on the other end was the right one . . . and it was.

"You're probably wondering why I'm not there yet," Griffin said.

"It's good to hear your voice." Then she cringed. What a teenage-crush sort of thing to say. "What I mean is, it's good to hear from you."

"I wanted you to know what I was up to."

"That's nice. How did you get my number?"

"Detective work. I went back to the office this afternoon and checked the phone log. Because you called the office yesterday, I was able to get the number."

"Ingenious." She couldn't help noticing that he'd checked the phone log this afternoon, but he hadn't contacted her until almost ten at night. It looked as if he'd found more remedies for the spell and was using them to keep from hanging around like a puppy. "Where are you?" She hoped he was in a cab headed toward the Bubbling Cauldron.

"Out on a walk with Daisy."

"You *are*?"

"I hope you don't mind. I'm sure you're really busy down there, considering it's Saturday night. You wouldn't have time to talk to me, anyway."

"That's true." She ducked behind the counter when she saw Devon come out of his office. "In fact, I have to hang up now."

"Okay." He didn't sound upset. "I'll see you when you get home."

She stood, the phone still in her hand, and Devon was right there, staring at her.

He popped his gum and leered at her. "You wouldn't be taking personal phone calls during work, would you, Lily?"

She adopted her haughtiest manner. "There are party details to iron out. I want everything to be right, especially because Anica invited Dorcas and Ambrose Lowell." All of that was true, even if the phone call hadn't been related to any of it.

Mention of the Lowells wiped the leer off his face. "Right, right. It'll be a good party. With Dorcas and Ambrose here, I figure it'll get a mention in *Wizard World*. I'll send the editors a few pictures, in case they want to run those."

"They might at that." Personally, Lily wasn't looking forward to interacting with the Lowells tomorrow. Dorcas would have too many questions.

"I want to make sure I get a picture of me with them," Devon said. "You'll do that for me, right?"

"Sure, Devon. I'll do that." But for the most part she planned to avoid the Lowells. Maybe they wouldn't say anything incriminating in front of her parents, but they'd probably be evaluating the situation with Griffin. She knew they didn't approve because they'd tried to enlist Anica to stop her.

Everything should be fine if she stayed away from them and made sure Griffin did, too. Fortunately he didn't know anything about them. To him they'd just be another couple at the party, somebody he met once at the beginning of the festivities and then promptly forgot, because she'd steer him in another direction. She'd been to plenty of parties in her life. She ought to be able to manage this one.

Chapter 22

Griffin was impressed with how the polished black stone in his jeans pocket had affected him. He was still eager to see Lily, and he was really excited about having sex without bothering with a condom, but he wasn't feeling obsessed about any of it anymore. He'd even called Kevin to report on the effect of the stone.

But the power of the stone was about to be tested. Lily was due home any minute, and he'd stashed the jet inside the pillowcase on the right side of the bed, where he'd slept each time he'd spent the night in her apartment. Other than that, he hadn't set the scene, hadn't provided flowers or wine.

He had spent more time reading her magic books, though, but now those were all carefully put away so she wouldn't suspect he'd been gathering more information. He'd concluded that Kevin was right—he had to find out how to break the spell. Being tied to Lily because he had no choice wasn't good.

She kept a basket full of magazines in one corner, and he'd settled on the couch to read one about dogs when he sensed that Lily was near. A moment later he heard steps in the hallway, and Daisy left her spot by his feet to stand near the front door, tail wagging. Griffin found it amazing that he'd known Lily was home before Daisy had sensed it.

The key turned in the lock, and his heart rate went up. He'd managed to get through the evening without needing to be with her, but now that she was here, all he could think about was holding her, kissing her, making love to her until they were both exhausted. He tossed aside the magazine and stood.

She came through the door with a smile that made his breath hitch. Logically he knew there were women out there more beautiful than Lily, but at the moment, he couldn't imagine how that could be. He would never tire of looking at her.

Shrugging out of her backpack, she dropped it to the floor and greeted Daisy.

He waited, letting Daisy have her moment.

Once Lily had finished petting the dog, she straightened and gazed at him, her eyes shining. "Hi, stranger."

He swallowed. "Dear God, I've missed you." Closing the distance between them, he pulled her into his arms and groaned with relief as he held her tight and lowered his mouth to hers. One kiss and he was desperate for her.

She seemed equally desperate, backing him toward the bedroom as she fumbled with the buttons of his chambray shirt.

They'd become more efficient at undressing each other, and soon they were both naked and rolling together on the bed, each of them laughing with joy. Griffin stroked and kissed every part of her he could reach before changing positions so he could stroke and kiss whatever he'd missed.

They tumbled about on the bed, teasing each other with the promise of what was to come. At last he pinned her down, unable to wait another second. The laughter faded from her eyes, replaced by smoldering heat.

Slowly he lowered his head and kissed her, giving her his tongue as he probed her wetness with his cock. With a soft moan she lifted her hips in invitation, and he thrust deep. His heartbeat thundered in his ears as he reveled in the glory of making that connection.

And yet there was a subtle difference. Tonight he wasn't crazed by the need to drive into her. Tonight he had no dreamy illusions that he should spill his seed and make her pregnant. Tonight was about pleasure, not obsession.

As he began a lazy rhythm he lifted his head to gaze into her eyes.

She was watching him, almost as if she sensed the difference, the added control he had over his emotions. "Something's changed," she murmured.

"Has it?" He angled his hips, increasing the friction. Tonight he had the presence of mind to make those slight adjustments. Tonight he was less of a wild man and more of a lover.

"Yes." She arched her back so his strokes came in closer contact with her clit. "I can feel you . . . thinking."

"I am thinking." He moved a little faster. "I'm thinking about making you come."

She gasped. "Exactly."

He looked deep into her eyes, wanting her to hear him. "I can't let you be in charge forever, Lily."

Her gaze didn't waver as she dug her fingers into his hips and met him thrust for thrust. "I know."

"Then let go."

She was breathing hard. "I want to."

"And you will." Pumping faster, he tilted a fraction more, and felt the first ripple move over his cock. He'd brought her there without losing his mind, without letting a haze of lust obscure everything. As the first ripple turned into waves, as she cried out in surrender, he allowed himself to come.

It was good . . . very good . . . but not like before. He would miss that hedonistic rush that had claimed him when he was fully under the spell. But the price for that kind of tumultuous passion was losing control of his body, his mind, perhaps even his soul. And that was a price he was unwilling to pay.

They made love again that night, and Lily could tell that Griffin was less in control the second time. He'd weakened the effect of the elixir with some sort of countercharm earlier that day, but apparently good sex would eventually tip the balance in the other direction. He would need to keep using countercharms to keep the spell from overwhelming him. . . . Or give up sex.

The countercharm idea sounded a lot better. She wondered what he'd come up with, but didn't dare try and find out while he was still in bed with her. She waited until morning and pretended to sleep when he got up and headed into the bathroom.

She listened to the sounds of splashing in the sink, which meant he was shaving. She didn't want to begin her search until he was in the shower. Once the water was running and he was whistling away, she began her investigation.

Although she didn't want to interfere with his work to dilute the spell, she needed to know what it was. He and Kevin weren't wizards and they were messing around with things they didn't completely understand. Better that she discreetly check it out for them.

First she looked under the bed and found nothing, although she had to brush off the salt from her knees when she stood. Just the salt couldn't have created this change in Griffin, though. For one thing, he hadn't been surrounded by salt all afternoon and evening, when he'd found the intestinal fortitude to keep his distance from her.

There had to be something else. She ran her hand between the mattress and box spring, but nothing seemed to be there, either. Whatever it was had to be small, something he'd carried throughout the afternoon and then transferred to . . . then she knew exactly where it was. Grabbing the pillow from his side of the bed, she stuck her hand inside the case and found the stone.

She recognized immediately that it was jet, which would bring him more emotional stability and self-confidence. Good choice, whether it was his idea or Kevin's. The stone had been working hard and had a slight crack in it that she'd bet hadn't been there originally.

Sitting cross-legged on the bed and holding the stone between her palms, she closed her eyes. *"Piece of jet stone, black as night, be whole again so you can fight."*

Secretly helping Griffin dilute the spell that she'd cast on him was totally weird, but she didn't know how else to handle this awkward situation. How ironic that she'd given him the elixir because she'd wanted a respectable boyfriend around when her parents came home to celebrate Anica's engagement and wedding. Her plan had worked perfectly with her dad, who now saw her as having the maturity to accept more family responsibility.

Her plan had also worked well for her sex life. But her heart—her heart ached with the knowledge that she'd enslaved this man. Love from a bottle, so to speak, wasn't love at all. Sometimes she could almost convince herself that Griffin really cared for her, but as long as the spell was still in effect she couldn't trust any of his behavior as being genuine.

She opened her hands to find the crack in the stone gone. As an excellent witch with good magical skills, she'd expected as much. It was a small spell she'd created, so her adrenaline level would spike for only an hour or so.

But it was spiking, which meant that climbing in the shower with Griffin sounded really good right now. Talk about counterproductive. She'd just repaired the jet in order to bring him back into balance after the sex they'd had during the night.

"Lily?" He came to the door of the bathroom with

a towel draped around his hips. "Were you talking to somebody just now?"

She closed her hand over the stone and glanced up. "Just saying my morning ... affirmations."

"Here's an affirming idea." There was a definite gleam in his eye. "Hop in the shower and I'll wash your back."

And wouldn't she love to do that? But she had a responsibility to him now that she'd created this situation. "Nice idea, but I have to get going. I'm meeting Anica and the folks down at the Bubbling Cauldron in ..." She glanced at the bedside clock. Yikes, it was later than she'd thought. She couldn't dally with Griffin in the shower even if she could justify having more sex with him. "I'm supposed to be there in an hour to decorate."

"I'll come with you and help."

She recognized the signs of dependency returning. "Oh, Griffin, that's sweet, but I'm sure you have plenty of things to—"

"Nope. I'm coming with you." He walked over to the duffel he'd brought with him and rummaged through it. "Let me get some clothes on and I'll take Daisy out while you shower. We can pick up some breakfast on the way over there."

"Uh, okay." She started to put the jet back in the pillowcase, but he stood and turned toward her. She jerked her hand back.

"How about we pick up muffins and coffee for everybody?"

"That would be nice." The jet was warm in her hand as she sat on the bed, trying to decide how to replace it so he could find it again. He needed that stone. He was reverting back.

"Go on." He made shooing motions with his hands. "Get in there and shower. I'll take care of Daisy. I'll feed her, too."

She couldn't leave the room without putting the jet back inside the pillowcase. Once she went into the bathroom, he'd get dressed and look for it, so he could put it in his pocket. But he was standing right there, watching her.

The door was still closed, so Daisy couldn't come in and occupy him for the few seconds that she needed. But wait. If she concentrated very hard, she could make the front doorknob rattle, which would cause Daisy to bark like crazy to alert them to a potential intruder. Lily didn't do telekinesis very often, so she was a little out of practice, but she needed a distraction and she needed it now.

"I appreciate all your help with Daisy." She remained where she was, because she needed to be quiet and centered to accomplish this. Besides, the minute he left the room, she should be right by the pillow so she could replace the jet in a hurry.

"No problem. I like her. She—"

Loud barking—Daisy sounding the alarm—came from the living room.

Griffin spun toward the closed bedroom door. "What the hell?"

She forced herself to sound scared. "I don't know. From the way Daisy's barking, she must think somebody's trying to get in." She started to stand up. "I should go see if—"

"I'll go." Griffin knotted the towel more securely around his waist.

She gave him points for chivalry. She couldn't remember the last time a man had been ready to defend her against an unknown enemy.

Griffin's protective stance was sexier than she'd figured. She wanted to jump his bones even more now. But she'd created a diversion so she could replace the stone he'd hidden inside the pillowcase. There was no real threat, although now she'd jacked up his adrenaline level as well as her own. Bad combination.

"Stay here." The low command thrilled her to her toes, even if there was no danger.

"I will." She played the meek maiden in distress, although in a true emergency she would have been right beside him, ready to face whatever he might encounter. She wasn't a fan of shrinking violets, but in this case it suited her purposes to adopt that role.

He opened the door. "Hey, Daisy. What's the matter, girl?"

Lily stopped the rattling at the same moment she shoved the jet inside the pillowcase.

The sound of Daisy's whine drifted through the partly open door.

"Go to Lily, girl. Stay with her while I check this out."

Lily was doubly touched. He could have kept the dog with him, but he preferred to have Daisy watch over Lily instead. One glance at the clock told her this little maneuver would make them late to the Bubbling Cauldron, but it couldn't be helped. He had to have that piece of jet, and he couldn't know that she'd discovered it. She scooted to the side of the bed so she could pet Daisy.

"We have a winner in that guy," she told the dog.

Daisy wagged her tail vigorously and smiled her doggie smile.

"Yeah, I know you like him, too. Let's hope this works out for all of us." Lily hadn't considered the impact of bringing Griffin into Daisy's life when there were no guarantees he'd end up staying. In a sense, she was toying with Daisy's affections by allowing Griffin to become the dog's friend. If he left, Daisy would probably mourn his loss.

That was one more reason why Lily couldn't arbitrarily break the spell. She'd traumatize her dog. Jupiter's balls, what a complicated situation. She'd never anticipated things would get so messy.

Griffin came back in. "I checked the peephole, and nobody was out there, so I opened the door and took a quick look around. Nothing. You have good locks, though. If someone tried to get in, they wouldn't have much luck."

She nodded. "True. Still, that was brave of you, to go out there virtually naked to scout around."

"Brave or stupid, I'm not sure which. I'm glad it was a false alarm, because I've never tried to fight someone while I was wearing nothing but a towel."

"Have you ever had to fight someone at all?"

He looked somewhat wistful. "No. I was big for my age, so nobody ever picked on me. And I don't have brothers or sisters, so I didn't have those kinds of fights, either."

"I had some knock-down, drag-outs with Anica." Lily remembered wands had been raised and half-baked spells had been used, which only got them in bigger trouble with their parents.

He smiled. "I'll bet you were a fierce little fighter."

"I don't like to lose, I'll tell you that."

"Neither do I, Lily." He gazed at her with a million questions lurking in his hazel eyes. "Neither do I."

She hated that they were on opposite sides of the fence, but then, she'd been the one who'd put them there.

Chapter 23

Griffin rode the bus with Lily to the Bubbling Cauldron. He didn't want to show up looking like a snob who only took cabs. With his jet back in his pocket, he felt more in command and ready to take on her family. By now he assumed the whole kit and kaboodle were magical, except Jasper, of course.

Although he hadn't wanted to go along with Kevin's conclusions that Lily was a witch, he couldn't very well deny it now. He was relatively sure she'd made the door rattle so Daisy would bark, thus getting him out of the room for some reason. He was guessing she'd found his stone and then wanted to put it back while he wasn't looking.

He'd never before had a sexual relationship with somebody who kept huge secrets from him. And that forced him to keep huge secrets from her, too, although he doubted either of them was fooling the other. They were both too smart. So instead they played this complicated chess game to see who would blink first.

He was determined it wouldn't be him. If he was in luck, Jasper Danes would be on the decorating committee this morning, and he'd have a chance to talk to him, man to man, about what to do when the woman you were sleeping with happened to be a witch. Griffin didn't know if Jasper would talk or not. But surely he'd take pity on another guy who found himself trying to navigate this unusual landscape.

After they got off the bus, Griffin had to hurry to keep up with Lily, who was barreling down the sidewalk as if she'd taken up race walking.

Griffin had never seen her move that fast. "Does it matter so much if we're late?"

She slowed down. "I guess not. But I'm always late, and I'm just . . . tired of being labeled the screwup of the family."

"Blame it on me."

She glanced over at him and smiled. "Thanks, but there's no way it was your fault, and hiding behind you wouldn't speak very well of my maturity level, now, would it?"

"Who said you're not mature?"

She sighed. "Nobody's said it in so many words, but look at my life compared to Anica's. She owns a business and she's been working toward that goal for several years. She's getting married to a guy who adores her, and she adores him. Her apartment is always cleaner than mine—well, now she has the condo that she bought with Jasper, but it's always clean, too. She—"

"Lily." Griffin took her arm and pulled her around to face him. The street was nearly deserted this time of the morning, and he was tempted to kiss her and see if that made her feel better. It probably would, but this wasn't about endorphins.

She gazed up at him, her jaw set in a belligerent line. "Listen, I didn't say all that just so you could tell me how wonderful I am, so don't start."

"You are wonderful, but I'm not going to harp on that if you don't want me to. I don't have any brothers or sisters, so maybe I don't get the whole sibling rivalry thing, but it can't be good to compare yourself to Anica. She's a different person from you."

"No kidding." Lily gave him a smile filled with sadness. "She's goal-oriented and I'm not. She's organized and I'm not. She gets places on time and I don't. She knows what she wants out of life and I don't."

He rubbed her upper arms. "I'll bet you do know what you want, deep down."

She looked at him for a long time without speaking. "Maybe. Maybe I do."

"So what do you want out of life, Lily Revere?"

For a second there was a gleam of self-knowledge in those big brown eyes that he hadn't seen before, and he thought she might open up and tell him. He suspected one of the things she wanted was a guy who adored her, a guy she adored in return. She'd sounded wistful when she'd mentioned that about Anica.

Then she shrugged. "It's too early in the morning for this kind of discussion. And now we're even later." She drew away. "Let's go in, Griffin."

He sighed and opened the door for her. He understood her better now, but he didn't know how to help her. Hell, he couldn't guarantee he could help himself now that she'd created this magic spell that bound him to her.

Her reason for timing it the way she had was more obvious, too. With her sister getting married and her parents coming back from Peru, she'd wanted a guy around so she wouldn't look quite so aimless in comparison.

Choosing that route was a screwup of major proportions. He knew he was sexually attracted to her because he'd wanted her even before she'd slipped him that potion. The only difference was that now he had less ability to resist her.

But could he ever love her? He wouldn't know as long as he was under this spell. He had to get free of it, for both their sakes.

The bar took some getting used to. He'd never seen it like this, virtually empty under the glare of the overhead spots. The place looked a little shabby in that unforgiving light. The tables and chairs that had seemed rustic now simply looked battered and old. He'd never noticed that the wooden floor could use refinishing or that the wall around the dart board needed patching and painting.

Lily's father, Lionel, was in the process of climbing a tall metal stepladder, holding a mirrored ball. Jasper was steadying the ladder and offering encouragement, while Simone and Anica moved chairs and tables back against the walls, probably to create a dance floor under the revolving ball.

Griffin thought Lionel and Jasper should have traded jobs. The weight of the ball was throwing Lionel off balance.

"He's going to drop that thing." Lily started forward.

Griffin moved faster and was almost under the ball when Lionel and the ball toppled sideways, pulling the ladder with them even though Jasper tried manfully to hold on to it. As everyone in the room started yelling, Griffin had a choice as to whether to try for the ball or Lionel. He chose Lionel.

As the ball crashed to the floor beside them, Griffin did his best to control Lionel's fall, but the guy still took Griffin down and knocked the breath from his lungs. Everyone else pressed closer, trying to help while they cried out in alarm.

Griffin picked out Jasper's voice right away because he was cussing while everyone else was yelling. Jasper was saying things like *God damn it* and *shit*, but those weren't the words everyone else used. Indeed, Griffin noticed the women were saying things like *Zeus's balls* and *Apollo's ass.*

Come to think of it, Lily had used a phrase like that once or twice, and he'd thought it was something she'd heard on TV. Apparently witches and wizards swore differently, too.

Lily crouched next to him and touched his face. "Are you okay?"

"Breath knocked out." He sounded about ninety years old. "How's your dad?"

"I'm good, thanks to you breaking my fall." Lionel held out a hand. "Let's get you up and make sure you're still in one piece."

Griffin took Lionel's hand and felt a sudden jolt, as if he'd touched a live wire. And then, miraculously, he could breathe easily again. Once he was on his feet, he held Lionel's gaze, so like Lily's. "Did you just do something?"

The man's eyes didn't even flicker. "I helped you up."

"I know, but I felt . . . like, an electrical charge."

Lionel regarded him steadily. "There are some people who say I have a touch of the healer in me. Maybe it's true."

"Yeah, maybe." Griffin looked over at Lily, who was watching the exchange with a worried expression. No wonder she hadn't wanted to bring him to this little decorating party. Some of those secrets they were keeping from each other might leak out.

Simone touched his shoulder. "I'm *so* sorry, Griffin. Are you truly all right?"

"I'm fine." Griffin walked around a little and shook out his hands. "But I can't say the same for that mirrored ball."

"I'm about to take care of that." Anica came over with a plastic garbage pail that held a long-handled dustpan and a broom.

Griffin picked up the dustpan as she began sweeping the glass. "I'll help."

"Then I'll go work on tablecloths," Lily said.

Anica smiled at Griffin as she started to sweep. "Thanks for coming down today. I'll bet you didn't expect things to get so exciting."

"I'm just sorry the mirrored ball is history. It would have been a fun thing to have tonight."

"We might still be able to do it."

"Not with this one." *Unless you use magic to fix it.* Griffin was surprised at himself for even thinking such a thing. Was he getting used to this weird situation?

But the proof of magic was all around him. He'd definitely been given a potion, and he'd been able to modify the effects using salt and the jet in his pocket. That didn't make him magic, but it meant he was accepting possibilities he'd never have believed before.

After the fall he'd experienced what he thought could have been a magical healing touch from Lionel. No telling what sort of sprain or dislocation he might have suffered without the jolt he'd felt coming from Lionel. Now he wanted to talk to Jasper and find out how much he knew.

Creating that opportunity might be tricky, but he would give it his best shot. Thinking of Jasper made him wonder about the other man's parents. Were they in on the magic secret?

He decided to go on a fishing expedition with Anica. After dumping a load of glass into the garbage pail, he turned back for another load. "I guess Jasper's folks didn't come down to help."

"No." Anica kept sweeping. "They both seem to be plagued with allergies, so between pollen blowing around and the dust we knew we'd stir up with this project, we convinced them to spend the day relaxing at the Art Institute of Chicago."

"That sounds like a good plan. So you'd never met them before this?"

"Sure hadn't." Anica said it brightly, a little too brightly.

Griffin laughed. "I detect some reservations about your future in-laws."

"Oh, they're okay. Just not . . ."

Griffin filled in the blank with no problem. *Not magic.* But then, neither was Jasper, and she was obviously head over heels in love with him. "You mean they're not like your folks?" he asked.

"Nobody could be like my folks. I knew Jasper's parents were on the conservative side, but—" She paused to glance around. "I hope they'll have a good time tonight."

"I guess Lily's going to do some magic tricks."

Anica stopped sweeping to gaze at him. "Yes, she is. Lily's very talented with magic."

"So I hear."

Anica leaned on the broom. "She's very creative, too, much more so than I am. Lily has style coming out her ears."

"I agree." Griffin paused. "But mostly she wants to be like you."

Anica blew out a breath. "I wish she'd stop thinking like that. Lily needs to be the best Lily she can be, which means wearing outrageous clothes, decorating with lots of color and expressing herself with an interesting job." She gestured toward the bar. "Like this. I don't think I ever appreciated before that she's great at bartending. She has a gift."

Griffin nodded. He hadn't been so good at recognizing that, either, he realized. He'd been somewhat of a job snob, to be honest. Shame on him.

"Devon doesn't give her enough leeway," Anica said. "She could create signature drinks for this bar, and she offered to do that when she first was hired, but he has zero imagination and thinks everyone just wants the same ol', same ol'. Either that or he's afraid she'll get too good and someone else will hire her away from him."

"Signature drinks sounds like a great idea. She does so well with the basics that she should try branching out."

"Absolutely." Anica started sweeping again.

Griffin put the dustpan back in position, but he couldn't resist one last comment. "I'll tell you this: Lily makes a hell of a Harvey Wallbanger."

Anica glanced up and he could tell from her expression that she knew exactly what he was talking about. Like her father, she didn't allow her gaze to flicker even a little. "I'll bet she does."

After that, as if by mutual agreement, they moved away from the subject of Lily and onto more neutral ground. They talked about their jobs, and Griffin could tell how much alike he and Anica were. She'd invested time and money in her coffee shop, Wicked Brew, with the same sense of dedication he'd brought to his law practice.

"There was a time not long ago when I thought I might lose the coffee shop," Anica said. "It wasn't a fun moment, knowing all I'd worked for was at risk because of an impulsive move on my part." She swept the last of the broken glass into the dustpan. "But I can't regret that impulse, because I ended up with Jasper."

"Did I hear my name?" Jasper came over and wrapped his arm around Anica's shoulders. "I hope you were telling Griffin what a prince I am."

"I hadn't gotten to that part yet."

"Damn. I showed up too soon." Jasper smiled at Griffin. "I have a confession to make. You remember that night several weeks ago, when Anica and I came over and crashed your table?"

Griffin remembered it well. "You said we'd met at the gym, but I couldn't place you."

"That's because I made up that story. I was on a reconnaissance mission for Lily, to find out more about you. You know, doing my good deed for the future sis-in-law."

Anica poked him in the side. "You didn't even know she'd be your sister-in-law at that point."

"Yeah, I did." Jasper beamed at her. "In my heart of hearts." He turned his attention back to Griffin. "That's been bugging me, knowing I fibbed a little bit, but it looks like it worked out okay."

"It's worked out." Griffin wasn't quite ready to put the *okay* label on it. But he was now convinced Jasper knew nothing about the potion. He was being too open and friendly to be concealing that kind of information.

Griffin had been hatching a plan while he worked with Anica, and with Jasper standing right there, it could be put in motion. "Listen, now that Anica and I have this glass under control, I was thinking we probably need some signage out front, to direct people to the right place. That freestanding blackboard they usually put out announcing drink specials would work, but I could use a hand getting it out there."

"Absolutely. Great idea. Just so you're not expecting me to do the lettering. I suck at that."

"Let's just get it out there and then worry about the lettering." Griffin wanted to jump on his idea right away, before something came up to interrupt what he thought was a brilliant plan. Without the jet in his pocket to subdue his obsession with Lily, he might never have thought of it. He owed Kevin a drink, probably several drinks.

"I'll get the blackboard," Griffin said, "if you'll hold the door and then come on out and help me decide the best place to put it."

"I like a man with a plan." Jasper walked ahead of him and positioned himself by the door.

Griffin hoisted the blackboard, which was more bulky than heavy, and carried it out the door Jasper opened for him. In seconds they were both on the sidewalk with the heavy bar door closed behind them.

The sun was bright and almost directly overhead. Griffin squinted a little as he looked at Jasper. "Now I have a confession to make. I didn't ask for help with the blackboard because I was focused on the need for signage."

Jasper leaned against the brick building, arms folded. "I didn't think you did."

"The Revere family is . . . unusual."

"Yep."

"This isn't easy to admit, but I'm not sure how to deal with . . . a woman like Lily." He waited, wondering if he'd have to be more specific. He'd rather not get into details in case for some weird reason Jasper was still in the dark.

"Then you're aware that she has special abilities."

Griffin's shoulders sagged with relief. "Yes. But she doesn't know I know. Or rather, I think she knows I know, but she's not willing to admit to me that she knows that I know." He peered at Jasper. "Does that make any sense, because listening to myself, it makes no sense whatsoever."

Jasper laughed. "And you're a lawyer who's used to that kind of wording. But yeah, I get it. Lily's not ready to reveal her magical status, because then the two of you have to talk about it, and she doesn't want to rock the boat right now, with her folks in town and the party tonight."

"Exactly. Plus there's . . . there's something else, but I'd rather not go into that."

Jasper held up both hands. "Hey, I have several things I'm not prepared to go into involving Anica. This is a complicated world you've stumbled into, buddy. I remember how lost I felt. Still feel lost sometimes. Incidentally, my folks know *nothing*, and that's how I want it. They would freak."

Griffin nodded. "So I gathered. That whole allergy ploy sounded bogus."

"Oh, they have allergies, all right. Thank God. It was the perfect excuse not to have them come down here today. The less time they spend in the Bubbling Cauldron, the better. Anyway, this isn't about me."

"In a way it is. I want to know how you've handled being with Anica, when she's a . . ."

"She's a witch, Griffin," Jasper said quietly. "And so is Lily. Simone is, too, and Lionel's a wizard. For all four of them it's an essential part of their being, and you have to be okay with that or you'd do well to bow out now."

Griffin decided not to reveal that he didn't have that option at the moment. "I'm ... very attached to Lily." That much was true. "But obviously I'm feeling out of my depth. I'd appreciate any words of advice."

"I have two suggestions. One is to enjoy the hell out of the magical aspect, because, as I'm sure I don't have to tell you, these two women are hot."

Griffin heaved a sigh. "Yeah."

"But there are bound to be issues regarding the magic. Turns out you're in luck, because Dorcas and Ambrose Lowell are coming to this party."

"And they are?"

"A matchmaking witch and wizard."

Griffin's gut clenched. "I'm really not sure that's the sort of thing I—"

"Hold on. Yes, they're matchmakers, but they're also experts in the field of magic, and they helped Anica and me work through a very difficult situation. I don't know where we would have been without them. They're completely discreet, and they know a hell of a lot. I'd lay it all out for them, if I were you."

"I can't believe I'm going to a witch and wizard for advice."

Jasper smiled. "I know the whole idea of magic takes some getting used to. Believe me, I understand what you're going through. I'll introduce you to Dorcas and Ambrose. If they can't straighten out your problems, then nobody can."

"Thanks." Griffin offered his hand, which Jasper took in a firm grip. "We'd better get back in there. I'm sure Lily knows why I dragged you out here."

"You're allowed to have some backup," Jasper said. "After all, she has Anica." Clapping Griffin on the shoulder, he followed him back inside the bar.

Once they were inside, Griffin glanced around for

Lily. She was up on the ladder, stringing paper streamers. She looked over at him, her gaze knowing. She understood what he was up to.

He was going to break the spell. She had to know he would try everything. Dorcas and Ambrose, if they were as powerful as Jasper had said, should be able to tell him how to do it. What would happen after that was anybody's guess, but Lily looked worried—very worried. He was sorry about that, but as he'd told her last night, she couldn't be in charge forever.

He was so caught up in Lily and her reaction to his trip outside with Jasper that at first he missed the most amazing thing in the room. Hanging from the ceiling, in perfect condition, was a large, multifaceted, mirrored ball.

Chapter 24

After the decorating was finished, Lily's parents took everybody out for lunch. Her mom and dad seemed in their element, obviously delighted with Jasper, their future son-in-law, and Griffin, who seemed very interested in Lily. They made it clear they would welcome Griffin into the family with the same enthusiasm they'd shown Jasper.

But Lily knew Griffin was testing the bars of his cage and gathering information that would help him escape. She couldn't blame him for talking to Jasper. In his shoes, she would have done the same thing.

After lunch, while everyone stood out on the sidewalk prior to heading home to get ready for the party, Lily took Anica aside. "I don't know if you saw, but when we were at the bar Griffin managed to get Jasper alone for a conversation." She kept her voice low.

"Actually, I do know. It was pretty clever the way he did it, too. He's a smart man, Lily."

"I know. He's figured out that I gave him some sort of potion and that's why he's so tied to me."

Anica nodded. "I thought so. He made a pointed reference to the great Harvey Wallbanger you mix, and I decided that must have been the delivery system."

"It was, and with a little help from his friends Miles and Kevin, he's trying to break the spell."

"Oh yeah?" Anica's eyebrows lifted. "How's he doing that?"

"Salt around the bed for starters, and now he's carrying a piece of jet around in his pocket."

Anica looked impressed. "Not bad."

"I can't blame him for trying, but I'd like to stay one step ahead of him, so that I won't end up in some embarrassing situation, especially in front of Mom and Dad. If you can subtly find out what Jasper told him, I'd be eternally grateful."

"I'll do my best."

"Thanks, An. I've been driving myself crazy wondering what they talked about. You don't suppose Jasper would tell him the cat story, do you?"

"Absolutely not." Anica glanced over at her fiancé, who was joking around with their father while their mother talked quietly with Griffin. "Jasper doesn't want that story going *anywhere*. I suspect you and I may be the only two people who will ever know about his days as a cat."

"And your former neighbor Julie, the one who's convinced her calling is to become a witch."

"Right, Julie. She won't tell, either. I'm her connection to the world of magic, and she's not going to screw that up by broadcasting my secrets."

Lily lowered her voice. "Okay, you can tell me. Your future in-laws are awful, aren't they?"

Anica glanced over at her fiancé again. "I wouldn't say that. . . . At least not to anyone but you." She grinned. "Yeah, they're awful."

"I had a feeling they were when you made sure they didn't come down to help decorate."

Anica groaned and covered her face with both hands. "That would have been a nightmare. They're convinced the big city is full of germs waiting to give them some terminal disease, and muggers intent on stealing their money."

"Lovely."

"I know. I've never seen two people more afraid to live their lives. Mom and Dad go off to primitive villages in Peru where they can run into all sorts of unexpected dangerous situations, while these people are afraid to leave their sanitized and heavily patrolled gated community."

Lily put an arm around her sister. "I'm sorry, An. Are you sure you want me to do magic tonight? I don't want them to run screaming out of the Bubbling Cauldron."

"Oh, I do." Anica's smile became uncharacteristically devilish. "I would pay to see that."

"Except that wouldn't sit well with your sweetie pie, now, would it?"

"I suppose not." Anica sighed. "And I doubt they'll run screaming out of the building because you perform a few illusions. As we've said, they'll think it's a trick."

"Then we'll continue as planned, but if you find out anything about that conversation between Jasper and Griffin, call me on my cell. I don't want to be caught with my pants down."

Anica began to laugh.

"Bad choice of words," Lily mumbled.

"Oh, no." Anica wiped at her eyes. "I think it was the perfect choice of words."

Lily had reason to think of that word choice once she and Griffin arrived back at her apartment. He'd held her hand during the entire bus ride home, and once they'd closed the apartment door and properly greeted Daisy, he drew her into his arms.

He gazed at her with frank appreciation in his hazel eyes. "I told Anica you wanted to be more like her."

"Now, there's a news flash." She wound her arms around his neck, loving the feel of him, the scent of him. "She knows."

"And she thinks that's crazy." He massaged the small of her back slowly, seductively. "She told me you're far more creative than she is and she admires your sense of style."

His touch created predictable results—she wanted him, even if having sex would counter the work of the stone in his pocket. But his words had an even greater effect on her than his touch. They filled a place in her heart she hadn't realized was so empty.

"That's nice to hear," she said.

"I guess Devon shot down your idea of creating signature drinks for the bar." His hands slid lower, cupping her and bringing her into alignment with his growing erection.

"Uh-huh."

"You should suggest it again." He pulled her tight against him and heat shot through her. "You have loyal customers now, and you have more power than you think. If you threaten to walk, he'll let you create those drinks."

"Could be."

"I want you to make one called The Lily." He ground his hips gently against hers.

"Is that so?" In no time she was wet and ready for him.

He leaned down and ran his tongue over her lower lip. "It should be one of those flaming drinks, the kind made with a-hundred-and-fifty-proof rum and topped with cinnamon."

Her heart pounded with anticipation. "Sounds potent."

"With a name like that, it needs to be." He kissed her with easy deliberation and left her breathing hard. "I'm going to make love to you, Lily."

She had no doubt. As he led her into the bedroom and carefully undressed her, she sensed a difference in his touch, a difference in his eyes. She dared to hope that the emotions driving him came from somewhere deeper than the elixir could reach.

They came together as lovers who knew each other very well, as if they'd spent years learning the exact way to kiss, to stroke, to please. The beauty of it brought tears to her eyes, and at the moment when he entered her, the tears slid unchecked down her cheeks.

As he moved surely and steadily within her, he kissed her tears away. "Don't cry," he murmured.

"I'm . . . afraid." *Afraid I'm going to lose you.*

His smile was tender. "Me, too." And then he took her to a climax so filled with wonder and love that she sobbed in reaction, knowing he'd given her all he could for now, knowing he'd made no promises. She could expect none.

As Griffin was dressing for the party in gray slacks and a black silk shirt, Daisy lay in a corner of the bedroom, her head between her paws. Griffin found it interesting that she'd chosen to stay here even though Lily had left the room to answer a phone call. Daisy seemed to be getting attached to him, which felt good, but might not be wonderful for the dog if Griffin didn't stick around.

Griffin had recognized Anica's ring tone, so he knew Lily was talking to her sister, probably about some new glitch with the party. They'd have a little more trouble fixing it with magic during the event, when someone— like Jasper's parents, for instance—might notice something fishy going on.

Thinking about magic, Griffin remembered the jet stone in his jeans pocket and decided to transfer it to his slacks. He reached in to get it and discovered it had cracked neatly in two.

"Huh, that's weird."

Daisy lifted her head and thumped her tail on the carpet.

"I wonder if that's because it was working so hard, it cracked."

Daisy began panting and gave him a doggie smile.

"I swear you understand every word I say." Griffin crouched down and rubbed behind Daisy's ears as he continued to study the two pieces of polished stone. He'd suspected that sex made the spell stronger, and the cracked stone might be evidence of that. He'd put a strain on its healing power by taking her to bed.

And yet he didn't regret giving in to that urge, in spite of the cost. Yes, he had to break this spell, but he couldn't shake the thought that something was happening that had nothing to do with her potion. As he'd learned more about Lily, he'd come to admire who she was.

That didn't erase what she'd done, of course. Giving him a potion to make him want her was an extremely self-centered thing to do, but hanging out with her accomplished family made him understand why she might think she had to create a facade. She'd done it at his expense, but he'd enjoyed some great sex as a result, so it wasn't all bad.

He'd also expanded his knowledge of the possible. Until this past week he would have sworn that magic was only in the movies or what kids wanted to believe. He'd thought a witch and wizard were Halloween costume choices.

Now he knew that people who looked exactly like anybody else on the street could possibly possess magic powers. One of those people had put him under a spell, and while it hadn't been a malicious thing to do, it had affected his ability to choose for himself.

That had to end ASAP. He was reasonably sure Lily sensed his resolve, too. She'd told him in the midst of their lovemaking that she was afraid.

So was he. He wasn't sure what sort of side effects he was looking at, and he didn't know how he'd feel about Lily once the potion was no longer working. He might get very angry—probably would get very angry. After all, she'd messed with his life, big-time. If Kevin and Miles hadn't stepped in, his career could have been put on the line. He'd still have to make amends with Biddle for missing that lunch on Friday.

Daisy nudged his hand with her nose.

"Want to take a look?" Griffin held the broken stone in the palm of his hand and allowed Daisy to move it around with her nose. She snuffled a few times, her warm doggie breath tickling his palm.

"Sorry, it's not food. It's only . . ." He stared in fascination as Daisy nudged the two pieces of the stone so they touched along the break line. Had to be coincidence. She thought if she moved the stones around enough, they'd magically transform into dog cookies. For all Griffin knew, Lily could change rocks into dog cookies and had done that for Daisy.

"I'm not magic," Griffin said. "I can't turn these into treats for you. Sorry."

Daisy glanced up at him with an expression that clearly labeled him a moron. It was so obvious he had to laugh. Then she began licking the two pieces of stone.

"You just don't give up, do you? After all this work, you deserve a real dog treat. Let's go in the kitchen and see what we can find." Griffin ruffled her fur and closed his fingers over the stone as they both got to their feet. Then he stood very still and opened his hand.

The stone was whole again.

He looked at Daisy, who stood there wagging her tail and giving him that goofy grin of hers. "Well, I'll be damned. You, too."

Daisy whined and wagged her tail faster.

"It's to Lily's credit that she hasn't tried to make you into a movie star," Griffin said softly. "You could earn her a bundle. But she doesn't want a bundle of money, does she? She just wants a dog." Griffin stroked Daisy's silky head. "Okay, let's go get you that treat."

Tucking the stone in his pocket, he walked into the living room, where Lily sat on the couch, strapping on another pair of sexy sandals, black this time, to go with her short black dress. Her cell phone was pressed between her shoulder and her ear while she talked to her sister.

He continued into the kitchen, and after opening a few cupboards, found an open box of large, bone-shaped biscuits. He gave one to Daisy, who carried it over to a corner and plopped down to enjoy it.

With one last glance at the dog, who looked so normal lying there munching on her treat, Griffin walked back into the living room. Lily didn't sound very happy as she talked with Anica. He'd already heard a couple of magical swear words.

Then she sighed. "No, I don't blame Jasper. Thanks for letting me know. At least I'm—" She glanced up, saw him standing there, and didn't finish the sentence. "Anyway, gotta go. Yes, I know it's getting late. We'll catch a cab over there." She closed her phone and tossed it on the couch next to her.

"Everything okay?" He could tell it wasn't because she fumbled with the strap of her sandal, and Lily was usually well coordinated.

"Just fine." She fumbled some more. "Blasted thing."

"Let me." No wonder she couldn't do it. Her hands were shaking as if she'd had six cups of coffee. Sitting next to her on the couch, he leaned down and neatly buckled the strap. "There you go." He glanced up and met her gaze.

"Thanks." Anxiety lurked in her eyes. She opened her mouth as if to say something, then seemed to change her mind. Her lips, covered in a deep red lip gloss, settled into a firm line of what looked like resignation.

"The cab should be down there," he said.

"You called one?"

He nodded. "I keep a cab company on speed dial, so as long as I have my phone, which I do today, I'm set. I called after I got out of the shower." It was efficiency, not magic, but she seemed grateful.

"I appreciate your doing that." She sighed again and picked up her cell phone, tucking it into the small black purse beside her on the couch. "And for giving Daisy a biscuit. I can hear her crunching away in there. She likes you a lot, Griffin."

"The feeling's mutual." He thought again of how Daisy would react if he and Lily eventually split up. Then he remembered that Daisy had repaired the stone that was helping counteract Lily's spell. Maybe the dog was on his side.

He and Lily didn't talk on the way to the Bubbling Cauldron. He was busy with his thoughts, and obviously she was busy with hers. She spent most of the cab ride staring out the window.

When the cab pulled up in front of the bar, the door was propped open and music and laughter poured into the street. Griffin chuckled to himself. Nobody would need signage to figure out where the party was.

His date, however, didn't look to be in a partying mood. She insisted on paying for the cab, and when he thanked her, she seemed to have trouble dredging up a smile.

"Is there anything I can do?" he asked as they started toward the open door.

She paused and faced him. "No, but it's nice of you to offer." Then she hooked her purse over her shoulder and reached out to cup his face in both hands. "Thank you for . . . everything." Then she kissed him quickly, turned and hurried inside.

He groaned softly, wishing things could be the way they appeared to her parents—that he and Lily were headed for a serious commitment. But total honesty demanded that he admit the truth: If Lily hadn't given him the potion, they would never have come to know each other in any sense. And once he'd broken the spell she'd cast, they might become strangers again.

Following her into the bar, he had to pause and let his

eyes adjust. The mirrored ball revolved slowly, and although the effect could have been cheesy, it wasn't. The Bubbling Cauldron sparkled as if it had been touched by magic, which, of course, it had.

Jasper stood just inside the door, where he'd apparently stationed himself as a greeter. He shook hands with Griffin and leaned close. "Just so you're aware, when the sisters talked today, it was about you."

"Me?" Griffin was completely taken aback. "Why?"

Jasper gestured with both hands. "It's that complicated family interaction thing. Lily got Anica to find out what I told you outside this morning. I don't keep secrets from Anica, so now Lily knows that you're planning to talk to the Lowells tonight. She's not happy about it."

"Duly noted." Griffin's felt his jaw tighten. "But whether she likes it or not, I'm going to talk to them. If you'll point them out, then I'll—"

"Hold on." Jasper glanced out the door. "The Lowells are over talking to my folks, so I'll introduce you to all of them at once. I don't think you'll have any trouble figuring out which couple is which."

As Jasper led the way toward a far corner of the room, Griffin could see what he meant. One couple there looked as if they'd dressed for church, or maybe a business meeting. The man, an older version of Jasper, wore a neatly pressed pinstripe suit. Jasper's mom, whose brown hair was short and poufy, wore a little black suit with a conservative hem. The scarf tucked into her collar was a swirled pattern of gray, black and white.

The Lowells, on the other hand, seemed to have stepped out of the pages of a glossy urban magazine. Dorcas Lowell's purple dress hugged her curves, and her necklace, made of purple stones that Griffin now recognized as amethyst, could have come from Tiffany. Her brunette bob was streaked with highlights that caught the light from the rotating mirrored ball.

Ambrose Lowell wore an open-necked white shirt

that looked like silk, a navy blazer that also might be raw silk, and slacks with a European flair. He was graying at the temples, which made him seem even more sophisticated.

After getting to know the Revere family, Griffin no longer had a stereotypical picture of witches and wizards wearing pointy hats. Even so, he was impressed with the Lowells. And that was important, because he was counting on them to give him critical advice, advice that would change the course of his life.

Jasper introduced his mother and father, Janet and Fred, first, and mentioned that Griffin was a lawyer. Jasper's parents fell on that information as if stranded on a desert island with nothing fit to drink. Jasper moved on to the Lowells, who smiled and shook hands.

But Janet and Fred Danes were hungry to meet people with normal jobs, and they monopolized Griffin, much to his frustration. Meanwhile Jasper had to get back to his other guests. With a shrug of sympathy he left Griffin to sort it out.

As Fred Danes launched into a diatribe about the quality of the hotel service in Chicago, Dorcas touched Griffin's arm and leaned in. "We'll talk later," she said.

Then the Lowells were gone, abandoning Griffin to Jasper's parents, who apparently had a laundry list of complaints about their treatment in the Windy City. To his dismay, Griffin finally concluded that they were contemplating legal action against their hotel and were hoping Griffin would handle that for them.

"I'm in family law," Griffin said. "So I don't usually—"

"Griffin's a brilliant lawyer." Lily came up and linked her arm through his. "But lawyers, just like doctors, specialize these days."

"Damn nuisance, all this specializing." Fred swallowed the last of his drink. "In my day, we—"

"Hold that thought, Mr. Danes," Lily said. "I promised Griffin a dance, and I've requested that the DJ play our song. Let's plan to continue this discussion later." Depositing her drink on the nearest table, she led Griffin to the dance floor and stepped into his arms as the DJ played a slow song Griffin didn't recognize.

"I didn't know we had a song." He drew her in close. "But thank you for rescuing me."

"You're welcome." She snuggled against him. "We don't have a song. I couldn't tell you what this one is, either. I just made all that up to get you away from them. Poor Anica."

"Yeah. Good thing they don't live nearby. You know, I kind of like this song." And it was a love song, Griffin realized. Of course it would be, because this was an engagement party, which was all about love.

He nestled his cheek against hers. "God, you smell good. What is that? I keep meaning to ask you, because it's very nice." They moved well together, as if they'd been dancing this way for years.

"I make it myself."

"Of course you do." Heaven was holding Lily in his arms. He could cuddle like this forever.

"Griffin?"

"Hm?"

"What would it take for you to stay away from Dorcas and Ambrose Lowell for the rest of the evening?"

His mellow haze dissipated and he drew back to look into her eyes. "Why?"

"I'd . . . rather you didn't talk to them."

He felt the heat of the stone in his pocket. "I'm sure that's true. Jasper mentioned it, in fact. But, Lily, I will talk to them."

She took it with the fatalistic bravery of a soldier facing the firing squad, and for that he had to give her credit. "All right," she said. "I guess that's how it has to be."

"Yes, it is." And he pulled her close again and danced the rest of the song. After all, she had said it was theirs.

Chapter 25

At the end of the dance, Lily's mom claimed Griffin for the next one. Lily surrendered the dance, just as she would be forced to surrender the magical field to Dorcas and Ambrose sometime tonight. Once Griffin enlisted their help, her spell would go down in flames.

At this point she was into damage control. If Griffin broke the spell, she hoped he wouldn't become enraged. She couldn't blame him if he did, though. Once released he might feel like a wounded animal set free from a trap.

She hoped his anger wouldn't cause him to spill the whole sordid story to her parents. But if he did, she'd have to accept the consequences. Her dad would probably withdraw his offer to make her coexecutor of their wills.

Anica should handle all of that, anyway. Just because Lily could inventory the contents of the storeroom with one hand tied behind her back didn't mean she was up to this coexecutor nonsense. She should never have become so excited about the prospect in the first place.

Daisy would miss Griffin terribly. Lily felt sorry about that. She focused on Daisy's misery, because that allowed her to block any thoughts of her own. She didn't want to think about that. Not tonight.

Anica came over and stood beside her, both of them

watching Griffin dance with their mother. "He hasn't had a moment alone with the Lowells yet," Anica said. "I've been keeping track."

"Thanks, but you're not supposed to be worrying about me." Lily wrapped an arm around her sister. "You're supposed to be enjoying your engagement party."

"I am." Anica glanced over at her sister. "Thank you for being willing to go along with it. This is way better than Donatello's."

"If you think that, you've had too much wine."

"No, I mean it. This is perfect. How soon are you going to do your magic act?"

Lily noticed the Lowells moving in Griffin's direction. "Now. Right this very minute. Get on the PA system and announce it for me, will you? Say I've played Vegas with this act."

Anica grinned. "Well, you could have."

"Damn straight I could have. Build me up, Buttercup."

"You got it."

Moments later, before the Lowells had managed to connect with Griffin, Anica took over the microphone and announced Lily's act. While Anica broadcast Lily's talents to the guests, embellishing the facts like crazy, Lily scampered back to the storeroom and retrieved the wand she'd stored there last night after she'd arrived at work. She'd also hidden a black cape in an empty box that used to hold Jose Cuervo Gold.

Her wand tucked in her cleavage, she tied the cape as she came down the narrow hallway toward the main room. Once the cape was tied, she pulled out the wand and held it at the ready. This was her favorite wand, purple with sparkles and stars on it. She wondered what Griffin would think when he saw her in full witch mode.

Although she hadn't acknowledged it until now, she

wanted him to be blown away. He might be chafing against the spell she'd put on him, but she wanted him to be fascinated with the woman who could create such a spell. She wanted him to consider how dull his existence would be if he went back to a life without magic.

To that end, she strode into the middle of the room, lifted her wand and created the illusion of sparkling rain falling on the guests. The DJ had been forewarned to cue up his most dramatic music, and he came through.

All the nonmagical people in the bar gasped in surprise. Her parents, Lily noticed, looked proud. Now *that* was very cool.

She captured Griffin's gaze and was gratified to see that he was watching as if mesmerized. Excellent, because this show was all for him. Arching an eyebrow, she pointed her wand at the floor and sent undulating beams of light into the circle of friends and family surrounding her.

She didn't dare look at Jasper's parents, for fear she'd giggle. No doubt they were in a state of shock. Later they would find a way to explain it all. From meeting them, she knew that they'd rationalize everything they'd seen.

Lily couldn't tell for sure how Griffin was reacting. He seemed riveted but not necessarily awed. She wanted awe. Pointing her wand straight up in the air she created a swirling, multicolored mist that surrounded her.

When the mist cleared, her black dress had been replaced with a garment of silver threads that caught the light from the revolving ball and flashed it throughout the room.

The room exploded in applause. More important, Griffin was grinning at her and looking proud. A surge of adrenaline filled her with creative confidence. Lifting her wand again, she conjured a mini fireworks display near the ceiling. Bursts of color transformed into blossoms that drifted slowly toward the audience before winking out right above their heads.

When the music swelled she swept her wand around the room, creating more colored mist that gradually shaped itself into a twenty-foot dragon with purple and silver scales. She'd chosen the dragon to represent her power and her dreams. She wondered if Griffin would understand.

The crowd gasped again as the fantasy she-dragon circled the room, beautiful and fierce, her tail whipping, her eyes glowing red. Lily's exit required split-second timing, but she was in the flow. She could do this. Beckoning her dragon illusion toward the center of the room, she lifted her wand and called forth its fire. As the flames roared down, she disappeared.

She didn't really disappear, of course. She used the she-dragon and its imaginary fire to distract her audience so she could duck back down the hallway and run into the storeroom. She made it before the flames and the dragon dissipated.

Even inside the storeroom with the door closed, she could hear the crowd's reaction. She was a hit. If Griffin chose to get advice from the Lowells so he could break the spell, so be it. If he left her once the spell was gone, she couldn't stop him. But she'd allowed him to glimpse the spirit and inner power of the woman he'd be giving up.

Griffin hadn't wanted to be impressed by Lily's display of magic. Maybe he'd expected her to pull rabbits out of a hat or saw Anica in half. He was used to magic like that and knew it was all illusion.

But this . . . this was incredible. *She* was incredible, as magnificent as the dragon she'd created out of thin air, the dragon that made him think of Lily in all her untamed beauty. No, he hadn't expected that. He hadn't expected to have his heart swell with pride as she dazzled the crowd.

Most of the people here would think that she'd used

special effects—lights, mirrors and hidden cameras—
to create the show. He knew she'd had none of those
things, which made everything so much more amazing.
She could do all that and yet she'd chosen him, a man
who seemed boring by comparison, to be the recipient
of her love potion.

That didn't make what she'd done right, but it did
make it flattering. He had to break the spell, though, or
they would never meet on a level playing field. She was
more powerful than he'd imagined, and he could no longer be her puppet.

A woman like Lily might not require a magical man,
but she certainly required a man who could think for
himself, act on his own. As the mist cleared and the
guests began returning to their drinks and their conversation, Griffin scanned the room.

Dorcas and Ambrose Lowell weren't far away. Each
held a martini, which seemed to go perfectly with their
look. Griffin caught Dorcas's glance and started toward
them. She touched Ambrose's sleeve. Carrying their drinks,
they moved in his direction. They met near the bar.

"That was quite a show," Ambrose said.

Griffin nodded. "Quite a show. Lily's an amazing
woman."

Dorcas set her martini on the bar. "Even amazing
women can make mistakes."

"Even you, dearest."

Dorcas flicked a slightly annoyed glance at her husband. "We don't need to be going into that right now,
darling. We have limited time. So, Griffin, what can we
do for you?"

"How much do you know?" When Griffin looked
into Dorcas's amber eyes, he had a feeling she knew a
great deal.

"We've been in touch with Anica." Dorcas kept her
voice low. "We know about the elixir."

Griffin's heart hammered. This woman, so far as he

knew, was a witch, and she'd just confirmed that he'd been put under a spell. This wasn't Kevin making wild guesses anymore. It felt frighteningly real.

He swallowed. Jasper seemed to trust these people, but Griffin didn't know Jasper all that well. Still, there weren't any other options. He gazed at Dorcas. "Can you break the spell?"

She shook her head. "No."

Panic climbed from his chest into his throat. "But I thought—"

"Daisy can."

"*Daisy?*" Griffin stared at her. From the corner of his eye he noticed that her husband was also staring, which was not a good sign. "The dog?"

Ambrose put a hand on his wife's shoulder. "I assume you've researched this."

"Of course." Dorcas folded her arms and gazed up at her husband. "Will I ever live down that incident, or will you bring it up every blessed time?"

"It's just that—" Ambrose glanced apologetically at Griffin. "A few years ago my dear wife created a spell that went awry."

Griffin's confidence, not in great shape to begin with, wavered even more. "What happened?"

"Well, she—"

"Let me tell it, Ambrose." Dorcas picked up her martini and took a healthy swallow. "It was an impotency problem, Griffin, something I'm sure you've never experienced. The man's wife wore panty hose, so I created a spell that made him aroused by the sight of her panty hose. I simply forgot to limit the spell to her particular panty hose, so he . . . well . . ."

"Became quite uncontrollable, actually," Ambrose said. "Wanted to do the nasty with every panty hose–wearing woman he came across. Unfortunately, he was the brother-in-law of the Grand High Wizard, so we were banished."

"Which turned out very well, if I do say so." Dorcas lifted her chin. "We've rehabilitated a problem dragon, found a mate for a lake monster and helped four wonderful couples find happiness. None of that would have happened if we hadn't been banished to Big Knob."

Griffin gripped the edge of the bar. He needed something real to hang on to, and that was the closest thing. Dragons? Lake monsters? Obviously repairing a mirrored ball was child's play compared to what these folks could accomplish.

Ambrose handed over his martini. "Drink this, dear boy. You look as if you could use it."

"Thanks." Griffin knocked back the entire contents of the glass.

Dorcas gazed at him in sympathy. "I know it's a lot to absorb."

"Yeah." He set the glass on the bar because he was feeling a little shaky and didn't want to drop it. "So what about Daisy? I know she's an unusual dog."

"She's magical, and Lily used her qualities of love and devotion when she created the elixir. I checked through all my resource books, and—"

"Did you check online sources, too?" her husband asked. "I wish you'd told me you were researching this matter."

"I didn't tell you, Ambrose, because you wouldn't have approved."

"Well, there's that."

She glanced at Griffin. "You and Lily are out of our jurisdiction. We couldn't offer you advice until you asked. But now that you have, I'm free to tell you how to break the spell. The more time you spend alone with Daisy, the quicker you'll break it."

Ambrose nodded. "It does make sense."

Nothing made sense to Griffin in these uncharted waters, but spending time with Daisy sounded innocuous enough. He'd been afraid his cure might have involved toads and snakes. "How much time do I have to spend?"

"It's hard to say exactly." Dorcas sipped her martini. "Every time you have sex with Lily, you increase the power of the spell, which means you'll have to counter that with more Daisy time."

Griffin's face grew warm. He'd never met this woman before tonight, and now she was discussing his sex life. He took a deep breath. "Okay. What if I don't sleep with Lily again? How long do I have to hang out with the dog?"

Dorcas set her glass on the bar and slipped her hand in a pocket hidden within the folds of her curve-hugging dress. She pulled out a piece of lavender paper and handed it to Griffin. "Here are my calculations."

He studied the paper covered in an elaborate gold script. Dorcas had style, even in her penmanship and her choice of ink color. He'd never been handed a note written in gold before.

She'd set it up as a series of equations. Griffin scanned the first four of them.

1. Five-minute quickie = fifteen minutes with Daisy
2. Twenty minutes, missionary position = forty minutes with Daisy
3. Ten minutes oral sex (for Lily) = fifteen minutes with Daisy
4. Ten minutes oral sex (for Griffin) = thirty minutes with Daisy

The list went on, with various addendums and asterisks. He glanced up. "Are you saying I have to go back and figure out how many minutes I need with Daisy based on the sex I've already had?"

"That's right, plus any future sex you will have."

"Considering I'll have to get out a slide rule to figure out what I owe so far, I'm thinking there won't be any. It's just too complicated."

Dorcas's eyebrows rose. "You obviously have tremendous willpower, then."

That was his dearest hope. "I want to beat this spell, which means I have to play catch-up on my Daisy minutes. I don't have time for backsliding and recalculating."

"I don't know," Ambrose said. "She's a very good-looking woman."

Griffin was well aware of that. "I also have a piece of jet in my pocket."

"Is that like a rocket in your pocket?" Ambrose laughed at his own joke.

"Ambrose." Dorcas frowned at him. "This is not a time for levity. Griffin has a serious problem."

"Oh, I agree. But I sometimes think it helps to inject a little humor, and when he talked about the jet in his pocket, I started thinking of the kind of jets that are planes, which made me think of rockets, so that's why I—"

"Right, dear." Dorcas patted him on the arm. "Why don't you go see the bartender and order us all another round of drinks? He's at the other end of the bar."

"Excellent idea. I'm on it." Then Ambrose leaned close to Griffin. "There's that other funny line—*Do you have a gun in your pocket, or are you just glad to—*"

"Ambrose. Drinks."

"Yes, my love. Right away." Ambrose turned and walked to the other end of the bar.

Dorcas shook her head as she gazed after him. "Wizards. Can't live with 'em, can't play strip poker without 'em." Then she turned back to Griffin with a gentle smile. "I know this isn't going to be easy."

"You mean the math or the self-control?"

"Mostly the self-control."

"I know, but this is important. And as for hanging out with Daisy, that part will be fun. I love that dog." He thought he might love the woman, too, but while he was under this spell, he couldn't know anything for sure.

"But in order to hang out with Daisy, you'll have to spend time with Lily and somehow resist the urge to go to bed with her."

Griffin rubbed the back of his neck. "I know. I've been trying to figure that one out. For example, if Lily and I go back to her place after the party tonight, the most I can expect is ten or fifteen minutes alone with Daisy, and that's assuming Lily agrees to let me walk her by myself."

"And then Daisy goes to sleep."

"Right. It's bedtime."

"Bedtime?" Lily walked up to them wearing the slinky black dress she'd arrived in. "Did I hear somebody mention bedtime? It's barely ten!"

Griffin could tell from the slight tremble in her voice that she was nervous. "Great job out there." He couldn't stop himself from giving her a hug, which meant he was surrounded by her warmth, her softness, her signature scent that drove him wild. He released her with difficulty. Oh, boy.

"Yes," Dorcas said. "It was a fantastic show. I loved the purple-and-silver dragon."

"Thank you." Lily looked pleased but still nervous. "It's an honor to perform for someone who could do far better."

Dorcas shook her head. "No, I couldn't. I'm not good with performing in front of crowds. You have a talent for drama that would probably serve you well if you decided to go on the commercial circuit."

"There's our girl!" Lionel, wearing his Peruvian headdress, hurried over. Simone followed close behind and the two of them spent the next several minutes fawning over their daughter and raving about the show.

Griffin watched Lily blossom in the midst of the praise and attention. Shortly afterward Jasper and Anica arrived to offer their congratulations, and Griffin edged away from the crowd surrounding Lily.

He still tingled from the brief contact of their hug. Reaching in his pocket he closed his fingers around the piece of jet. Already he could feel the crack widening, and if he spent much more time with Lily, the stone would probably break apart again.

Considering what he had to do regarding the spell, it made no sense for him to go home with her tonight. He'd get very little time alone with Daisy, and the way he felt now, he'd surely take Lily to bed. But he didn't know if he could walk out of this bar without her.

Chapter 26

The moment Lily had stepped out of the hall she'd spied Griffin talking to Dorcas and Ambrose. Her first impulse had been to rush over and interrupt whatever they were talking about. High on the adrenaline pumping through her system following her magic show, she wanted nothing more than to dance the night away with Griffin and then take him home to bed.

Dorcas could at this very second be putting a serious crimp in that plan. Lily might still be able to stop it though. She might still . . . and then, despite the adrenaline rush and her desire for Griffin, she paused.

For the first time she could remember while under the influence of doing magic, she paused to consider her course of action. She found it to be selfish and dangerously impulsive.

Despite the needs raging through her, she thought of Griffin and what he needed. He was looking for a way out, and the time had come to let go with as much grace as she could muster.

That would mean disguising how much she dreaded what was about to come. In binding him to her, in creating that forced proximity, she'd opened herself to loving him. And she realized the loving thing to do now was to back away.

And she would . . . when it became obvious that's

what he wanted. She'd temporarily arrested the course of her adrenaline surge, but it wasn't gone. Controlling it would be a constant battle.

She'd walked over to him, prepared for any reaction, and then he'd pulled her into that hug and all her good intentions had disappeared. She craved him all over again, wanted to make love to him for hours, even though she knew, she *knew* that was a bad idea.

As her family surrounded her with compliments and hugs, she tried to keep track of Griffin, who'd moved aside. She loved her family, but she wanted Griffin. She kept glancing his way but never seemed to catch his eye.

And then she did. His gaze locked with hers and no one else mattered. Anica and her mother were in the middle of a discussion about whether Lily should hire an agent and pursue bookings as a magician. Her father and Jasper were arguing about the best venue for her next performance.

With a murmured excuse she extricated herself from the group and walked over to Griffin.

His hazel eyes were filled with longing as he reached for her. "Dance with me."

"Okay." Technically speaking, they weren't even on the dance floor, but she didn't care. Technically speaking, they weren't dancing, either.

He wrapped his arms around her waist and she wound hers around his neck. Pressed together, gazing into each other's eyes, they swayed to the beat of the music. His body heat called to her as memories of all they'd shared swirled around them.

His grip tightened and desire burned in his eyes. "I need you so much."

At that moment she knew that the spell was more powerful than she'd ever imagined it could be. He would beg her to take him home with her tonight and make love to him all night long. Even though Dorcas and Ambrose surely had given him instructions for breaking the spell, he wouldn't be able to do it because he wanted her so fiercely. If she chose, she could have Griffin as her love slave forever.

Still on her adrenaline high, she struggled with her conscience. Ah, he was so warm. And she was so willing. And this was so wrong.

Sick with disappointment, her heart aching, she stepped out of his arms and backed away. "Griffin, it's time . . ." The words wouldn't come. She had to force them out one by one. "For you . . . to go . . . home."

He looked confused, as if he'd lost his place in the middle of a book. "But I planned to stay until you were ready to leave. We'll leave together."

"No. You need to go now. You have to work tomorrow." She reached for the cell phone clipped to his belt and neatly unfastened it.

He still looked disoriented, as if trying to remember what was supposed to happen next. "What are you doing?"

"I'm calling you a cab." She was sure he'd forgotten whatever plan he'd had. She backed away from him as she flipped open the phone.

His gaze cleared, became more focused. "Oh, for Pete's sake. I don't need a cab. Give me that." He made a grab for the phone.

"For *your* sake, I'm not doing that." Dancing out of reach, she glanced up at the revolving mirrored ball and muttered a quick incantation. *"Mirror flashing to the max, stop this human in his tracks."*

Just like that, Griffin could no longer move his feet. His eyes narrowed. "Lily, damn it, what did you just do to me?"

"I'm keeping you from making a mistake." She found the cab company among his stored numbers and quickly arranged for a cab to come to the Bubbling Cauldron. Fortunately the dispatcher said a taxi was parked a mere block away.

He watched her, disbelief shining in his eyes. "You're actually sending me home?"

"Yes."

He lowered his voice. "But you want me. I know you do. When we were dancing you melted against me. I know you, Lily. I can tell when all you really want is—"

"Never mind that, Griffin." Sad to say, he probably could tell exactly what she wanted. He'd learned her responses well in the past few days. "It doesn't matter."

"The hell it doesn't!"

Lily became aware of her parents watching the little drama, along with Anica and Jasper. Obviously they hadn't decided whether to become involved, but that indecision wouldn't last long. She'd have to work fast.

His voice rumbled with anger. "And what if I don't want to take this cab you've called? What will you do to me then?"

"Take the cab, Griffin. Once you're in it, you'll remember that's what you intended to do in the first place." Gazing upward again, she drew in a quick breath. *"Mirrored ball, release his feet, send him out his cab to meet."*

Neither of her incantations was particularly strong. She'd linked each one to the mirrored ball, which retained traces of magic from being repaired earlier in the day. Such a spell could work only if the subject had an inclination to do the thing the magical person had suggested.

She was counting on the urge that had made him consult with Dorcas and Ambrose and the plans he'd made as a result. Those plans combined with her spell could send him out the door.

He gazed at her and finally spoke softly in surrender. "All right, Lily. Make my apologies to your family." Then he turned and left the bar.

The magic-induced adrenaline rushed through her

again, and she gripped the back of a nearby chair to keep herself from running after him.

"Lily?" Her father must have been designated as the emissary. He walked over, his Peruvian headdress bobbing, his forehead wrinkled with concern. "What's the problem?"

If you only knew, Dad. But she didn't intend to unburden herself now, and probably never would. "Nothing," she said. "Griffin just needs to get home. He has to be up bright and early for work."

Her father didn't look convinced. "I can understand that, but I thought the guy had better manners. He didn't even come over to say good-bye."

"He asked me to do that for him." She turned and gave her dad a hug. He smelled like incense, which probably came from the ceremonial headdress. "Don't blame him for leaving abruptly. He and I have ... a few issues."

"I was afraid of that." Her father sighed and hugged her back. "It's not my headdress that bothers him, is it?"

"No, certainly not! It's a fine headdress."

Her father smiled. "It is, isn't it? Your mother says I look like an Incan god."

"You most definitely do."

"I hope he's not upset about the magic."

She was touched by how much her father wanted Griffin to approve of them. "Not magic in general." Her magic, however, the magic she'd foisted on him—now *that* he wasn't so crazy about.

"Well, that's something, at least." He pierced her with his dark-eyed gaze. "And he knows you're a witch, right?"

"Oh yes. He definitely knows." She'd now placed spells on him right in front of his face. He couldn't doubt her magical powers at this point.

"I hope you can work out your problems with him,

Lil. I always wanted you girls to end up with wizards, but now that I've met Jasper and Griffin, I'm becoming a fan of integration."

If she hadn't been so heartsick, she might have smiled at that. For all his virtues, her dad had been prejudiced against nonmagical people for years. She was happy to see him giving up his long-held belief that magical people were somehow superior.

She responded with forced gaiety. "Let's drink to integration, then! Where's your drink, Dad?"

"Your mother's holding it. I was sent over to—"

"I know. And I seem to have misplaced my drink, too. Let's go find ourselves some full glasses. I don't know about you, but I'm ready to party."

"Attagirl." His expression was approving. "I can always count on you to put a little life into the proceedings. By the way, your friend who runs that Hangout place, the café and late-night coffee shop, was asking me where you were. I guess he came in late."

She'd forgotten all about inviting Brad. It was just as well that he'd missed the magic show, because he didn't need any more reason to be fascinated by her. She could dance a few fast dances with him, though, and work out some of her adrenaline rush.

"I'll find him in a minute," she said to her dad. "First we need to locate our drinks!"

Her father laughed. "You bet we do, party girl."

Arms around each other, they returned to her family, where her father assured everyone things would work out between Lily and Griffin, and now it was time to make this old bar rock. Lily backed him up with an enthusiasm that she didn't feel.

Her mother beamed at them both. "I think this is the perfect time to open the gifts!" She put an arm around Lily and leaned close, laughter in her voice. "Aren't you dying to see Fred and Janet's reaction to the fertility symbol?"

"Mom, it's going to be worth the price of admission." Lily winked at her mother. "I can hardly wait."

She was beginning to understand her role in this family, which was to be the life of the party. By Hera, that's exactly what she would be, even when her heart was breaking.

Lily was right. Once Griffin moved out of her orbit he remembered the plan. He took Dorcas's calculations out of his pocket and studied them.

In order to figure out how much time he should spend alone with Daisy, he'd have to recall every sexual experience he'd had with Lily and he'd have to estimate the amount of time they'd spent on it. The calculations were daunting enough, but the emotional toll would be worse as he relived each of those scorching sexual encounters.

If he tried to do that alone he'd crash and burn. He'd be over at her apartment, ringing her doorbell like a maniac and begging to be let in. Not dignified. He speed-dialed Kevin.

As Kevin's phone rang, Griffin glanced at his watch. Ten twenty on a Sunday night. Kevin could be sleeping already.

But his buddy answered on the second ring and sounded wide awake. "So how's the stone working? Are you still at the engagement party? What's—"

"I'm on my way home from the party, but I have a spell-breaking assignment from a certified witch and wizard."

"Cool."

"It, uh, involves doing some calculations. I could use some help." Griffin decided not to mention what the calculations would involve.

"I'm all over that, buddy. Direct that cab straight to the home of the Kev-man."

"Thanks." Griffin felt the tension in his shoulders relax. "I'll be there in about five minutes."

"Is this a beer occasion or a caffeinated occasion?"

Griffin thought about that. "You got both?"

"Always. I just wondered whether to pop the top on the brewskies or put on the coffee."

"Let's start with the coffee. We may have to move to the beer before we're done, but we'll start with a couple of cups of coffee."

Kevin sounded excited. "Should I call Miles? I think he's still hanging out with the natural foods clerk, but I could call him. He helped on Friday, and he might want to be in on this."

"Sure. I can use all the help I can get."

Thirty minutes later the three of them sat at Kevin's small dinette table, each with a steaming mug of coffee, a yellow legal pad, and a pen with BIDDLE, RYERSON & THATCHER printed on the barrel.

Miles tapped his pen on his legal pad. "How many minutes are we giving to that first blow job?"

Griffin ran his fingers through his hair and tried to think of this as a legal case. "Uh . . . maybe fifteen, maybe a little longer."

"Can't we make it ten?" Kevin punched in numbers on a calculator. "We have guidelines for ten, but not more than that, unless we start going into the addendums, which are way complicated. I don't think this Lowell chick figured on a blow job taking more than ten minutes."

Miles blew out a breath and threw his pen down. "I'm jealous as hell. Fifteen minutes, maybe longer? I'm dating a health food nut, for Christ's sake, and I can't get more than ten out of her. Who wants a beer?"

"Me." Griffin put down his pen.

"I could tell," Miles said. "You're getting a crazed look in your eye."

"I'll get it," Kevin said.

Griffin scrubbed a hand over his face. "This is tough. No matter how much I try to think of this in clinical terms, just talking about it makes me want to head straight to her apartment."

"Hell, it makes me want to head straight back to my health food chick." Miles sighed. "But I won't. I'll stay here and help." He glanced over at Griffin. "Want me to tie you to the mast?"

"Excuse me?" Kevin returned, open beer bottles dangling from his spread fingers. "Are we taking this project out on the lake?"

"Nah." Miles picked up one of the bottles Kevin set on the table and took a swig. "I was thinking about that Ulysses story we had to read in humanities, where the guy had to be tied to the mast so he wouldn't be tempted by the Sirens." He gestured with the bottle. "I thought we needed a little culture around here."

Kevin pulled out his chair and sat. "We need a plan for Griff, is what we need. He'll have to have a fair bit of uninterrupted time with Daisy when Lily's not around to sabotage the program. Maybe while she's at work tomorrow."

Griffin had already thought of that. "She doesn't work tomorrow. She has Sundays and Mondays off. There's no way I can be alone with Daisy tomorrow."

Kevin exchanged a look with Miles. "I'm feeling a guys' night out coming on. We can monitor you at work, but after work anything could happen."

Miles nodded. "Strip club."

"Nope." Kevin shook his head. "Too close to home for Griff. We don't want him getting worked up. The Cubs are away, but I think the White Sox have a night game. We'll do that."

All that time without seeing Lily. It stretched ahead of Griffin like the Sahara—featureless and frightening. "This feels like detox."

"That's because it is like detox," Kevin said. "We'll get you through until Tuesday. Assuming we do that successfully and there are no incidents—"

"Aka sexual encounters," Miles added helpfully.

"I know what he meant." Griffin was feeling more miserable by the second. "I'm going cold turkey."

"For your own good," Kevin reminded him. "You'll thank us."

"I'm already thanking you." Griffin took a swallow of his beer. "But that doesn't mean I'm going to enjoy this."

Kevin made a note on his legal pad. "Okay. Tuesday you can leave the office early so you'll be at Lily's right after she goes to work. If you spend her entire eight-hour shift hanging out with Daisy, you *might* break the spell."

"Maybe." Miles looked over his figures. "Obviously, some of these estimates could be off, but damn, you had a lot of sex in a very short time."

"Yeah." Griffin was already mourning the loss of it. "What if the spell made me more studly than I really am? What if after I break it, I can't keep up the pace?"

"I dunno." Miles took another swig of his beer. "Were you any good before?"

That cracked Kevin up. "How do you expect him to answer, moron? You think he's going to admit that he wasn't?"

Miles gazed at Griffin across the table. "I think you would, Griff. You're not hung up on your rep like some guys in this room."

Kevin continued to chuckle. "Speak for yourself, Miles."

"At least I admit it." Miles turned his attention back to Griffin. "So, were you any good in bed before Lily zapped you?"

"I was okay, I guess. Nobody ever complained. But with Lily, it was like ... like going from analog TV to high-def with Blu-ray."

"Whoa." Miles reared back in his seat. "I need me some of that potion."

Kevin shook his head. "No, you don't, Miles. It might sound great, until you think about the total loss of control over your life."

"Hey, it might be worth it!"

"It almost was," Griffin said. "Believe me, it almost was."

Chapter 27

Lily was extremely put out with her dog. She'd taken Daisy to the dog park and tried several times to coax her to play the way she had with Griffin, but Daisy refused. Instead she flopped down on the grass with her head on her paws, looking as depressed as Lily felt.

Crouching down next to Daisy, Lily stared into the dog's expressive brown eyes. "Hey, Daisy, don't you know dogs are supposed to be cheerful, bouncy, and generally the sort of animal you want around to improve your mood and make you laugh?"

Daisy let out a little doggie sigh but didn't change position.

"At this rate I might have to get you some doggie Prozac."

Dogs weren't supposed to be capable of rolling their eyes, and yet that's exactly what Daisy did.

Lily blew out a breath in surrender and stood. "Okay, babe. You can do this kind of thing at home. We don't have to be down here at the dog park for you to lie around moping."

"Is she feeling okay?" A guy in jeans and a sweatshirt came over, a standard poodle at his heels.

Lily vaguely realized he'd been at the park when she and Daisy had arrived, but she hadn't paid much attention to him. She was in her own fog, too. But she should at least be polite and answer a well-meant question from another dog lover.

"I think she's fine," she said. "All her vitals are good, and she's eating normally. She's used to having a certain person around, and apparently she misses him a lot."

"The divorce lawyer."

Lily did a double-take. "You know Griffin?"

"Not really. We met briefly when he brought Daisy to the park a few days ago. I remembered Daisy because she's so intelligent and . . . I don't know how to put it . . . sensitive, I guess."

"Maybe too sensitive." Lily shook her head. "I didn't think having Griffin gone would bother her this much, but she's been in a mood ever since last night."

"So he's on a trip of some kind?"

Lily finally tuned in to what she usually noticed right away. The guy was interested in her. Because she was here without Griffin and because Griffin seemed to be gone somewhere, the guy wanted to know more, like whether Griffin would be coming back or if the field was clear.

"He, um, has some things to take care of." That sounded lame, exactly as if they'd broken up. She didn't know if they were broken up or not, but Griffin hadn't contacted her since the party.

"Well, seeing as how your dog doesn't want to play, and Max doesn't have the cocker spaniel around this morning, how about we walk them over to the nearest Starbucks?"

"Thanks, anyway." She smiled to take the sting out of the rejection.

"So, you and the lawyer are involved, after all."

"Yes." Or at least she was. The idea of going for coffee with someone other than Griffin held absolutely no appeal. She'd forced herself to party hearty last night, and then she'd had to fend off Brad toward the end. Apparently her heart belonged to a man who might or might not want it. The jury was still out on that.

"Let me know if anything changes. The name's Mitch Adams."

Lily knew she was supposed to introduce herself after that, but she didn't. "See you."

The guy inclined his head, as if he'd gotten the message. With a wave he and his poodle left the dog park.

Lily looked at Daisy, who continued to act as if she'd lost her best friend. "I didn't want to exchange names with that guy, but you don't have any reason not to sniff that poodle. Isn't that what dogs are supposed to do?"

Daisy gave her a glance that clearly said some things were beneath her.

"We might as well head on home, then." Lily reached down and snapped the leash onto Daisy's collar. "This dog park has memories for me, too, you know. I'm not having a picnic with this situation, either. Come on. Haul yourself up."

Daisy stood and walked toward the gate, but there was no bounce in her step. Once Lily got her back to the apartment, she decided to leave her there and go over to Anica's coffee shop, Wicked Brew. Hanging around with Daisy was only making her feel worse.

She could go see her folks, but that wouldn't help, either. They'd only ask about Griffin, and because they didn't know the whole story she'd have to skirt the subject as best she could. Anica was the only person who knew the truth and would understand what she was going through, and now that the engagement party was over, Lily didn't feel so guilty unloading on her.

She took the bus over to Anica's shop and tried not to think of the times she'd ridden the bus with Griffin. They'd created some potent memories, and now she had to live with them. She'd worn a favorite pair of red high-heeled boots today along with a red blouse and denim short-shorts.

The effort seemed wasted, but she was determined not to look as bad as she felt. Although she checked her cell phone constantly, it remained silent. Griffin was keeping his distance, probably because he was in the process of breaking the spell.

Wicked Brew was busy, and Anica was behind the counter helping her two employees keep up with the orders. Lily stood in line and waited her turn while trying not to fidget. By the time she got to the counter she discovered that she'd managed to knot the straps of her backpack together so that she couldn't get to her money.

Anica waved away her promises to pay later for the triple-shot espresso. "It's on the house. The rush should be over in a few minutes, and then I can come over and talk to you."

"Thanks. I'd appreciate that." Lily felt better just being in the cheerful bustle of Wicked Brew. Office buildings, including the one where Jasper worked, were a short block away, and Anica catered to that crowd by opening early and closing in the late afternoon and on weekends.

She used magic to keep the white Formica tables and the black-and-white checkered tile spotless. She always placed red carnations in bud vases on every table, and made sure the coffee was some of the best in town. Lily wished she lived a little closer to Wicked Brew, but there hadn't been any apartments available in that neighborhood when she'd needed one.

Now she was settled in a spot she liked, or at least she had liked it until she'd brought Griffin into the mix. Now she could barely stand to be in the apartment, because Griffin wasn't there and might never be there again.

Anica called her name for the coffee drink, and Lily carried it over to one of the few vacant tables in the place. Fortunately the nice weather meant Anica could set some tables and chairs out in front. Everywhere Lily looked, people were laughing and smiling, enjoying the lovely spring morning.

Anica was probably happy, too, on the heels of her rousing engagement party. Lily felt guilty for coming into such a positive environment, trailing black ribbons of depression.

The triple-shot espresso helped. A few sips of that and she began feeling loads better. Maybe if she kept herself jacked up on coffee for the next few days, she'd barely notice that she wanted to crawl into a drainage pipe and never come out.

Anica hurried over and sat down, wiping her hands on a paper towel. "You look like crap."

"I know." She started to get up. "I didn't mean to come here and bring you down. I'll just take my coffee and—"

"Hey, hey." Anica grabbed her arm and urged her back to her seat. "I didn't mean to drive you off. But judging from those dark circles under your eyes, I'd say you haven't slept much."

Lily allowed herself to be coaxed back into her seat. "Stupid concealer is no good. I should have taken time to brew up an under-eye potion, but all I could think of was coming over to see you."

"Poor Lily." Anica stroked her arm. "You haven't heard from him."

Lily shook her head. "How about the Lowells? Have they called?"

"No, and just for the record, I have no idea what they told him. They never divulge that kind of information."

"But they told him something." Lily sipped her coffee drink. "I'm sure of that."

"Oh, I'm sure they did, too. The very fact that he's changed his pattern and is staying away is proof."

Lily rotated her coffee cup between her palms, mixing the contents some more, although they didn't really need it. "I've thought about trying to take Chad's shift tonight, in case Griffin and his friends come in."

"Don't do it. He'd know why you did, and you don't want to signal that you're needy."

"But I *am* needy!" Lily heard the unattractive whine in her voice and grimaced. "Forget I said that."

"Lil, what caused him to leave last night?"

Lily described the circumstances, and when she was finished, Anica reached over and stroked her cheek.

"I'm so sorry for what you're going through, but you should be proud. You beat back that adrenaline rush and did the right thing."

"It may be the right thing, but it feels like doggie do. And that's the other thing. Daisy, the turncoat, is in mourning because Griffin's not there. Isn't she supposed to be offering me comfort?"

Anica took a deep breath. "Normally, yeah. But you used her to create the elixir, so there's probably a strong bond between them now. She might really need him around."

"Well, that's just great. Griffin's definitely not around, and if he's this good at staying away, he might not ever be around again. What am I supposed to do about Daisy?"

"I don't know, Lil. You could ask Dorcas and Ambrose."

"No, thank you very much, but I think I'll forgo that option. I'll let Griffin be the contact point there." She glanced across the table at her sister. "Aren't they supposed to be matchmakers?"

"That's one of the things they do. They certainly helped Jasper and me."

"So far all they've done for me and Griffin is drive us farther apart." She met Anica's sympathetic gaze. "But I have to thank you, sis, for not saying *I told you so.* You could say it and nobody would blame you."

Anica gazed at her, a hint of humor in her blue eyes. "Want me to say it and fulfill my job as a big sister?"

"Zeus's balls, no! In fact, let's talk about you. My life

is too depressing. How are Fred and Janet, your soon-to-be in-laws?"

Anica made a face. "They flew out of O'Hare this morning, and I swear, a big black cloud moved away from the sun the minute their plane took off."

"I'm afraid they didn't appreciate Mom's fertility symbol gift."

"And the more they criticized it, the more I came to love it, which is not a good sign." Anica sighed. "I should try harder to like them, but they are beyond dull, and they have such a negative attitude toward everything. I'm sure the hotel was delighted to get rid of them."

"Are they going to sue? They tried to rope Griffin into helping them do that." Lily was proud of herself for saying Griffin's name without breaking into tears.

"I'm not sure if they'll sue or not. I think that's still on the table. The only good news is that they never suspected that your magic show was real, because they wouldn't dream such things could happen. The bad news is that their lack of imagination is really depressing."

"Looking forward to that relationship, are you?"

Anica groaned. "I'd rather take a sharp stick in the eye than deal with them, and yet they're Jasper's parents, so what am I going to do?"

"Give them an imagination elixir so they'll become more interesting?"

"That's not even funny."

"Yes, it is." Lily discovered that making Anica feel better buoyed her spirits more than the triple espresso. "You're trying not to laugh." She pointed a finger at her sister. "See, you think it's funny. You're already planning how you're going to slip an elixir in their decaf or their diet ginger ale."

Anica covered her mouth but the giggles escaped, anyway. "That would be a kick. Hera's hickeys, I'm tempted."

"I'll help. We can test whether it's working by bringing out the fertility symbol to see if their reaction improves."

"And if they're still horrified by that gigantic penis, we'll keep dosing them with the elixir until they covet the fertility symbol for their mantel at home." Anica's cheeks were pink with laughter. "Tell you what. We'll see how bad things get between now and the wedding."

"Which is a mere four weeks away."

Anica looked heavenward. "Don't remind me."

"Too late. I just did."

"And I have *so* much to do before then."

"Put me to work," Lily said. "I have a wand and I know how to use it. Besides, as it turns out, I'll probably have tons of free time."

Without constant surveillance from Kevin and Miles, Griffin wouldn't have made it through until Tuesday afternoon. They checked on him at work all day Monday, took him to the ballgame Monday night, and camped out on his floor after the game. Without them he would have given in to the overwhelming urge to see Lily.

But with such dedication to the cause, he felt honor-bound to be strong. They wanted to come with him to Lily's when he was ready to go over late Tuesday afternoon, but Dorcas had been very clear. He had to spend time alone with Daisy.

"Call us if you start to weaken," Kevin said as Griffin left the office at four. Miles had a client and couldn't be part of the bon voyage party. "Think of us as your help line. We'll talk you down."

"I can handle this," Griffin assured him. "I can already tell the spell isn't as strong, just because I've stayed away from her."

Kevin put a hand on his shoulder. "Yeah, but one romp on that innerspring and all our hard work will be for nothing."

"She'll be at work."

"You'd better hope she's at work. She could've called in sick." Kevin studied him. "I'm not heartened by your look of excitement when I mentioned that possibility."

Instantly Griffin wiped the smile of anticipation from his face. His friends had put themselves through plenty of inconvenience so that he could successfully break this spell. Kevin was right. A slip-up now would cancel that noble effort. He couldn't do that to Miles and Kevin.

"I'll do what needs to be done." He met Kevin's gaze with as much confidence as he could muster. "You can count on that."

"I am counting on that. I want my buddy back, the one who was in charge of his own destiny."

"Right." Making sure Lily's key was tucked in his pocket next to the jet stone, he walked out of the office. "See ya," he called back to Kevin.

"Next time we meet, you'll be a free man!" Kevin called after him.

Griffin kept that thought foremost in his mind as he took a cab over to Lily's apartment. On the climb up three flights, his heart was pounding, and not from the physical exertion. He wondered if Kevin could be right and she'd called in sick.

He was supposed to hope that she hadn't. He was supposed to be praying for an apartment that contained only a dog—a dog he needed to break the spell Lily had cast over him. But if she was there for some reason, if he could see her for only a few minutes, if he could only kiss her . . .

Fitting the key in the lock, he opened the door and knew immediately that Lily wasn't there. But Daisy was, and she danced and carried on as if he'd been gone a week. It felt like a week, maybe two.

Disappointment at Lily's absence made his knees buckle and he dropped to the floor and wrapped his arms around Daisy. "I need her so much," he said, his voice choked with emotion. "Daisy, I really, really need her."

But then, as he clung to the dog, a strange thing began to happen. He could feel the debilitating urge to be with Lily start to ease. Although he still longed for her to come through the door, he wasn't quite as desperate for that to happen.

His cell phone, which he'd clipped to his belt, sounded Kevin's ring tone. Releasing Daisy, Griffin unclipped the phone and answered it. "I'm here."

"Is she?"

"No."

"That's good, Griff. That's really, really good. I was scared that she'd be there, and you're still a little shaky."

"Not so much now that I'm with the dog." Griffin stood and looked around the apartment. First he'd take Daisy on a long walk that would include the dog park. Then they might watch some TV together. For the first time since Lily had given him the elixir, he had hope that he could break the spell. "Yeah," he said to Kevin. "This is going to be okay."

Chapter 28

When Kevin and Miles walked into the Bubbling Cauldron at happy hour without Griffin, Lily was disappointed but not surprised. She was dying for information about him, but she had to play it cool and not let her anxiety show.

She walked over to their table, as always. "Hey, guys! You seem to be missing someone tonight."

Kevin shrugged. "You know that guy. He has a million irons in the fire. He wasn't available to drink with the peons."

"Yeah," Miles said. "But we weren't about to miss happy hour on account of him being too busy. So here we are."

"Well, that's great." Lily gave them her best bartender smile. "What will you have?"

"I'm going to start out with a draft," Kevin said. "I'm in the mood for some onion rings, too. It's been a long week."

Lily gazed at him. "It's only Tuesday."

"You're kidding! It feels like Friday already."

Lily knew exactly what Kevin meant. Monday had been the longest day of her life, and Tuesday had dragged by, too, until she'd come to work. Then she'd spent every spare moment staring at the door to see if Griffin might show up.

Well, he hadn't, and she would love to know where he was. She didn't think these guys were going to tell her. "Miles, what about you? What can I get for you?"

"I'll take a draft, too," he said. "And some garlic fries. I'm not likely to be kissing anyone tonight, so I might as well indulge myself."

"Excellent. Coming right up, gentlemen." She had the ignoble thought that if they'd switch to hard liquor, she could double up the shots and maybe loosen their tongues. But as long as they stuck with beer, she couldn't do anything except drop broad hints.

"I hope Griffin's not still hungover from the engagement party on Sunday night," she said about two hours later as she delivered the third round of beer and two hot pastrami sandwiches.

"Nope," Kevin said. "He's arrived at the office right on time both mornings."

Lily balanced the tray on her hip. "I suppose he had a meeting with a client that ran late."

"Not exactly." Miles wrapped his hands around half of his pastrami sandwich. "But he did have some business to take care of." He bit into the fragrant sandwich.

"He's dedicated, all right," Lily said.

Kevin nodded. "One of the most dedicated lawyers I know. But I guess we're all kind of like that. I mean, Miles and me, we'd do about anything for that guy."

"It's nice to have friends like that. Well, let me know if you need anything else."

As she walked back to the bar a thought hit her. Miles and Kevin were spending more time than usual in the bar tonight, and yet they didn't have their good buddy here with them. Why were they staying so long? She could only think of one reason. They were here to keep an eye on her, in case she decided to go somewhere. And where would she go that might somehow be connected with Griffin, that might somehow endanger whatever plan was in place?

Her own apartment.

It made perfect sense. Griffin would want to stay away from her when there was any chance they'd end up in bed together. But now when she was at work, he could set up whatever counterspell Dorcas and Ambrose had suggested. He had a key.

While she was willing to allow him some leeway in his attempts to break the spell, she wasn't comfortable with him invading her space to do it. She had some special things there, like her crystal ball, her wands, her books, her herbs. Surely Dorcas and Ambrose wouldn't recommend that he destroy or steal any of those things, but she didn't know them well. She couldn't be absolutely sure the counterspell wouldn't involve messing with her stuff.

She might be able to get Sherman to cover for her while she went home to check on things, but then Kevin and Miles would probably alert Griffin with a call to his cell. For now she'd have to wait them out and hope they weren't planning to stay until the end of her shift.

An hour later, they finally settled their bill and left. Business had slowed down, so Sherman was willing to hold the fort for an hour so she could run home. She made an excuse that Daisy hadn't been feeling well, which was true.

She was set to head out the front door when she paused. What if Kevin and Miles had moved their surveillance operation to the restaurant and bar across the street? That place had window tables with a good view of the Bubbling Cauldron.

She waited until Sherman was too busy to notice before ducking into the hallway and going out the back door into the alley. Better safe than sorry.

On the bus ride home, she tried to talk herself out of this bout of paranoia. She'd probably get home and discover nothing but a morose Daisy waiting for her. Just because Griffin wasn't at the Bubbling Cauldron didn't

mean he was skulking around her apartment. Maybe
he'd finally decided to make good on that dinner invitation to Debbie.

Now, there was an unhelpful thought, imagining Griffin with another woman. Lily ground a little enamel off
her back molars thinking about it. Griffin had every
right to date someone else, of course. Everything he'd
said to her had been under the spell, so it didn't count.

Sad to say, she hadn't convinced her heart that his
devotion was bogus. Her heart wanted to believe that
Griffin was committed to her and her alone. She'd have
to have another stern conversation with her silly heart.

A million butterflies had taken up residence in her
tummy by the time she stepped off the bus at her stop.
Despite all her arguments with herself, she believed that
Griffin would be in her apartment when she opened the
door. She could weave a fantasy and pretend that he'd
come back because he wanted to welcome her home at
the end of her shift. But she didn't think that was his
reason.

She climbed the stairs softly, not wanting to announce
herself. By the time she reached her door her heartbeat
thrummed in her ears, making it hard to hear.

But even so, a familiar sound filtered through the
door. Her TV was on.

She supposed Daisy was capable of pushing the button on the remote, but Daisy had never shown the slightest interest in TV. That left Griffin as the obvious TV
watcher. Maybe he really had decided to hang out here
and wait for her to come home. Maybe he'd been unsuccessful at breaking the spell and was ready to spend
another night in her bed.

Although she shouldn't be happy about that possibility, she was. A girl could only be so noble before crack-
ing, and without Griffin in her life she was coming apart.
She could be forgiven for wanting one more night in his
arms.

Her hands shook as she fit the key in the lock. With the TV on, Griffin probably wouldn't hear her doing it. Taking a deep breath, she opened the door.

Griffin's expression told her he hadn't expected to see her. There was no smile of welcome, only shock that they were face-to-face. Daisy simply looked guilty. She was sprawled on the couch, a place Lily didn't allow her to be, with her head in Griffin's lap.

Lifting her head, she gazed at Lily as if trying to find out if she was in big trouble.

"It's okay, Daisy," Lily said.

With that reassurance, the dog climbed down and came over, tail wagging, to greet her. Lily reached down to pet her dog, but her gaze never left Griffin's.

Slowly he got to his feet. "Why did you come home? Are you sick?"

Heartsick. "I had a feeling that you'd be here." She searched his eyes for any sign of impending lust and found none. *None.* Her stomach began to churn. Maybe he'd done it. Maybe he'd broken the spell.

She glanced around, checking that her crystal ball was in its place and her books hadn't been disturbed. Everything seemed perfectly normal, exactly as she'd left it, except that Daisy was much happier than she'd been when Lily had gone to work. But after greeting Lily, Daisy moved away and returned to Griffin, looking up at him in adoration.

The realization of what had happened slammed into Lily, leaving her feeling dazed and disoriented. He'd broken the spell. That much was obvious from his manner, but somehow in the process he'd won Daisy's allegiance. She was his dog now.

Lily took a long, quivering breath. "How did you do it?"

"Until you walked in the door, I wasn't sure I had. But I'm standing here looking at you, and that manic urge to grab you is gone." His words were laced with wonder and, unmistakably, relief.

Deep sorrow threatened to swamp her. So it was over. Really over.

"All I had to do was spend time alone with Daisy." He seemed stunned by that fact. "Amazing. That was the whole deal. I've been with her ever since you left for work."

Daisy shoved her nose into the palm of his hand, and he scratched behind her ears while he continued to stare at Lily, as if expecting the spell to come back at any moment. "I guess it really worked."

"Apparently." She couldn't help herself. She had to ask. "Do you have . . . any feelings for me at all?"

"I'm still—" He cleared his throat. "Still processing everything." He hesitated. "But now that you mention it, now that the shock of seeing you is fading, yeah, I have feelings for you." He clenched his fists and heat filled his gaze, but it was the heat of anger, not desire. "What the hell did you think you were doing? What gave you the right to put something in my drink like that?"

"I . . ." She swallowed the lump forming in her throat. She was determined not to cry. "I was wrong."

"No shit you were wrong!" His chest heaved. "You messed with me, Lily, big-time!"

"I did, and I'm sorry, Griffin."

"Well, *sorry* doesn't cut it." He grabbed a light jacket he'd left on the arm of the couch. "I'd better get out of here before I do or say something I'll regret."

Daisy whined and danced at his side.

"No, Daisy. You can't come." He started toward the door.

Daisy ran to the door and placed herself next to it.

"No, Daisy." Griffin's voice sounded rusty. "You're not going."

Daisy pawed gently at his leg, her tail swishing against the carpet.

Griffin sighed. "Daisy, move away from the door. You can't come with me."

Daisy's tail slowly stopped wagging. Then she looked at Lily and the plea in her eyes was impossible to ignore.

"Yes, she can." Although Lily's throat was tight with grief, she managed to get the rest out. "Take her, Griffin. She's not happy with me anymore. She wants to be with you."

He scowled at her. "If you think giving me your dog is going to make up for—"

"No! This has nothing to do with us. It's for her! Can't you see how she adores you? If you leave her here, you'll break her heart." Since Lily's was already broken, the least she could do was try to save Daisy's from complete destruction.

Griffin gazed at the dog, and his expression softened. He crouched down in front of her. "Hey, Daisy. Want to come home with me?"

Daisy whined and her tail started up again. Leaning closer, she licked his face.

Lily figured she had about another five seconds before she completely lost it. "Just go," she murmured. "Take her leash and go." Then she turned and fled into the bedroom, closing the door behind her.

Leaning against it, she allowed the tears to slide silently down her cheeks, but she pushed her fist against her mouth to stifle the sobs. She heard the front door open and close.

Unable to stand it, she wrenched open the bedroom door to see whether Daisy was still there. Griffin was gone, and so was Daisy. She was utterly—and deservedly—alone.

Griffin was furious for days, but having the dog around helped. He located a dog park near his apartment and whenever he wasn't working, he was romping in the park with Daisy. Fresh air and exercise did wonders to clear away the rage he felt whenever he thought about what Lily had done.

While under the spell he'd looked for ways to excuse her behavior, but now that he was free of that magical connection, he'd decided there was no valid excuse. She'd screwed up, and she deserved every bit of his anger.

But the more he played with Daisy, the less he could hold on to that anger. After all, Daisy had been part of some fun times with Lily. He tried to forget about that, wipe the slate clean and be with Daisy without thinking about Lily. Turned out he couldn't.

Kevin and Miles were convinced she'd given him the dog on purpose, to manipulate the situation so he'd be forced to think about her, about going back to her. They thought it had been a last-ditch effort to save the relationship.

Griffin didn't think so. Daisy had been the one who'd indicated her desire to go with him. True, Lily could have refused, but Daisy had been pretty damned touching, with her big sad eyes. Griffin wondered more than once whether Lily regretted the impulse of giving him the dog.

That wasn't all he wondered about, either. As the days went by, he wondered how she was doing—if she was sad, lonely, sexually frustrated. Kevin and Miles had suggested finding a different happy hour spot, which made sense. The new place had a guy behind the bar, and the setup felt strange after Griffin had become so used to the Bubbling Cauldron. To Lily. He never stayed long.

Besides, he had Daisy to think of. He'd arranged for a dog walker to take her out around noon on weekdays so she wouldn't be desperate for his return. Even so, every time he came home she greeted him as if he'd been on a monthlong trip to China. He loved that. Lily must have loved it, too, and now that comfort had been taken away.

But he didn't feel guilty. She'd brought it on herself. That didn't keep him from feeling sad, though. There was no magic spell forcing him to stick to Lily like glue, but . . . he missed her.

A week after the confrontation in Lily's apartment, Kevin walked into Griffin's office, waving baseball tickets. Kevin and Miles seemed determined to take Griffin's mind off Lily one way or the other. They'd put him through a round of sporting events, either live or on Kevin's plasma TV. Over the weekend they'd rented a sailboat and taken it out on the lake. They'd played tennis and eighteen holes of golf.

Kevin slapped the tickets onto Griffin's desk. "Tomorrow night, right behind home plate."

Griffin picked up the tickets. "You know, I appreciate what you and Miles are doing."

"What are we doing? Having a good time now that the weather's nice, that's all we're doing. Last spring we promised ourselves we'd get out more, so this spring we're following through for once. Simple as that."

"It's not as simple as that. You're keeping me occupied so I won't miss Lily."

Kevin shrugged. "That might be part of it, but—"

"I still miss her, Kev."

"Sure you do. That's natural. It'll pass, especially—" He glanced out the door to make sure no one was listening. "Especially now that you've broken the spell she put on you. That was some weird shit, man. You need to give yourself time to get over something like that."

"I was thinking that maybe . . . maybe if I took her out to dinner, then—"

"Nix to that noise! Are you insane? She could have a vial of something in her purse. You turn your head and whammo, she dumps it in your wine. She is a *witch*, buddy boy. We got you out of that mess, and we don't need you tempting fate by going anywhere near that chick."

Griffin thought about the magic show Lily had put on

for the engagement party. "She's not just a witch. She's an extremely talented one."

"My point exactly! She could tie you up again without you even knowing it. You listen to the Kev-man on this one. She's—"

Griffin's phone buzzed. "'Scuse me." He picked up the phone and Kevin started out of the office. "Don't leave, okay? We need to talk about the baseball game." Griffin wanted to back out. He'd been entertained enough recently.

"Sure." Kevin returned and plopped down on one of two chairs positioned in front of Griffin's desk.

Griffin punched the button that connected him to his secretary, Marcie. "Hi."

"I have Lily Revere on line one. Will you take the call?"

"Give me a second." He disconnected the line and held the phone until his heart stopped pounding.

Kevin sat forward in his chair. "I'm going to take a wild guess and say that's Lily calling. Nobody else puts that expression on your face."

Griffin nodded. "It's her."

"Has she called before?"

"No." Griffin drew in a breath and let it out slowly. "This is the first time since that night in her apartment."

"Don't take the call, Griff. That's what secretaries are for. Have Marcie say you're unavailable."

Griffin gazed at his friend, who had been there for him through this whole ordeal. Kevin wasn't going to like what he was about to do. "I'm taking the call."

Kevin threw his hands up. "Go ahead, then, but I promise you'll regret it. She's going to try and rope you back in." He settled into his seat with a bulldog look that announced he wasn't going anywhere until the phone call had been concluded.

Saddled with Kevin's resolute expression, Griffin connected with his secretary. "I'll take the call, Marcie."

"I'll connect you." Her prim response made him wonder if office gossip had linked him with Lily, although he
knew that Kevin and Miles wouldn't have talked about
the witch angle. They might have said he'd escaped from
a bad relationship thanks to them. Yeah, they might
have said that.

He waited for the click saying the line was open between him and Lily. He felt her waiting on the other end
and had the crazy urge to crawl right through that tele-
phone line. That probably wasn't good.

He swallowed. "Hello, Lily." His voice sounded like
tires on a gravel road, but he couldn't help that. "How
are you?"

"I'm okay. How are you?"

The sound of her voice nearly flattened him. He'd
heard it so many times in his head, in his dreams, and
now here she was at last. He sighed. "Okay."

Then he glanced at Kevin, who was glaring at him as
if he'd committed some huge crime. No doubt the sigh
hadn't thrilled Kevin.

"How's Daisy?"

"She's good. I take her to the dog park every morning
before work, and then for a walk after work, and I've arranged for a dog walker to come at noon because I don't
want to make her wait all day to go out." He was bab-
bling. If he hadn't recognized it, Kevin's slashing motion
across his throat would have alerted him.

"I'm glad you two are getting along," Lily said. "Look,
I'll come straight to the point. I feel as if I didn't say
all I needed to last Tuesday night, but then again, you
might not have been ready to hear it, either. Anyway, I
certainly didn't say a proper good-bye to Daisy. I'd like
to meet you tonight somewhere. Maybe at the old dog
park, if you'd be willing to bring Daisy over."

His heart leaped with excitement and he was ready
to say yes immediately, but Kevin was there, making him

feel like an impulsive fool. "I don't know, Lily. It might upset Daisy to see you."

Kevin gave him a thumbs-up.

"Don't worry. If it does, I'll leave right away. But she's a special dog, and I think . . . I think she deserves to know that I still . . . that I still love her."

"I hope this isn't some attempt to get back together, because I—"

"I promise it's not. But our last conversation was rather abrupt, and I have some things to say that I think are important. Plus, I really want to connect with Daisy one last time. I was thinking around six o'clock."

Griffin glanced at his calendar to confirm that it was Tuesday. "Don't you have to work?"

"With the hope that you'd agree to this, I got Chad to take my shift."

From the moment she'd proposed this meeting he'd known he'd be there. He'd only put up the roadblocks to show Kevin he wasn't a complete patsy. "I'll be there at six."

"See you then."

"Right. Good-bye." He hung up the phone with what he hoped was a show of authority. "It's about the dog. She wants to say a proper good-bye."

"Bullshit. She wants to manipulate you into getting back with her."

"Well, she won't be able to, okay? I'm not going to let that happen. I've worked too hard—we've all worked too hard—for me to fall into the same trap."

Kevin shook his head. "I hope so. But I predict she'll try to make you feel sorry for her, and you, poor sap, will want to make everything better."

"If she pulls anything like that, I'll shut her down."

"See that you do. I have half a mind to come with you."

"Kevin, I'm a big boy. I can handle this."

"I sincerely hope so, buddy."

Griffin hoped so, too. But he couldn't tamp down the excitement churning through him at the thought of seeing Lily again. After what he'd been through, he had to wonder if the spell was completely gone. Yet there was nothing manic about his mood. For the first time, his feelings might be real.

Chapter 29

Lily arrived at the dog park fifteen minutes early. With daylight savings time in effect, there'd be enough light for her to easily see Griffin and Daisy arrive. She wondered how Daisy liked cab rides. Lily had only taken her on one, when she'd brought her home from the animal shelter.

That seemed so long ago, but it had only been weeks. Daisy had become such a big part of her life so fast that Lily had trouble remembering a time when the dog hadn't been around. But the solitude of her apartment during the past week had been a poignant reminder of what life without Daisy had been like and would be from now on.

Lily knew she'd done the right thing, even though her heart ached as she watched people play with their dogs in the park. Daisy had chosen Griffin, and that wasn't surprising after Lily had included Daisy in the adoration elixir she'd used to snare him. Lily had one clear purpose for this meeting tonight—to let Griffin know that she understood the extent of her crimes.

As a bonus, she'd get to see Daisy one last time. She didn't want the dog to ever imagine that giving her up had been easy or impulsive. Daisy needed to understand that the gesture had been made out of love, not disinterest. That might be a complicated concept for most dogs, but not for Daisy. She'd get it, as long as Lily could see her once more.

Dressing for this meeting had been a challenge. She'd changed her mind a dozen times about what to wear. No one knew she'd set up the face-to-face, not even her sister. This was something she had to do on her own, without coaching. She had to prove that she was strong enough to say what had to be said and walk away.

Because of that, she'd rejected any outfit that was the least bit provocative. That left very little to choose from, because most of her clothes, including her casual wear, were designed to show off her figure. But she had a faded pair of jeans she'd owned since high school and a loose-fitting Cubs T-shirt somebody had given her several years ago. It was a typical bargain shirt—bright blue with the logo in front, boxy cut, and flappy short sleeves.

She couldn't make herself any more unattractive without going shopping, and shopping for baggy clothes wasn't in her blood. Bypassing all her sexy footwear, she put on her running shoes. Then she pulled her hair back into a simple ponytail and called it good.

Well, except for makeup. She did apply that, because Lily Revere didn't step outside her door without makeup. She aimed for understated and thought she achieved that. Most men wouldn't notice her makeup at all and assume she'd decided on the natural look.

Nerves made her heart beat faster and her palms sweat. She paced around, glancing at the street every few seconds in case Griffin showed up early.

He did.

When he climbed out of a cab at ten minutes before six, her heart rate kicked up another notch. She wondered if he was early because he was eager to see her or because he wanted to get the meeting over with. He'd changed out of his suit, and she couldn't decide if that was good or bad, either.

She was probably searching for meaning and signs where there were none. At any rate, he looked way more fashionable than she did in his jeans and a chambray shirt open at the neck with the sleeves rolled back. He turned and helped Daisy out before glancing toward the park.

Scanning the area, he spotted her in no time. For a moment he stayed very still, as if getting his bearings. Everything about his body language said that he didn't trust her, and that lack of trust tightened her throat with grief. But she had only herself to blame.

Daisy had no such issues. Tongue hanging out, doggie grin in place, she strained at the leash. Griffin kept her close to his side as he opened the gate, walked through and closed it behind him.

Then he started toward Lily, his grip tight on the leash. She held her breath, as if that would control the yearning that threatened to sabotage her plan. She was not here to beg him to take her back. No matter how powerful that urge was, she'd resist it with all her might.

Someone had cut the grass in the dog park earlier today, and the fresh smell would probably always remind her of this moment. Behind her, a young dad and his two daughters romped with their border collie. She'd remember those happy sounds, too, which were so at odds with the way she felt inside.

She'd never forget the way Griffin looked, either. He'd shaved before coming here. Not only was his chin smooth, but there was a small speck where he'd cut himself with the razor. The closer he came, the more she could see the uncertainty in his eyes.

Not surprising. He might wonder if she'd whip out a wand and put another spell on him. Meeting her had taken courage. Or love. She didn't dare think about the second option.

He stopped about ten feet away from her, as if wanting to keep some kind of distance. She couldn't blame

him for that, either, although ten feet wouldn't have protected him if she'd had devious plans.

She held out both hands in front of her, palms up. "I
promise not to do anything magical to you or Daisy."

"Okay." He didn't sound convinced. "But I'll stay
here, if you don't mind."

She nodded. She'd have to speak loud enough that
the dad and his kids might be able to hear, but maybe
that was fitting, that her apology be a semipublic one.

Meanwhile Daisy was going nuts wanting to close
the distance between them. She whined and pulled
at the leash, while her tail whipped back and forth in
anticipation.

Lily started to give her a command to calm down, but
Daisy wasn't her dog anymore. Griffin might resent her
attempt to control Daisy's behavior.

Instead she focused on what she had practiced in
her head a dozen times. "Thank you for . . ." She had to
stop and clear her throat. "Thank you for meeting me
tonight."

"You're welcome." His voice was grave, all laughter
and lightness gone.

She regretted that, too. She'd always loved Griffin's
laugh. "Last Tuesday night was a charged environment,
and although I said I was sorry that night, I'm not sure
you were in a mood to hear it."

"Oh, I heard it. It just seemed . . ."

"I know. Not enough. And it wasn't enough. So let
me try again." She took a deep breath and held his gaze.
"Griffin, for my own selfish reasons, I took away your
free will and caused you pain through no fault of your
own. That was unforgivable, and I'm ashamed of my actions. I can't give you back those days and nights I took
from you, but I want you to know that I'm deeply sorry
for the problems I visited upon you."

He stared at her in silence for many long seconds.
"That's it?"

Her stomach churned. She hadn't made things right with that apology, but then, a mere apology really wasn't enough. "If there's anything you want me to do that would in some way make up for—"

"No, no. I'm not looking for payback. I just ... I just wanted to know if you had anything more to say."

"No."

He nodded, and some of the tension eased from around his mouth. "Okay."

"But I would love—"

"What?" Instantly the tension was back. His shoulders stiffened and the suspicion that had begun to disappear from his eyes returned.

"I wanted to give Daisy a hug and tell her I love her. That's all. You can stay there if you want, but if you'd let her come over to me, I'll send her right back." She clenched her hands together and held her breath. Surely he would give her this one small thing.

He hesitated.

"Griffin, this isn't a trick or a maneuver. I just ..." She ran out of things to say. Either he would let her give Daisy one last hug or he wouldn't.

His chest heaved. "All right." He leaned down to unhook Daisy's leash.

As Daisy broke free, Lily dropped to her knees and held out her arms. Daisy bounded into her embrace, moaning with delight.

Lily tried to be stoic, but having an armload of warm, wriggling, joyous dog broke through the tight control she'd had over her emotions. But she didn't want Griffin to see her cry, so she buried her face in Daisy's fur.

She did a very poor job of telling Daisy all she'd intended to say. The words came out all choked and soggy. Daisy seemed to understand, anyway. She kept trying to lick whatever part of Lily's face wasn't pressed against her silky coat.

With great effort, Lily reined in her emotions. Keeping her head down in the hope Griffin wouldn't notice she'd been crying, she stood and gave Daisy one last scratch behind her ears. "Good-bye, Daisy," she murmured. "Now go back to Griffin."

Daisy stood, tail wagging slowly, and gazed up at her. "I mean it. Go to Griffin."

With obvious reluctance, Daisy turned and walked back to him.

Lily swiped at her eyes. "Thank you, Griffin." She didn't dare look at him or he'd know how upset she was.

"No problem."

She detected sympathy in his voice, and she didn't want that. As she heard the click of the fastener on the leash, she lifted her head briefly. "Good-bye." Then she walked briskly, keeping back and shoulders straight, toward the gate.

Once she was home she could give in to the sorrow cascading through her at an alarming rate. But not now, when Griffin was watching. After walking through the gate, she turned for home.

She'd gone nearly a block when she heard a shout behind her. She turned in time to see Daisy, leash and all, leap over the gate and race in her direction. Next came Griffin, who vaulted the gate and sprinted down the sidewalk, calling Daisy's name.

Like a linebacker going for a touchdown, Daisy dodged the pedestrians and kept her eye on Lily. When she arrived, she screeched to a stop and sat at Lily's feet, panting and smiling.

"Oh, Daisy." Lily fought the tears she'd just recently brought under control. "That wasn't good." Then she took Daisy's leash and held it while she waited for Griffin to catch up.

Breathing hard, he came to a stop in front of her.

"Here." She handed him the leash. "I guess you need to hold on a little tighter."

"Yeah."

"I do hate long good-byes." She managed a watery smile. "See ya." Then she turned and continued down the sidewalk.

"Wait."

She paused and slowly turned to face him. "I can't hold on to my emotions much longer, Griffin."

He stepped closer, close enough to touch. "Then don't."

She lifted her gaze to his, afraid to hope but afraid to lose sight of what might be right in front of her face, too. "What . . . what do you mean?"

"Let go." He dropped Daisy's leash. "I'll catch you."

"You can't drop Daisy's leash so you can catch me. You need to hold on to her."

"Where do you think she'd go? She's with the two most important people in the world to her, the two knuckleheads she's trying to bring back together."

He sounded almost as if he might want that, too. Lily swallowed. "I suppose we must seem pretty stupid to her. She doesn't understand how complicated this is."

"Maybe it's not so complicated." Griffin drew her into his arms. "When I saw that you were willing to walk away, I realized something."

Being held by Griffin was so wonderful she closed her eyes to savor it.

"I love you."

Her eyes popped open. "What?"

"That's a hell of a response." He smiled. "You're not supposed to question it. You're supposed to say it back."

"But maybe you don't really. Maybe it's an aftereffect, a holdover from the—"

"Nope. It's the real thing. I know what a love-potion crush feels like. It blurs stuff and makes a guy dazed and confused. This is a whole other feeling. Instead of blurring things, what I'm feeling for you now is bringing everything into focus."

"Oh." She could believe he was focused, because he totally ignored the people passing by on the sidewalk, people who had to walk around them, wheel baby strollers around them, even steer skate boards around them.

Griffin gazed at her intently. "In fact, this feeling snapped into focus about the time Daisy ripped the leash out of my hand and came after you."

"But then you were forced into following her. Maybe if she hadn't run, you wouldn't be standing here."

"Maybe I wouldn't be. Maybe it would have taken me a few hours before I pounded on your door." Keeping one arm firmly around her, he cupped her cheek in his hand. "I'm not as impulsive as you are. I need you to teach me to act on the spur of the moment and do crazy things."

"Like cast a spell on you?" She didn't want him to ignore her previous crimes now and bring them up later.

"Thank God you cast that spell." He stroked her cheek with his thumb. "I was too stupid to realize how much I needed you. The potion would never have worked so well if I hadn't wanted you desperately. And I still do. Daisy understands that. She knows we belong together."

At the look in his eyes, Lily's knees grew wobbly. "We do?"

"Yes. Especially if you can find it in your heart to love me."

Now she was *really* wobbly. To steady herself, she wrapped her arms tight around his neck. "I can find it in my heart." Pressing closer, she lowered her voice. "To be honest, I can find it in all sorts of places."

"Mm." He leaned down, his mouth hovering over hers. "But this is about more than sex, you know."

"I know." She felt so good that it was a wonder she wasn't giving off tiny sparks. "It's about love. I love you and you love me."

"For real this time."

She sighed, filled to the brim with happiness. "Yeah, for real." And so it was. Of all the times Griffin had kissed her, and there had been some spectacular kisses among them, this one was the best.

Epilogue

Griffin stood next to Jasper at the end of a carpeted aisle between rows of white folding chairs. At the other end a rose-covered gazebo decorated with white ribbons awaited him. The gazebo was surrounded by brilliantly colored flower beds and emerald stretches of manicured grass.

Beyond it, Lake Michigan sparkled in the sun, and the swish of the waves blended with the notes of a white baby grand positioned to the left of the assembled guests. A slight breeze from the lake brought with it the scent of roses and cut grass.

The setting was magnificent, designed to be savored. Griffin wasn't in a savoring mood. He wanted this part over with, and the sooner, the better.

Jasper spoke in a low voice so the man standing a short distance behind them, Ambrose Lowell, wouldn't be able to hear. "I still can't believe it's legal for him to conduct the ceremony."

"I ran his credentials through the system. He's licensed to do the deed." As the only lawyer in the family, Griffin knew he should be more concerned about the legality of being married by a wizard.

But he really didn't care, just so he made it to the honeymoon. In his briefcase lay airline tickets to Paris. The prospect of seven days and six hot nights with Lily in a city designed for lovers had wiped out any other thoughts.

"I'll bet there was some magical funny business involved in those credentials," Jasper said.

Griffin looked over at him. "Jasper, do you really give a damn?"

Jasper grinned. "No. I'm just looking for a way to distract myself so I won't go crazy waiting for the whole thing to start. Why the hell didn't we just elope?"

"Hey, don't look at me. I suggested it several times. It wasn't a popular choice."

"You'll both be glad you went through with this," Ambrose said from behind them.

Both Griffin and Jasper turned. Griffin hoped the wizard hadn't overheard the comments about his legal status. "I'm not so sure I'll be glad," he said. "Getting married is fine, but going through all this—"

"Gives it added significance," Ambrose said.

"Speaking for me," Jasper said, "the wedding's loaded with significance already. I don't need the fancy outfits and the hordes of people."

"Ditto." Griffin looked forward to having Jasper as a brother-in-law. They thought a lot alike, and Jasper would be the brother Griffin had never had.

"You probably don't need the fancy outfits," Ambrose said, "but it gives the hordes of people something nice to look at. And you definitely need the hordes of people."

Griffin shook his head. "Not this guy. I'd be happy to stand in front of a JP with my best friend and both sets of parents as the only witnesses."

Ambrose rocked back on his heels and looked wise. "Are you feeling joy at the thought of this marriage to Lily?"

"Oh yeah." Griffin wasn't sure *joy* even covered it. Such deep happiness filled him every time he thought about spending a lifetime with the woman of his dreams that he caught himself smiling constantly. "I'm bordering on ecstatic. I don't know how well you know Lily, but she's the most beautiful, most—"

"Well, except for Anica," Jasper said. "Anica's an incredible, amazing—"

"I suggest you two avoid that argument," Ambrose said. "But you've made my point. You're both filled with joy, as are your two brides. Can you even imagine how much positive energy that will generate? Are you so selfish you wouldn't want to share it with as many people as possible?"

Griffin stared at him. The guy had a point. His divorced parents had been kind to each other for the first time since the divorce. Kevin and Miles had been in exceptionally good moods lately because they could see that their friend was genuinely happy.

"I hadn't thought of that," Jasper said. "But I have to admit, I've never seen my parents looking so happy."

Ambrose smiled. "There you go. Aha! The processional music is beginning. Remember, you're not just getting married today. You're spreading joy."

With those words Griffin's perspective shifted. He found himself cherishing every moment that followed. The colors glowed brighter than before, and when he reached the gazebo and turned, he looked, really looked, at the face of each guest seated before him. Ambrose was right. They all reflected the joy he felt.

In the name of simplicity, each couple had chosen only one person to stand up with them. Lily and Griffin had decided on Kevin, while Anica and Jasper had picked Anica's former neighbor Julie. As Kevin walked Julie down the aisle they seemed touched by magic, and Griffin wondered if a romance was brewing. More potential joy.

Then Daisy arrived bearing four rings tied to her collar, which created merriment among the guests as they applauded the prancing dog. Daisy radiated joy right back to them.

Finally, the most joyous moment of all convinced Griffin that Ambrose was very wise, indeed. Lionel appeared with Lily on his right arm and Anica on his left. Griffin's breath caught as he gazed at Lily, the most beautiful bride in the world.

Her white satin dress was sleek and sexy, exactly like the woman wearing it. A crown of flowers held a veil that cascaded down her back. No hiding behind a wisp of white for his lady. She looked directly at him, her gaze warm, and his heart swelled. Yes, this was joy, joy enough to share, joy enough for a lifetime of loving.

Have fun with Lily?
Read on for an excerpt from
her sister Anica's story in

Blonde with a Wand

A Babes on Brooms Novel

Available from Signet Eclipse

The night Anica Revere turned Jasper Danes into a cat started out innocently enough.

They'd dated for nearly three weeks, and tonight lust ping-ponged across the restaurant table. Anica had anticipated this moment since she first glimpsed this dark-haired Adonis with golden eyes. Although Monday wasn't a common date night, Jasper's favorite restaurant was open and he hadn't wanted to wait for the weekend to see her again. All the signs pointed to finally Doing It.

He studied Anica as if he wanted to lick her all over, which sounded great to her, except ... she still hadn't mentioned a significant detail, one that could be a real buzz kill. She hadn't told him she was a witch.

With chemistry this strong, she was so tempted not to tell him, but one mistake with a nonmagical man was enough. The image of Edward racing out of her bedroom a year ago still pained her.

He hadn't even bothered to grab his clothes. Sad to say, a Chicago police squad car had been cruising by the apartment building and poor Edward had been arrested using a *Keep Lake Michigan Clean* leaflet as a fig leaf substitute.

She'd heard all about it from her neighbor Julie, who kept a video camera running from her third-story window in hopes that she'd get something worth airing on her brother's independent cable show, *Not So Shy Chi-Town*. That clip made it on the show, no problem. To avoid legal repercussions, Edward's features had been scrambled so no one except Julie and Anica knew who it was.

"You're frowning," Jasper said. "Anything wrong?"

Good thing he wasn't a mind reader. "No, no. Sorry." She smiled to prove that everything was hunky-dory.

He reached for her hand. "What do you say we get out of here?"

Whoops. She wasn't quite ready to be alone with him. Better to reveal her witch status in a public place, where she could resist the urge to prove that she had special powers.

That had been her biggest mistake with Edward. He hadn't believed her, and she'd worked one teensy spell to convince him and had been inspired by what was at hand, so to speak. He'd left before she could explain that his penis would return to its normal color in a few hours.

"I'm fine with leaving," she said. "But there's choco-late mousse on the dessert menu. Let's get some to go. Mousse could be . . . a lot of fun."

"Mm." His gaze grew hot. "I like the way you think."

As he signaled their waitress, Anica searched for the least threatening way to explain her unique gifts. After her experience with Edward, she dreaded broaching the witch situation. Maybe she should retreat to a quiet place for a few minutes and ask for guidance.

She pushed back her chair and picked up her purse. "I need to make a trip to the ladies room."

He stood, a perfect gentleman. "Hurry back."

"You bet." All the way to the rear of the restaurant, she thought about how gorgeous he was and how much she wanted him. She imagined how his eyes would darken during sex. So far his lips had only touched her mouth and neck, but she could mentally translate that delicious sensation to full-body kisses. She longed to feel his dark chest hair tickling her breasts as he hovered over her, poised for that first thrust.

Despite her parents urging her to find a nice wizard boy, she'd always been attracted to nonmagical guys. Because they couldn't wave a wand or brew a potion to create what they wanted, they had to make it through life on sheer grit and determination. She admired that.

She'd noticed Jasper the minute he'd stepped into her downtown coffee shop. What woman wouldn't notice six feet of gorgeous male with a physique that did great things for his Brooks Brothers suit? She'd become his friend once she'd learned he was suffering from a broken heart. Sure, he probably had the ability to recover on his own, but she wanted to help.

They'd progressed from conversations at Wicked Brew to a lunch date. That had been followed by two dinner dates, and after the last one he'd kissed her until she'd nearly caved and invited him upstairs, rule or no rule.

He had a right to know the truth before the kissing started again, though, and most likely he wouldn't believe her. If he didn't, she had to let him go. No clever little tricks to convince the guy, this time. But letting him go would be very difficult.

The bathroom was empty, which pleased her. She'd been hoping for time alone to prepare. Jasper was special and she didn't want to muck this up if she could possibly help it.

Closing her eyes, she took a calming breath and murmured softly. "Great Mother and Great Father, guide me in my relationship with this man. Help me find the best way to tell him of my special powers. May we find a kinship that transcends our differences. With harm to none, so mote it be."

The bathroom door squeaked open. Anica quickly

opened her eyes, turned toward the mirror and unzipped her purse as a tall brunette walked in. Moving aside the eight-inch rowan wood traveling wand she carried for emergencies, Anica pulled out her lipstick and began applying another coat of Retro Red.

She expected the woman to head for a stall or take the sink adjoining Anica's to repair her makeup. Instead the woman clutched her purse and watched Anica. Weird. Maybe this chick needed privacy, too.

Anica capped her lipstick, dropped it in her purse, and closed the zipper. Turning, she smiled at the woman, who didn't smile back. Instead her classic features creased in a frown. Troubles, apparently. She looked to be in her late twenties, about Anica's age.

"It's all yours." Anica started toward the door.

"Damn, I can't decide what to do."

Oh, Hades. Anica tended to invite confidences and she was usually willing to listen and offer whatever help she could. But now wasn't a good time. "I'm sorry. I have to get back to my date."

"Jasper Danes."

Anica blinked. "You know him?"

"Yes." The woman sighed. "I stopped by here for a drink hoping to run into him, because he comes to this restaurant all the time. I should have realized by now he'd be involved with someone else."

Anticipation drained out of Anica so quickly she felt dizzy. She looked into the woman's soft brown eyes. "You're Sheila."

The woman nodded.

In the spot where hope had bubbled only moments ago, disappointment invaded like sludge. If Sheila was having second thoughts about breaking up with Jasper, then Anica should step aside. What Anica shared with him was mere lust, which might disappear once he found out she was a witch.

She made herself do the noble thing. "We're not really involved." *Yet.*

"I was afraid to ask if it was serious between you two, because it looked as if—"

"We were heading in that direction, but when I first met him, he was devastated over your breakup. If you regret leaving him, then maybe there's still a chance to start over." Anica wanted to cry. Jasper was the first man she'd had any real interest in since Edward and she was giving him back to his ex. Nobility sucked.

"Excuse me, but did you say *I* left *him*?"

"Yes. He said that he begged you to reconsider, but you—"

"Oh, my God." Sheila gazed at the ceiling. "It's *déjà vu.*" She closed her eyes and let her head drop. "I thought I was smarter than that. Guess not."

"I don't understand."

When Sheila opened her eyes to look at Anica, her gaze had hardened. "I didn't understand, either, until now. Tell me, did he say that I broke his heart?"

"Sort of. You know how guys are."

"Apparently I don't know enough about how guys are, but I'll learn. Let me guess what he said." Sheila deepened her voice in a pretty good imitation of Jasper. "*I thought we had something special. I was all set to take her home to meet my folks in Wisconsin when she lowered the boom. Maybe I should have seen it coming. Maybe I dropped the ball somehow, didn't live up to her expectations. I tried to get her to reconsider, but she was finished with me.*"

Uneasiness settled in Anica's stomach. Sheila had quoted Jasper almost word for word. What if this woman was a nut case who'd been lurking in the coffee shop behind a newspaper while Jasper spilled his guts? "That's . . . approximately what he said."

"I'll bet a million dollars that's *exactly* what he said.

Because that's the speech he gave me about Kate, his previous girlfriend. It touched my heartstrings, which appear to be directly connected to my libido. A few dates, and we were in bed, where I could mend his broken heart." She blew out a breath. "I didn't leave Jasper. He dumped me three weeks ago."

Three weeks ago Jasper had walked into Wicked Brew for the first time and she'd elbowed her employee Sally out of the way so that she could personally serve him a latte. Jasper had shown up the next morning, and the next, and on the third morning he'd announced that his girlfriend had left him.

But Sheila couldn't be telling the truth about that breakup. Anica prided herself on her ability to read people, and Jasper had been one forlorn guy three weeks ago. If he'd made up that story—no, she couldn't believe that he'd do such a thing.

"I want to hear Jasper's side," she said. "I don't see any reason why he'd—"

"Don't you? He's figured out that women are suckers for a sob story. He hangs with a woman until he finds somebody he likes better. Then he dumps the current girlfriend and works the heartbreak kid angle with the new one. I fell for it. And the worst part is, if I could have him back, I'd take him, even knowing what I know."

Anica shook her head, still unwilling to accept what Sheila was saying. "I'm sure there's an explanation. Maybe you two misunderstood each other." That still left Anica out in the cold if Sheila and Jasper reunited, but she'd rather see that happen than discover Jasper was a louse.

"It's hard to misunderstand when someone says—*it's been lots of fun and you're amazing, but it's time to move on*. That's pretty damned clear, don't you think?"

"Did you two fight about something?"

"No. All was peaches and cream. I'm guessing he met you and decided to trade up."

Had Jasper lied to her? Anica couldn't believe it, but there was only one way to find out. "I'll talk to him."

"You do that, and if you decide you don't want him after you find out the truth, let me know." Sheila thrust a business card in Anica's hand. "He might bounce back my way."

Anica stared at her in disbelief. "You'd still want him, even if he lied to you?"

"'Fraid so. I shouldn't, but . . . he's just that good."

Also Available

FROM

Vicki Lewis Thompson

Blonde with a Wand
A Babes on Brooms Novel

Sexy witch Anica Revere has one rule: never
under any circumstances get involved with a
man before telling him she's a witch. Still,
what's one silly rule? Especially when the
guy in question is as cute as Jasper Danes.
But when Anica and Jasper have a spat, she
breaks an even bigger rule of witchcraft and
turns him into a cat. Bad news for him.
Worse for her...

S0005

Also Available

FROM

Vicki Lewis Thompson

Casual Hex

Gwen Dubois lives in Indiana, but her heart is in France with Marc Chevalier, a man she met online. Now he's come to Big Knob to show Gwen the meaning of amour and spirit her back to Paris. But stiff competition is coming from another part of the world—if not exactly this world. Prince Leo of the Atwood fairy kingdom has his own plans for Gwen, creating a romantic mishap that only Big Knob's resident witch and wizard can untangle.

"Count on Vicki Lewis Thompson for a sharp, sassy, sexy read."
—Jayne Ann Krentz